EASY STREET

by

MICHAEL SHEPHERD

Michael Shepherd
Visit my website at www.michaelshepherdwriter.com

Printed in the United States of America

First Printing: November 2012

DEDICATION

For my wife, Peggy,
who believed I was a writer long before I believed it myself.

CHAPTER 1

It wasn't the booze Frenchy was drinking that overly concerned me, nor was it the subsequent anger he'd generated while looking at the photos I'd provided that showed his wife and brother doing the deed.

No.

My first hint of concern surfaced when he picked up a gun. And pointed it my way.

That's when I thought I might be in a pickle.

It would take some pretty cagey thinking on my part to make my situation improve.

And thinking has never been my strong suit.

Doyle, I thought, you sure know how to pick a case. That was immediately followed by another thought: this case might be my last.

I didn't like that thought much.

A couple of weeks earlier Frenchy had hired me to find out if his wife was sleeping around. My general opinion is when a guy hires you to prove that, he already knows deep down in his heart the truth, that he married a lipstick-wearing, gold-digging pit viper in stilettos who couldn't wait to pierce his tender heart with her freshly-sharpened fangs. It hadn't taken me long to prove Frenchy's beloved wife Hannah Mae was no exception. Telling him this though…that turned out to be the hard part.

As in gun-pointed-at-my-chest hard.

When Frenchy first asked me to take the case something told me to leave this one alone. But then I remembered the good old days. After all, it was Frenchy who'd introduced me to the whimsical, fun-filled Jekyll-and-Hyde properties of alcohol about twenty years before. He'd provided the intoxicating Mad Dog stimulation and I'd provided the subsequent puking. Still, a first drink is a first drink, so how the hell can you turn down a guy like that when he's in need?

Judging by the gun, he no longer held me in the same high regard.

I stood frozen to my spot, staring at Frenchy's gun barrel for what I thought would be the rest of my life, when his pistol began to wiggle and wobble. I attributed this to the half-bottle of Wild Turkey he'd worked his way through. He stole another glance at the pictures that I'd laid out on the coffee table. They were damn near incriminating.

No. They were indisputably incriminating.

"To tell you the truth, I've been there too," I said, as if his knowing my wife had also cheated on me would help him deal with the pictures.

"Whatever. That don't make us like brothers," he grumbled. Which was an odd thing to say, seeing as who was "coitally involved" with Hannah Mae.

"Not brothers like this anyway," I said, tapping one of the pictures.

"My big fuckin' brother," Frenchy wailed. "Why'd he hafta do this to me?"

I rejected an urge to bro-hug him, because I figured that'd get me shot quicker than anything. I needed to focus on surviving. Priority one.

Frenchy finally let a juicy sob escape. He glared at me. "You shouldna oughta done this, you piece a crap," he howled. "You made Hannah Mae look like a whore slut."

I cleared my throat. "Point of clarification. Hannah Mae made herself look like a whore slut. I merely captured the event for posterity. Look real close at what she's doing right there," I said. I tapped at one particular picture where it was hard to tell where Hannah Mae ended and Frenchy's brother began.

Frenchy dropped his eyes and squinted at the photo.

While I hightailed it for the door.

The first shot exploded out of the living room and into the hallway wall over my head.

I spun right and crashed down the stairs like I had a fair piece to go and a short time to get there.

Frenchy lunged out to the top of the staircase. Two more shots blazed past me and whined off the concrete floor at the base of the stairs.

I hit the sidewalk, dashed across the street and dove into my rustbucket '73 Nova for a tire-squealing get away.

I turned the key. The engine coughed and backfired, then started.

I slammed it into gear.

It lurched forward.

It shimmied. And died.

She had a flair for the dramatic.

Frenchy's next shot blew out a passenger side window, showering me with glass. I threw the door open, dove for the pavement, and landed with an impressive bellyflop. My head slammed against the concrete and a knifing pain ripped through my ribs.

But my various maladies wouldn't stop Frenchy's relentless pursuit, so I rapidly scrambled behind the rear tire and squatted there, shaking like a schoolgirl on her first trip to second base.

Some people would say this is fun, getting shot at and all. But then again some people eat octopus, so there's just no accounting for taste. Anyway, my life hadn't always been quite like this. Straight out of high school I had a real job, operating a crane for my dad's construction company. After that went away, this private eye thing caught on. Life was good for a few years.

Good enough, anyway. Until my ex-wife Eileen started screwing around. And once she got a taste of the wild-as-a-hawk party life, it seemed like she didn't want to let it go. So she didn't. She ran the streets till even the streets gave up and called it a night.

Funny thing was, Eileen had always dreamed of being famous. And now, strange twist of fate, she was famous as hell—she was the talk of the whole damn town.

And in the painful aftermath I'd had a tough time stopping the Paul Doyle freefall. But I thought I might finally have hit bottom today.

I struggled to get my impressive bulk less impressively bulky while Frenchy peppered three more shots my way.

The first two hit the Nova.

The third ricocheted off the sidewalk and hit me.

Right in the ass.

Now I was at the bottom. Me at forty, fat as a summer seal, floating in the shallow end of the IQ pool, with a bullet wound in the butt.

I felt my backside and gauged the blood flow as less than life-threatening.

But it hurt like hell.

To make matters worse I'd gone into Frenchy's 'perfectly safe' apartment unarmed. Now, while I was cowering on the garbage-strewn sidewalk, I thought about the great equalizer, the ender of all arguments, my beloved .357, as it sunned itself on the passengers' seat.

Perhaps I hadn't thought this out as thoroughly as I could have.

A bullet slammed into the car. This time a tire blew.

Another shot, and I felt a gentle tug under my arm. I looked down.

Bullet hole. In my Patriots hoodie.

Frenchy was taking this 'kill Paul Doyle' thing way too seriously.

When it stayed quiet for a few seconds I crawled into the Nova, grabbed the .357 and took a bead on Frenchy's open second-story window.

Then he was there. Taking dead aim at me.

I gulped like I'd never breathe again.

Held my breath and pulled the trigger.

The EMTs who responded told me Frenchy would live. Drunks and fools usually do. Good guys that they were, the EMTs patched me up as a personal favor and didn't insist on taking me to the hospital. After the cops were done hearing my side of the story I changed the tire, got the car running, cleaned the glass up, and babied it home.

I pulled up to the curb outside Ma's house, where I'd returned to live after my marriage went the way most marriages do, opened the car door, and hoisted my beat-up body out.

I stretched a little and began the slow walk inside.

The curtains in the front room moved. Vanessa Doyle, checking on her baby boy.

I gave her a slight wave. Her eyes never left me.

My cell phone rang. Lou Principi.

Lou ran The Limit, Westfield's only strip club, which I occasionally frequented. Purely for investigative reasons.

"Hey Paul, you lookin' for clients?"

I'm always looking for clients. Like I have a choice. I pay the mortgage on a house I don't live in and a healthy dose of alimony to a freeloader who can't spell work if you spot her the W and O.

"Depends on the job," I gruffly said, although we both knew I'd take it sight unseen.

Lou said, "I got a girl gone missin' and Yvette told me to find a good private eye. I don't know any, so I called you."

CHAPTER 2

The Limit is a low-end, working man's shot-and-a-beer strip joint. The weathered, splintered plywood outer walls are a garish two-tone mess, as if someone made an untimely run on purple paint at the hardware store when the job was half-done. So one side and the back gleams neon pink. It looks classy that way.

Anyway guys come for the girls, not the building. A guy wants ambience, he packs up the wife and the kids and goes to IHOP or Applebee's or the Italian restaurant downtown with the plastic grapes, the bathtub fountain and the artsy guy statue with the fig leaf.

The Limit's windows are blacked out, save for two broken ones covered with plywood. The broken marquee offers HAPP HOUR $10 LAP DANC, 4-6 PM.

Yvette Monfort, Lou's fading lady friend and part-time dancer, was sitting at the front desk. I'd had the misfortune of seeing her tired body up on stage twice. Hers was a performance that begged no encore.

Yvette wore jeans and a ragged, scoop-neck sweatshirt that draped her emaciated frame, hiding any hint of definable shape. Her hair color was a ghastly black rinse a couple of months overdue for a tuneup. A half inch of gray roots burst from a ragged part that started one way, lost itself in a frenzied debate, and gave up all hope of organization. The rest hung limp, bedraggled, defeated, at the base of her jaw.

"Yvette," I nodded to her as she sat in a cloud of her own cigarette smoke directly under the NO SMOKING sign. "How they hangin'?"

"Down to my knees," she cackled and fell into a severe coughing fit that wracked her bony frame. Finally she spit out, "Ain't that a bitch?"

"Yeah, gravity sucks. Anyone new dancing?"

"You mean younger, dontcha?" Yvette pulled her elbows together, trying to generate cleavage from her meager offerings. "Come on, ain't these babies good enough?"

"Too good. You're too good, Yvette."

She rolled her tired eyes. "Bullshit. I'm way past my prime."

"Aren't we all, dear? But at least you're still above ground. Got that going for you."

She smirked. "Jeez, ain't you a ray of sunshine on my ass? You're right, I got the world by the short hairs. How can I ever give all this up?"

I looked past her at the mismatched vinyl chairs ringing the double stages, and the stained, crushed velvet lounges in the corner where the girls took customers for private dances. I'd been there before, once with Yvette on a particularly miserable evening for both of us.

I started to slip by her, then stopped. "Lou here?"

"He's in the office. Give him ten minutes."

Inside the club, two of my favorite things beckoned. Topless women and cold beer. I'd give him twenty.

"You know what he wants to talk to me about?" I asked.

She grimaced. "We own this place together so yeah, I probably do."

"You want to beat him to the punch?"

Yvette glanced toward the office's closed door. "We got a problem we need fixed. But I'll let him tell ya. He likes to be the one who tells folks stuff."

Yvette coughed and cussed and jammed her cigarette into the half-full ashtray, and went to the pack at her elbow and dug another one out. Smoke billowed as she got it going good.

She caught me watching her. "Yeah, I know. Each cancer stick is like five minutes off my life."

"Hard habit to break." I stopped counting butts in the ashtray when I ran out of fingers.

She ignored my gaze. "Like you care. But you want to know what? Today I heard the damnedest thing. You know Alexis, right?"

I nodded.

Yvette shook her head. "That dumb bunny uses her own name here. I'm A Lexus. Drive me. You ever hear of such a thing?"

I didn't give a crap one way or the other. I'm a Chevy man.

Yvette said, "So, Alexis goes to church every Sunday morning. Religiously." She barked a laugh, then cocked her head like a mutt hearing a dog whistle when I didn't join her.

"Anyway," she said, "you know the Castle View Free Church, right? The one the great Reverend Johnny Virdon preaches at? Alexis said old Johnny went on a rant today about women. They gotta be all wifey. They gotta wear a dress. They gotta have a drink and a BJ for their husbands when they come home from work. And he told his congregation about the evil going on…well, try to guess where."

"Between his ears? In his heart?" I heard rumors Reverend Virdon had more than a passing interest in his congregation's fairer sex and, if you believed the word on the street, he concluded most of his private counseling sessions with broken-hearted housewives in bed.

His.

"No, you friggin' retard. He told them about our place. Called it a sinner's paradise."

"Of course it is. And him bringing it up will be good for business. More fellas swing by to get a look at what all the fuss is about."

"Oh, but that ain't all. Reverend Dumbass said shutting us down is his personal vedenta."

"Vendetta?" I helpfully offered.

"That's what I said. Vedenta."

"Oh." The State of Maine hadn't bothered wasting a high school diploma on her. I was now certain of this very fact.

Reverend Johnny Virdon ministered to the largest congregation north of Portland. Around 400 members packed into Sunday service, and Virdon had also finagled Westfield's only television station to broadcast his sermons.

Not a crap PBS station either, but a real one. N-B freaking C affiliate. The big time. Or at least as big time as you could get in Westfield.

So the poor, downtrodden members of Westfield who could not find the impetus to make it out of their houses could still witness Johnny's antics, live and commercial-free, from 10 to 11 every Sunday morning.

Hope you enjoyed the show. Donations welcome.

No.

Expected.

Yes, my central Maine cow town had a rising star. Reverend Johnny Virdon.

And now, apparently, he wanted to use his star power to shut down The Limit.

I figured I better drink a beer and see some more boobs before he did.

Two beers later Lou threw his office door open and motioned me back. He stood short and bowlegged, with an enormous belly he'd spent most of his life constructing. It strained against the buttons on his blue-striped shirt, exposing a ribbed white tee through the gaps. Only the double action of belt and red suspenders kept his pants somewhere near his hips.

He wore his black hair in a comb over that started above his left ear and petered out in wisps and tendrils halfway across the crown, which left his liver spotted scalp looking like a weed infested lot. But given the whole Sweet Lou Principi package, the hapless hair fit him.

He sat at a gray metal desk that had absorbed more than its share of anger from the highly dissatisfied. Dings and dents marred the thin metal and a large section of the kick panel bore no paint at all.

I sat in the chair opposite him. I wanted to give the desk a good kick myself, if for no other reason than to leave my indelible Kilroy. Paul Doyle was here.

Lou smiled like we were friends and asked, "Havin' a good time tonight?"

This was the tag line for everyone who worked at The Limit, from door girls to bouncers to bartenders to waitresses to dancers. Lou probably figured I hadn't heard it a dozen times yet tonight.

"Sure," I said. "The beer is cold, the girls are hot. But you didn't invite me here to see what kind of night I'm having. Spill it so I can hang out with ladies who think I'm the greatest guy in the world. Until my wallet runs dry."

Lou leaned back, laced his fingers across his gut, and rocked.

I stood up. "You didn't prepare a welcome speech? I'm crushed."

"How about you zip your lip a little? Jesus, I forgot what a pain in the ass you are."

"Indescribable greatness bears a heavy price tag."

He shook his head. "Great you ain't, but I'm a little short on options. Any chance we could do this without you runnin' your yap quite so much?"

I know me, so I wouldn't make any promises. I sat.

Lou said, "Most of these girls, they think strippin' is easy money. Pull their tops off, shake their stuff, and end up with their own reality show on the tube. It ain't like that, though. They get up on stage a couple of times, don't make enough to pay the babysitter, and crawl away to work at Mickey D's."

"Business that bad?"

He sighed. "That's the least of my problems. And have you took a look at a few of these heifers? I could name a dozen that guys would pay 'em more to keep their clothes on."

Harsh assessment. But I'd seen a couple like that.

Such as Yvette.

I decided not to bring her up, what with Lou banging her and all. I said, "So the missing girl, couldn't she have split? Maybe she's working somewhere else."

He shook his head. "The missing girl weren't lackin' money. She's Cherry Delight."

Twenty-year-old Cherry was the closest thing The Limit had to a headliner. On my birthday, two months ago, she'd been my present to myself. Pretty face. Blazing blue eyes. Full lips. Fiery red hair that hung to her waist. An explosion of freckles across fair, bare milky skin.

She was long, lean and curvy, with legs that went on forever.

Cherry Delight.

For the man who deserves the very best.

I felt her hair brushing my face.

I remembered her perfume.

Haunting.

Hypnotizing.

Yeah, I knew Cherry.

And now she'd disappeared. Mankind's loss.

Lou growled, "So you takin' the job, hotshot?"

"You tell me." I gave him two options: my bargain-basement, absolute cheapest, I-need-a-customer daily rate, or my awful convenient, one-price-fits-all flat fee, plus miscellaneous expenses.

He balked at both. "Get the fuck outta here, you sleezebag!"

I stood. "Happy hunting. Of the million people in Maine, about a million of them are as white as her. Tracking her down will be like finding a grain of salt in a sugar bowl. Let me know how that goes for you." I walked to the door and gave the knob a turn.

"Hold on, damn you," Lou sputtered.

I turned. "So you do like me. You really like me."

"Go find the girl, Doyle."

We settled on a flat fee for the job, plus expenses. Nothing exorbitant, but I could afford to eat now. Maybe buy a new spare tire. Become a better tipper. The world was my oyster.

But something didn't fit. I said, "You told me girls drop like flies around here. What's so special about Cherry that you'll pay me to find her?"

He grimaced. "She's my niece."

"Cherry Delight is your niece?" My niece, sixteen-year-old Vicky Morrissette, lives with her dad three towns over in Albion. I pictured Vicky at six with pigtails, long legs and skinned knees, as she raced around my yard and chased the dog.

I pictured Vicky at eleven, the last time she'd visited my ex-wife Eileen and me, wearing her one piece pajamas with the feet, a huge bowl of popcorn in her lap and a goofy smile on her face as we let her watch a movie her parents wouldn't have allowed.

I pictured Vicky at fourteen at my sister's funeral, wearing a black dress, her mother's necklace and high heels, forced to be adult in a world she was wholly unprepared to meet head on.

But never, ever could I picture my niece Vicky Morrissette up on stage, shaking her newfound chest for the classy clientele that frequented The Limit.

Lou looked at me as if I spoke Latin. "Yeah, she dances for me. Hell, she lived with me for a couple years when her mom split. I'm her family. I gotta take care of her."

Apparently we had a different definition of family and taking care of someone. He seemed satisfied. I wasn't.

But she wasn't my niece.

And he was my new employer.

I'd just lowered my standards another rung. Although, I conveniently rationalized, they'd never been sky high to begin with.

Cherry. I thought about her eyes that sparkled with excitement. The galaxy of freckles that splashed across her cheeks. The tempting smile when she cranked it up for a customer.

But I liked her other smile more. The one she used when she didn't want a customer's whole paycheck. The flat out 'good to see ya' grin. Like the one she gave me a while back when we hung out together for a half-hour with nothing better to do and I wowed her with my encyclopedic knowledge of World Series winners.

The last time I'd seen her she was sitting at a table with another girl, giggling endlessly over text messages. Cherry Delight. Just another twenty-year-old woman. A woman you'd see every day at the coffee shop or the mall.

Who'd gone missing.

Lou leaned forward. "Cherry wouldn't just up and leave here. This doesn't sound right."

He hit the nail dead on the head with that one. It didn't sound right at all.

Even less right than allowing your niece to be a topless dancer in your club.

CHAPTER 3

Annette Begley. Lou told me Cherry Delight was really Annette Begley. When I kicked it around, the name didn't match the spectacular girl I knew as Cherry. The Annette Begleys of the world spent their free time in the library. Then marrying vice principals, driving Saabs and organizing fundraisers for animal shelters. Or something similar. But whatever they did, the last thing I expected a girl named Annette Begley to do is strip.

When I asked about her family, Lou told me he had no idea where Annette's mother ran off to. But her journey would likely end with her acquiring future ex-husband number four.

"How about Annette's dad?" I asked.

He scratched himself down below and made a major adjustment. "Me and him used to get together time to time. Shoot some pool and get shit-faced."

"He a Begley?"

"No, he's a fuckin' Hershey Bar, Doyle. I told you Annette's name is Begley, didn't I?"

"Easy, little man. Trying to get down to the facts."

"Yeah, but you're asking stupid shit! Shit that don't make no difference to nobody."

"Stupid is in the eye of the beholder." I looked him up and down. Surprisingly, my subtlety eluded him. "Humor me, how about?"

Lou threw his hands up. "Steve Begley, okay? So one night, Annette musta been eight or ten, and Steve and I go out. Celebrating Arbor Day. Hump Day.

Canadian Thanksgiving or some damn thing. Anyway, Steve drove like God gave him a lead foot and it had to be used to be appreciated. Speed limit says fifty, Steve goes seventy. Sign says forty, that means double or nothin'. And the sign says…" He paused for a moment as his voice cracked, "the sign says slow the fuck down, and Steve laughs his ass off and jams his foot to the floorboard and we hit a place where the side of the road is…all washed out."

Lou rubbed between his eyebrows. "I live and the bitch of it is, Steve don't. Now Annette's got no daddy so I pitch in. Then my sister decides I'm a better daddy than she is a momma. So one day I go to her house before the snow flies to make sure the furnace still works, and Annette is alone takin' care of herself. Said her momma had been gone for three weeks. I told her to come on if she's comin' and she grabbed her suitcase and followed me out to the car like she was my new puppy. And she's been with me ever since."

Heartwarming, I wanted to say. You and Annette. And when she turned eighteen you put her up on stage like any caring uncle would.

Lou said he'd already checked the Principi side of the family, but no one had seen Annette. He told me Annette's dad had kin scattered around and if he did my job, he'd start there. He admitted he'd already burned more than his share of Begley bridges for a couple of lifetimes. Prudence dictated I pick up the phone instead.

Because I'm brilliant I looked in the phone book. I found two Begleys in the greater Westfield area.

I called the first one, Abram and Myrna, who lived in Fairfield.

A wavering female voice answered. "Hello?"

"Hi, I'm Ernie Callas from the *Morning Constitutional*. We're interviewing redheads to dispute the notion that blondes have more fun."

She screeched, "Abram? Phone for you!"

The phone clattered as she dropped it on a hard surface. Soft footsteps.

"Hello?" Abram Begley barked, loud enough for the neighbors to hear. In New Hampshire.

"Mister Begley, I'm looking for Annette."

"What you need a net for? You going fishing?" He cackled a loud, long laugh that drifted away and ended in a wheeze.

"Hoo boy," I said. "I haven't laughed that much since you put Prince Albert in a can."

He cackled again. "Prince Albert in a can. Ayuh, I used to tell that one too."

"Does Annette live there?"

"I don't know Annette. 'Course, my wife says I don't know my ass from a hole in the ground, so that don't mean much. Hold on a sec." Once more the phone clattered. And I heard him yell, "Hey, Ma. Phone for you!"

A familiar screech came back on the line. "Hello? Who is it?"

I thanked her. And crossed Abram and Myrna Begley from my 'most helpful' list. Forever.

Goble Begley's number went unanswered. No voice mail. No answering machine.

I checked the address. Euclid Road in Clinton.

I had to drop my car off at Grenier's Auto Glass in Clinton the next morning to fix the window Frenchy shot out. Before I did, I'd swing by Goble Begley's house for a little look-see.

CHAPTER 4

Euclid Road wound its way from downtown Clinton, past a couple of dairy farms and the local grass strip airport, which consisted of two single-engine airplanes, a helicopter that hadn't moved in at least five years, and a battered windsock that fluttered with frequent uncertainty.

Goble Begley's house sat close to the road on a hard right hand bend. Fresh tire tracks careened across his lawn, immortalizing someone's recent unplanned excursion that ended at the base of a freshly-scarred three-foot stump. A forest green bumper from a Pontiac Grand Prix leaned against the stump, undeniable evidence against its assailant.

The house walls were discolored plywood, half-covered by peeling tarpaper. Two bare windows peered outward at the world. Junk cars, partially concealed by waist-high weeds, littered the yard. I saw a yellow Mustang fastback, a white Dodge Dart, an old GMC pickup with no bed. Beside the house stood a ramshackle garage suffering from a severe list to the north. A canvas lean-to nailed to the garage covered a tricycle-wheeled, rusty John Deere tractor with no motor. A pile of scrap wood sat beneath it.

An edgy pit bull, chained to a metal rod in the center of the lawn, protected Goble Begley's empire. He eyed me as I pulled into the yard. He seemed glad to see me.

Or, more likely, hungry.

As I climbed from my car, I gauged the length of chain and the wooden stairs leading to the front door. It would be close.

I walked in an exaggerated arc, about thirty feet from the dog. He lay in a small, dusty pit and continued to eyeball me.

16

Shoot, I congratulated myself as I neared the stairs. I'm home free.

With a wolf-like howl he exploded toward me, paws tearing up the ground, teeth bared.

I grabbed my pistol. A hell of a way to introduce myself to Goble Begley. By ventilating Rover. I drew a bead on his fast-approaching chest.

He hit the end of the chain, yelped and flipped ass-over-teakettle not three feet from me.

He struggled to his feet and shook the dust off. He looked confused. He walked back to the pit and lay down, his head resting on his paws.

"Now you know," I said.

When my heart rate returned from the stratosphere, I climbed the stairs and pounded on the door.

No answer.

I pounded again.

Shuffling footsteps approached.

The door opened a crack. I saw a skinny, unshaven chin with egg yolk dribbling from the corner of his mouth. A flushed, bright red rose. Rheumy, faded blue eyes. Bushy eyebrows topped by greasy, uncombed gray hair. The smell of booze oozed from his pores.

Goble Begley, I presumed. In all his glory.

I stuck my hand out as an introduction, but apparently none was needed. He swung the door open and leaned on the door frame for support as I slipped by.

The kitchen had one chair, which I figured was reserved for the owner. I leaned against the edge of the counter.

Begley flopped into the chair and sat, spread-legged, with his elbows on his knees.

He wore green wool pants that hung on his skinny frame, held in place by off-white, dirt-specked suspenders. His fly was unzipped and filthy undershorts showed through.

He wore a misbuttoned green work shirt with a huge oil stain on the left breast pocket and unlaced black tennis shoes with no socks. The finest in casual home wear.

"Whaddaya want?" he slurred.

"You know a girl named Annette Begley?"

"Never had no girl." He grabbed a red plastic tumbler from the table and took a gulp. He shuddered as he swallowed. "Whaddaya want?"

Whiskey can slow a man's thinking down to a crawl. And in Goble Begley's case, slower. "What I want is to find Annette Begley."

He ponderously shook his head. Slow, looping back and forth. "Who?" He struggled to focus on me.

He took another slug and wiped his mouth with his sleeve. "Whaddaya want?"

In the style of dashing television private detectives, I wanted to make a dramatic exit. But given Goble Begley's lack of interest in my departure, walking straight out the door did the trick.

I skirted the pit bull. He glowered at me.

"I know the feeling," I told him.

He didn't bother to respond.

As dusk slunk over the foothills to the west, I made my way twenty miles down the Interstate, took the first Augusta exit and drove toward the Pop Warner football field for my weekly liaison with Mikey Cross.

A man of magnificent gestures, a couple of years before Mikey had built a football field complete with artificial turf, pro-style lights and real stands for the fine folks of Augusta.

So every Monday night during the fall local sixth and seventh graders enjoyed the immense privilege of playing under the lights on the Mikey Cross Football Field, in the middle of Cross Park, donated to the city by the estimable, ubiquitous Mikey Cross.

Who as a side note killed my father.

So I didn't love him quite as much as the kids and parents and community leaders and State Representatives. Even if he did referee all the games for free.

I watched the black hair-dyed Wayne Newton look-alike dash up and down the field, whistle jammed between his bleached white teeth, demonstratively waving and blowing and posturing and posing. And smiling. One thing about being in the same zip code as Mikey Cross, you'd get lots and lots of smiles.

Like a great white shark smiles just before it rips you apart.

Once or twice he serenely looked my way. And once or twice I fantasized about emptying my pistol into his chest and giving every fool in the stands my biggest, dumbest, goofiest bleached white Mikey Cross smile and saying, "How you like your hero now?"

As the quarterback brought the offense up to the line Mikey again looked at me.

And motioned my way.

But I knew he wasn't motioning to me.

Because I heard car doors open and close behind me.

Two guys who looked like they could bench press a minivan walked toward me.

Before they made it, I climbed into my car.

Locked the door.

Drove away.

And cursed myself all the way home.

When I got there, I had a drink to perk me up. Then a quick refill or two in case dehydration set in.

Three double rum and cokes drew the shades on my once-promising evening.

The next morning I woke up late, still dressed, on the couch. But what the hell, I started my day closer to the bathroom this way.

When I came out of the shower, a towel wrapped around my waist and my wet hair sticking up in four directions, Ma stood at the stove flipping pancakes. Bacon sizzled on another burner, and coffee aroma wafted throughout the house.

Ah, the life of a sophisticated forty-year-old bachelor. Who'd returned home after a failed marriage to live with his mother.

After a quick change I sat at the table, watching her. She wore a threadbare blue housecoat that came to mid-calf and didn't hide her swollen, arthritic ankles. She moved like every step hurt. And I knew it did.

My mother called the whole family big boned, but she tipped the scales a bit north of two-fifty when she wasn't retaining water, so I didn't consider her to be the most objective source. Glandular, she called our problem. All the Doyles and Hendersons were glandular she loved to say, usually while she enjoyed a mound of Chunky Chocolate ice cream on top of an equally chocolaty wedge of cake. With Marty Doyle and Vanessa Henderson marrying, she couldn't help but remind me, I lucked right into a double dose of glandular.

I maintained no such delusion. When I stood in front of the mirror, it didn't lie. I was a fatass. Plain and simple.

But Ma had been through a lot. Husband Marty who died at fifty-nine, daughter Vivian a victim of breast cancer at thirty-eight. With all that had happened, Ma could be as glandular as she wanted to be.

And now she was going through her Golden Years with me in tow. Lucky girl. I poured two cups of coffee, and gave her a kiss on the forehead as I handed her one.

"How you doing today?" I asked.

Ma forced a tired smile from her jowly face. "Three pancakes or four?"

"Four." I hated to see all her hard work go to waste.

She piled them on my plate, slapped butter on top, and handed me the bottle of syrup.

"Thanks, Ma."

She dropped into the chair beside me with such force the legs splayed slightly.

"Bingo tonight?" I asked. She'd won two hundred dollars at the local church last month, and what was once an occasional occurrence now bordered on outright obsession.

Ma shrugged. "Maybe I won't go. Maybe I'll stay home with you tonight."

She probably had her Bingo Survival Kit, full of daubers, doo-dads, her Lucky Stiff coffee mug and her toilet seat-shaped comfort cushion already locked and loaded.

Bingo night was Ma's night.

"No, you go ahead Ma," I said. "Take all their money this time."

As I wolfed my breakfast down I caught her looking at me, a slight smile on her face.

"What?" I asked, around a mouthful of pancakes.

"Nothing."

But it's how Ma always looked at me.

Like after Bingo, I was all she had left to live for.

No pressure or anything.

CHAPTER 5

After Ma dropped me off at the glass shop and I picked up my car I drove to Annette Begley's apartment. The stately elm and maple trees that lined her street had already shed their splendor and the fallen leaves, once red and gold, now littered the narrow drive. After last night's rain they looked limp and brown. Dead.

Annette lived on a dead-end street in a rundown house that had been carved up into apartments. On each side of the house a staircase led to the second floor. Two apartments up, one down. After checking the ground floor and the upper left apartment with no luck, I climbed the stairs on the right. They creaked with every step I took.

At the top, an unpainted gray door with the letter C nailed beside it told me I'd found Annette's apartment.

I banged on the door. No answer. I tried the knob. Locked.

I looked at the filthy, unscreened window beside the door. One whack with my elbow. One whack and I'd be in. I pulled my arm back, ready to smash the glass.

I thought about it for a second.

I lifted the welcome mat, found the spare key and unlocked the door.

The apartment was tiny, even by tiny apartment standards. Pops would have said it was so small you had to go outside to change your mind. I went into the miniscule kitchen and opened the cupboard. Five packages of ramen noodles sat on the first shelf, along with a box of cereal, two cans of tuna fish and a bottle of ketchup.

I looked in the fridge. Three eggs, butter, two slices of cheese and a half package of ham were on the first shelf. On the top shelf I found an inch of milk in a half-gallon container. I gave it a sniff.

And wished I hadn't.

I checked the combination living room and dining room. An octagonal glass table held an arrangement of dried flowers. I picked up the vase. A little bit of water sloshed in it.

The dried flowers weren't intentional.

One back leg had broken off the couch. It now rested on a brick.

I sat on the couch and looked around the room. I took it all in, hoping for a case-breaking clue to jump out at me.

After about five minutes, I realized I'd wasted a small part of my life I'd never get back.

I walked into the bedroom, hardly larger than the full bed centered in it. A beige comforter covered the mattress. I glanced at the end table where a small lamp with a yellowed, cracked plastic shade and a book sat. I picked up the book. Tolstoy's *War and Peace*. What I also would choose for a little light reading.

Except not.

Three steps to the neat-as-a-pin bathroom. A place for everything and everything in its place. Ma could learn a thing or two from Annette Begley.

I looked at her makeup. Eyeliner. Mascara. Eye shadow. Blush. And many colors of lipstick. It looked like she hadn't packed much when she left.

That seemed odd. Most of the girls I saw wandering around town wore two or three coats of the stuff. In case the first one wore off.

I returned to the bedroom and looked in the tiny closet. An overnight bag sat on the floor. Four pair of shoes. Black heels. Clear plastic heels. Black flats. A pair of sneakers.

I checked the worn four drawer dresser in the corner. Bras, underwear and socks in the top drawer. Stripper outfits in the second. Shirts in the third. Jeans in the bottom.

I studied the stacks of underwear but couldn't tell how many she'd taken.

The shirt drawer seemed almost full. The jeans drawer, too. So she hadn't taken much.

If she'd had time to pack at all.

But nothing led me to believe she'd been forced to leave. Nothing broken, nothing damaged, nothing scattered around the house. No sign of forced entry.

Annette Begley was just…gone.

A dark jewelry box sat on the dresser's right corner. I opened each drawer. One held earrings. A few pairs, some singles. The other drawer had three pictures.

One showed a topless girl, shot in the mirror. Relying on my expert detective skills, I determined the impressive body belonged to Annette. Because I could see her face as well.

The second picture showed her again, sitting on a rock on the edge of a river. She had a peaceful, contented smile. She wore jeans and a white sweater, and her hair flowed like lava from her ponytail. The quintessential girl next door. Who also gave one hell of a lap dance.

In the third picture I saw a shirtless man. He looked my age. He had a decent smile, brown hair, and a muscular, shaved chest. The type of chest that makes a girl swoon.

I tried to convince myself I once had a chest like his.

I looked closer. He had a tattoo over his heart. I couldn't make it out.

But I knew someone who could.

Every time I saw Westfield Police Sergeant Venus Robinson I thought about high school, where she and I had been classmates about a million years ago. I played football, she played field hockey. You know what they say about field hockey girls. The only boyfriends they can get are the softball girls.

Throughout high school, Venus had kept her head above all that talk. She wore makeup and perfume every day, her hair looked shampoo commercial perfect, and her short skirts showed off her great legs.

Venus Robinson was all girl, all the time. And back then, the girl of my dreams. Once or twice during senior year when I caught her smiling at me in the lunch room I thought maybe she wanted me, too.

But I remained ridiculously shy and monumentally awkward. As it turned out, stupid to boot.

Because one day she stopped smiling. Not long after, I saw Venus walking arm in arm with Larry Pottle, a trumpet player in the school band.

A trumpet player, for Pete's sake. With runaway acne and coke bottle glasses.

They married after college. Remained married to this very day.

Larry Pottle was the luckiest damn trumpet playing jerk in the world.

Venus's dad had been a career cop in Westfield, and she'd followed the old man at a time when few women chose to be police officers. She became the first female patrol officer in Westfield as a cute twenty-two year old, and didn't that get the boys talking.

She made Detective in seven years. Five years later she was promoted to Sergeant and ran the Communications Center. Three years ago she took over the Detective division when Orel Cluck had a stroke that drove him into retirement.

If you listened to the folks around City Hall, there were multiple reasons why Venus Robinson achieved her rapid climb. She was good in the sack. She was Don Robinson's baby girl. The Chief was a complete feminist lunatic.

In my eyes it was because Venus was the best cop around, bar none, but my judgment might have been clouded a tad by how she still smiled at me when I made her laugh.

As I approached her office on the second floor of the Westfield Police Department, she looked like she still kept herself above the foolishness. As always, her makeup was perfect. The hair that once hung to her waist now brushed the midpoint of her shoulder blades. It remained a beautiful rich brown, one I suspect Clairol helped from time to time. Her dark blue semi-conservative skirt forever answered the question about whether she'd kept her field hockey legs. A resounding yes. She wore the top two buttons of her light blue blouse undone, showing she dared to be an attractive woman in a male-dominated profession.

Venus looked at me. "Well, if it isn't the great Paul Doyle?" She stood and gave me a hug. She still smelled good, too.

Venus Robinson. And me. The return engagement.

I sat in the chair beside her desk. "The great Paul Doyle all right. Great big."

"No," she said. "Just great." Her eyes softened. Years ago, that move would have slain me. But she had Larry Pottle's picture on the corner of her desk. I drove by their house often. It was blue with white shutters, had a white picket fence and a well-trimmed hedge. A rambunctious Irish Setter ruled the yard. The house had a big picture window that she could look out, every day, and gaze toward her future.

Not her past.

I thought about the lunchroom and her smile. About me being too stupid to act on it. And knew for the hundredth time a moment passed is a moment lost.

"It's you who looks great, Venus," I said.

"Listen to the crap that comes out of your mouth. Only thing I look is old." She laughed and patted her nearly flat stomach. "And where did this come from? Shit, I have a pooch that would make the kennel club proud."

I snuck a peek. You could iron clothes on her abs. "Guess you'll do for an old broad who cranked out a couple of rugrats."

She glanced at the picture frame that held photos of her two boys at various ages. She beamed like only a mother could. "The little buggers. When I get big and fat I'll tell them, 'Your momma looked hot before you came along.'"

She still does, I almost said. But that might have upset the applecart. And I needed that applecart to remain right where it sat. Instead I said, "So lady, can you talk about a case?"

"What's on your mind?"

"A woman named Annette Begley. Twenty years old. Her uncle says she's missing." I leaned back in the chair and winced as it creaked.

Big Paul Doyle. Too damn big.

Venus flipped through her notepad. "Nothing about a missing woman named Annette Begley. Nothing that I've heard, anyway."

I pulled the pictures out of my pocket and put them on her desk.

When she saw the topless one, she sighed. "Mine used to look like that before they starting heading for my belly."

"Ah yes. I remember them well."

"How sweet of you." A hint of color danced in her cheeks. "I think. And when you're done reminiscing, can we move on?"

"If we must. But the guy with the tattoo on his chest. If I were a world-class detective, I might think that's important. What does a professional say?"

She tapped the photo. "That's a nice chest."

"I know, right? I don't recognize the face, but I thought if we identify the tattoo we might figure out the wearer of the brand. Find out who Annette was playing footsies with."

"I get you," she said, tapping her temple. "You think it might be a clue."

"My humble opinion. Can you guys blow it up and get a better look?"

Her face looked like she just sucked a lemon. "Oh, that's where the 'we' comes in. When you mean 'me.' I love it when a private citizen comes in and wants to use taxpayer dollars for his benefit."

I gave her my full-power lady killer smile.

She shook her head and took the photo. "Nice try with the pearly whites, Doyle. I'll see what I can do, anyway." She pushed the others toward me. "You want to keep these?"

I took them. "Annette dances at The Limit. She goes by Cherry Delight. Her uncle is Lou Principi. Classy guy. Lets his niece shake her stuff up on stage."

"I know all about Lou, trust me. We tapped one of his girls for prostitution when she offered to provide extra loving for an off-duty cop. We tried to get her to roll on Lou for other stuff we've heard rumors about, but she refused to talk. We're still looking."

"Good to know. Since I work for him I'll tell him to watch his back."

Venus chuckled. "That'll give me another excuse to pistol whip you. As if I need more incentive."

"You guys have anything even close to concrete on Lou? Something that can get my case moving?"

She leaned forward and doodled on her note pad. Tapped it with her pen. "Is this an 'I show you mine, you show me yours' kind of thing? Because right now I'd say I have a hell of a lot more to show than you do. As usual."

I looked her up and down. "I won't deny that."

She shoved my arm. "Bite me, Paul. You know what I mean. We've been looking at Lou for quite a while now but we haven't cracked the nut yet. We have rules. That whole ethics-integrity thing puts a damper on our fun sometimes."

The good humor seemed to vanish from the room. "And you're thinking, 'Here's where Paul Doyle comes in. He's not bound by any of that.'"

I'm sure I looked like a basset hound, because Venus shook her head. "It's not like that."

"No big deal. I can sniff around a bit. Garbage man at your service."

She gave me a cheerleader smile. "Thatta boy."

"I'll take solace in the fact Lou is paying me to find his niece. Let's say in the course of trying to find her, I ask a few of the girls a few questions. Maybe I'll learn something that can help us both."

"And then you'll be willing to show me yours?"

"I always have been, dear. Apparently you never noticed."

She waved her arms in a safe sign. "You ever hear of subtle innuendo?"

"Come on, nothing I do is subtle. Why would innuendo be any different?"

Venus tapped her pen on the desk. "Speaking of subtle, Lou says his niece is missing but hasn't talked to us about it. Wonder why?"

I puffed my chest out. "He cared enough to hire the very best."

"Is he paying you what you're worth? Like three bucks?"

I told her how much. "Apparently *he* recognizes true quality when he sees it."

She scrunched her eyebrows together. "For a skinflint like Lou that's a king's ransom. He could have us for free. Or he could overpay you. I'm thinking if he's willing to lay out that kind of money, maybe he hopes he can keep it under the radar."

"And I put it smack dab in front of you."

"Don't sweat it, Paul. Lou isn't very high on our list right now. Bad time for the crime busters. The yearly pot harvest bust is wrapping up. We have the annual shoot-'em-up bloodbath in two weeks when deer season starts. And about a thousand other tasks the city says we're manned to do, but can't quite fit in to the daily rotation. In short, we're busy as hell, and Lou's still a rumor. But keep your eyes open? You ever decide you want to show me yours, you give me a call."

And then Venus Robinson gave me one of her lunchroom smiles from a million years ago. "You play your cards right, I may even buy you a beer."

CHAPTER 6

The girl who worked The Limit's bar doubled as waitress on a slow afternoon. With four patrons she could easily handle both jobs and still have time left over to contemplate the mysteries of the universe.

I studied her disinterested face as she pulled a couple of beers from the cooler. It didn't look like she'd made much headway on those mysteries yet.

But the day was young. And I'm an optimist.

I watched as she made her way down the bar to me. Her black hair hung to her jaw in a wedge. She had purple nails, green rimmed sunglasses that rested on top of her head and held her hair back, red shorts and a black blouse with a wide white collar. I'd found my rainbow.

"Coffee," I said.

She brought me a heavy white mug. "Two bucks."

I shook my head. "I think I'm supposed to be comped. I work here."

She cocked her head and squinted. "You a dancer?"

I rubbed my impressive gut. "Like none you've ever seen. Or ever want to. What's your name?"

"Tori."

"I'm Paul. I drink a lot of coffee. Ask a lot of questions."

Her smile told me she'd talked to too many flirty, intoxicated men for the too few tips she earned. In short, she barely tolerated me.

I sized her up. Early twenties. Likely a college girl.

I slid her a dollar tip. "For textbooks."

She shook her head. "Dude. Erstwhile Chemistry major. Books are awful pricey."

I sipped the coffee. Not bad. I pushed another bill her way. "Earn 'em a cup at a time."

Two dancers hovered near the bar. I zeroed in on the big-chested one with the turned-up nose. The other one gauged my disinterest, gathered up her purse and headed toward the back door for a smoke.

The woman who remained was about average height, but there was nothing else average that I could see. She had more curves than a Rocky Mountain back road, ice blue eyes, jet-black hair and a face that belonged center stage in an oil painting. She gave me a pleasant smile. "What's up, Superman?"

"Close," I said. "Paul Doyle."

She looked suitably impressed. "I'm Veronica. Cute as a bug in a rug, huh?"

"Indescribably. You danced here long?"

She giggled. "I'm the extremely talented new talent."

She looked like a polished pro. "Is this the only club where you've danced?"

Veronica laughed. Long and utterly happy. "Heck no, techno. I danced in Chicago. Florida. California. Now I'm cooling my heels in little old Westfield Maine. Came here to take care of some family things."

"Quite a fall from the big time."

Her eyes gleamed. "Here's a bigger one. Thirteen years ago I had a *Hustler* cover. Nineteen years old and I was big time. Now I'm raising two kids and trying to buy a house."

I wanted to ask her about the perishable nature of a dancing career. While doing math in public isn't my forte, she was thirty-two now. In ten more years…few men wanted to see a forty-two year old stripper. Even one with a *Hustler* cover on her resume.

Instead I asked, "Have you been here long enough to see any behind the scenes activities at the club?"

"You mean like drugs? Girls who screw customers when their rent is due? Handjobs under the table for an extra hundred?"

"If you say so."

"Not a thing." Another bubbly laugh.

"You say you're new here. You know Cherry?"

Veronica shook her head. "Cherries are just about nonexistent in this place. If ya know what I mean." She gave me a shoulder check for emphasis.

"Got it. But I'm looking for a dancer named Cherry."

"I know, handsome. Just pulling your leg. My first week here Cherry and I did a two-girl lap dance for a bachelor party. I made out with her on stage and the guys loved it." She tapped her chin with her index finger. "Come to think of it, I haven't seen her since. You think maybe I should change my flavor of mouthwash?"

I chuckled. "I'm sure that wasn't it."

She put a hand on her hip and shook her impressive assets like a poor man's Mae West. "Trust me babe, me neither."

"Moving on. How about Lou? Anything interesting going on there?"

Veronica's face lit up. "Did you know someone beat him up last night?"

"Bad?"

She rolled her eyes. "Is there another kind?"

"Guess not."

"By the look of his face, someone has an anger management problem."

Lou came out of his office and started toward the door. When I caught his eye, he pivoted and pointed toward the office. I turned to follow him.

Veronica took my hand. And held it like she meant it. "Hold on a sec. It's slow right now. You want to go in the back for a dance?"

I sighed. "If only I could, Veronica. But alas, I'm on the clock."

Lou had a black eye, a split lip and a busted nose. He motioned to the chair in front of his desk.

He caught me assessing his remodeled visage. "What you lookin' at?"

"You should have hired me to be a bodyguard instead."

"I can take care of myself."

"I can see that. But for the record, how does the other guy's fist look?"

He grimaced. "Only one, I'd still be kickin' his ass. But one grabbed me from behind. And the other whacked me."

"They disagreed with the cover charge?"

"Doyle, you ain't nearly as funny as you think you are."

"Look, if I'm even half as funny as I think I am, I'm still freaking hilarious."

"Whatever. I ain't payin' for no damn comedy show."

His cheek had started to take on a yellow glow. He touched his split lip.

I could relate. I'd burned mine on Tori's coffee. I gave it a sympathetic lick. "Tell me about the boys that hit you."

His lip curled. "Big black one. Fat Italian one."

"Come on Lou. How do you know he's Italian?"

"I smelled the garlic."

"Skills like that, you should be a detective. Tell me about the other one."

"You wanna know how I knew he was black? My goddamn eyes told me."

"Oh, now you got jokes. But for fun, can you tell me anything else that might narrow down the field?"

Lou muttered, "The black guy was like six-three. Taller than you but not so fat. Bald with a goatee. He wore a black leather coat. The Italian was wide as a door. Black hair in a ponytail. He's the faggot who hit me."

"Is there anybody mad enough that they'd want to beat you up?"

He fidgeted with a pen for a moment. "My ex-wife. An ex-business partner. An ex-customer. Pick one."

But he was bullshitting me and we both knew it. "Nice list. Now how about you tell me what's really going on behind the curtain?"

Lou shrugged. "When I fall in the shit, it's my job to get out of it. So how about you keep your nose outta my business and find Cherry like I'm payin' you to do. Before things get worse."

Just because someone says it doesn't mean I have to do it. Lou told me not to worry about his beat down, but I couldn't help but wonder why two guys had hit him. Since my luck had run snake eyes so far on finding Annette, I turned my attention to him.

The guys were likely pros. But who would send real muscle after a small-timer like Lou Principi? I thought about guys I knew. Guys who might not be the most understanding if you disappointed them.

Patches Cole out of Bangor. Lucien Leroux, who does cross-border work from Quebec. Local guy Pete Neff.

I tried to place the strong-arms. Tall, black guy. Big Italian. Nothing came to mind. But boys like that didn't often run in the elegant circles I did. While I didn't know all of the thugs and lowlifes in the area, I knew a pond where the scum sometimes congealed.

I walked into Chelsea's Pub soon after dark, smack dab in the middle of Happy Hour. The time when you expect it to be packed. Chelsea's was empty, save for the guy behind the bar.

His nametag said Marty, which saved on introductions. I ordered a beer.

He brought it over and hovered near me. My animal magnetism snared another unsuspecting victim.

Or maybe he was simply bored beyond words.

I decided to break the ice. "What's up, Marty?"

He glanced at the door. "You're the first one to come through there in an hour."

I looked around. "That's progress, right?"

Marty leaned hard on the bar in front of me. "If I want to stay in business, sure. This place used to be hopping. Then I decide to shut the kitchen down and just do booze. Save a little overhead and a lot of hassle. By the looks of it, I'm a far sight short of a genius."

"You just don't ever know, do you? Like my ex-wife used to tell me, no matter how good things seem, you're still only one step from the gutter."

"Cheery thing, wasn't she?"

"Among other redeeming qualities."

Marty wiped the bar down with a damp rag, neatly folded it, put it beside the sink and came back to me. "This place is such a loser, I'm about an inch from torching it and taking the insurance." He cut his eyes to my face. "You ain't a cop, are you?"

I shook my head. "Insurance adjustor."

He chuckled nervously, and I enjoyed it a while longer than I should have. His mood improved significantly when I waved him off and said, "I'm a private investigator. If this disappears in a cloud of smoke, my lips are sealed."

Marty looked relieved.

"Unless the insurance company hires me to investigate."

He shook his head. "One step from the gutter. Maybe your old lady had it right."

If Marty was going to continue to hover, I might as well use him. "Since we're good buddies and all, maybe you can help me with a couple of boys. A big Italian guy who wears his hair in a ponytail. With a black guy. Think Shaft without the cool music."

Marty reached over and grabbed the rag. He wiped the bar down again.

When he came close, I slammed my hand on top of his. "The bar is pretty clean already. How about we talk instead?"

Marty gave me nervous baby blues and said, "Look, mister. Here's where I find myself. There are good guys and bad guys in the world. But with some it's hard to tell." He looked at me hard, like he was trying to decide on which side of the equation I fell.

I slid a fifty across the bar to help with his math.

He crammed the bill in his shirt pocket like it belonged there all along. "Those boys come in from time to time. But you don't want to mess with them. They busted a guy up a couple of weeks ago because he stepped on the black guy's shoe."

"Well, you can't let just anyone do that. You are your reputation."

Marty snickered. "Their reputation is asshole times two in my book."

"Any guess where I can find these two respectable, law-abiding gentlemen?"

He shook his head. "You didn't get it from me."

"Get what?"

"You know…oh, you're playing along. I got you." Marty's face turned a rosy shade. "So they're paying customers. And as you can see," he looked around the empty bar, "I can't afford to lose any."

"Even assholes?"

"Especially assholes like those two. I piss them off, who knows what they'll do? It's hard to earn a living from a hospital bed."

I'd been there twice before. Once for a day. That wasn't bad, except for the fifty dollar pills they force-fed me. The next time had been six days. I fingered my left shoulder an inch below the collarbone. Bullets will keep you down a bit longer. Even if you think you're Superman.

"Yeah I know," I said.

"You going to mess with them? They don't seem the type who would cooperate much."

I patted my side. "I carry my cooperator right here. You know who those boys work for?"

Marty scurried away like a cockroach when the light comes on. He stayed away for a couple of minutes.

When he came back, he seemed edgy. "You've got to promise you won't let anyone know I told you."

"Shouldn't be hard. You haven't told me anything so far."

Marty fidgeted with his apron. "Yeah, you're right. These guys you asked about. I hear they work for Mikey Cross."

Mikey Cross. Holy shit. Lou Principi hit the big time.

CHAPTER 7

I couldn't wait to tell Lou the good news. I'd snooped uninvited into his business and I'd discovered his secret Mikey Cross connection. Sadly, when I went to The Limit to see Lou he wasn't in. But since I made the drive I figured I'd stay a while.

I was bushed, so I mentally punched the time clock.

I counted nine customers, which didn't overly surprise me. Wednesday evenings at The Limit are notoriously slow. Notoriously slow means it's bad for the dancers and their cash flow but good for the customers. The girls are chattier, more inclined to spend a few minutes talking before they make the glorious, headfirst plunge for a customer's wallet. But on a night like this, dancers might not earn enough to cover the kids' babysitter tab.

Observations. As a detective that's what I specialize in. I can't turn it off. So I remained fully in character when I observed, with great interest and a dash of good old-fashioned carnal lust, the slim, breathtaking raven-haired beauty, wearing a sparkling silver mini that reflected the overhead lights like a prismatic disco ball, who slipped from the shadows and glided near me.

Not near me.

To me.

Directly.

The tables at The Limit are round, big enough for three chairs. As the woman came closer she looked at the stage to my right where Desiree, with her cartoonish fake boobs, gyrated for four men who were mesmerized by the wonders of implants.

She glanced to my left where a tall girl, flat-chested and heavily-tattooed, danced poorly. No men surrounded her circular stage. The brunette chose tattoo girl as her backdrop, placed her purse on the table, and sat near me.

She leaned over. "Having fun tonight?" I didn't move, so she leaned a bit closer and nudged me. "I'm talking to you, handsome."

Handsome. So she could lie with a straight face. Useful quality for a stripper. I stuck out my hand. "Paul. And you're…?"

She took it. "Ecstasy."

"Dancer name?"

She chuckled. "No, I'm really that good. Aren't all women?"

"Not the ones I've been with."

Ecstasy rubbed a small scar on her chin. "Let's see. Appears to me the only constant in this equation is you."

I must have looked mildly irritated, because she clutched my arm. "I'm sorry. I wanted to make you laugh."

"Fair enough. When will you start?"

Her shoulders drooped and she sighed. "Of all the strip joints in all the towns in the world you had to walk into mine." She dropped her head into her hands, peered at me through her spread fingers, and waited until she heard me chuckle. When she popped her head up she gave me double-barreled dimples and the warmest smile I'd seen in years.

And something long-dormant in me fluttered. Just the tiniest bit. I reached out and brushed a loose tendril of hair away from her eyes. "Nice to meet you, Ecstasy."

She nodded. "And you as well. Although I think I've seen you here before."

"I think I've seen you too. But you never made it over to me. Popular girl."

She looked around the nearly empty club. "I'm not too popular tonight."

"So you can fit me in."

"Yes Paul, tonight I can fit you in. And now that we've met, I'll fit you in a lot more often."

That thing in my chest fluttered again and I didn't mind one bit. I studied her features. Not your white-girl-from-the-trailer-park face that dominated The

Limit. Latina? Maybe. Regardless, she was different than what I expected from a tiny, trashy strip club in the center of Nowhere Special, Maine.

I liked different.

Especially as it was presented by the woman next to me.

Ecstasy patted my arm. "So Paul, what do you do?"

"Detective."

"You're a policeman? The fuzz? The heat? The man?"

"No, not a policeman." Did it matter what I did? But she was talking to me, and talking with women had been pretty unproductive lately. I'd try to keep it going. "I'm a private investigator."

She wrapped her arms around my left one like she was drowning and I was a life preserver. "Ooo," she cooed. "Like Magnum, P. I.?"

I patted my expansive belly. "Yes. Exactly like Magnum, P. I., except it snows more here and I don't quite measure up to Tom Selleck in the looks department."

Ecstasy knew the Stripper's Code: Always find a way to flatter the customer. "Not everyone has to look like Tom Selleck to be sexy."

I sighed. "You stretched too far, girl. The only sexy part of me is my wallet. Don't try so hard." I probably said it more firmly than she deserved. But you put yourself out on the tightrope, you just might fall off. Them's the breaks, kid.

The Stripper's Code, especially on a slow night: Backpedal, but continue to flatter. Ecstasy said, "Don't underestimate yourself. Women find different things attractive." She gave my arm another squeeze. "I didn't walk over here for your wallet."

"Right," I said. I studied her. Five-foot-six in her heels, no more. Black hair cascaded in waves over her shoulders. It framed her face and caressed her cheeks when she moved her head. She had flawless light brown skin and chocolate eyes that danced the jitterbug when she laughed. The tiniest lines formed around the corners of her mouth when she smiled. I gazed at her athletic body and made a snap assessment.

I might be the bottom, but she's the tops.

So I had two choices. Tone it down, or watch her walk to another table where three guys in dress shirts and loosened ties were making lover boy eyes her way. As they built a stack of cash on the table.

I toned it down. "Ecstasy, are you a local?" I saw a cloud cross her face. As quickly as it came, it blew away.

"No, Paul. I relocated here for the career opportunities."

"Really?" I looked around the shabby club. "Yeah, I'd move here if I wanted to improve my standard of living."

She looked amused. "Again, not everything's like Tom Selleck. The handsomest one doesn't always win."

"You haven't been here for a winter yet, I'm guessing?"

She shook her head.

I said, "After it hits twenty below and the snow comes in November and stays until April, we'll see if you still like it."

She gave a big, fake shiver. "Twenty below? Where I come from…"

I picked up her sentence. "Where you come from it doesn't hit twenty below?" That narrowed it down. A little. I tried to read the truth in her face.

But I was sidetracked at her eyes. Appearing nearly black in the low light, they seemed so deep I could bathe in them.

They flickered.

Then smoldered.

Then glowed.

As a smile tugged at the corners of her mouth, her eyes…invited me in.

I took the plunge.

In a flash she swept me away from the club. From the case.

But mostly, from being Paul Doyle.

I was adrift in the magnificence of her. For the first time in my life I felt incapable of rational thought.

I gulped, utterly befuddled. She was just a stripper. Nothing more.

But my lonely heart thought otherwise. It wasn't only that I couldn't take my eyes off her. I felt I needed to hear her breathe. I needed to watch the lights dance across her face. I needed to watch her smile slowly crescendo. I needed to feel her close to me. I needed…her.

More than anything I could place my finger on, at that moment I determined the solution to my life thus far was her.

Yet I was paralyzed. I yearned to take the next step, but I had no earthly idea what the next step was. Or how to take it. Or where it would lead.

Or if she'd skitter away like a dry leaf in the wind if I so much as flinched.

So I did…absolutely nothing. The ultimate no-risk move.

Ecstasy dropped her gaze, fidgeted in the silence that followed, tore small pieces from a napkin and looked down at the table. Finally she said, "Well Paul, you're a sweet guy, and I enjoyed talking to you. But I must make some money tonight." She put the napkin down, picked up her purse and swiveled around to the tie wearers.

Moment of truth. Customer and client, if I so chose. "Ecstasy?" I blurted.

She swiveled back. "Yes?"

"I'd be interested in you making money. With me."

She nodded, seemingly pleased. The next step of the Stripper's Code: Sort out the financial details before things progressed any further. She patted my hand. "That's very sweet of you. It's twenty dollars a song for topless. Thirty dollars for nude."

I gulped. "You do nude?"

"Spectacularly so."

My love life had been slower than cold molasses running uphill on a winter day. The last nude woman I'd seen was one who went by Forna Kate, a faded stripper with dirty blonde hair, a baby belly, and a tattoo on her rapidly spreading behind. Luckily, I hadn't seen old Kate dance at the club in a while, and had no immediate need to see her again. Nude or no. But Ecstasy?

"Nude," I mumbled.

She reached for my left hand with her right. "Let me entertain you."

My father endlessly reminisced about watching TV and seeing Neil Armstrong walk on the moon. My mother recollected every detail of the moment when she received the call saying her father had died.

And when I went home, lay in my bed and closed my eyes, I relived each moment I had spent with Ecstasy. From the first, when she walked me to a private booth in the back, to the second when she slipped off her silver dress, to the next when she removed her tiny thong. To her tipping my chin up. To her pulling my eyes into hers. To her sliding onto my lap. To her brushing my face with her hair.

I remembered her looking at me.

Her eyes.

Welcoming me. Wanting me.

Me.

And I remembered watching her dance.

And I remembered my near panic at the last notes of the song during the fastest three minutes of my life.

And I remembered Ecstasy bringing her lips to my ear and whispering, "Do you want another dance?"

And I remembered gasping, "Yes."

And I remembered her smiling.

Of course I remembered those eyes.

And the way her lips brushed my neck when she pulled me close as the music ended. Not like I was a customer. I'd been a customer with Yvette and Forna Kate. No spark. No connection. No breathless excitement.

But with Ecstasy it felt like we could be any two people who, on an off-chance, might meet. Two people who might experience an instant attraction. Who might decide to act on that attraction.

And who might one day share something more.

She curled up in my arms for a minute more as I ran my index finger down her nose, over her lips, and traced a circle around the scar on her chin. Then Ecstasy patted my chest, stood up, slipped on her thong and her dress. I paid her in twenties and she caught my hand, led me to the front desk where Yvette watched a *Three's Company* rerun on the black and white, gave me a hug and thanked me.

Ecstasy said she'd like to see me again.

See me again because we'd shared a pleasant conversation? Because I made her laugh? See me again because I'd spent over a hundred dollars on her?

Or see me again because, just for an instant, she felt what I felt?

I turned the light on, stood up and looked at my body in the mirror. I had a heavily muscled frame from hours I'd spent at the gym. Good hours from the years I was married and I cared about how I looked.

But now a layer of fat had taken over. Ma's home cooking. Too many hours in front of the TV. Too much time feeling sorry for myself, and too little time changing. Dejected, I dropped to the edge of the bed.

She was Ecstasy, after all. And here I sat, forty pounds past my prime.

I had a few scattered gray hairs dotted amongst my brown ones. Mine were tired hazel eyes. Eyes that used to speak to a woman, I'd hoped when I was young. But now I feared they only said that I had failed.

I needed to snap out of this funk.

Without a doubt, I needed Ecstasy.

So like my father remembering Neil Armstrong walking on the moon, and like my mother reminiscing about every detail of the moment when she received the call saying her father had died, I once again let my mind wander and pored over every detail about the time Ecstasy and I had spent together.

When, for the first time in a long time, I had felt like a man.

CHAPTER 8

When I awoke the next morning I still couldn't get Ecstasy out of my mind. I guessed her age at late-twenties. I'd recently hit forty, limping along in the breakdown lane to middle age. She had a slim, athletic body. Mine was…no other way to say it, kind of thick. Emphasis on thick. Not kind of.

Men fall for hard bodies every day. It's our own little fantasy. No matter how old, fat, out of shape or stupid we are, we feel we deserve to be loved by a young, hard-bodied woman.

But Ecstasy seemed to be more than just a hard body. I chased the thought of her around, trying to touch what made her different. For starters, she'd done a pretty good job carving me up with her one-liners. The funny one at cocktail parties? That was my domain.

I liked the competition.

She was playful and smart. Sexy? Sure, but overt sexuality would go away over time. Something else attracted me.

I narrowed it down to her eyes.

They had depth, like they'd seen the yang that countered the ying, the pain that matched the joy. While they offered to be a life preserver to a drowning fool, once or twice I'd thought her eyes had asked me if I might offer them the same. If I could, just for a moment, give them what they'd given me. Hope…or understanding…or maybe acceptance.

Maybe no more than a simple acceptance of the person in front of me.

And because of that, I was smitten with a stripper named Ecstasy.

Still, as if a guy like me had a chance with a girl like her.

43

But miracles happened from time to time, every other millennium or so. Who's to say one couldn't happen again? Right here, right now?

Yet sometimes even miracles need a shove in the right direction. If I had a snowball's chance in hell, I had to take the first step. I'd sat on my ass for a year. I'd gotten fat, then rationalized it was normal, a guy filling out as he aged.

Except I'd done most of my filling out around my waist. And now that I'd met a girl who sucked the breath out of my lungs, who made my head spin like a tilt-a-whirl on steroids, and who made me start to feel alive again, I had to change.

Not next week. Not next month or next year.

So I'd rolled out of bed and dragged myself for a jog around the streets near my house.

Getting back into shape had sounded like a swell idea when I sat on the couch drinking beer. But the light-headedness, the pounding heart, aching knees and rigid back I'd felt soon after I'd finished sent me straight to bed for the rest of the day.

Which, in hindsight, was mild compared to what I felt when the alarm went off today.

It hurt to breathe. I felt knife jabs in my back, set in deep like they planned on staying a while. Last night's pills hadn't impressed them much. They kept digging into the depths of my spine, angry pokes that only abated as my left hip became numb.

Yeah, working out. The cat's meow.

I slid to the edge of the bed, swung my feet down, and winced. A vise had a death grip on my spine and it appeared to be tightening.

But sitting here feeling sorry for myself wouldn't cut it. I had to get up and work the pain out now. I struggled to stand and the vise loosened a bit. I hunched forward, afraid of another jab.

No jab, but no day at the beach.

I cursed. I couldn't go through the day hunched over like I was trying to see my nuts. I forced myself upright, every inch a battle.

I won, with only minor casualties. I had a hamstring so taut I could hang laundry on it. I threw the offending leg forward. Now my hip and hammy rebelled.

But I was tired of being a fatass. Tired of saying I'd start a diet tomorrow, or I'd go to the gym tomorrow. I always said tomorrow.

I thought about Ecstasy. Excuses wouldn't fly if I wanted a girl like her.

Screw the back, screw the hammy. I gritted my teeth and stepped again. Again.

I peered outside. The treetops, whipped by the wind, waved at me. I gauged the temperature, went the conservative route, and decided on sweatpants and a windbreaker. Plus a windbreaker gave me the chance to slip a snub-nosed .38 in the right front pocket. Because not everyone likes me as much as I like me.

Hard to believe, but true.

I leaned down.

Jesus.

Four-year-olds can tie shoes. Even arthritic old ladies can tie shoes. But yesterday's workout had left me so damn sore it was an accomplishment to get my shoes on, never mind tie them. But I stuck with it, got the job done, and gingerly made my way to the door.

Water Street paralleled the Pessamoc River. While I enjoyed the view, nothing stopped the wind from roaring across the street and ripping its teeth into me. Still, I made it a mile downriver. Then, in a fit of sheer idiocy, I decided to plod along a little further. I had some thinking to do.

Why would Mikey Cross's boys visit Lou? Only one reason came to mind: Lou had something Mikey wanted. And, as a general rule, Mikey had a knack for making something that was yours into something that became his.

What did Lou have? The Limit. Maybe it was as simple as that. Mikey wanted The Limit. But why? I continued to mull it over.

The only problem with exerting so much brain power on Mikey and Lou was that I kept jogging away from the house while I was ruminating. Realizing that, I turned on a dime.

And reality set it. I'd never noticed before the entire jog home was slightly uphill. And today it was dead into the wind.

I closed my eyes and remembered Ecstasy when she curled up in my arms. Her smell. Her laugh. The electricity in her touch. The way it felt when I traced her face with my finger. The way she smiled when I did it. Like she liked me.

Her eyes. Most of all, her eyes.

That was enough to get me moving. I flipped my hood up, Rocky-style, and began the slow shuffle home.

"You want breakfast, Paul?" Ma waved the spatula at me, motioning me to sit.

Sweating like a pig and barely able to breathe I made it to the table, running a body health inventory with every step. Lower back? Steadily tightening. Hammy? Ehhh. Aching knee? No change.

I slid the end chair out and dropped into it. Ma handed me a cup of coffee. Better.

She returned to the stove. "How many eggs?"

Cholesterol bombs, some people call them. With Ma, everything screamed cholesterol. Eggs. Bacon. Pancakes with lots of rich butter and heavy syrup. And her specialty, French toast, the dreaded combination of bread, eggs, butter and syrup in one artery-clogging treat.

I patted my love handles. "Ma, do you like fruit?"

"Fruit? What kind of fruit?"

"I don't know. Bananas. Do you like bananas?"

"Eat your eggs." The plate clattered on the table in front of me.

Our conversation wouldn't go well, but I had to do it. "Doc Mitchell said I need to watch my cholesterol, and when we eat breakfast we go pretty heavy on the cholesterol."

Ma hovered near the table. "So now you don't like my breakfasts?"

We were headed down a well-traveled path. Ma met anything resembling dissent, anything that remotely sounded like disagreement, with ridicule and a generous side helping of guilt.

I said, "I like your breakfast just fine. But he said I should lose weight, and he worried about my cholesterol. Eggs are high in cholesterol. I think." I weakened slightly. "Aren't they?"

I read her face. Mostly cloudy with a good chance of a nasty storm on the horizon.

She slapped the table. "My breakfast fed your father. It fed your sister. It fed you well enough until today. And now, apparently it's not good enough."

When pushed into a corner by Ma, I'd learned to play rope-a-dope. Defend until she became word-weary. "Ma, it's not like that. It's…." The moment of truth. "Ma, I'm fat. And I don't want to be fat. I'm forty years old, and I want to see eighty. Right now, I don't think I'm going to get there."

Deep creases etched her forehead. She barked razor sharp words. "You're not fat, Paul. You're big-boned."

"Ma!" I groused, louder than a man should talk to the woman who made him. "Look at me. My belly is not big-boned. My butt is not big-boned."

I wiggled my arm and meat shook underneath. "This isn't big-boned. I'm fat, Ma. But I'm tired of being fat. And I'm tired of it being okay that I'm fat."

Her jaw chewed up a storm, though she hadn't touched her food. She ground her teeth back and forth.

She took my plate, walked to the trash can, and scraped the eggs in. She walked to the sink, rinsed the plate and dramatically flipped off the water.

When she turned to me I could see the storm had arrived. "You want fruit, mister? There's a diner up the street. I bet they'll serve you all the fruit you can stand." She stomped across the kitchen, through the living room, turned left into her room and slammed the door.

CHAPTER 9

It was time to talk to Lou about his Mikey problem and to see if there was any tie to Annette. I swung behind The Limit but didn't see Lou's pink Cadillac, which put me back in 'questioning strippers' mode. Annette might not have anything to do with Lou's troubles, but she'd shared the stage and the dressing room with more than a few women. Someone was bound to know more about her than I.

A grouchy bartender with two-toned hair and cutoff shorts that exposed too much of her falling bottom hadn't made coffee when I walked into The Limit. I'd have to introduce her to Tori. Tori always had coffee going. Tori is my girl.

I pointed to the empty pot. "That thing work?"

She crossed her arms. "It's after lunch. Who in their right mind drinks coffee this late?"

I stuck out a hand. "Paul Doyle. Pleased to meetcha."

She eyed me like an ornery teenager. "You want coffee now?"

"Naah. In five minutes will be fine." I motioned toward the pot. "You just do what you have to do there."

She muttered something, shook her head and dug a filter out from under the bar.

I scanned the room for a certain someone and came away disappointed.

I tapped the bar with my knuckles. "Hey Sunshine, you got a sec?"

The bartender spun on a dime. "Try Lola, it works better. And you don't have to knock. You're already here."

"Got it. Hey, by the way," I said, trying to act cool as a cucumber, "Ecstasy working?"

She rolled her eyes. "Jeez, you ain't one of them, are ya?" Lola looked me up and down with a level of animosity I hadn't seen since my ex-wife came by my office one time demanding a late alimony payment. "We got a whole smorgasborg of white girls and you want the sneak-across-the-border one? Typical."

I could tell cultural bias wasn't a problem with her. She had it down in spades. Where was Tori when I needed her?

Lola got the coffee brewing, then came near me. She exhaled. "There ain't no way you're the guy she was talking about."

Ecstasy was talking about…me? "What did she say?" I asked, way too quickly. Premature excitation, as it were.

"She said she met a guy. Sweet and awful funny, she said. Kinda described him like he was you." She looked me up and down again. "Though to be honest, I don't know what she sees in you."

I looked for something redeeming in her and came up empty. "I gotta say the feeling's mutual on this one."

Lola stared at me. "Well, we can scratch the sweet part. Say something funny, wiseguy. Let's see if she got that wrong, too."

I thought for a moment. "Guy wearing only cellophane walks into a psychiatrist's office. Says, 'Doc, is there something wrong with me?' Doc takes one look at him and says, 'Well, I can clearly see your nuts.'"

Her head twitched a couple of times as she worked through it, then she cracked the tiniest smile. "Funny enough. Ahh shit, I guess I'll tell ya."

"Tell me what?"

"Your little girlie is supposed to come in around seven tonight. She thinks you're nice so don't screw it up, okay? This stuff ain't easy as it is. Don't make it harder by messing with her heart."

Lola handed me the coffee. I turned from her, slightly confused and possibly overjoyed. Ecstasy thought I was nice? I inventoried the women. One who called herself Trouble sat at a small table by herself. I joined her.

Most dancers wear layered clothing, hiding their bodies until the big unveiling. Build up the mystery. Trouble, on the other hand, wore a simple white bikini, white heels and nothing more. No air of mystery. No intrigue. No salesmanship.

Trouble showed it all from the get go. Take it or leave it, mister. You don't want it, likely someone else will.

She had first-class legs, a good tummy with no baby bump, a nice, full chest, and lots of tattoos. My favorite one was in three-inch script from shoulder to shoulder just below her collarbone. My Life…My Way. Hard to argue with logic like that.

I looked at her face. She had swelling under her left eye and a bruised cheek that makeup and low light couldn't conceal. Her lip was split.

I touched her arm. "What happened?"

"My stupid boyfriend. When he gets crazy drunk he pops me. But this time he got it worse."

Trouble couldn't weigh one-twenty soaking wet. "How did he get it worse?"

She held up her right hand. "He got his nose broke by a girl."

One thing pissed me off more than about anything else in life. A jerk who punched women. "You need me to lay him out?"

Trouble shook her head. "Nah. He pulls that shit again, I'll lay him out my-self. For good."

She sounded like she meant it, and I had a better appreciation for why she called herself Trouble. "So girl, do you know Cherry?"

Trouble nodded. "Redhead. She dances nights and I do mostly days. I ain't seen her in a while." She grimaced. "My damn language. I haven't seen her in a while."

"She's missing. I'm trying to find her, but I'm pretty short on information right now."

Trouble closed her eyes and tapped her nose with her index finger. "You talk to that guy she dances for?"

"What guy?"

"Good looking. Wears a coat and a tie. Nice shirt. Nice shoes. He dresses like it's prom night and she just got elected queen."

"Haven't heard about him yet. Did he only come to see Cherry?"

"Not at first. You know them guys." She grimaced again. "Not them. Those. You know those guys who hover around like they have nothing better to do but look at our tits and think they're in love? He was like that until he saw Cherry." She sniffed. "Then he was exclusive. He smelled some good, too. Seductive."

"Nice vocabulary."

Trouble rolled her eyes. "I ain't an idiot, you know. I go to night school. I'm going to be a teacher."

That would give the students something to talk about. My teacher is hotter than yours. She's a stripper. And her name is Trouble. She can kick your teacher's ass, too.

The waitress brought my coffee and a drink for Trouble, which I covered. I asked, "Why do you think he only came for Cherry?"

Trouble thanked me for the drink. "You don't know anything, do you? We all have regulars. Guys who only want a certain girl." She ticked off her fingers. "There's guys who like black girls. Fat girls. Girls that look like their daughters. Girls with tattoos. Big tits. Small tits. So we're like a fast food restaurant. Come to The Limit, where you always get it your way."

"Do you have regulars?"

She tried smiling around her split lip. She gave it her all, but it came out cock-eyed. Still, I appreciated the effort. "Even the waitresses have regulars. When you get some guy who's hooked on you, you text him and say you're working, and he comes running like his butt's on fire. I have a grandpa says I look like his dead wife. He holds my hand and cries when he talks about her. I always cry too, but I feel like I'm his therapist, you know? There's one guy who tells his wife he's bowling. He calls my legs 'pins' and keeps saying he wants to nail the 7-10 split. I tell him he can as soon as he shows up with sixteen-pound balls. Two guys from my college class stop in sometimes. That gets a little weird when I see them on campus. But what are you going to do? Girl has to pay her bills."

"Is it hard doing this?" I asked. "Taking your clothes off for guys who only want to see you with your clothes off?"

Trouble sipped her drink a bit and glanced at me over the rim of her glass. When she put the glass down she said, "Girls don't set out to do this when we're playing with dolls, but one thing leads to another and some of us end up here. Me? Too much weed and no high school degree. But now I have a GED, I go to night school. Even though I do this now, the first thing I had to get right in my head was that I still respect me. Makes it easier to pull the top off after that, you know?"

Embracing self-respect. Interesting concept. "You mind if I ask you a few more questions about Cherry?"

"It's talk to you or talk to no one. You win by a nose."

"Despite the stiff competition. So, other than the first guy, how about other regulars for Cherry?"

Trouble's face wrinkled. "Like most of us, she had occasionals. Even her regular guy, he got two lap dances from me before she came along. But when he saw her he was a goner."

I thought about the picture I'd given Venus, the one of the guy with the tattoo. "You say you danced for him. Do you remember anything else about him?"

"He never tried to suck my tits or feel me up, so in my mind—good guy."

I was looking for a guy who didn't fondle strippers. Still…maybe I'd dig a little deeper. "Was he closer to your age, or mine?"

"He was old, like you." Trouble giggled, then batted her eyes and leaned close to me. "I like you a lot. You want a dance?"

I felt flattered that she'd fallen for me so quickly. Still, I had work to do. "How about I pay you to talk to me instead?"

She took my rejection well. She shrugged and adjusted her bikini top to better cover her impressive accoutrements. "Your money. Suit yourself, cowboy."

"Does Cherry have any close friends she hangs out with? Other dancers, maybe?"

Trouble's eyes drifted. She shook her head and started to get up. "You talk to Sexy yet?"

I wasn't sure if that was a description. "Who's Sexy?"

"Well you are, Big Guy." She giggled again. "But I'm talking about Cherry's friend with the purple hair."

Purple hair. My heart sank. "Tell me about her."

"She's like my size. Cute kid with nice tits. And hers are real, lucky bitch. Anyway, I guess she wanted her hair the color of grape jelly. You tell me why and we'll both know."

There might be a lot of purple-haired, big-chested girls in thriving metropolises like Portland or Bangor. But here in the Westfield area, I only knew of one: Shari Tappey. Who, last time I'd seen her, worked at her uncle's convenience store in Benton. With her clothes on.

Shari Tappey was now Sexy. I never wanted to consider that connotation. Ever again.

I asked, "Is she dancing tonight?"

Trouble shook her head. "She hasn't been here for a week at least, but I think her daddy was one of Cherry's occasionals. Story was one night he came in when Sexy was dancing and she ran off."

I knew her daddy. I bet he ran as fast in the other direction.

Trouble said she'd ask around a bit and see if any other girls knew anything about Cherry or Shari. I slipped her my card and matching twenties, which earned me a hug and a kiss on the cheek.

On my way out the door I called my old friend Sheriff Gerald Tappey and told him I was on my way.

CHAPTER 10

Clinton is a small town about fifteen miles outside of Westfield, and Sheriff Gerald Tappey graduated from the same high school a couple of years before me. We played football together and one time we double-dated the Carrington sisters, he far more successfully than me. He married Katherine. I conked little sister Kim on the nose with my elbow when I tried to put my arm around her. That signified the highlight of our date, and the end of my double-dating career.

Gerald sat on the side porch in an old rocker that offered a good view of the town dump, although I doubted that was his intent. But the wind came out of the north, sending any lingering smell away from him. So it wasn't a bad seat, or a bad view.

As far as dumps went.

He nodded as I stepped onto the porch. I chose the white wicker love seat pushed up against the side of the house.

Gerald looked toward the dump. I looked as well.

"How far inland you figure we are?" he asked.

I shrugged. "Seventy, eighty miles."

"So why is the dump full of seagulls? You ever wonder?"

"Are we playing stump-the-dummy, Gerald? How do I know?"

"Because they're rats with wings. What else could be so easy, living life like that?" He turned from the seagulls. "You said you wanted to talk."

"I do. About a tall redhead named Annette Begley."

He picked up a pitcher of cider, filled two glasses, and offered me one. He placed the pitcher on the table between us, picked up his glass, and took a long swig.

"Gerald."

He put the glass down and ran his fingers through his hair. "I'm acquainted with the redhead of whom you speak." His face said it wouldn't be that easy.

"Better known as Cherry Delight."

Gerald grimaced. "I might have cruised past The Limit a time or two when Cherry worked."

I raised my eyebrows. "So I hear."

He tried to sound mad. "Oh, don't look at me like that. Married don't mean I can't look at another woman."

"Even one Shari's age."

"Exactly."

"How did you get tangled up with Annette in the first place?"

Gerald looked at me funny. "I guess I never thought of her as Annette. Always Cherry. Something appealing in a stripper name. Anyway, I stopped at The Limit for a beer one night and she was there. We talked and we talked some more. And then we got to cuddling in the corner like customers and strippers are known to do. Pretty soon she told me everything about herself but her shoe size."

"Eight."

"What the hell is eight, you numbskull?"

"Her shoe size, Gerald."

He busted a laugh. "Eight. Ain't you a card?"

He watched the gulls while I thought about Annette. And Shari. And Ecstasy. And wondered long and hard about what made them take the stage.

Some said because stripping was easy money. I'd always believed there was nothing easy about easy money. Especially earned that way.

Gerald fidgeted in his chair. "So, I'm a flipping idiot, Paul. But that girl, she done it to me. All hair and legs and giggles and smiles, and…"

I put my hand on his arm. "Yeah, I know the feeling. How well did you know her?"

"If this is what you don't have the cojones to ask, I did not have sexual relations with that woman. That should keep me from losing the next election, don't you think?"

"So, what did you do with her?"

"You're full of questions, ain't you? Yet I don't suppose it'll hurt to answer a few. Cherry came out here one day, me and her. Now, would we do it? Part of me hoped like hell we would. She wore a little flippy miniskirt and a white halter top that didn't leave no secrets. And lacy red underwear that I caught a peek of and…well, you know."

Not really, but I wasn't here to pass judgment. I was here to find Annette. "Okay, she spent some time with you. What happened?"

He glanced at his feet. "Cherry and I were in the kitchen. Verbal foreplay, I guess. Not the real thing, but a helluva warm-up act. Then who walks in but Katherine and Shari. Now Katherine didn't say boo, but I could see her jumping to about sixteen conclusions a second and they all pointed back to me being a dick.

"And Shari, she walked right over to Cherry and gave her the biggest hug and thanked me for keeping her company. And they walked out the door together and sat down on the porch and started yammering like they was the closest of friends."

He sighed, long and loud. "Christ, now I got my girl covering for my stupid butt."

"Katherine buy it?"

"Maybe," he said, his voice weighted by sadness. "For a week or more her eyes shot me daggers like she'd caught me doing the neighbor's sheep. After a while she found other stuff to be mad about."

He finished the cider and looked at the empty pitcher. "Why does this bring you out?"

"Annette is missing. Seems like nobody knows anything. But I heard about a girl with purple hair who Annette is friends with. So…Shari."

"Purple hair? Jesus Christ, what kind of a moron lets his kid wear purple hair? Oh, wait. The same moron who tries to nail her stripper friend." He turned his sad gray eyes toward the dump.

"You didn't, though."

He nodded without conviction.

"Talk to me, Gerald. You have something weighing pretty heavy on you."

He watched the sea gulls swoop and dive. "It's the whole thing about Shari. I didn't want it like this. She could have gone to night school. The Vo-Tech. Me and Katherine set aside some money in case she wanted to go to a big school like Orono or Farmington. But college didn't fit her any better than it fit me when I was her age. She's wilder'n a hawk, you know it's true. Just like I was. Guess I still am."

Finding nothing of value to add, I remained silent.

Gerald said, "And I decide to run my mouth to her. I say 'You gotta get off your ass, girl. You don't want to end up here.' I say 'You don't want to get stuck working in a grocery store or the mill.' Almost like saying she didn't want to end up like her mom and me."

I nodded.

"Finally," Gerald said, "she had enough of my bull, we went up like the Fourth of July, and she moved out and shacked up with some loser who didn't deserve her. And then I missed the hell out of her, you know? Used to be when Katherine went on the warpath, me and Shari would lean on each other. But all of a sudden..." He shrugged.

"You had to find another way to escape?"

He looked at me like we were kinsmen. "Exactly. So when things got bad here, I'd go downtown and blow off a little steam. One night I swung by The Limit. I paid my five bucks. I ordered a beer. And I waited around for the next girl on stage...and...and...it was Shari."

His shoulders slumped. "I ain't never told Katherine. A mother don't need to know that about her baby." He stared at the gulls.

"They tell me Shari's not dancing there anymore," I said.

Gerald looked at me like he couldn't comprehend what I was saying. "She's not?"

"Apparently she hasn't danced in a couple weeks or more."

"You ask them where Shari went?"

"That's why I'm here. To track her down."

He grabbed my arm. "Ain't nothing bad, do you think? Nothing bad happened to my girl?"

"Doubtful. Sometimes people just have to get away for a while. Away from work, or away from life…"

"Or away from an asshole. Especially when I saw her up on stage." His eyes went wild. "What kind of a sick-ass father sees his daughter like that? Shit."

The seagulls swarmed over the dump. They continually wheeled into the sky in a small cloud, then spun down to the garbage. Gerald turned and watched them.

"What about Katherine? Might she know where Shari is?" I asked.

He spit over the porch railing. "Hard telling. We don't talk so much lately."

"Think she'll talk to me?"

"Roll the dice, man. I keep coming up snake eyes."

Gerald turned back to the dump. To the sea gulls. Who continued to search through other folks' trash, thinking for all the world they were on easy street.

"Katherine?" I called out as I skirted the kitchen island.

"Back here."

I stepped into the living room dominated by a huge, L-shaped brown couch that faced a flat screen TV. A fire crackled in the fireplace. Katherine Tappey sat on the couch, a book in her lap, and her legs curled underneath her. She wore faded jeans and a blue turtleneck sweater. She wore no makeup. No jewelry.

Including no wedding ring.

"Hello, Paul."

"Hey, Kats."

She motioned for me to sit. "I heard you and Gerald talking."

Time to play it cool. "What did you hear?"

She snorted. "I heard you and Gerald talking."

"So you know I'm trying to find a girl."

"Annette." The name hung in the air.

Katherine glanced out the window as a black stake-body truck rattled by.

"Yes, Annette," I said. "She disappeared a while back. Her uncle hired me to find her."

Katherine snapped, "I'd think that stupid sonovabitch would know where to find her." She turned toward me and her eyes pried into my face, watching for any telltale tweak or twitch. Any confirmation of her suspicions.

I think I passed. "The fool girl ran off. She didn't see fit to tell anyone her destination."

Katherine clucked her tongue. "Women."

"I hear you, sister." I slid closer. I wanted us intimate. Co-conspirators.

She glanced at the window, then back to me. She leaned so close her left breast rested in the cradle of my right arm. "Paul, you ever think about fooling around?"

I bugged my eyes. "Come on, Kats. Gerald is right outside."

Katherine Tappey owns the prettiest laugh I've ever heard. It's smoky, warm, and rich with life. She's a tough Maine girl living a tough Maine life, and she doesn't laugh often. But when she does, she means it. I don't think she'd had many laughs like this one recently.

"Not with me, doofus," she said. "I mean with Eileen. Did you ever fool around on her?"

"That'd kind of negate the whole 'together' thing. No, I never fooled around when Eileen and I were married."

Creases tore her brow. "You know I saw her recently."

My stomach tumbled. "Eileen?"

Katherine closed her eyes, then nodded her head. When she opened them she said, "She's having a tough go, Paul. Things have gone pretty bad for her since the divorce."

Oh.

She'd taken Eileen's side. Simple as that. "Look," I said, for an instant wanting to pile-drive my Eileen-fueled anger onto Katherine.

Women.

I hated them.

Every single one was out to get me.

Katherine included.

Then I looked in her eyes and saw the truth.

She was concerned about me.

She was concerned about Eileen, too.

Because once upon a time she'd been equal friends with both of us, and now she was in the middle of a mess she couldn't clean up. So she cared enough about us not to take sides. That was all it was.

I counted to five, then five more. It helped. Some.

I reached out and touched her arm. "Look…give Eileen an extra hug the next time you see her. No need to tell her who it's from."

Katherine wore a crestfallen smile that never made it to her eyes. "That's so sweet. I always thought I went with the wrong guy on that double date."

"You'd probably have gotten a nose full of elbow, too."

She twisted on the couch. "It'd be better than what I live with now, Gerald sniffing after every girl eighteen and older. Him thinking there's something new and fresh around the corner." Her voice strained. "Him thinking maybe it's time to be done with me."

I glanced around the homey interior, at the wide board floors, the sage colored walls and the white painted trim that glistened in the low light. They had a nice home.

By all outward appearances.

Katherine sighed. "It isn't much, but it's ours. See that chair?" A weathered mission oak rocker stood in the corner, a green cushion on the seat and a blue and green knitted throw draped on the back. "Gerald and I found that at a yard sale in Belfast. Now it's nothing special. It has a twist in it, and when you get it going good you think the floor is warped. But we bought it just before Shari came along. It's where I used to feed her. It's where she and Gerald would nap when he rocked her to sleep."

She wiped her eyes. "It's only a chair, I know. But it's part of us, and I want to be able to rock my grandbabies in that chair. In our house. In our front room. With my husband watching us, or snoring on the couch, or anything. As long as it's us. Together."

"What I don't want," she said, her nostrils flaring, her voice filling the room, "is that miserable, crooked, squeaking chair to show up in a property settlement because a stupid old goat thinks he's in love with a stripper!"

I rose, walked around the couch, and stood behind her. I reached down and rubbed her shoulder.

Katherine looked up at me with defeated eyes. "You know what I'm saying?"

"The further Annette Begley is from here, the better."

"Awful, isn't it?"

"I must find her, though. Her family's worried about her."

She patted my hand. "Of course you must, Paul. I'm just getting old. My belly is too big, my butt is too fat, and my hair is too gray. Here I am talking about rocking chairs and grandbabies and feeling sorry for myself and you're trying to find a missing woman."

"Trying is right. I'm spinning my wheels so far."

Two ladies in black spandex and pink windbreakers power walked past the window. "Spinning my wheels," Katherine quietly said after they disappeared from sight.

"You're doing fine, Kats," I said, although I was probably less convinced than she.

She gave her nose a good blow.

I said, "Annette and Shari are friends. I'd like to talk to Shari, if you know where I can find her."

Katherine quickly stood up, walked to the door, and peered outside toward Gerald.

She came back to the couch and wiggled into the cushions until she got comfortable. "I never told Gerald. It would kill him the way he loves her. But when she wasn't making enough money at the store she started stripping at The Limit to pay her bills. She's been doing it a couple of months. I don't like it one bit, my baby stripping. But I might have made it up on stage once or twice when I was her age and I didn't have two nickels to rub together."

"And the world's a better place for it, I'm sure."

"No doubt." She didn't bother blushing. Katherine and I were way past that. "But Shari's grown, and she's headstrong like Gerald, and she makes her own choices no matter what I say. Stripping, though. A father doesn't need to know, Paul. Please."

"No, he doesn't." I leaned closer to her. "Kats, she's not dancing there anymore. They say both girls left a couple of weeks ago."

"You saw her on stage?" Her scowl accused me of being a jerk.

"No, I haven't. But they told me about a girl with purple hair."

"That does narrow the field a tad, doesn't it?"

"I wouldn't push like this but I think I'm out of options. I could walk away from this entire mess right now, and part of me wishes like hell I'd never gotten involved. But I am involved, and I'm going to find Annette. And Shari as well, if the girls are together. This is one of those times a little help might go a long way."

Katherine dug into her pocket and grabbed her cell phone. She jabbed a few buttons.

She waited.

After maybe thirty seconds she sighed deeply and said in her most bubbly, 'Mom's not worried' voice, "Hey sweetie, give me a call when you get this and we'll go shopping. Okay, love you...bye."

When she put the phone down her face twisted. "Shari didn't answer."

I patted her leg. "Has she not answered before?"

She shrugged, tightlipped. "Normally when I call and Shari doesn't answer, I figure she's just busy. Now...something doesn't feel right. Ever have that, when things don't feel right?"

While I was working on an answer that would calm her, Katherine clutched my arm, her nails digging into my bicep. "Why didn't she pick up?"

"Easy," I said. "It's probably nothing, and getting yourself all spun up when she could be in the shower or taking a nap isn't going to help, now is it?"

She sighed after a few beats, and released my arm. "You're right. Lately I've been so...sometimes my imagination gets away from me. Like you said, she's probably taking a nap." Katherine's face said she didn't buy it.

"Where does she live now?"

"She moved in with Sam Rosewood off Unity Road in Burnham." She gave me his address.

When I stood to go, she touched my arm. "I need to see Shari at the dinner table laughing with Gerald again. Will you make that happen for a lonely old girl?"

"Yes." Which meant I'd try.

She hugged me longer than usual. "Thanks for talking, Paul. Not a lot of that going on around here lately."

As I drove to Sam Rosewood's trailer I thought about Shari. She used to play soccer in high school, and when she was a senior she invited me to watch one of her games. I stood in a steady fall downpour on a muddy sideline in Westfield and watched her dart around the field, slide tackling anyone who dared to come close, racing full speed from sideline to sideline like she was having the time of her life.

After the game, her body covered with mud and her hair plastered to her face, Shari skipped like a kindergartener over to her parents. She curtsied to her mom, gave Gerald a greasy hug and stuck her tongue out at me.

We all laughed and went for hot chocolate. She called me Uncle Paul and then she decided I needed a greasy hug, too.

Now I was looking for another girl. A girl who felt compelled to wear Easter-egg purple hair. Who decided stripping was a viable solution to her cash flow problem. Who didn't give her dad muddy hugs and who didn't curtsy to her mother and didn't stick her tongue out at me. A girl who'd probably forgotten she'd ever done those things before.

I had a bad feeling about Shari Tappey.

It improved a little when I pulled into Sam Rosewood's front yard. Shari's car was the only one in the drive.

Sam Rosewood's place looked different than I expected. He kept a small flower garden beside his short dirt driveway. The flowers hadn't succumbed to the frost yet. A dozen or so sugar maples stood about eight feet high around the trailer. Their unfallen leaves proudly burned a brazen cherry red. They reminded me of teenage girls who recently discovered they had something worthwhile to show and couldn't resist sharing it with the world.

I banged on the door, peeked in the windows, and scouted around the trailer. Nothing.

I went around the trailer again and checked the windows. One in the back was unlocked.

I found a couple of cinder blocks under the trailer. I stacked them, climbed on, and shoved the window open.

I hoisted myself up and tried to force my way in.

The window was too small, or I was too big.

No, the window was too small, damn it. But I had my head and one shoulder inside. I could see part of the bathroom.

And I could smell the air inside the trailer. It smelled…clean. Not like it had been closed up for two weeks with the body of a purple-haired girl decaying inside.

I climbed down, slid the window closed, threw the cinder blocks under the trailer, went back to my car and waited until dark.

Sam Rosewood never showed.

Which was par for the course I was playing.

CHAPTER 11

As my eyes became accustomed to the low light inside The Limit, I scanned the interior. I saw my favorite table, the one strategically placed so I could watch both stages at once. It was already shaping up to be a good night.

I leaned back, hammered the beer a waitress brought me, and watched men flock to the dancers like flies to honey.

The evening got even better when Ecstasy came around the corner, smiled like she meant it, gave me a Grade-A hug and sat with me.

"Hi," she said. "Paul, right?"

"Bingo."

"No, it's definitely Paul," she brightly said. "You can't fool me."

I was happy, bubbly, approaching downright sheer giddiness, because a client had squared his bill with me a couple of hours before. He'd also paid in cash, which made it much easier to stimulate the local economy that way. No taxes, no IRS. No problem.

I'm a giver. It's who I am. So most of the money would end up at The Limit. And since Ecstasy was here tonight, she'd be the main beneficiary.

She wore a Catholic schoolgirl outfit, complete with pleated plaid skirt, white thigh highs, black heels, and a midriff-baring white blouse. If I'd known girls looked like her growing up, I'd have gone to Mass a lot more often. And I'm not even Catholic.

"Any money tonight?" I asked.

"Slow so far." Ecstasy slid her chair closer and placed her hand on my thigh. "Maybe you'll speed it up?"

"Maybe I will." I decided to go for it. "Under one condition."

"One condition?"

"Tell me your real name."

"You're a detective. Figure it out." Her words were playful.

Her tone wasn't.

I'd learned over time that strippers live by an ironclad rule: don't let customers too close. Their money might all spend the same, but the world inside the club and the world outside remained decidedly different. Although a woman stripped down so she didn't have a single secret left, in here she had an identity she chose in a world she created.

But outside the club she had a different life. She had friends, she had a family. Often they didn't know she danced. Inside, her life was fantasy. Outside, it was real. And 'real' was no place to invite customers.

I'd have to go to 'subtle mode.'

I pulled a handful of twenties out of my pocket and placed them on the table. Ecstasy warily looked at them, then back at me.

I leaned toward her. "Since you don't know any better, let's say I'm a brilliant detective. The first time we talked, you told me you weren't from around here. Where are you from, if you don't mind me asking?"

She checked my face to see if I was a pervert or a mass murderer or something. I'm not sure what she came up with, but she said, "Down south."

"Down south? Like Boston?"

She put her hands on her hips and leaned back. Her eyebrows ratcheted up. "Wow, broaden your perspective. Real down south. Like below the Mason Dixon, y'all."

I slid her a twenty.

She smiled. Kind of.

"And west of the Mississippi?"

She hesitated. Her eyes darted to mine and she looked into them for far too long. She bit her lower lip. She nodded.

I slid a half tank of gas her way. I was leaking bills like my car leaked oil.

I asked, "Are we talking desert and cactus, or bikini-clad surfer girl?"

She shook her head, agitation leaping to her face. She was cat-on-a-hot-tin-roof tense. Too many questions. Too much prying.

Which put a tourniquet on the cash flow. As I stuffed the remaining bills in my pocket I heard her sigh. It sounded like relief.

Ecstasy snatched up a flyer from the table that advertised Amateur Night. She deftly shaped it into a small paper boat. When she completed it she gave a small nod and exhaled deeply, still watching her hands.

"Hey," I said and reached a finger out to touch a small mole near her mouth. "You okay?"

Her eyes seemed to flicker between 'hell yeah' and 'help me' for a second. I cupped her jaw with my fingers and caressed her cheek with my thumb. Stress slowly melted from her face, as if a mini-demon had just been exorcised.

Ecstasy gently rolled her head away from my hand, quickly nodded a couple of times as if reassuring herself, gave me a smile that approximated a real one in shape if not sincerity, and said, "So tell me Paul, are you married?"

I held up a left hand with no ring. "Not anymore."

"Are you happy or sad about it?"

"A little bit of both. We had fewer good times than bad. But still, we were married. Occasionally I miss the fact we aren't married anymore."

Ecstasy said, "My dad left when I was a teen. I miss the fact he isn't here anymore." She started tearing the paper boat she'd made.

I said, "It's been a year. It doesn't hurt every day now."

"Over ten years here. It doesn't hurt every day now for me, either. But there are still things a girl needs to say to her dad. And I can't anymore."

Things had gone decidedly south again in about three sentences. And that takes skill and commitment on both sides.

But before we wallowed too far in self-pity, Ecstasy and the Stripper Code kicked in. A strip joint is not a place for sadness. She triple-tapped the table with her fingers, and she was back in the game. "Paul, we had fun the last time you came here. Would you like to have fun again?"

I almost choked on my beer. "I would."

"Now?"

"Let me finish my drink first. I like talking to you."

Her eyes locked onto mine and stayed a while, like she was looking for something. "I like talking to you too, Magnum P.I. with a real Maine accent. You make me laugh. I like it when a guy makes me laugh."

"Oh," I said, unsure for a time what to say next. "By the way, I really enjoyed spending time together. You are a wonderful conversationalist."

She blushed. "You're so sweet to say that."

That was it. She thought I was sweet and funny. The same two words Lola the bartender said Ecstasy had used when talking about...me, apparently. "Well, you're very sweet too," I stammered.

The DJ butted in and broke up our mutual appreciation fest when he said, "Okay boys, get your hands off your peckers and put them together for Jasmine on stage one, Ecstasy on stage two. Jasmine on one, Ecstasy on two."

She reached for her purse. "I'll be right back."

Eight chairs ringed the stage. Men filled each one as she undressed, moved, writhed, shook, and smiled. As she flirted and cajoled. Singles coated the stage. She slid them out of the way as she neared one customer after another.

A bearded man scored big when she wrapped her legs around his neck. An old man with coke bottle glasses got her boobs in his face. A fat man received a wet kiss on his bald pate. With each one, she'd hold out the waistband of her g-string until they slipped a few more singles in. That earned them a kiss on the cheek.

And on and on, one man to the next and the next and the next until the music wound down and the final bills hit the stage. She raked them into her purse, pulled her skirt up, and tied her blouse in front.

The bald man caught her arm as she walked down the steps. She flashed him her best 'I think you're the one for me' smile and whispered in his ear. His fat face exploded in a huge smile. Paradise was only a lap dance away. As she left, he looked longingly her way.

As she walked back to me.

Ecstasy slipped into her chair and whooshed a sigh. "There, that's over with."

"Do you like to dance on stage? I mean, you make more on a couple of lap dances than for three songs up there."

She bit her lower lip. "I guess. But I need to show the men what they can get for their money. It worked on you, right?"

I clutched my beer a shade tighter. Was she insinuating I was like the men for whom she'd just performed? Had I been so quickly reduced to seeing Ecstasy as no more than an erotic fling in the shadows? And when my money ran out and she went to another, what would I walk out of The Limit with? Besides an empty wallet, of course. Not much. Nothing real, anyway.

And suddenly 'real' was what mattered.

Damn crossroads.

Ecstasy leaned against my arm, and I trembled as I noticed every bit of her that touched every bit of me. Christ, I felt like a hormonal teenager. I wasn't overly proud.

Her lips touched my earlobe. "Are you ready for me?"

I said, "Let's talk about that."

She jerked away from me, cocked her head and caught my eye. "Okay, but talking won't get you the good stuff."

"I…I…" I couldn't believe what I was going to say. "I respectfully disagree."

Ecstasy looked down at herself, her brow wrinkled. "I'm not sure stuff can get much better."

I touched her hand. "Everything about you is, as you put it, 'the good stuff.' But I don't want you to dance for me. That's not what I'm looking for."

Ecstasy's face glazed over. She quickly picked up her purse and stood. Very precisely she said, "Well, I hope you find the girl you want."

I panicked. "Wait. You misunderstood. Please sit."

She waited. But she didn't sit. I don't think she bought the 'misunderstood' piece. And she didn't look like she planned on staying long.

I touched her arm. "Sit? Please?"

She stood a moment, her face still taut. Then she placed her purse on the table and, without turning toward me, sat. She watched a dancer do her magic on stage one.

I watched Ecstasy. And only Ecstasy. "Thanks," I said to the side of her head. "What I meant to say is, getting to know you is the good stuff I'm interested in."

Ecstasy slowly turned. "What are you talking about?"

"I already know when your smile is real and when it's a customer smile. I know when you're happy. I know when you're bored. I know what your body looks like and I'll never forget that. But that's Ecstasy the dancer. I want to know the woman, not the fantasy. What she thinks about. Why she thinks that way. I want to know who she really is." I reached out to caress her cheek.

Her face tightened and she again rolled away from my hand. "For heaven's sake Paul, I'm a stripper. Get a grip."

Desperate times called for desperate words. "I think you're the most exciting woman I've ever met."

She snorted. "That means I'm doing my job, you knucklehead." Her eyes glittered like hard, black diamonds. "But this isn't real. Who we are here, it isn't real."

"It could be."

Her face pinched. "No. That's ridiculous. No."

I stammered, "But Lola said you told her...about me...and...I thought..."

"Well, you thought wrong," she said. "Strippers don't like customers."

Ecstasy stood, snatched her purse from the table and took two steps toward the dressing room.

She stopped and stared at the bank of lights over the stage. For an eternity.

She turned with agonizing slowness. "You don't know me," she said as her eyes sought mine. They appeared to be pleading for something. Right then it was hard to tell.

"So let me know you."

"No Paul," she whispered. "No."

"Why?"

"Because..." Her voice cracked, and she stopped to compose herself. "Why do you have to make this so damned hard? You're a customer. I'm a stripper. Customers don't care about strippers and strippers don't care about customers. Don't you know that?"

"But I do care. And I want to know you more."

"And I," Ecstasy said, "will not allow that to happen."

"Tell me why."

She bit her lip and again looked at the lights above the stage for more than a few seconds. Her voice wavered as she said, "Because I need you to keep looking at me the way you do now."

"I don't understand. We could…"

"No." She motioned toward the stage nearest us. "This is the me you want to know. Trust me. You don't want to see the rest."

I didn't agree. Not in a million years did I agree.

I've always been a sucker for a woman's eyes. Ecstasy turned hers to me. Again they bored into me, causing my stomach to instantly cartwheel out of control.

And I was hers. Completely.

"Tell me what to do," I said. "Tell me, and I'll do it."

Ecstasy spoke so quietly I had to strain to hear. "Don't try to get to know me. Please let it go at that."

Please. She said please.

I could beg. I could cajole. I could push her. I could make it about me.

Instead I stood, kissed her on the forehead and whispered, "Goodnight, Ecstasy."

The clock said 2:37. I couldn't sleep. I had a case to solve, and so far I'd barely made a dent.

For whatever reason, Lou Principi decided to tangle with Mikey Cross. And nothing about that sounded good.

I had a wealth of knowledge upon which to base my assessment. After my father lost his construction business and drank himself to death, I'd swung by Mikey's place to—hell, I don't know, the modern version of challenging him to a duel, I guess. But before we could march ten paces, turn and fire, a couple of his boys had thrown down on me and I'd woken up in the back seat of my car, beaten to crap.

A salmon continually hurls itself upriver to spawn, expending every ounce of energy to lay its eggs. A soldier will fight to the death for his country. He knows at any second a fatal bullet might come his way. He knows he might never see his children again. Yet he marches on and fights on, selfless and heroic.

And when it came to squaring up with Mikey Cross, I'd made one half-hearted gesture and backed away.

Talk about failing to announce my presence with authority. Since then I hadn't made it past hovering menacingly around football games or flipping his office the bird when I drove by.

They don't come much tougher than me.

I tried to ignore the fact that I hated every fiber of Mikey Cross's being. I tried to pretend I didn't want to see him die a horrible, pain-riddled death. I tried to pretend we were square, Mikey and me.

The only problem is Mikey didn't have to pretend anything at all. He'd won in a landslide. Without a fight.

If it came to it again, could I challenge Mikey face-to-face? At this time of the morning when I couldn't hide from much, I thought long and hard.

And I decided our saga might not be quite done yet.

But if I had to see Mikey again, I wouldn't fly solo this time.

Solo.

The word rattled around in my brain. Solo.

Unaccompanied.

Alone.

Since Eileen left, I'd convinced myself that I would spend the rest of my life that way. Solo.

Unaccompanied.

Alone.

And then, out of left field when I least expected it, came Ecstasy. As the alarm clock clicked off the minutes, I held my own internal debate.

She seemed to like me.

I paid her to like me.

Her eyes never left mine.

She made a living that way.

She told me she wanted to see me again.

She knew the way into my wallet.

My heart soared whenever I thought about her.

My heart ached because I knew the truth.

She was Ecstasy.

But not mine.

I shook my head. Solo was a hell of a lot easier.

But not nearly as much fun.

CHAPTER 12

Shortly after sunrise the next morning I drove twenty-five miles north toward Sam Rosewood's place. Rusted trailers dotted roadside lots. Dogs scrambled to get out of my way as I bounced along aged, cracked and poorly-patched asphalt.

A green Ford Ranger pickup sat beside Shari's car. I stepped past it onto the gray-painted steps and rapped on the door. It took more than a minute before a young man with dark, curly hair and dark blue eyes opened it.

"Help you?" he mumbled. His eyes were barely open, and his hair stood up at odd angles. The classic bed head look.

I stuck my hand out and we introduced ourselves. I said, "Did I wake you?"

A huge yawn shook Sam's body. He covered his mouth. "Whew, a big one," he mumbled through his hand. "I work nights at the mill up by Skowhegan. I get off at seven." He glanced at his watch. "I haven't been asleep long."

"I'll talk fast, so you can get back in the rack. I'm looking for Annette Begley. Shari too. Katherine Tappey sent me to see you."

He held the door open and motioned me in. He sat in the easy chair and pointed toward the couch.

He wore a green sweatshirt with a picture of a huge whitetail buck jumping over a fallen log, and blue plaid pajama bottoms. He settled deeper into the chair. "I know Annette."

"Her uncle says she's missing. He owns The Limit."

"He owns the place where she dances? Kind of a close family, aren't they?"

"My thinking also. But he hired me to find her."

Sam looked around. "And you made it all the way out to a forty-five foot trailer halfway between Burnham and Unity? You're good."

I chuckled. "None better. But I figured since you and Shari…"

Sam blurted, "Shari and I finished a couple of weeks ago. She picked up the cards, folded the table, and put away the poker chips." His eyes looked more sad than tired.

"What happened, if I may ask?"

"What always happens?" he said, with a little extra bite. "We were on different career arcs, is the nice way to put it. I worked at the mill. She did her thing. We hardly ever saw each other. When we would get together, it didn't seem long until we ran out of things to talk about. Me, I wanted to talk about forever. She wanted to talk about work and a new church she'd found. The Castle View Free."

I leaned forward. "Tell me about the church."

"Shari took me there once and I saw the great Reverend Johnny Virdon with my own eyes. You know what I remember most? Him saying over and over again, 'Give the Lord a handclap of praise,' and folks would start this rhythmic clapping. Even the keyboard player helped out. Every time Virdon said something the guy would smash a few keys, like he was revving up the crowd at a baseball game. I'm surprised Virdon didn't tell the congregation to do the wave for the Holy Ghost."

"You don't think very highly of Johnny Virdon?"

Sam scowled. "Sometimes I kind of blame him for Shari leaving me. That's the easy way. We lived together. She started going to his church. Now she's not here." He stared past me. Hoping to find answers, maybe.

He stewed for a while, his brain chasing the right image. "The church, I'm going to say it's like a mud hole. You see it, but it doesn't look so bad. So you drive toward it. You get near the edge, and it's a little slick, but you're still chugging along. You go a little further. All of a sudden you start spinning. Pretty soon you can't back up. You can't go forward. You keep spinning and spinning, and all you do is get buried deeper in it."

He seemed satisfied. The Castle View Free Church was like a mud hole.

I asked, "Did she live with you for quite a while?"

"For almost a year, after she and her dad had a falling out. Her being here, it seemed like a honeymoon every night. For the first couple of months."

It sounded exactly like my marriage.

For the first couple of months.

Sam said, "And then Shari started talking about the church and Reverend Virdon. And about her new friend Annette. And one day she stopped talking to me altogether, except to ask me to drop her off at the church. You been there?"

"Haven't had the privilege."

"You've got to go see Reverend Virdon preach, for the entertainment value alone. And he has another place over behind the college. It looks like a dormitory. He says he's providing a home to the destitute. I say he's building himself a new God Squad. Whatever he's doing, it's his gig. My gig was providing him two boarders."

The girls were at the Castle View Free Church dormitory. But I wanted to know more. Mostly, I wanted to know why two girls would pull up stakes and leave their homes and lives behind. Because one thing I'd learned in life is there's always more to the story. I just didn't know what the rest of the story was.

I said, "Why do you think they went to the dormitory?"

"I think it's because Reverend Virdon is a snake oil salesman, selling the next great thing. Except he's selling the goodness of the Lord and, from the looks of it, people are buying. The dormitory was pretty packed."

I didn't even know the place existed. I asked Sam where it was.

"You go past Aberle College, turn by the football field, and there's a road that goes back in the woods. Looks like it ends at nothing. But you go around a corner, and you see the dorm. I talked to one guy who lived there, Rufus Bentley. Said he and his wife and three kids lost their house in a fire, and couldn't make a go any more. Said the Reverend puts them up, and they work for the church to cover room and food. Bentley said they work together, live together, pray together. Sounded kind of strange."

I had to admit, it did sound strange. But who was I to judge? As I passed forty I'd returned home to live with my mother.

I said, "Tell me about when you dropped Annette and Shari there."

His face darkened. "I think it was eight or nine days ago. Something like that. I've been on mind-numb since Shari left. I get up, I eat, I go to work, I come home, and I sleep."

I remembered the feeling when Eileen invited me to leave our house. It was pretty close to Sam's description. I nodded encouragement. Because there were some days I'd needed it pretty bad.

Sam said, "I came home from work one morning around eight. Shari sat right here, suitcase all packed. She said she needed a ride to Reverend Virdon's place, but we had to pick Annette up first. I didn't know what to think."

He stood up and grabbed a bottle of water from the fridge. I shook his offer off. After he took a big swig he said, "Shari said Annette had to get away for a while, but when she was talking she wouldn't look me in the eye. I think Shari was talking about herself. Like she was the one who had to get away. Maybe she wanted to spare my feelings, but you know how sometimes what someone doesn't say is more important than what they do say?"

I fed him what he wanted. "Sure."

"So I picked Annette up and went to the dorm. Shari, she started hugging people like she'd die without them. And she introduced Annette, and Annette started hugging everyone, and pretty soon I noticed nobody was hugging me...so I left."

"You haven't heard from Shari since you dropped her off?"

Sam went to the kitchen and opened a small drawer. He motioned me over.

I looked inside.

There were two cellphones. I picked them up. They both had batteries. But no SIM cards.

"The red one's Annette's. The black one's Shari's." Sam rolled his shoulders. "I found them in Shari's car after she left."

"You haven't gone to see her since? Find out what's going on?"

He nodded at the drawer. "Those phones said enough. I never saw the need to have a follow-up conversation with Shari about 'hey, you want to come back' or anything like that. When I dropped them off..."

Sam sighed. "Everything Shari didn't say meant goodbye."

CHAPTER 13

Something told me to drive straight from Sam's place to the church dorm to talk to Annette and Shari. That something was my impulsive, impetuous nature.

But with age, I'd also attained a modicum of wisdom. Not a lot, but enough to keep me from pulling a Don Quixote routine every time I sighted a windmill. Sometimes, sure. But not every time.

Instead I'd learned…I'd learned before I made a complete and total ass of myself to think things through by bouncing my bright ideas off my good buddy Cash.

Winfield Romero Cashman III is a younger, stronger, handsomer version of me. For which I never fully forgave him. He grew up a rich, bigshot football player in Portland who wrangled an appointment to the Air Force Academy. Of course, Winfield Romero Cashman II had a bit to do with that. What with him doing multiple tours in Congress.

"Hey Dad, can I get an appointment letter to the Academy?"

"Sure son, as soon as you clean your room."

Cash played football for the Academy back when they beat Navy occasionally. And Army all the time. When he graduated, he learned to fly.

During the second Gulf War Cash became an all-star flying Warthogs, providing close air support for ground troops.

A reporter from Portland caught wind of his heroics and wrote a feature about local boy done good. It ran nationally, and all of a sudden you couldn't swing a dead cat without hitting someone who knew nearly everything about Winfield Cashman III.

Including how on one sortie his aircraft was hit by anti-aircraft artillery.

How shrapnel shredded his right leg.

How doctors did all they could.

And how they removed it just below the knee anyway.

Cash came home, medically retired from the Air Force with full disability augmented by a nifty trust fund Grandpa Cashman had left him. He'd never need to work again.

Winfield Romero Cashman II, who Cash referred to as The Deuce, wanted his son to follow him into politics. The war hero/sympathy vote would surely propel him into the House. The Senate. Maybe one day Pennsylvania Avenue.

Cash had his own agenda. He decided his injury wouldn't slow him down. He became a triathlete. Short ones first, then Olympic distance. Eventually, Ironmans. With a prosthetic leg, a made-for-TV movie story and a matinee idol smile, Cash became the poster child for amputees everywhere. He spoke to groups around the country about overcoming obstacles. About setting goals and achieving them. About not letting your loss become a disability.

I, on the other hand, knew the non-sound bite side of Cash. For he hadn't lost his pilot mentality when he left the Air Force. But with no call for that, with no plane to fly or war to fight, he drifted.

Until one day when we bumped into each other in a Rockport bar. He told me he felt bored to the gills and needed some fun to keep from going off the rails entirely. Because you can't find a more fun guy than me, I offered to let him hang out and watch me work.

We'd never termed it a partnership. But more times than not, it ended up that way.

So when I called to ask for his two-cents worth regarding Annette and Shari, he agreed to join me for a late lunch.

Harry's is the perfect guy's bar. Sawdust on the floor, neon beer signs, two pool tables, a shuffleboard game in the corner. Three TVs, normally tuned to a Sox game. Except baseball had already stumbled to a close in Red Sox Nation for the season. Today they showed some soap opera, which I mostly ignored.

Two spectacularly-tattooed waitresses who looked like they tied for first place in a 'most wicked cool ink' competition, Gina and Rachel, worked the lunchtime crowd.

Gina made eye contact and hollered out, "Whaddaya want?" as I walked past the bar.

I gave her the two beers sign and pointed at the table where Cash sat.

Gina brought us two heavenly draft beers. Cash ordered the Philly cheese-steak. I never had much luck with drippy, greasy food so I ordered the club sandwich. And hoped I could keep the tomatoes off my shirt.

When our sandwiches arrived Cash dove into the cheesesteak like he hadn't eaten in a week.

"You starving?" I asked.

"Not anymore," he mumbled around a mouthful big enough to choke a horse.

"But don't you have a race in New Hampshire tomorrow? Half-marathon or some ridiculous thing?"

Cash swallowed. "That's like seventeen hours from now. This'll all be digested." He jammed a handful of fries in his mouth.

I felt my arteries hardening. "I thought you superstar athletes carbo-loaded before a race."

He tapped his beer. "Liquid variety goes down easier."

"You leaving this afternoon?"

"I have an old Air Force buddy who lives in Fryeburg. I'll crash there tonight, do the race, drink some more liquid carbs with him, and come home on Monday." He studied me. "Why?"

I told Cash about Annette's case.

He waved a droopy, ketchup-soaked French fry at me. "You want to swing by the dorm this afternoon?" He stuffed the fry in his mouth, and checked his watch.

Cash has always been there to help me out, and he's never taken a nickel for any of the work he's done. Last thing I wanted to do was put him out to help me yet again.

I waved him off. "Sam left the girls there a little over a week ago. They can lay low for a bit longer. Monday morning, meet me at the office and we'll swing by for a visit with Annette and Shari."

"You were only hired to find Annette, right? You keep mentioning 'the girls'. I want to make sure I understand the objective. It's Annette."

I nodded. "It's Annette. I'm just doing some pro bono work for Shari's parents while I'm at it."

Cash grinned. "I'm intimately familiar with the pro bono concept. But whether it's one girl or two, it'd be kind of important to figure out that 'why are they there' thing, don't you think?"

"It's church-run, and Sam said Shari had found religion. Maybe Annette did too, and God told them to get off the stage and put their damn clothes back on."

Cash said, "It's a possibility."

I pulled the toothpick out of the club sandwich before I got careless and swallowed it. I'd come dangerously close once before. "That's what I'd like to get my mind around. What are they really doing there?"

"And when we see Annette, and she leans close to you and whispers in her husky, sultry stripperfied voice, 'None of your business, stud' where will you be?"

"Same spot I'm in now. But at least I can tell Lou I found her." I frowned. It had sounded like a much better idea before I said it out loud.

"What about the guy you mentioned, the one who was Annette's regular? Any luck tracking him down yet?"

"I left my card with Trouble, and she said she'd ask around."

"Stripper doing your dirty work. Nice. You going to split the take with her if she finds something?"

I sucked my teeth. "That's not all I've done. I've also been back there twice to talk to girls. The customers seem to be pretty compartmentalized, and the girls do too. It's not like they're a big country club and they all get along." I also told him about Venus checking the guy with the tattoo in Annette's picture.

Rachel couldn't resist ruffling Cash's hair when she came by to clear our plates. She took one look at my head, grabbed my plate and left. Cash said, "If

Annette is running from something, you think she'll up and leave with you when you go waltzing in there?"

"If I knew that, it would sound suspiciously like I had this all thought out. The last time I saw her, I was sticking singles into her g-string. Not much to define a relationship with."

Cash finished his beer and motioned Gina for another.

I waved her off. Two is my limit.

Per hour.

Cash grabbed a handful of round pretzels from a bowl. One at a time, he tossed them in the air and caught them in his mouth. He never missed.

When he finished his trained seal act, he looked back at me. "I can blow off the race, man. Screw it. Let's talk to the girls now."

The race Cash was scheduled to run honored POW/MIA, and as a semi-celebrity and former military man he needed to be there. I shook my head. "They'll be fine for a couple more days."

"You sure?"

I was pretty sure. "Definitely."

"I'm sure you've already hit upon the irony in this, but after the vote went the way it did, why would girls from The Limit end up at Reverend Virdon's church dorm? And what does he think about them in light of their chosen profession?"

I had no idea what vote he was talking about.

Cash looked at me. "You have no idea what vote I'm talking about, do you?" He grabbed his laptop and fired it up. After a quick Internet search he spun the laptop so I could see it.

I read how a Westfield city referendum to outlaw adult entertainment had been voted down two months ago. I was surprised as hell, mostly because I was a registered voter and I didn't remember it ever coming up. But I was probably chasing a vicious criminal.

Or taking a nap. Either way I missed it.

I scrolled to a video clip showing when the referendum had been debated on one side by Reverend Virdon, and on the other side by…none other than Lou Principi.

I watched as Lou stood, in a blue-checked suit, striped shirt and tie, in front of the television camera. But I had to say this for him, he made his point about free enterprise and how if people don't like anchovies they can pick them off the pizza, and if they didn't like nudity they didn't have to look at it. He even threw in a zinger about how government shouldn't try to legislate morality, and capped off his bravura performance by saying, "We gotta make our own decisions in life. When the time comes we'll have the opportunity to discuss those decisions, good or bad, with our Maker."

Touché.

Reverend Virdon, on the other hand, preached hellfire, brimstone and utter damnation, that adult entertainment establishments would be the ruin of women and children in our society, and how left-wing Liberals needed to be more like their God-fearing Conservative brethren and vote to close all adult entertainment establishments.

The referendum was voted down by a two-to-one margin.

I lived in Sin City. Who knew? I decided to personally hug Lou Principi the next time I saw him.

Cash took the laptop back. "For the record, I voted for boobs."

CHAPTER 14

While Ma had made it eminently clear that anything that resembled a health-nut breakfast was now my responsibility, a bunch of bananas had magically appeared on the counter. Gotta love Ma. The next morning I sat at the table, worked on hard-boiled eggs, oatmeal, bananas and coffee, and stewed. I was getting pretty impatient about my newfound patience. The old Paul Doyle would have already swept into the church dormitory like a one-man SWAT team, snatched the strippers, returned them home safe and sound, and been home for a nap before lunch.

But I'd learned that while one-man SWAT teams may be a ton of fun and are sure to cause a general ruckus, they're not especially effective for covering all the escape doors. Good things come in twos—like me and Cash. I would wait for him to return, and we would do this together.

I'm a gut-feel kind of guy, and this didn't feel good in my gut, or anywhere else for that matter. A twenty-year-old girl had gone with a friend to lay low in a church dorm. Why?

People disappear for a reason.

Therefore it was logical that Annette had disappeared for a reason. Was she hiding from something, or hiding from herself?

My swooping in to rescue her—especially when I didn't even know if she needed rescuing—seemed like a weak option, at best. Maybe it was as simple as...she'd found the Lord.

Today was Sunday. Best day of the week to find out.

I glanced at the clock. Cash would already be halfway through his thirteen-mile fun run by now. But he was still a full day away from coming back.

Therefore, I had a full day to get my arms around this problem a little better.

The part I wanted to get my arms around the most was Reverend Johnny Virdon. In the last few days, Yvette had mentioned him. I'd seen the video where Lou had debated him. Annette had been dropped off at his church dorm.

Everywhere I turned, it was Virdon, Virdon, Virdon.

What was the big deal about Reverend Johnny Virdon?

It was time to get me some religion. And maybe see if Annette and Shari were similarly moved.

The parking lot at the Castle View Free Church was packed. I pulled into one of the back rows and followed a young couple with three kids and abundant forehead worry creases inside.

The first thing I noticed was good music. At least good and loud. When I was younger church music had always been an annoying pipe organ, a choir of screechers, and an old minister who believed he needed to sing loudest of all as if to reaffirm his devotion to the Lord.

But today, to steal a phrase, the joint was jumping. A rock band inspired the masses to sway and dip their heads while a thin, black-haired woman with gauze-white skin and a full dose of rapture painted on her face sang about finding salvation. I actually found myself bobbing along to the music.

So church was cool after all. Who knew?

When the woman stopped singing, she sat and fanned herself with a program. But the music continued.

The bass line pulsated, low and stirringly sexual. It didn't sound like *Bringing In The Sheaves* to me. It sounded like…well, it sounded a helluva lot like sin.

A pretty brunette girl of fifteen or so sat to my left. She wore a flowery white dress that looked a little too short and a little too tight. At least a little too short and a little too tight for a girl of fifteen or so. Her face glowed like she'd just earned a summer sunburn and her eyes sparked as she bounced on the pew. Her white high heels tapped out the rhythm of the music. She had feet made for dancing.

They performed admirably.

A woman, who I assumed was her mother, sat next to her and didn't even bother to scowl when she caught me watching her daughter. Because the woman was getting cranked up, too. Her face was as flushed as the girl's. As was the face of the man next to her.

And on and on. Every face I saw, everyone I watched, every move a person made, seemed amped up, over the top, electric. Like they'd just done lines of coke and topped it off with a pot of coffee and a four-pack energy drink.

I searched around me, hoping to see Annette or Shari. All I saw were a sea of faces, glowing in anticipation. Alas, none of the faces were familiar.

The girl beside me jumped to her feet and screamed, "Jesus loves me!" She pranced like a cheerleader, nearly conking me when she threw her arms above her head. I didn't dare look anywhere near her hemline for fear of her exposing things best left unexposed. "Jesus loves me," she yelled again.

"Amen!" her mother screamed. Amens and Praise the Lords echoed through the church. Now mother was on her feet. And dad. The whole row.

And the whole damn church.

Except for me.

I caught the eye of an older man who glared my way. He kept waving me to stand in the presence of the Lord. Or at least in the presence of Johnny Virdon.

Right then, it was hard to tell who had top billing.

The girl hooked my arm with hers and pulled me on my feet.

She grabbed my left hand and raised my arm over my head. When I stood there, one arm sticking up and the other hand buried in my pocket she laughed, threw both arms around my waist, and gave me a hug.

"Like this!" she shouted. "Watch!" She whipped her arms sky-high and swayed like a hula girl, then turned and smiled at me.

Oh, youthful exuberance. She and her mother did the hula act together. They bumped hips and swayed, their arms floating above them.

"Now you do it!" the girl shouted. She wiggled her hips and gave me a huge, encouraging grin. He eyes gleamed like Casco Bay at sunrise.

I looked forward through a sea of waving arms. The band continued to grind out a joyful song. I debated joining the masses.

An elbow whacked me on the hip. It was my little cheerleader friend in the tight dress. "Both arms, dude!" she shouted.

I thrust my other arm in the air. The music seemed to get louder. More intense. I caved. I wiggled like I had ants in my pants. "Like this?" I yelled.

She wildly shook her head, tossing her hair, her face beaded with sweat and burning with excitement. "What did you say?" she yelled. She swung her hips toward me. In the heat of the moment I forgot to listen to the band. Instead I was fully committed to bumping her back. I was deep into the groove.

"How do you like *my* shit now?" I hollered at the top of my lungs moments after the song stopped dead.

My eloquence reverberated in the near-noiseless vacuum.

Glares from the closest dozen or so people burned my face. I could feel angry eyes tattooing the back of my head. Including those of increasingly uptight mom and dear old dad.

I looked helplessly at the girl. "Too much excitement?"

She giggled. "It's all good in the 'hood." She patted my arm. "God is glad you're here today."

Exhausted, flushed with exuberance, the crowd slowly settled into its seats. I looked around. People were laughing, hugging, chattering away. This wasn't the church of my youth. This…this was something else.

The energy didn't let up, even though the band had stopped. It continued to bubble like a pot of water over high heat.

The drummer thrust his sticks above his head and whacked them together. The band cranked it up again…and this time, as the congregation jumped to its feet and began to scream, Reverend Johnny Virdon swept up on stage like a rock star.

A group of six or seven wildly-dressed black women, who were sitting in the front row, started doing what I decided to call the 'We Love The Lord, Y'all' dance. Pale white women, who tried in vain to hide the thirty pounds they'd gained since high school, shimmied right along with them. Bearded men dressed in flannel, jeans and work boots, clean-cut men dressed in suits, kids in t-shirts, and the young and old dressed in everything in between, either pushed themselves out into the aisle or turned the tiny spaces between the pews into their own personal dance floors. There was a whole lotta love for the Lord going on.

Johnny Virdon danced right along with them.

A slim, light-skinned black man of medium height, with just a touch of gray hair touching his temples, Virdon wore no robes, but instead bounded across the stage in a dark purple suit and a mustard colored shirt. His leather shoes were a patchwork of both gaudy colors.

Virdon worked his way to the choir and swayed with them, dipping his shoulders and double-clapping to the music. He had dance moves that would make a teenager envious, the smile of a fool in love, and the presence of a man who knew inner peace.

I couldn't take my eyes off him.

And he hadn't said a word yet.

Virdon motioned to the band to bring it down. Lower. Lower.

When it was just the keyboard tapping in the background, Virdon said, "Do I look good?"

The keyboard blared.

"Amen!" the girl beside me squealed. Amens rippled throughout the church and echoed off the walls.

Amen.

Virdon stomped his feet. "Do *I* look good?"

The place erupted in a maelstrom of Praise the Lords. One might have slipped from me.

Virdon popped the lapels of his loud jacket and pantomimed primping himself in the mirror. "Sho'nuff, I look good."

The keyboard wailed.

"But it don't matter what we look like on the outside, y'all."

"Testify!" An old woman in front of me screeched.

Virdon shuffled sideways across the stage. "'Cause we're being changed, oh Lord, by the power of God!"

The Castle View Free Church exploded.

"We're being changed, changed, changed," Virdon intoned. The keyboard tapped, tapped, tapped the same rhythm.

"I don't know what you been told," Virdon bellowed, swinging his arms wide across the congregation, "but G-O-O-O-O-D-D-D is about to transform us."

Two rows in front of me a heavyset woman threw her arm across her forehead and crashed against the pew in front of her.

Three muscular young men, dressed in tailored black suits, jumped to her aid.

Virdon held his hand up to quiet the crowd, and glanced her way. When he saw she would recover, he swept into a sermon about what he called indulging in the lust of defiling passion. Which, given many lowered eyes and chagrined looks, appeared to hit close to home for more than a few.

Virdon shouted, "There is a den of iniquity!"

Keyboard.

"Bad for our community!"

"Praise Jesus!" a skinny black man with a huge afro sitting behind me yelled. Others echoed him.

"But we got a plan to purify!"

The crowd shouted approval. Another woman went down.

Virdon smiled wickedly. "Disinfect and sanitize!"

"Tell it, Reverend!" the old man behind me yelled.

Virdon's voice became deep. Soulful. He held up his hand to still any interruption until he got it out of his system. "Hear me good people. One day we will take the key from the hand of the man who cannot see. We will lock the door and end that day, this blight upon our fair city."

A low chant started somewhere behind me. Just a murmur. "The key. The key. The key."

Virdon motioned for quiet. Once the audience noise abated he smiled. "I don't know how and I don't know when, but if it is God's will it shall be done."

You could almost hear a pin drop in the cavernous church.

Then keyboardist leaned close to his microphone and bellowed, "Y'all rear back and say yeah, yeah!"

The church exploded.

Virdon let them go for an extended period, not exhorting them. Not needing to. Finally he waved to the keyboardist to stop tickling the ivories, then he motioned the crowd to sit. To wind down. To listen, and listen good.

When they were all seated, he said, "We lost the first battle."

The keyboard player rolled through the keys.

Virdon whipped his head around. "Do the Lord's will," he said to the keyboardist, smiling. "God's people, I say we lost the first battle."

"Amen!" rained from the balcony.

"The battle of sin and degradation."

Keyboard.

"The battle of poor-nog-a-phy."

The black women in the front row jumped up and praised God Almighty.

Virdon looked their way. "But with God on our side."

"With God on our side," the girl beside me repeated. She'd slammed her eyes shut like she was reciting a bedtime prayer.

Virdon said, "We still can win the war!"

The House of the Lord sprang to life.

Virdon let them carry on. His eyes sparkled as he surveyed his throng.

When their response faded to murmurs and they took their seats, Virdon said, "Remember, enclaves of sin, they do not last."

The keyboard danced.

"They will be expunged from the world."

Frantic Amens rained down on Virdon.

He leaned back, threw his arms heavenward and howled, "And as the Lord of Lords destroyed Sodom and Gomorrah..." Virdon stamped his feet on the last three syllables.

The keyboardist hammered out a series of chords.

"So will He strike down the palace of sin constructed among us!"

The band kicked in, the crowd once again erupted, and a hundred or more folks jitterbugged down the aisle.

I was stationary. Given my employer I thought it best to remain neutral on the topic.

I continued to search the crowd. And I continued to be disappointed. No Annette. No Shari.

Virdon motioned for the congregation to sit.

I stood and swiveled, hoping to see the girls. After a moment I noticed I was the only person still standing. And many, including Reverend Virdon, observed me like I'd peed in the punch bowl. I dropped like I was shot.

Virdon smiled and said, "You can always tell how blessed you're going to be tomorrow, by how much hell you're going through today!"

A three chord burst from the keyboard.

"You can say I'm limping, but I'm holding on. I've got scars, but I'm still holding on."

The bass burbled along with the keyboards.

"And though you and I came up the rough side of the mountain, the Lord was there to lend a hand."

A middle-aged bald man in the row in front dropped to his knees and wailed, heartfelt sobs that shook him.

Virdon pointed skyward. "With Him, we made it here today! And with God's grace we ain't going away!"

The band kicked into another song, and Virdon soulfully sang, "They said we wouldn't make it, but we're on our way, and we're growing stronger, each and every day."

The crowd stood, linked hands, and began to sway and sing along.

The girl beside me reached for my hand.

I looked over and caught her mother's eye.

Mom hesitantly nodded yes.

I took the girl's hand and swayed along with her. A pimply-faced boy on my right side meekly took my right hand, probably wishing he could trade places with me. Sorry bud. Her momma wouldn't like you either.

When the song ended, the crowd dropped hands but continued to stand and sway. Virdon waved his hands over them, as if he were blessing them.

A large man and woman across the aisle from me stood to leave. When they moved, for the first time I could see an extremely handsome, deeply tanned, spectacularly dressed man of forty or so. He wore a perfectly fitted dark blue suit, a mint green shirt and a striped blue and green tie. He wore a ruby pin in his lapel and a white pocket square. To top it off, his hair looked perfect, as if God himself had given him a heavenly haircut for the occasion.

Mikey Cross. Who I loathed, even on the Lord's Day.

Certain folks, you always know where you stand with them. They tell you what they think, and they usually don't give a damn one way or the other how you take it.

I saw none of that with Mikey Cross. On the surface, Mikey would pat your back, tell you what a super guy you were, and he'd always try to stay in camera range on the off chance someone would notice him. But when the cameras went away the real Mikey Cross came out. The ruthless, heartless, cutthroat bastard the rest of us knew.

I'd watched him from a distance as he'd put the screws to my old man. Pops had owned Cloverleaf Construction and over twenty-five years had grown it from a backhoe and a pickup truck to a multi-million dollar company with fifty employees. Ma told me once after Pops died that his enduring dream had been for me to take it over.

But before that happened, Mikey Cross cast his eye on the business. And when Mikey put his mind to it, whether it meant buying apartment houses for a steal, acquiring prime riverfront property for next to nothing or owning a construction company for pennies on the dollar, well that's what he did.

Pops, stubborn as a Missouri mule, told Mikey to take a long walk off a short dock. So one day some of Pops' trucks exploded and some scaffolding collapsed, putting a handful of men in the hospital. A lawsuit ensued and not long afterward Cloverleaf Construction became Cross Construction.

Pops sat quietly by like he'd given up, drank like he didn't give a damn about anything anymore and failed to see the year out.

To top it off, Mikey Cross had come to his funeral. And the prick seemed genuinely sorry that Pops had passed away.

Years later, Mikey and I shared the same church. How lovely. For both of us.

Cross looked at me. Irritation flickered across his face.

I glanced around. I didn't see anyone near Mikey who looked like a strong arm thug.

Therefore I had something I needed to get off my chest. I mouthed 'Fuck you' to him.

He turned his gaze to the front.

As the offering plates were being passed around, I could feel my blood boil. Mikey Cross. Sitting twenty feet away.

The man responsible for my father's death.

With no one here to protect him. And me with a full head of steam.

The time to square things up, once and for all.

I stood, tapped the three guys next to me on the knee, and scooted past them. I crossed the aisle.

Two women, both about my age, looked up as I loomed over them.

"Want to slide just a bit?" I asked. "I got to see a man about a ass-kicking."

Cross, still sitting, turned again. He measured me. "Not here, Doyle," he hissed. "Outside." He jerked his head toward the door.

Outside. I could do outside.

I slipped out the back of the church and waited.

After ten minutes or so, the doors flew open, and hundreds of people poured out. The same energy that had buoyed them inside now seemed to snap around them like an electric storm. They carried it in their hearts. They carried it in their souls.

I hoped they'd carry it home. And keep it awhile.

I wouldn't mind a dose of it myself.

I searched for a particularly well-dressed man with great hair.

More and more people poured past me. Young ones.

Then families.

Then older, slower moving people.

The band, carrying their packed-up instruments.

The doors closed.

I was alone.

CHAPTER 15

I stood in an empty parking lot. Beaten by Mikey again.

I'd decided to go all tough guy on him. And he'd slipped out the side door.

One day I'd corner him, when slipping out the side door wasn't an option.

I hoped.

I dropped to a bench near the sidewalk. Nothing was going right. Not a goddamn thing.

A friend. I could use a friend today.

But Venus was busy being a mom and a wife. Cash was recovering from his run and drinking beer in Fryeburg with a war buddy. It probably wasn't a good time for me to butt in.

Other than Cash, I really hadn't talked with anyone lately...except Ecstasy.

Last night I'd talked to Ecstasy.

We spent over an hour together. When I'd tried to steer the conversation to our parting from a couple of nights earlier, she'd quickly brushed it off. No need to talk about it, she said. I can't change how I feel. She was very clear. I wouldn't understand. Which, given that she'd told me nothing, was a pretty accurate assessment.

So Ecstasy and I found other things to chat about instead. People do that, they work their way around uncomfortable topics until they find things they can talk about. It's better than the alternative, incapacitating loneliness. I knew that for a fact.

Despite her earlier protestations about allowing me to see the real her, Ecstasy and I were two people getting to know each other. Sharing milestone moments like Santa Fe. She'd grown up in Santa Fe. She graduated at the top of her high school class and she had a twin sister named Tanya who was studying fashion design. Ecstasy had dreamed about fashion design herself before embarking on her current career. When I started to ask why she hadn't followed her dream, she shook her head.

Conversation halted.

Abruptly.

But she found her smile when I prepared to leave, and she gave me a peck on the cheek.

Which I chose to build a dream on.

I looked at my watch. Four minutes past noon.

On a Sunday.

I'd just gotten a heavenly dose of religion, and all I could think about was going to a strip joint. Maybe she'd be there.

I sighed.

I walked to my car, started it up, and drove to The Limit.

I asked for Lou first, but Tori said he'd gone to visit his mother's grave. Her birthday, Tori thought. I left a message for him to call me when he got back in town.

I'd just started on a beer when the DJ called for Ecstasy.

She appeared from the back and stepped on stage wearing a man's sports coat. No pants. No shirt. Nor much else that I could see.

She had her hair pulled back in a tight bun, wore oversized glasses and, instead of a purse, carried a briefcase that she placed on the edge of the stage. The hot businesswoman takes the stage.

I took the last empty chair near her.

Ecstasy crawled to me and leaned close. She whispered, "Three days in a row you've come, Paul. Welcome home." She kissed my forehead.

"There's this awesome girl, don't you know," I said, and hoped she'd smile.

It started with her eyes. They caught mine, held them and refused to let go. They became almost invasive in their intensity, in their insistence to look into me. They bored deeper, unrelenting, until my heart did the now-familiar

Ecstasy-induced barrel roll. Feeling disoriented, I gulped in a ragged breath, thankful that I still could. She blushed slightly and dimples appeared on her cheeks. One side of her mouth tightened and pulled slightly up. A smile line appeared as the other rose. Finally, like sunrise cresting the horizon, a broad smile beamed across her full, bright red lips.

I felt like I needed a cold shower. And a cigarette.

"Come join me when you're done?" I shakily asked.

"Of course," she said and caressed my face. The warmth of her affection was real. You can't buy something like that.

Well, you can. But it seemed real. To me anyway.

I picked up my beer and returned to my table.

Ecstasy slithered over to a handsome man about her age who belonged shirt-less in a magazine ad. He waved a couple of bills at her. She gave him a full dose of the 'I'm so glad you're here today' smile.

The same smile she'd just given me.

My stomach rolled.

He smiled back. Interested.

She hooked her arm around his neck and pulled his face into her chest. He came out looking like he longed for more.

I knew the feeling.

Their eyes locked. Like ours had.

She kissed him on the cheek and whispered something in his ear.

They laughed like lovers.

I hit the bricks.

Lou called me a couple of hours later and said he was back in town.

But I wasn't going to the club to see him, on the off-chance Ecstasy and her boy toy were still there. I told Lou to meet me at my office.

Twenty minutes later he clumped up the stairs and sat on the couch. Now that the swelling had set in, his face looked like he'd lost a fight with a cement mixer. "I heard you come by the club earlier."

"We need to talk about your problems."

"We don't need to talk about shit when it comes to me. What did you find about my girl Cherry?"

"Following a few leads."

"That's all you got? You bleedin' me dry, you fuckin' chiseler?"

"Whoa!" I jumped from my chair, ready to knock him into the middle of next week. "Easy on the fucking chiseler remark."

He rose to a half-crouch. "I paid you two bills and you ain't found her yet! You tryin' to get more outta me, ain't ya, ya lousy bastard!"

I fought the urge to beat the life out of him, mostly because corpses don't look good on a resume. Instead, after my blood pressure came down from the ceiling, I said, "Detective work goes step-by-step. These are the steps I've taken. Annette doesn't have her cell phone anymore. I've checked with every Begley I can find and she hasn't been in contact with any of them. I found no clues in her apartment. None of the girls have seen her since the last time she danced. So yes, I'm following a few leads."

I glowered at him, still fuming, my tension rising like the incoming tide.

He put his hands up. "You don't gotta get all defensive."

"Whatever. If you're dissatisfied with my service, I guess you could go to the cops."

Lou's face paled. "Can't have no cops in the middle of this mess, Doyle."

"Yeah, I guess they'd frown on the quality of your business associate."

A strawberry flush worked its way up his neck. He stammered, "What do you mean?"

"You and Mikey Cross. What are you in for, Lou?"

"I ain't in for nothin' from nobody! What the hell you talkin' about, you goddamn idiot?"

"Hey, dipstick!" I snarled. "Dial your friendly refrain back about four notches or you can shove your precious two bills up your ass and waddle out of here and find her yourself. Got it?"

Lou sunk a little lower in his chair. He got it.

I said, "It was Mikey's boys who tap-danced on your lovely mug a couple of days ago. What's the story?"

"I ain't gotta tell you nothin'," he groused.

"No, you don't. But I'm looking around the office here and I don't see a helluva lot of friends gathered at your feet. You got me, or you got no one. And you can't do Mikey alone."

"Says you." But Lou's feisty confidence had been replaced by what appeared to be a thin veneer of false bravado. Lou's goose was cooked. And he knew it.

He dropped his head in his hands and massaged his scalp with his fingers while he spoke. "Fine. I'll tell ya. The shit all started after the woolen mill closed down last year. Before then, I had the seven-to-three shift that weren't in a rush to go home to a bitchin' old lady, and the three-to-eleven shift that wanted a beer with a pretty girl before callin' it a night. But when they locked the mill up things went to shit and suddenly I got nothin' but dust bunnies in the corner. Then Reverend Virdon decides I ain't been kicked in the jimmy enough, so he comes up with his stupid-ass porno vote."

"I saw you on the Internet." I decided to leave out my praise for his bravura performance, what with him pissing me off as much as he was right at this moment in my life.

He shook his head. "I had to pay the TV station for that, plus a donation to the Reverend's church or he wouldn't a showed up. I needed a shitload of cash to do this right, and it don't grow on trees. When the banks wouldn't lend me nothin' I got a wild hair and talked to Mikey. I told him I needed money to classy the place up. I figured I beat the vote, more swingin' dicks hear about us, we get more business, and I make enough to pay him back. We all win."

"Didn't turn out quite as brilliant as your forecast, did it?"

Lou's blush deepened. "You think I'm shit on a shoe, dontcha?"

He had me there.

He closed his eyes and rubbed his neck, trying to knead out some nagging pain. When he opened his eyes he said, "I ain't got a entrance exam at the club. Girl wants to shake her stuff, who am I to say no? I ask 'em, 'You a single mom?' Most of 'em are. 'You got a diploma?' One in three."

Lou rubbed his neck again. "One in three, Doyle. The majority, they can't do nothin' else. But I was lucky enough to get out of the shitheap. Be kind of nice seein' others get out, too."

"Except now you're back in it with Mikey."

He looked crestfallen. "Turns out maybe I only thought I was out of the shitheap."

"How bad with Mikey?"

"Bad enough. Fifty G's."

Fifty thousand. Mikey Cross would bust you up for cab fare. He probably ran the lunch money shakedown in grade school. I could almost hear the bugler warming up for Taps. The fat lady gargling before she sang.

Lou's jowls shook as thrashed his head from side to side. "But am I employin' you to snoop around in my business? Or am I employin' you to find my niece? Which you consistently fail to do. I got no idea why I thought you could help."

I felt my defenses rise. Time to protect my professional turf. "Get off my ass, Lou. I have a solid lead on where she is."

"Jesus, you think she's alive? You think she's still alive?"

'Alive' had never crossed my mind before. Why did he think she'd be anything else? "Far as I can tell she is."

He smacked the desk with both hands. So what the fuck you doin' here? Go get her while she's still breathin'!"

"She's fine right where she is," I said, trying to soothe him. "I guarantee she's safe."

"You found her? No shit, you found her?"

"I believe so."

He smacked the desk again. "Damn it all to hell! If a bozo like you can find her anyone can find her. You gotta get her, Doyle. Before Mikey Cross kills her!"

My head swirled. "Why would Mikey kill Annette?"

Lou knocked my question away like a horse swats a fly. "It's like I'm talkin' to a child. He don't actually want to kill *her*. But he wants what I got, and if I don't give it to him…"

"He'd kill her over fifty thousand?"

"No," he said, wincing. "It's like this. I won the vote and I think I got the world by the balls. I make a couple of payments to keep him happy, but then his song changes. He doubles what I gotta pay him, right outta the blue. Doubles that shit. Not like there's rules in this game, but who can make double payments? Nobody can. So I miss like two, and he says he'll take the club and we'll call it square."

"What's the Limit worth?"

"A damn sight more than fifty G's even with what I owe, so I tell him to get bent. But then one of Mikey's boys comes to see me on the sly. Says it's important. Says he's in love with Cherry."

I thought about the picture Annette had. The guy with the tattoo. Who apparently worked for Mikey...Annette's mess had just gotten exponentially worse.

Lou snapped his fingers. "I'm payin' you Doyle, so focus. This jerk says Mikey is gonna kill Cherry if I don't give him the club. He tells me Mikey might even offer to buy it. Well, I tell him I ain't gonna do shit for Mikey Cross. So this guy's face goes about four shades of red, and he starts babblin' that Mikey's serious about killin' her. Then he goes chargin' outta my office and about takes the hinges off the door when he slams it. I go lookin' for Cherry in the club and her shit's gone. I go to her place. Nothin'. When she didn't come in the next day, that's when I called you."

"How do you know that guy didn't take her somewhere?"

Lou grumbled, "Because for a couple of days he hung around like a lovesick calf askin' me and every other Joe if we knew where she went when she took off. So loverboy don't know shit either. Which is the league you're playin' in. The Don't-Know-Shit league."

I thought about what Trouble had told me. A well-dressed guy with a thing for Annette. After he'd come to see Lou he'd told Annette to go into hiding. She listened.

And that was why she was hiding at the dormitory. Bingo.

Deep creases ravaged Lou's swollen face. "When Mikey found out she was gone and he thought I hid her, his boys done this." He pointed to his face. "It never turns out right with me. It don't ever."

I felt for him, but I couldn't resist saying, "I wish you'd shared the Mikey Cross link with me earlier. I could have started with him, instead of chasing my tail for a week."

His head bobbed like a car's back-window Chihuahua. "We're all a lot smarter lookin' backwards than forward. I figure she's on the run, so where would she go? Family, right? I check my side and nobody seen her. So I tell you about the prize-winning Begleys. Bastards won't talk to me no more, so I need you to do the legwork. You strike out. You talk to the girls, but they don't know nothin', either. But whether I tell you about Mikey or not, them things still had to be done to run this to ground, right?"

I read his face. There was more. But I wasn't going to make him say it. There was no value in him saying what I already knew.

It was the 'shit on a shoe' comment. Getting in the crap with Mikey was bad enough. But he couldn't bear to have people look at him like he was shit on a shoe. He needed me to look at him like he was somebody. Not like someone who'd fucked up. Royally.

I stood, walked to him, and patted him on the back. "I'll go get your girl right now."

CHAPTER 16

The setting sun was buried behind heavy clouds. Cold rain fell from a steel gray sky. The drops hit me like ice. Five degrees colder and it would be snowing.

I flipped my collar up, hunched my shoulders, and tried to keep water from slipping down my back.

I walked down the alley behind my office, and saw a parking ticket under the wiper of my car.

A parking ticket. On Sunday? In an alley?

Angrily, I strode to the car, snatched the ticket, wadded it up, turned and pitched it away.

I stepped in a puddle.

Water oozed into my left shoe.

It squished as I walked over to the wadded up ticket. I lifted it from the damp sidewalk, smoothed it out, folded it, and stuffed it in my pocket.

I climbed in my car and headed for the church dormitory to rescue Annette Begley.

Darkness crept over the hill as I stopped down the road from the church dormitory, flipped my headlights off, and parked. The dormitory's only outside light was over the main entrance. None of the windows were lit, and it was shrouded in misty rain and a creeping curtain of darkness.

Before I charged into the unknown I wanted to do a little reconnaissance work. I wouldn't mind surprising the occupants of the dormitory one little bit. What I would mind, however, is if I went in blind and was the recipient of my own nasty surprise.

I jammed my .38 in my jacket pocket and fished a small flashlight out of the glove box. I exited the car and quickly stepped into the brush. I pushed through it and began a slow circle around the building.

I didn't see anyone or anything moving. Still, I fought my way through the branches, unwilling to step out into the open.

The rain had nearly stopped, but the brush was soaked.

Soon I was too.

I stood in the middle of some raspberry bushes behind the dormitory. I played the flashlight beam toward the building. I counted the windows along the back of the dormitory. Three stories. Nine windows on each floor. Twenty-seven rooms per side. Fifty-four rooms in the building. Oh, the lifelong benefit of basic math.

I continued circling. Nothing remotely interesting happened.

Except for me getting wetter and wetter. Screw it. I flipped the flashlight off and charged though the brush until I came out on the lawn. I walked around the dormitory and strolled up to the front door like I owned the place.

Locked.

I beat on the door. The sound echoed through the foyer.

No one came to escort me.

I walked to the south end of the building and checked the first floor door. Locked.

I climbed the outside metal staircase to the second floor.

Locked as well.

I looked at the door on the third floor. What were the odds?

I climbed up, gave the handle a yank, and the door swung open.

I checked all eighteen rooms on the third floor. None of them looked like they had ever been occupied.

I went down to the second floor. Twelve of the rooms had made beds. Toiletries in the bathrooms and clothes in dressers.

On the first floor, every room looked lived in. Yet for all that living, I saw…no people.

A door clicked shut. I ran to the hallway, just in time to see a flash go out the front door.

I hustled to the main entrance to get a better look at them.

The light over the door barely illuminated the circular driveway in front of the dorm. For just an instant I saw a set of blue jean-clad legs dashing into the shadows. Had a sneaky suspicion who owned them. My girls were on the run.

I debated following them, even though they had a healthy head start. I decided people are generally like dandelions. Where you find a couple, more are sure to appear. I retraced my steps. I checked the first room a little closer this time.

I looked under the bed. Zip. In the closet. No. The bathroom.

They say insanity is doing the same thing over and over and expecting a different result. So maybe I was nuts, but I might as well look in every...

When I stepped into the bathroom of the fifth room, I heard a muffled squeal.

I drew my gun and pulled back the shower curtain.

A man, a woman, and two kids were huddled in the tub. They looked terrified. Of little old me. Hard to believe.

"I won't hurt you," I said.

The woman stared at the gun I'd forgotten to holster. She said in a wheezing tone, "Leave us alone, you monster! Cory, you make him leave us alone."

"Easy, Irmalee," Cory said.

I gingerly put the gun back in my shoulder holster and offered my empty hands to them. "I'm not here for you. I'm here for Annette Begley and Shari Tappey."

Hearing their names, Irmalee jumped.

"You know them?" I asked.

Irmalee shook her head.

"I'm here to help," I said. "I really am."

Irmalee scowled. I knew how to make a good impression.

"Sorry," I said. "How many more of you here?"

Cory said, "Eight families, thirteen singles." He did a quick calculation. "But since you showed up I'm thinking eleven singles."

"Where are the rest?"

"I sent 'em all down to the basement. But Annette and Shari were some skittish when I mentioned a big feller slinkin' around with a flashlight. Last I saw them they was headin' for the front door with their eyes on the horizon."

I looked at the four of them, a tangle of arms and legs, crammed in a tiny bathtub. "You folks want to come out of there? We can go in the room and talk."

Irmalee held up her finger. I waited while she coughed. She closed her eyes and sighed. She nodded when she felt ready. "It's especially hard on Cory's back, and it won't get no better."

Cory looked at her. "It ain't easy for you with the pleurisy either. Come on, dear."

He stood and helped the children climb out. Then Irmalee. He brushed a wisp of hair from her face.

She smiled at him like she'd married the greatest guy in the world.

The same way he looked at her.

We walked into the small bedroom and the children sat on the bed. Cory took the wooden chair by the desk in the corner. Irmalee sat between her children and hooked an arm around each.

I stood and debated how much I should tell them. After all, the targets of my interest were likely doing wind sprints toward the city while I was making small talk.

But I wouldn't learn anything until I began to get along with my hosts. I stuck out my hand. "Paul Doyle. Private investigator."

Cory offered his. "Cory Fettig. My wife Irmalee. Our kids Ethan and Ruthie. Reverend Virdon has me here running things."

"Why were you hiding just now?" I asked.

Cory rubbed his neck. "I didn't come here with a gun, mister. You did."

"Fair enough. But the girls are in trouble."

Cory smirked at me. "We should all have troubles like this. Families come, the Reverend feeds them. Runaways come, Reverend takes them in. I got busted up working in the woods last spring, and we had nothing else so we came here. The Reverend put us up. No fuss, no muss." He licked his lips. "'Course, we ain't never had anybody come with a gun before. Little more fuss goin' on now. Caused principally by you."

Despite my gentle demeanor the kids still looked frightened. Maybe I should have shaved. I looked at Cory. "I wasn't sure what I was getting myself into."

Irmalee scoffed. "Still. A gun, Mister Doyle. We're church people."

Cory patted her thigh. "It's okay, honey." He looked me up and down. "So Mister Private Investigator, just what kind of trouble are Annette and Shari in?"

I glanced at Ethan and Ruthie. I'd give the PG-13 version. Or less. "There's a bad man after them, and they felt the best way to deal with him was to run. But they're going to need a lot of help to make him go away."

I pointed to Cory, and back to me. "Our help. You and me. But first..."

He interrupted. "You gotta see if that was them running off."

Give that man a kewpie doll.

Cory patted Irmalee on the leg again. "Come on, baby. Let's go to the basement."

I met the Bentleys, the Payettes, the Hassims, two families named Wilcox, and a host of others whose names soon left me. Plus nearly a dozen singles, who ranged from about seventeen years old to nearly thirty. But not a flaming redhead or a purple-haired woman in the bunch. In fact, not a single woman in the highly popular 18-to-21 year old demographic could be seen.

Most of the residents eyed me like I was the high school principal and they'd been caught skipping school. They lounged on the furniture, mothers with their arms around small children, fathers debating whether or not they could take me, and teens with their eyes downcast.

When I asked them what they knew about Annette and Shari, no one spoke.

Ahh, the silent treatment. I said, "I know you think you're protecting them by not speaking, but things are worse than they know. They need my help, but first I have to find them."

A short, chunky man with a full red beard spoke up. "Who died and made you savior?" A brave few tittered.

"I'm no savior. But I know the girls are in trouble, and it's not going to get any better if they keep running. They need my help."

Irmalee had slid up behind me. She said, "The Lord by wisdom hath founded the earth; the Lord shall be thy confidence, and shall keep thy foot from being taken." She dragged a breath through her nose. "Book of Proverbs."

The bearded man spoke. "The Lord, it says. I can't find you in the Good Book nowhere."

"Yeah, but it was a little hard to prophesize my coming way back then," I said. "If only they'd have known, you'd see me in a whole new light."

Cory tightened. "You're making fun of us."

"I'm not making fun of you. I just don't understand why you're not willing to help them. I'm asking you to trust me."

Cory said, "Making jokes about us kinda just set your fate in stone. It appears we trust in the Lord a little more than we trust in you." The others unanimously agreed.

I walked out of the Castle View Free Church dormitory alone.

The rain had stopped, but the pavement was still damp as I walked toward my car. The feeble porch lights of some neighboring houses shone through the trees, causing a patchwork of shadows on the dimly-lit pavement in front of me.

I mentally kicked myself, every step I took. This is why you don't do one man assaults. Because you can't cover everything by yourself. You walk in the back, they dash out the front. You think you're so smart, and they've out-thought you.

Again.

Until I'd brashly decided to storm the castle, Annette and Shari had had a roof over their heads, food in their bellies, and beds to sleep on.

Now they were probably hiding in the damp, near-freezing Maine woods with nothing but the clothes on their backs.

As I hammered myself for my foolishness, my foot struck something that skittered across the pavement. It made a metallic clinking sound as it slid away.

I fished the flashlight from my pocket and swept the beam back and forth across the road.

A glint caught my eye. I bent over and picked up…a small key ring with two keys.

Key rings on the ground might not mean much. Anyone who'd ambled along the road near the dormitory could have dropped it during the day. Any old one at all, except...

I fingered the keys. They were dry. They'd fallen since the rain had stopped.

Which was about the time I'd entered the dorm.

Still, they could be anyone's keys, really. Just because I was looking for Annette and Shari, and I'd found some keys on the same road I'd seen them running down thirty minutes earlier, didn't mean the keys belonged to the girls.

But I didn't discount the chance, either. I flipped the key ring over. The plastic tab was from Unity Raceway, a stock car track a handful of towns away. One of the keys was small, like it was for a suitcase lock, or maybe a diary.

The second key looked like it would fit a door. An apartment door.

It looked an awful lot like the key I'd fished from underneath Annette Begley's doormat recently. A piece of white tape had an ink C on it. Annette's apartment.

She was on the move.

I dropped the key ring in my pocket and turned to look down the hill. As I did, the beam of my flashlight washed over the edge of the road.

Muddy tire tracks came from the dirt shoulder and onto the asphalt. They'd been made since the rain stopped as well. The driver had gunned the engine, for a spray of mud had kicked onto the grass along the shoulder.

I'm no expert Indian tracker, but what even I could see as I squatted down and studied the area were two sets of large footprints. One with square toes, one with pointed toes. Men's size.

And distinctly different shoe prints from small, woman-sized sneakers.

I looked down the empty road and thought for a long time. What I came up with was, someone had followed me to the dormitory on the hill, hoping I'd lead them to the girls.

Which I had.

And because of that, I didn't think Annette and Shari were on the run anymore.

CHAPTER 17

After a nearly sleepless night I rose before 6 AM, threw my sweats on, and went for a jog along the river. The sky to the east was just beginning to lighten. Not enough to see much, but enough for me to tell which direction was east and which wasn't.

A heavy fog hung over the Pessamoc River and had frozen to the bare branches of the trees that lined Water Street. As my shoes scuffed along the pavement, ghostly white trees slipped out of the pre-dawn gray. This morning, everything was soft and gentle.

Except for the fact that Mikey Cross probably had Annette and Shari. There was nothing soft or gentle about that.

As I turned for home, I thought about the 'what's next' question.

It took me the rest of the jog to realize I had no clue.

When I can't sort things out, I either say it's not worth sorting out in the first place or I jump into the water head first and start swimming in whatever direction the tide takes me. Today was shaping up to be a swimming day.

And I had a feeling the tide was going to lead me to Mikey Cross.

I puttered around my office until I figured Cash was back in the area, and I called him.

He was less than an hour from home. "You want to take a field trip?" I asked.

"Sure, why not?" he said, and hung up the phone.

I called him back. "You want to know where? And why?"

"I figure it's high time we see Mikey Cross. How smart am I?"

"You're a freaking genius. You know when?"

"Now?"

"Yeah. Now."

We met at a parking lot in Augusta. When I pulled in Cash stepped from his pimped-out black Chevy Caprice with the chrome rims and the dark, illegally-tinted windows. He wore baggy jeans and an oversized Maine Black Bears hoodie. Blonde hair curled out from beneath his black watch cap. He walked with a slight limp. If you didn't know better, you'd think maybe he had blisters from running the half-marathon. You wouldn't think he'd lost his right leg from just below the knee.

Cash waved. "You ready to wreak havoc on the unsuspecting?"

"Mikey invited us for tea."

"I can do tea. But I'd rather bust heads."

"Save that aggression in case the tea sucks."

Mikey Cross ran his operation out of a strip mall. The ground floor consisted of a Laundromat, an adult bookstore, an insurance company, an Army recruiting station, two vacant units and a Korean takeout restaurant. They boldly claimed they made the best bulgogi and kimchee in the city. As far as I knew they made the only bulgogi and kimchee in the city, but who was I to quibble over a marketing angle?

Alongside the restaurant, a flight of stairs creaked like my back in the morning as we climbed. At the top were two white doors. I chose door number one for all the marbles.

Inside, an elderly lady with a bright copper dye job watched TV and smoked. She wore an aqua A-line skirt about four sizes too big, baggy support hose that failed to hide a spidery web of varicose veins, a long-sleeved beige blouse with a frilly lace collar and a double strand of yellowed pearls. Glasses hung from her neck by a faux-jewel cord.

She appeared fashionably dressed.

For 1958.

Two blocks of granite poorly disguised as cheap thugs sat behind her on a beige loveseat. I knew them from when they'd worked for other men. I hadn't heard they were working for Mikey. Maybe the tough guy trade was booming.

Chappy Quade's lumpy, worn-out body and salt-and-pepper hair made him look like he was about seven years out of warranty. When I was just getting into the game he should have been getting out.

But there's no retirement plan for muscle guys. One day someone's faster or stronger.

Or maybe one day your luck runs out.

Chappy looked like that day might not be far off.

The other man I knew only as Calderon.

I winked at them. "What's up, boys? Want to play a little two on two? We owe someone a beating for the one Lou Principi took."

Neither one said a word. In fact, neither one acknowledged our presence. Rude.

I said, "I'm going to pick first, since I'm the visitor. I'm going to take…" I looked at them. Back at Cash. Snuck a peek at the redhead in case she wanted to join the fun.

I said, "I think I'm gonna take my buddy Cash." I looked at Calderon. "I suppose you want the old man. That still leaves the unnatural redhead here."

She barely looked up, and kept the glowing cigarette in her mouth as she watched the game show. "What?" she croaked.

"Sucks to always get picked last, huh?"

She squinted. Without discernible humor.

I motioned Quade over to me and spoke softly. "You don't really want to do this, do you?"

He rolled his heavy shoulders. "If we gotta go, we gotta go."

"Let's sit this one out. We'll let the young guys dance."

He looked relieved. But loud enough for everyone to hear he said, "You ain't worth my sweat."

I looked at Cash. "Looks like I don't get to play after all. You going to take care of Calderon?"

Calderon was about Cash's size. Same age. Same general physique. From the look on Calderon's face, he thought he could win.

I didn't.

Cash motioned him forward. Calderon slowly stood. He measured the distance between himself and Cash. He took a sudden step forward to attack.

Whip-quick, Cash flashed a left-right-left-right flurry to Calderon's ribs and chin.

They weren't hard enough to take him out. Just hard enough to let Calderon know that Cash could, any time he wanted, do some serious structural remodeling.

Red grabbed a magazine off the desk, rolled it and swatted Calderon on the arm. "You two knock it off! Knock it off!"

Quade sat on the couch, picked up a newspaper and pretended he could read. Calderon sat and seethed.

I said to Red, "Please announce Paul Doyle and sidekick for Mikey."

Red said, "He ain't 'specting you fellas, is he?"

"No dear, he isn't 'specting us. But I like surprises. Does Mikey like surprises?"

"Not much, he don't. You wait a second." She walked a few steps and opened a door behind her desk. She mumbled a few words and turned to me. "He said he ain't in."

"A miracle, you talking to a fella who ain't in." I looked past her through the open door and gave Mikey a dashing smile and the double thumbs up.

He shot me a pained look. Probably wanted to shoot me the finger. Resigned to his fate, he waved us in.

"Thanks," I said to the lady. "As a door guard, you did real good."

"Screw you, jackoff," she mumbled. She went back to her cigarette.

I looked at Quade and Calderon. "You come through that door, you get one in the ribs." I patted my jacket pocket for emphasis.

Cash cocked and eyebrow and whispered, "You packing?"

"Naah. You?"

He scrunched his nose. "Don't judge me."

We stepped into a large office. Two men in black suits sat side by side on a white leather couch to my left, awaiting further direction.

"Sit. Stay," I said, waggling my index finger. "Good boys." I rummaged around my jacket pocket and came up empty. "Sorry, no treat."

The shorter one with the bad haircut and ears that looked like a dog's chew toys seemed excited to see me again. My old buddy Acie Doucette, who had ample reason to be overjoyed. He used to work for Marcus Caine, and after a disagreement a few years back I'd stuffed his head through a wall. I heard it came out harder than it went in.

The younger, beefier one wore a Marine-style flattop. His soft belly stretched the buttons on his suit. I reminded myself to tell him big guys like us should never button our suits when we sit. Too much stuff squeezing against too little cloth.

A lacquered black desk with a glass top dominated the room. Two black leather armchairs stood in front of it. The huge picture window behind the desk offered a wonderful view of a skeleton high rise under construction. Piles of trash littered the yard. Deep, muddy pools surrounded numerous construction vehicles, two of which were hopelessly buried up to their axles in the slop. A yellow crane hoisted a steel I-beam toward the top of the building where four men, buffeted by a stiff wind out of the north, waited to receive it.

I knew that crane well. Years ago I used to operate it for Pops. I wondered if I could still read the painted-over Cloverleaf Construction logo on the side.

Behind the desk, in all his glory, sat Mikey Cross. Tall, slim, and beautifully tanned. Each strand of his black hair lay perfectly in place. He had an innocent face. With a killer smile.

He gave me his biggest one. I tried to remain unimpressed.

Cash leaned against the wall by the door, right hand in his pocket. He looked disinterested.

"Nice view," I said to Mikey. "I bet they charge you extra rent for it, huh?"

His smile grew. "Paul Doyle. Minor league private eye. Major league pain in my ass."

I shrugged. "Just what I was aiming for."

Mikey smirked. "I own this building. You're eminently familiar with my humble construction operation. And I own more than you…it makes no difference what I own, if it were any of your business." He paused, as if weighing his next words. "But alas, it's not." He looked at Acie and Flattop. "Gentlemen, would you show Mister Doyle out?"

Cash slapped a vice-like grip on Flattop's shoulder, forcing him to stay on the couch. Acie, however, jumped up like a man who'd built up a hell of a grudge in the last five years, and charged at me.

Like the football lineman I once was, I set my legs and drove my left shoulder into his chest. He crashed into me full force, grunted like he'd just hit a wall, and staggered backward to regroup.

He gingerly rubbed his chest and glared. Given the way we'd collided I thought he might be done, but Cash chose that moment to snicker. Acie gave a banshee wail and came at me again.

I turned the smallest bit as Acie lunged. He glanced off me, staggered, and lost his balance. He crashed into the corner of Mikey's desk, causing it to skid a couple of inches. Two of the pictures on Mikey's desk fell over. He didn't bother setting them back up.

As Acie fought to steady himself I grabbed his arm, spun him around, and slapped him, open-palmed, on the left side of his face. I back-handed him on the right side, got a good grip on his jacket, and shoved him toward his buddy.

The sound of the slaps lingered in the room.

No man wants to get slapped.

Acie's eyes burned with hate. "I'm gonna kill you, fat boy!"

I was game.

He charged.

Blindly.

I blocked a few of his punches, ate a few more than I should have, and slipped a lucky one or two past his guard. But in the end I wasn't here to play pattycake with Acie.

No more screwing around.

I lunged forward and shouldered him off-balance. As he struggled to right himself, I feigned a left. When he clumsily turned to block it, I set my feet and hit him with a hard right to the jaw. The perfect shot to an undefended target. He didn't fall so much as crumple.

Flattop looked down. If he seemed surprised at Acie's sudden demise, he didn't show it.

He glanced at Cash, as if asking permission to go to recess.

Cash took his hand from Flattop's shoulder.

He stepped over his fallen comrade. In a voice way too close to tenor for a guy who wanted to be a badass he said, "I ain't gonna go down so easy."

Cash stifled a yawn and rolled his eyes. "They never do."

Flattop moved like a tank. Straight ahead. Predictable. Just the way I like 'em.

He launched a wild right that started from his hip and arced toward me. I blocked him with my left, did a quick shuffle step to get my timing down and jabbed him twice in the nose.

While he wiped the blood away and stared at his hand, I prepared for the next phase of the operation.

Shock and awe.

I took a quick step to my right, got my balance, made a full shoulder turn and cracked him with a right that felt good all the way to my toes. He fell beside Acie. Neither one would move for a while.

I looked at Mikey. He had his hand under the desk.

Gun.

Or buzzer. To tell the other two boys to get their asses in the office pronto.

I heard the doorknob rattle behind me. Buzzer. I relaxed.

I turned as the door slammed open. Cash smashed his fist on the point of the first chin coming through. Calderon's.

It quickly disappeared.

Quade's chin never showed.

The door crashed closed. The knob didn't turn again.

"I told them they'd get one in the ribs," I said.

"And that's why I popped Calderon in the chops," Cash said. "The art of misdirection."

I nudged Flattop and Acie with my toe and looked back at Cash. "Sorry, did you want in?"

He pulled a toothpick out of his mouth and pointed it at me. "Uh uh. There were just these two little ones."

"That's what I figured. Besides, Acie had a score to settle with me."

Cash leaned forward and glanced down. "He going to think you're even?"

"I don't think Acie will ever call us even." I turned and looked at Mikey. "You need any more cord wood stacked?"

He smiled. All teeth. Beautifully bleached. He was Bernardo-from-West-Side-Story cool. They didn't come prettier than Mikey Cross. "Nice work."

I cracked my knuckles. "I'm just getting warmed up. You next?"

He waved his hand. "Hardly. As you so succinctly said, sit. Stay."

I hate being told what to do. Especially by a pompous ass like Mikey. But my need for information about Annette and Shari far outweighed my need to be a stubborn jerk.

I sat. Cash stayed by the door.

Mikey threw me another big smile that was as insincere as it was cheesy. "Twice in one week Paul Doyle appears in my life. And that doesn't count your apparent love for my work during football games. To what do I owe the pleasure this time?"

"I wanted to wring your neck at church yesterday, but you chickened out."

Cash clucked like an old hen.

Crimson slowly crept up Mikey's face. I liked it much more than his smiles.

I said, "But I've controlled that impulse for now. So let's talk business. Man to man."

Cash cleared his throat.

I looked back. "Sorry. Man and man, to man."

Cash said, "Thank you."

I turned to Mikey. "I hear you're putting the squeeze on Lou Principi."

He tapped the desk with a pen. "A man with an entrepreneurial spirit is good for my business interests."

"Not good for Lou and your esteemed muscle boys. Gotta ask you, though. I saw some retreads outside. Not the A-team. Where's the big Eye-talian and the brotha who thinks he's a bad motha?"

Mikey said, "They are not in my employ." He didn't bother to elaborate.

"Can't afford 'em? I kinda figured times were tough, the dump of an office you have. But before you gave them the pink slip you sent them to see Lou.

They popped him a few in the chops. Didn't help his face much. Although it didn't hurt much, either. His mug like a catcher's mitt and all."

Mikey's smile disappeared. "That's a harsh accusation."

I said, "I hear you're a harsh man. I'd ask Lucky Valentine his opinion. But word on the street is you convinced him to try to fly from about a hundred feet up on the Messalonskee Stream bridge. He doesn't say much anymore."

The smile returned. "It was an un-Lucky end to his trip."

I glared at Mikey. "Let's get hypothetical. You know what that means?"

He impatiently circled his hand, motioning me to continue.

I said, "Let's say, for the sake of argument, a businessman looked for a lifeline to keep his operation afloat. And you acquiesced."

"I am forever a giver."

I probably rolled my eyes. "And let's say that same businessman struggled to reimburse you. Stars didn't align. Economy sucked. His dog died. You doubled the payments. Any old excuse. Is it safe to assume you'd look unfavorably on that person?"

He sighed. "You're a nosy jerk, Doyle. But I like you. I really do. So, to keep the conversation moving, let's say a businessman sees me as an avenue to achieve success. And he discovers success is…" He looked at me. Like he was searching for a word.

"Elusive?" I asked.

He smiled. "Elusive. He asks me for understanding."

Fair enough. "Let's say that. How would you respond to such a man?"

For the briefest moment, his eyes flashed anger. "I'd convince him to find a way to square the fuck up with me. While he's still breathing."

"And you told Lou to square up?"

Mikey shook his head. "Who's talking about Lou? Apparently you don't know what hypothetical means."

"You want me to use shorter words so you can keep up? We're talking about you shaking Lou down. Now he says you want his club instead. And you'd do just about anything to get it."

He clucked his tongue. "You're quite a storyteller, Doyle."

"You say it like it's a curse. I call it a gift." Some gift. I'd been here for ten minutes and I knew less than when I'd started. I needed to learn about the girls.

I tried a different tack. "Tell me about the good-looking redhead."

He scoffed. "I have no interest in Principi's niece."

I tried a Mikey Cross smile just for fun. "I meant the older model with the bad paint job out front. But now that you mention it…"

His eyes narrowed and his jaw clenched. Introducing the real Mikey Cross. He growled, "Stay out of my business!"

I leaned on his desk. "Mikey, right now those girls are *my* business. You do the right thing and maybe I'll forget what a piece of shit you are. And trust me, I know."

Mikey turned away from me. "You call detective work your profession, yet you continue to prove you don't know anything, Doyle."

"I know I want the girls. Both of them."

He studied his thumbnail a bit longer than necessary. When he looked up, he seemed puzzled. "I'm not sure what kind of game you're playing, but people play games with me, they die. Understand this. I lie to my friends, you lie to your friends. But Doyle…" He cracked the knuckles on his left hand. "Don't fucking lie to me."

Now I was puzzled. I didn't think I was lying about anything. But apparently Mikey did. Which may or may not work to my benefit. "They're just girls, Mikey. They aren't part of this."

He folded his arms across his chest and glared. "Girls, you say. And the lies, they continue. Pray I do not catch you in this lie, my friend. Or it will be your last."

We were like two kids chasing each other around the dinner table, yet no matter how fast we ran we'd never catch each other. I think we both knew it.

His eyes locked on mine. We stared each other down. A veritable dead heat.

But I wanted the last word. I said, "Maybe you can scare others, but I'm not like Lucky Valentine. I won't go away so easy."

A hint of smile returned to his eyes. "Of course you're not like Lucky Valentine. You are not dead. Yet. I offer you a chance to keep it that way. Stay out of my business with Principi."

I glared at him. Similar to the pit bull look I'd gotten a couple of days earlier. Yet just like me with Goble Begley's pit bull, Mikey remained beyond my reach. No matter how much I growled.

But for years I'd hated the way I'd been with Mikey Cross. Today he was dealing with the new and improved, industrial-strength Paul Doyle. "No deal." I smacked his desk with the palm of my hand for emphasis.

Mikey's warm, friendly smile came back. "You don't scare so easy. I forgot, you're a tough guy."

"Damn right." I swept my arm across his desk, knocking the pictures onto the floor. One picture frame broke when it landed. Mikey surveyed the damage. "Impressive. Do you wreak this much havoc everywhere you go?"

"Well, the buffet line for starters," Cash said.

Mikey's eyes bored into mine. "You are an annoyance, nothing more. I could crush you. You know this."

"You're pushing it Pretty Boy," I said. "I'm on your ass now. Me *and* the cops." I winced when I said that. Cops made it sound like I couldn't handle Mikey by myself.

Mikey said, "Principi thought he hired a man to do the job. Instead he hired you. Nice skirt, Paula."

I lunged across the desk to slug him.

As my fist whistled inches away from his jaw he effortlessly leaned back and laughed. "Maybe you should call the cops to help you do that too. But if I see you again, or the cops, someone will find out what a bullet in the head feels like, tough guy. I think you know who I'm talking about."

It hit me like a two-by-four between the eyes. Mikey Cross held the entire deck. All the chips. He was dealing, to boot. I realized I'd gotten a little too far out on the gangplank. And once you're out a gangplank, there's usually only one place you can go. Down.

Time to back off. Carefully. I said, "Got it."

I heard a murmur behind me. Acie had made it to his knees. "Don't get up on my account," I said, and crashed a right to his temple. He went back to sleep.

We weren't home free. We still had to make it past Calderon and Quade and, for all we knew, they were waiting with baseball bats, brass knuckles…or heavier artillery. Cash and I shared a glance as we passed through the door and prepared for one more battle in a lifetime of battles.

But Calderon and Quade had returned to their sullen, uncommunicative ways. They sat, side by side, studying the far wall, awaiting Mikey's further orders.

And Big Red never even bothered to wish us well.

"We got problems," Cash said when we reached the parking lot.

"I think Mikey has them. But we don't know where."

"Nice, the way he tried to put you on the short leash. *You are not dead. Yet.* Were you scared?"

"Yeah, I almost peed my pants." But the bad thing about Mikey saying that was I believed him. "I'm worried."

"Hard to fathom," Cash said. "Paul Doyle worried about anything. Despite what Mikey said, are you going to share his slip about his interest in Annette with our favorite flatfoot, the ultra-hot Venus Robinson?"

I shook my head. "For one thing, Mikey lives thirty miles outside her jurisdiction. But even if I could, what am I going to tell her? That Lou is an idiot who decided to do business with him? That Mikey wants Lou's club and Lou will only give it up over his dead body? That Mikey may have threatened Annette? For all we know he may have her. And, oh by the way, let's not forget Mikey's not-so-veiled threat to me. We keep working this, someone gets a bullet."

"He didn't actually say 'we keep working it.' He was pretty specific about you, however."

"Thanks for the clarification. But let's say the town cops here or the state boys get involved. What would they do, ask Mikey if he has the girls? I'm sure he'll say 'Oh, are they yours? My bad' and give them back. Except they're likely to be a little worse for wear. So how about you and I continue to creep around like the good little creepers we are, and we'll see what we see before the cops blow the cover off this thing."

CHAPTER 18

We ate at a local greasy spoon and debated our next move. Like my wardrobe after an eating binge, nothing fit exactly. We could go back to The Limit, pass around a few twenties, and see if any girls discovered an improved memory. We could hang out with Venus. We could stay here and eat another slice of pie. I wavered slightly when the discussion turned to a nap.

But instead we decided our best move would be to follow Mikey and his boys when they left. See where they went. Because I was positive Mikey's boys had taken Shari and Annette. I just didn't know where.

Cash would get first choice about whom to follow. But I already knew who I'd trail home. I had veto authority.

Mikey was mine.

We drove back to Mikey's place and swung into two empty spaces just down the street from his parking lot. We sat in Cash's Caprice, which had a better heater and a better view. My Nova was parked three spaces behind him. From our vantage point we could see the stairwell, and we could see the parking lot. We had them right where we wanted them. Bottled up inside.

It was nearly dark when Quade and Calderon clumped down the stairs.

Quade drove a silver SUV that had seen better days. Calderon drove a black Nissan Maxima with blackout windows and chrome rims.

"Whaddaya think?" Cash asked, as they drove out of the lot.

"Your choice."

"Quade. Don't want to be accused of ethnic profiling."

I climbed from his car. Before I closed the door he asked, "Sure you don't want Calderon?"

I shook my head. "I'm waiting for the big man."

He hesitated momentarily, then saluted and drove away.

By now the street lights on Belfast Avenue had come on, as well as the three in Mikey's parking lot. The restaurant had closed, along with the Laundromat, book store and insurance company. Even the recruiters had gone home.

Lights had gone out, employees had drifted out.

Including Flattop and Big Red.

But no Acie. And no Mikey.

Yet the parking lot was empty.

I glanced at the second-story windows facing me. Dark.

I walked around the side of the building and edged along the construction site. I poked along until I could see Mikey's picture window.

Black.

There had to be another way out.

I walked the length of the building, but could find no other staircase. No other exit. However, I saw some tire tracks next to the entrance of the now-deserted construction site. Maybe they'd parked there.

But if so, how did they get out? Like having all my bases covered, tonight was the night for me to learn how to have all Mikey's exits covered. For future considerations.

Because sure as hell, I'd be back to follow him soon. And this time I'd be on him like white on rice.

But for now, I had the place to myself.

I continued around the U-shaped building, checked the parking lot one more time, then walked up the main stairs.

I checked the first door I came to. It was locked.

The second was locked, as well.

I peered down the dark hallway, then overhead. Enough light crept up the staircase that I could see there was no bulb in the light socket.

Walk all the way across the parking lot and back to my car to get the flash-light, or follow the hallway? Surely at the end of the hallway was another flight of stairs that led somewhere.

The flight of stairs Mikey had used to elude me.

While I debated getting the flashlight, the hallway got a little darker.

Screw it. It was only a hallway. I'd been down hallways a million times in my life, and so far the worst that ever happened was…nothing.

I reached out until the fingers of my right hand found the wall. Slowly, I moved forward, counting my steps.

Thirteen. I'd taken thirteen tentative steps in utter darkness when my fingers found a corner. I turned to look where I'd just come. A shadowy haze outlined the stairwell.

I reached, found the corner again, and turned right.

A hammer-hard blow smashed into the side of my face. Multiple punches pummeled my ribs.

I was down. Down on my knees, trying to block the kicks that bounced off my legs, my chest, and my gut.

I dropped to the floor and rolled down the hallway, over and over, fast.

The blows stopped.

I scrambled up and pressed against the wall, trying to quiet my gasping breath. I thrust my left arm out, shoulder height, and held it there. If anyone came after me, I wanted that to be the way I found them.

Not by me absorbing another fusillade of blows.

I peered through the pitch blackness, trying to see something, anything.

I waited. I could hear nothing but absolute silence.

Time to move. I took one step toward the corner.

A floorboard creaked.

Before I could brace myself someone punched me in the gut, grabbed my arm and slammed me face-first into the wall.

Now I could see just fine. Stars, anyway. I sagged against the wall and tried to pull myself together.

A muscular arm wrapped around my neck and squeezed. Hard. My assailant's lips pressed against the side of my head. He exhaled in my ear.

He had me good. I couldn't…hardly…breathe. I rolled my neck, trying to loosen his grip.

I whipped my head to the side to hit his nose.

I hit the side of his head instead. It felt as hard as mine. Figures.

I kicked backward to nail him in the crotch. I missed.

I flailed my free right arm, trying to strike him. Nothing.

Darkness brushed the edges of my consciousness and crept toward me.

I was in the sunset of my years.

I would die in a pitch-black hallway in Augusta Maine.

But he loosened his grip enough so I could draw a breath. Another.

He whispered in my ear, "You ain't so tough now, are ya?"

He was right.

"I tell you to stay out of this, and you don't listen. You have trouble listening?" Despite the roaring in my ears he sounded an awful lot like Mikey.

I drew in a ragged, painful breath. "Apparently."

"You'll pay for that." He tightened his chokehold once more. When I struggled to free myself, he hissed, "Don't worry, I'm not going to kill you. I want you alive to see the fruits of your labor."

"Cool," I gasped.

"Not so cool," he said. "Because I don't like this little game you and Principi are playing."

Game? What you talking 'bout?" I forced out.

He yanked tighter on my windpipe. My knees buckled, but I didn't go down.

"One of you is jerking me off!" Mikey yelled. "I know you are. You will tell me who!"

I sagged toward the floor. "Don't. Know. Nothing."

He shoved me against the wall. "You fucking do!"

"Fuh. Kin. Doan."

He tightened his grip some more.

This was it. I was done.

Mikey spun me around like he was presenting me to an assailant.

Of course he was.

I pulled my knee up and caught someone coming in hard. Right in the jewels. I heard an agonized moan as he hit the floor. I believed I'd found Acie.

One down.

One.

One at a time.

Like how you eat an elephant. One bite at a time.

Mikey's grip loosened a bit. I gasped a desperate breath.

I could do this.

I could. I could take Mikey down. One little bite at a time.

And I knew. I would not cower here, not like this. Not anymore. When Mikey let go of me to check on Acie, I whipped a fist over my shoulder and nailed him in the nose. I felt it crunch. I felt the blood spray over me as he howled and let go.

The blood felt good. The howling felt better. The crumpled nose felt best. He'd never be Mister Pretty Boy again.

And he had me to thank for it. His arch-nemesis, Paul Doyle. I was one badass mother…

Mikey grabbed my head again and hammered it against the wall.

I came to in a dark, empty hallway. Blood ran down my face and into my eyes.

I felt for the wall and worked my way up so I could stand, fighting dizzy spells. Each breath seared my lungs. My throat felt like I'd been choked to death. Which I nearly had been.

I ran my fingers along my hairline. Mikey split my head open, and I'd need stitches. I didn't bother to stop the bleeding. I wasn't sure how far I lagged behind Mikey, but I wouldn't get any closer worrying about my face. It hadn't been much to worry about in the first place.

I worked my way down the hall, turned the corner, and eased toward the dim glow.

I made it to the stairs.

I made it down okay.

I made it to the bottom step.

Where I puked my guts out.

I staggered to the curb and sat, my bleeding forehead resting on my jacket sleeve.

Eating this elephant was gonna be a tough go.

CHAPTER 19

After a trip to the emergency room for stitches and a night with little sleep, the next morning Cash met me at The Limit to talk to Lou. Now more than ever, I knew Mikey wasn't playing around. I'd already tasted the sting, and the last thing I wanted was for Annette to get a similar dose of Mikey's medicine.

Cash whistled when I drove up. "Looks like your modeling days are over."

I slowly worked my way out of the car. "For a while, I thought everything was over."

"You did better than me. I watched Quade visit some old woman. Felt worse for him when I realized it was his wife. But you gave Acie one in the junk and broke Mikey's nose. Plus you got stitches. The thug trifecta."

My face hurt too much to smile. "The way I feel right now, they came out ahead."

Cash winked. "Well, there's ample time to even the score, slugger."

The Limit's front door was locked. We walked around the side of The Limit where Lou parked.

His pink Cadillac sat in its usual spot. The driver's side door was open. As I walked closer I saw Lou Principi dying on the front seat.

Yvette sat huddled against the far door, quivering slightly. Her vacant eyes stared at the windshield. I don't think she even knew we were there.

Another guy was on the ground by Lou's door. Someone I didn't know. Given he was dead, I determined Lou deserved my attention more.

Lou lay half-on, half-off the front seat, one leg protruding from the door. He still breathed, but not like he'd be doing it much longer.

126

Blood pooled around him. A lot of blood. He'd been shot in the stomach.

While Cash called 911 I gingerly knelt just outside the door, trying not to mess up the crime scene. I reached in and shook Lou.

His eyes fluttered. He struggled to open them.

Lou gave his head a tiny shake. "Jesus, it hurts."

I leaned in and touched his shoulder. "Who shot you?"

He took a deep breath and his head rolled back and forth as he tried to speak. He rattled a cough and winced in pain.

He closed his eyes. "Gonna die, Paul."

Soon he'd be right. Before he did I had to know. "Tell me who shot you."

He moaned, "I don't wanna die."

Since I had no control over Lou's outcome, I turned my attention to Yvette and gave her the once-over. No blood, no wounds that I could see.

I thought she might find it in her heart to comfort him. Spend the last few moments of his life together. But she sat like a concrete gnome perched on the edge of a garden. That was all she had to give.

I looked at the body a couple feet from my knee. He wore a black pinstriped sports coat, a red checked tie, and a white shirt that was drenched in blood. He'd taken one in the neck. Blood spatters painted the door beside me.

I glanced at the floorboard. Where a foot-long knife lay.

I reached over and slid the jacket away from the dead man's body. His pistol remained in the shoulder harness.

I touched Lou again. "Tell me what happened."

"Find Cherry. And don't say nothin' to the cops. Promise."

I promised.

While Cash picked the lock and poked around the club to see what he could see, I stayed with Lou and listened to him fight to breathe until an ambulance roared into the parking lot.

Uniformed EMTs rushed past me. Hearing them, Cash came out and joined me on the outskirts of the fray.

Two dark blue cars careened around the corner, tires squealing, lights blazing. There would be more. Soon it'd be as crowded as half-price lap dance night.

One car slid to a stop near us, tires squealing again as the brakes locked up. The other pulled closer to the Cadillac. Two officers hustled from the car and rapidly worked to set up a crime scene perimeter.

The doors on the nearest police car opened. The first cop out looked like he'd escaped from dress-up day at the junior high. He was short and slim, with a face thirteen-year-old girls would love. He wore his black hair close-cropped and his tailored uniform fit like a body suit. I didn't see an ounce of fat on him, which I considered a showoff move. His dark blue eyes crackled with excitement as he approached me.

"You stay put, you hear?" he ordered. When his voice didn't crack I think it surprised all of us. He'd graduated puberty. He dashed toward the Cadillac.

His partner climbed from behind the wheel. George Willoughby was the exact opposite of the little guy. He was older like me, leaned to the overstuffed side like me, and if I looked closely, I bet I could find remnants of his last meal on his uniform shirt.

Just like me.

I liked George.

He leaned against the wall near the club's front door. "What do you think about Westfield Police Department's Golden Boy?"

"My Ma would call him cute as a button and pinch his cheeks. Maybe make him hot chocolate and get him a booster seat. He's not my type though. I like 'em with a little more meat on their bones."

"Thanks." George eyed my face. "You going for a certain motif there?"

"Trying to match your ugly mug."

He grinned. "I believe you did."

George looked at Cash. "You couldn't choose better friends than Paul?"

Cash flashed a mouthful of pearly teeth. "When I start feeling bad about myself I hang out with this big lug for a while. Brings my self-esteem back up to level."

"Don't I know it," George said.

"Hey, you gonna do that cop thing they pay you to do?" I asked, after George continued to hover around me like I was the last cookie on the plate. "Right now everyone else is doing your job."

"Crime scene ain't going anywhere, is it?"

I had to admit it wasn't.

"And the paramedics are working on Lou?"

I nodded.

"The stiff's walking days are over, ain't they?"

Sure.

"Lou's woman doesn't seem like she's guilty, does she?"

Nope.

"You saw Golden Boy eager as a high school lad on prom night?"

I nodded again.

"Well, okay then. Detective's on her way. State boys are on the road, but it's a long road from Augusta. Crime Lab ain't here yet and I expect the ME to be fast on their heels. Now I'm probably going to be here all day and half the night while you're laying on your couch napping, so how about you let me have a moment of peace before all hell breaks loose?"

He pulled a cigarette from his breast pocket and stuck it in his mouth. He lit it and took a long drag. He looked utterly happy.

"That young feller you're partnered with have a little too much energy for you?"

George sighed heavily. "Now that's an opinion I won't refute." He scraped the pavement with his toe. "Oh, he ain't a bad sort, I guess. But he's all go, from sun to none."

"From the looks of him, he doesn't endorse the piss-poor diet you enjoy so much."

George grimaced. "Little feller loves his vegetables, that's the worst of it. I tell him, you're a cop, for Chrissakes! Eat a donut. Better, eat two."

"Does he listen?"

"No, he's like my kids. Every word I say, it's in one ear and out the other without touching anything on the way through. How it's supposed to work is they pair me with Wet-Behind-The-Ears, I say jump and he asks how high."

"Junior doesn't jump so high, I take it?"

"Little bastard asks how jumping's gonna benefit his law enforcement career. I tell him you jump, you're gonna miss my boot up your ass. That's your benefit right there." George finished his smoke, dropped the butt and ground it out. His hand hovered near his pocket.

"Go ahead," I said. "Just don't let Golden Boy see."

George rolled his eyes. "Marlene thinks he's the second coming. He tells her I been smoking, she'll cut me off in the bedroom entirely. And it won't take much snipping to get there." He fired up the cigarette. "I'm guessing your face is part of the story?"

"Another chapter."

He shook his head. "Looks like a tough read."

The young officer popped around the corner. George dropped his smoke and quickly covered it with his foot.

The youngster surveyed the three of us. My roughed-up face. George's chubby mug. He settled on Cash.

"You," he said. "Come inside. I have some questions." The cop didn't leave it open for debate. He turned and went into the club.

Cash shrugged. "Newest member of my fan club." He walked inside.

I looked at George. "Won't the boss be a little pissed when he finds out Golden Boy is talking to potential witnesses? Even if he is the anointed one?"

George looked toward the road and smiled. "Some lessons are learned the hard way. Officer Cameron Hedgepeth is about to discover that."

I followed his gaze to a fast-approaching green Chrysler Sebring. "Friend of yours?"

"Hardly. That's Mister Prima Donna in the flesh. The new Chief."

And his sidekick, Detective Venus Robinson.

CHAPTER 20

Chief Blue Porterfield pulled up beside us, opened the door, unfolded his six-foot-four frame and climbed from the car. Venus, who rode with him, glanced from George to me then slipped around the corner of The Limit to the crime scene.

Golden Boy dashed from The Limit and followed close behind. That left only George and me in the general vicinity of a full-blown local legend.

A few months earlier Porterfield had been all over the paper, the big deal about him getting hired as the city's top cop. And the hubbub wasn't only because he was the state's first African American Police Chief.

The excitement stemmed from the fact that Blue Porterfield once pitched for the Boston Red Sox. Four years as a reliever. He had decent stuff, and a southpaw who can get lefties out will always find a job in some team's bullpen.

But in late September about fifteen years ago he'd started getting hit. The Orioles took him deep twice in the eighth when the Sox had a one-run lead. He was trotted out two nights later in a tie game against the Royals, hung a belt-high curveball to a kid just up from the minors, and that had pretty much cinched the Sox's late-season playoff fade.

The team discovered Porterfield had been pitching with a frayed rotator cuff. A young pitcher, maybe he'd return after surgery. But Porterfield was already thirty-two years old and would never be more than a journeyman.

Journeymen pitchers with bad wings generally become insurance salesmen.

But not Blue Porterfield.

He retired without so much as a press conference and fell back on his Criminal Justice degree. He'd married a girl from Maine when he'd pitched in the minors, and she missed home, so after he left baseball he migrated to the Pine Tree State and worked his way up the law enforcement ladder. When the police chief position opened up Westfield was only too happy to hire a celebrity.

I found myself occasionally overcome with joy as well. I had to force myself not to hug him every time we met.

As Chief Porterfield approached us, he still walked with the easy gait of an athlete. Everything smooth and lubricated, like he moved in oil.

I moved like I was in peanut butter.

Chunky.

Porterfield stood an inch or two taller than me. I stretched my back a bit, tried to loosen my hamstrings, and believed we now stood eye-to-eye.

Although Chief Porterfield and I had met before, George went through the introduction parade to make sure the chief properly noticed him.

While we made small talk the paramedics loaded Lou into an ambulance. He had a mask over his face and an IV in his arm, which I thought was an exercise in futility.

Next was Yvette, on a gurney as well.

The incoming Crime Lab van swerved to miss Lou's departing ambulance. They quickly began unloading their gear.

As the commotion hit its zenith, Golden Boy charged from the crime scene and double-timed it over to us.

Porterfield asked Officer Hedgepeth about Yvette.

"Yvette Monfort. Caucasian. Forty-seven years old. Shock," Hedgepeth said. "A precaution."

Porterfield gave him a curt nod. "What else should I know?"

Hedgepeth stood stock still. I could almost feel his mind flipping flash cards, trying to hit on the right answer.

His right eyebrow cocked. "Sir?"

"Yes, Officer Hedgepeth?"

"The core area of the crime scene has been secured. Detective Robinson is now here and she has taken charge of the site until the State Police arrive."

Porterfield stifled a smile. "She rode with me."

Hedgepeth's ears turned red. "Yes, sir." He pivoted to leave.

"Officer Hedgepeth," Porterfield called.

"Sir?" Hedgepeth hopefully replied.

"One important task remains."

Hedgepeth beamed. "What is that, Chief?"

"I saw the bartender go inside a few minutes ago. Have her put the coffee on."

Hedgepeth stammered something before George caught his elbow and they left.

Porterfield studied me. "You involved in this mess?"

"I worked for Lou."

"I hope he paid in advance." As an icy gust of wind whipped across the parking lot, he pulled his camelhair overcoat tighter around him and shivered. "Damn, I should have married a Florida girl. Come on, let's take a look around back. Maybe the wind won't bite so much if we're moving."

A young officer was stationed along the perimeter of the crime scene tape, ostensibly to keep the riffraff away. Apparently I qualified as such, for he stopped me cold. He wavered regarding allowing the chief to enter, clutching the tape and lifting, then dropping, it twice.

"Sorry sir," he said to the boss. "Can't afford any extra traffic in here."

The chief nodded his acceptance. We walked a couple of steps away and found a spot out of the wind.

"You been here once already, haven't you?" Porterfield asked.

"I found them."

"You make a mess of the crime scene?"

I smiled warmly. "No more than usual."

"Shit," Porterfield grumbled. "That's what I was afraid of."

Venus and one of her young detectives was standing about five paces from Lou's Cadillac, scribbling notes. The County Sheriff, Alfred Cunniff, an ample man whose limber days were a distant memory, slowly ambled by.

"Chief," he said to Porterfield, and touched his fingers to the gray Resistol hat he sometimes wore when he wanted to look good for TV. "Always ready to assist."

Porterfield's smile was extra broad. "Do appreciate that, Sheriff."

Cunniff ambled over to a television crew that was setting up. He tipped his hat to the female reporter, then shook her hand.

"Cordial relationship you two have developed, from the looks of it," I said.

Porterfield shrugged. "First time we met, he told me his wife left him the night I lost a playoff game."

"Was he pissed off about it?"

"He continues to thank me daily."

Porterfield grunted as he watched Cunniff slip into in full gentleman mode with the cute young reporter, who wrestled to keep the wind from whipping her skirt up. "A little face time today can't hurt him come next election. And maybe he'll keep them occupied. I'm not ready to face the media just yet."

Porterfield and Venus made eye contact. He motioned her over.

She handed her notebook to the detective and wove her way to us. "We need to talk," she said.

Porterfield looked at me. "How about you see how the coffee is coming along? I'll join you in a minute."

I picked my way around the edge of the crime scene and headed toward the front door. Once inside, I walked by the small table where Officer Hedgepeth was intently talking to Cash. It looked like a fascinating conversation.

I swung a chair around to sit. "Hi, boys."

"No sir," Hedgepeth snapped. "Not here. Not now. And not you."

I leaned close and whispered, "Chief Porterfield is on my heels. My guess is he'll be pretty interested in why you're driving out of your lane."

Hedgepeth's head whipped toward the front door. To Porterfield's stern face. And cocked finger motioning to him.

Hedgepeth stood up, looking like a puppy who'd just peed on the floor.

I made my way to the bar. Cash mouthed 'call me' as he walked by.

Tori was changing a beer line. She looked when I sat down. "We have day-old popcorn and stale pretzels for brunch. You game?"

I turned to Porterfield, who was still in the office doorway, talking to Venus and a very chagrined-looking Officer Hedgepeth. I shook my head. "Just coffee, dear. Times two."

A couple minutes later she brought two mugs. Porterfield glanced over, said something to Venus, and joined me.

We each threw a ten on the bar to ensure Tori's eternal adoration.

Porterfield tapped the rim of the coffee cup with his fingers. "Crime Lab and the ME are here, so Detective Robinson has her hands full right now. This is just two guys talking, off the record, but what do you think about Lou taking one in the gut?"

"Painful way to go. I'll take one in the temple any time."

"What I meant was, any guess as to why someone would shoot him?" He waited for me to jump in.

I waited right back.

He took a sip of coffee, placed his cup down, and said, "This is how a conversation works. I say something. You think about it, and develop a response which you present to me. I reflect on your response, and offer a rejoinder. You ponder my witticism, and provide a snappy riposte. It bounces right along that way, a conversation. Good time to have one, don't you think?"

"Don't know why not. My expert opinion is Lou pissed someone off. Big time."

"Any guess who?"

I shrugged. "When it comes to detective skills, picture me in rookie ball. Not like you major leaguers."

"You're telling me you don't know anything?"

"I know most of the state capitals, if that'll help."

Porterfield stifled a cough. "You think you're even remotely funny?"

"Well, I crack myself up on a daily basis. But let's talk about you. Do you think I'm funny, Chief Porterfield?"

He gulped the last of his coffee. "I feel a headache coming on."

"Stress of the job. I'm not surprised."

He peered at me. "Let's go to the easy stuff. Want to tell me about your face?"

"I have my father's eyes and my mother's chin. The rest is uniquely me."

He looked like he was on the way to the dentist. He held his mug up for a refill. After Tori topped him off he said, "How about you knock off the comedy act? I'm going to ask you this and I'm willing to wait as long as it takes for an honest answer. Don't say anything until you're ready. Get all the facts straight in your mind, get them lined up just perfectly so you know what true and false is, and let it go. So…do you know the real story about what happened here?"

I shook my head. "Sad to say I don't."

Porterfield took a deep breath. "You're going to stick with that? You don't know anything else?"

I knew more. Of course I knew more. I knew Mikey wanted Lou's business. I knew he was perfectly capable of shooting Lou. And anyone else who got in his way. Plus he'd made it clear: cop involvement meant someone would get a bullet in the brain. I'd do everything I could to make sure it wasn't Annette.

Porterfield placed a hand on my arm. "How about you answer the question, Doyle."

"Chief, what I think about this case is far more compelling than what I know. Annette Begley is missing. Someone shot her uncle, who in turn took out the creep who hit him. What I still don't know is why. Where the girl is. Or if any of it is connected."

Porterfield pushed his coffee cup toward Tori and stood up. "That came across as eloquent, lucid, and utterly believable. Yet I don't think for one minute it's the entire truth."

CHAPTER 21

After my guy time with Chief Porterfield concluded, Venus and a State Police detective, a guy I'd never met named Dellacroce, were next. I gave the same answers the same way, except for the comedy bit. Venus had already heard all my A-material.

When they finished taking my statement I met Cash at Pearl's, a sub shop on Revere Drive. He'd eaten half a tuna sandwich loaded with onions when I arrived. I ordered a ham and cheese.

"So, did you sing like a jailbird once Venus started grilling you?" he asked after he swallowed a massive bite.

"I remained ice to her fire," I said. "But you knew I would."

Cash shook his head. "Fire melts ice."

"C'mon, man. Don't spoil my vivid imagery."

He said, "It has to be Mikey who hit Lou. Add everything together and it equals him in a nice, pretty package. What did the Venus think about your theory?"

I took a long sip of my lemonade. Another.

"You son of a…you didn't tell her, did you?"

I said, "I like to maintain an air of mystery."

Cash rolled his eyes. "Lou didn't tell anyone about his problems with Mikey. You see what that got him. Now you go mute with the city cops."

"I'm not that shallow. I didn't say anything to the State cop, either."

Cash whistled. "The Paul Doyle action figure. Comes complete with over-sized ego. So you're going it alone, huh?"

"You don't even know me. I'm never alone when I'm working with you."

He looked pleased. "But why didn't you tell her something? Enough to whet her appetite?"

I rolled my neck to work the kinks out. "To be honest, I'm not ready to learn if Mikey meant it when he said no cops." I rubbed my aching forehead and felt like bouncing it off the table. "Mikey told me he wanted me to stay alive to see the fruits of my labor. You think he meant this?"

"It crossed my mind that he was talking about Annette, not this. This could be random, after all. You think?"

"Sure," I said. "Another option is that with Lou gone, Annette moves up another notch on Mikey's hit parade."

Cash lifted his sub to take a bite, then jabbed it at me. "You know what I don't get? You start shooting people, and…"

I butted in. "And you don't leave a witness who can ID the shooter. But they left Yvette. What does that tell you?"

Cash held up a finger while he swallowed. "It looks like it was meant to send a message. Maybe to you, maybe to someone else. I was thinking that's what the knife was for. Motivation. Of course, motivation doesn't mean much to a corpse."

"But it would to a survivor."

Cash talked around a mouthful of tuna. "Let's run with the Mikey theory for a moment. If I had to pin this on someone's back, I'd pin it on his. Today."

"With Lou dying, I wouldn't mind giving Mikey another thump on the head and see where that leads. Miserable prick that he is."

Cash studied my face. "I hear you, but with your face all rearranged I don't think we should poke the Mikey piñata again. Not for a while, anyway. That piñata pokes back."

"That's what I'm afraid of. And if the cops come in I can see this going south in a hurry."

"Even further south than the mess we just saw? The cops are in now, whether we want them or not, and they're not going to leave a stone unturned. You may not have noticed, but they're not the most subtle bunch of cowpokes when it comes to solving crimes."

I said, "And it's not going to get better soon. Venus wants to sink her teeth into this and take a bite out of crime, and now the State cops have final say they'll be telling everyone it's fine to look, but mind the blood spatters, please. So while they're playing so nicely together, let's shake the Mikey tree for a couple of days while no one is playing with us."

"Good plan. But if Mikey finds out, maybe he'll split my head open next time." He thought about it. "Naah. He wouldn't split *my* head open. Not like he did your melon."

"Of course not. You're Cash the Magnificent. So, did you recognize the dead guy?"

Cash shook his head. "No idea who the stiff is. Of course, I don't maintain the type of police connections you do. Couple of beers and your sweet words, you could probably find out real quick."

"You think Chief Porterfield will come across that easily?"

"Oh, he might. But there's a pretty lady who definitely will."

"You wouldn't be talking about Venus Robinson, perhaps?"

"One and the same. You should talk to her, Paul."

I refused to mute my smugness. "She's meeting me for a beer after work."

He beamed. "You never cease to amaze me. How did you pull that off?"

"I was trying to think what you'd do in this situation. Then I did the opposite."

I'd staked out a small table by the bar and was eagerly watching the door when Venus came in. She wore faded blue jeans and a gray New England Patriots hoodie. She wore her hair in a ponytail that stuck out the back of a faded Red Sox cap. I couldn't help but admire her for a moment or two, for she remained stunningly gorgeous in a girl-next-door kind of way. Some things never changed.

She went straight to the bar and grabbed us each a beer.

When she sat down I asked, "Is Lou still alive?"

Venus shook her head. "He passed away when I was at the hospital this afternoon."

I felt unsettled. On one hand he was a rude, crude, pompous little man, and I wanted to slap common sense into him every time I saw him. But he kept the club running. He kept dozens of girls working. Although there were enough bad things to say about him to write a book, I hoped someone would remember some good things for his eulogy.

I asked, "You guys have anything so far?"

She eyed me for a moment. Probably admiring my profile. She said, "It's only preliminary, but we believe Lou killed the unidentified victim, and someone else shot Lou. Crime Lab tells me there were multiple people in and out of the crime scene, probably during and immediately after the shooting. You wouldn't know anything about that, would you?"

I shook my head. "Not a thing."

Venus was the first one to know about me getting married, and the first one to hear about Eileen and me splitting up. She'd been there for me when Pops died, and also when I was shot and spent nearly a week in the hospital.

Without a doubt, she is my oldest and closest friend. A friend who I'd chosen to tell next to nothing about the case we were now both involved in.

I had to tell her something.

Without telling her too much. Because I couldn't bear to see Annette Begley end up the way Lou had.

For then I'd be attending a funeral doubleheader.

I polished off my beer for an extra dose of courage. I glanced at Venus. Here goes.

She was into the hockey game on the TV by the bar. I thought a moment and decided it was pretty rude to interrupt her. After all, the Bruins only play about eighty games a year. I hated to have her miss a few crucial seconds of game number seven.

I redirected my attention to a pair of hotties in a nearby booth who were wearing painted-on jeans and scanty, cleavage-celebrating Patriots tank tops.

"Hey," Venus said, slapping my arm. "If I wanted a man to ignore me, I'd be home with my husband."

I cocked an eyebrow toward the TV. "Score?"

"Not so much since the kids came along, but if you care about the game the Bruins are up, 2-1. Third period's just about to start."

"Thanks for the update on your love life. Now, unless you're a big Zamboni fan, can we focus on the vic?"

She took a long pull on her beer. "Okay, Mister Serious. We can talk about work if you want. I'm going to dream about Bobby Orr."

"I'll keep that in mind if your attention wanes. You know the dead guy's name?"

"Chrome Livingston."

"Chrome, like the bumper of my car?"

She chuckled. "Hardly. The bumper of your car is pure rust. But no kidding, his given name is Chrome Elvis Livingston."

"Well, one thing about a name like Chrome. It makes Elvis sound a lot better."

She threw her arms up and pumped them. "Yes!"

"You liked my joke that much?"

"No, silly. The Bruins just came back on the ice."

"I forgot. Your mind is on the important stuff."

Venus smirked. "Screw you."

"Not now. I'm busy working, lady."

She reached over and patted my hand.

I didn't dare look at her eyes.

When I could breathe normally again I asked, "So what's the story on Chrome Elvis Livingston?"

"Two prison tours in Texas, both for assault." Venus raised her glass. "Here's to consistency."

"I guess when something works you stick with it, Detective Pottle."

"Hey. It's still Robinson. It'll always be Robinson."

"Funny you should mention that. I've known you since you were actually young, but I never asked before. You settled for marrying that trumpet-playing Toot Sweet instead of a real…"

"Come on, Paul." She sounded embarrassed. "*Toot Sweet?*"

"That's nothing. We used to call him Blow Boy back in the day."

"Oh, jeez." She picked at the cuff of her hoodie sleeve.

"Anyway, you married Larry *Pottle.*"

"That's better."

"But you kept the name Robinson. Why is that, if I may be so bold?"

Venus continued to pull on her sleeve. "Girl has to keep her own identity. I started life as a Robinson. I wanted to stay a Robinson."

"Says Pottle on the marriage license though?"

"It does." She traced a beer ring on the table with her index finger. "Of course it does. I'm married to Larry Pottle. Till the cows come home. Till death do us part. Forever and ever. Amen."

"And how does Larry feel about you and your identity crisis?"

She clucked her tongue. "It's been the topic of more than a few family discussions, believe you me."

"But you didn't bend on the matter."

"I'm like an oak tree," she said. "Not a willow."

"So let me see if I have this straight. You and Larry are at a bar. He sees a friend from work and waves him over. Larry says 'I'd like you to meet my wife.' What does he call you?"

Venus flinched. "Well, that's different. He calls me his prized possession. Giver of the Kitchen Pass. The old Ball and Chain. My Personal Baby Factory." Her voice became strident. Tense. "But the asshole never calls me the Goddess of Love anymore. I just want to know why he stopped calling me the goddamn Goddess of Love."

And for some reason she started to cry.

I know nothing about women. If there is a less-than-nothing category, that's where you'd find me. But I couldn't just sit and watch.

I stood up and walked to her. She slipped her arms around my waist and put her head against me and let loose with a good old-fashioned deluge.

When the floodwaters began to recede she leaned away and looked up at me.

"Now you're going to be really sad," I said. "The game's tied."

She tried not to laugh. Or cry. It was hard to tell.

I sat down. She slowly shook her head and the bar lights glistened like a rainbow on her ponytail. It looked as beautifully silky as I remembered it from way back when.

Me and Venus. Who'd never even gotten a proper start to our high school romance.

Tears stained the front of her hoodie. She looked down. "I should have worn black."

"You know what would have been way cool? If you'd worn heavy makeup, too."

Her shoulders quivered with stifled laughter. "Yeah, that would have been cool all right. I'd look like the Bride of Frankenstein."

"No chance. She had way better hair."

Venus seemed calmer now, as if she'd gotten over one hurdle. I debated telling her a few tidbits about Annette and Shari but given her current emotional crisis, I said, "Can I ask what brought that on?"

She shook her head. "Seventeen things. Maybe eighteen. You don't want to know."

"Prioritize them. Try me."

"It's work. I don't want the Bruins to lose. It's me and Larry. And so much more."

"You and Larry?"

She slapped the table. "No fair. You jumped to number three."

We talked for a long time about being one of four women on the Westfield Police force. The other three were administrative assistants. Though there were few steps remaining for her to climb, there were times when she felt the entire staff was waiting for that one moment when she would step on the banana peel of failure. And some days, she was pretty sure it would happen.

After dissecting the Bruins' chances for a Stanley Cup, I brought up her home life.

Venus let out a painful sigh. "It used to be fun. Like funhouse fun, you know? Now we have a house and a mortgage and kids and a dog and two cars and when I get home it's a machine gun attack of Mom this, honey that, Mom this, baby that. Ma, Mommy, Mama, Mom, Mom, MOM!" She slapped the table again, causing an empty beer bottle to topple.

She caught it before it clattered to the table and set it straight. "There are times I wish it would stop. Just. Stop. Because right now there's not a lot of Venus left over."

"What does Larry say?"

She scowled. "Larry doesn't say shit. Used to be, he waited on me hand and foot. He'd bring me breakfast in bed. We made love before work. He bought me flowers. He opened the car door for me. He put the toilet seat down. Stuff a girl likes. Now he just about lives in the basement and plays computer games. He probably doesn't know I'm gone. Probably doesn't care. Look at me, Paul. Look at every bit of me."

I gazed at one of the most desirable woman I'd ever known.

Her voice trembled. "I wear sexy undies, I do my hair, I smell nice, and I have a great body." She wiped her hands on her hoodie and locked eyes with me. "I still have a great body, don't I? Tell me the truth."

"Is there a higher category?"

She gave me a sad smile. "Larry hasn't touched me in six months. He acts like I'm not worth having any more. And it's silly, because I don't need a man to make me feel beautiful. But if he'd touch me, if he'd hold me like he used to, even for an hour, maybe I'd feel more like a woman. Right now, I'm just…blah."

"Drinking a beer with me doesn't help much, does it?"

She looked around, where numerous bottles cluttered the table. "*A* beer?"

"They're relatively harmless now. They're empty."

She patted my hand. "Paul, it's exactly what I need. Here, I'm not Honey. I'm not Mom. I'm not Head Pooper Scooper or Chief Cook or Errand Girl. I'm not Detective anything. I'm a girl watching a hockey game with her old friend."

We were done talking about Chrome Elvis Livingston. We were done talking about anything at all. Including Annette and Shari.

We walked to the couch in the corner. She curled up in a ball next to me.

We stayed like that and watched the Bruins cough it up in overtime.

CHAPTER 22

Just past noon the next day Venus swung by my office, dug a Coke out of the fridge and sat on the couch. "How you doing?"

"I'm sorry about how it ended last night."

"The Bruins game?"

"That too."

She chuckled. "We didn't exactly finish our talk about Chrome Elvis Livingston."

"No, you got sloppy drunk and passed out and…"

Venus snickered. I stopped while she still found me mildly amusing. Now wasn't the time to tell her what I knew about Annette. I figured I'd know it when I saw it.

She said, "I have two more things if you care to listen."

"All ears, dear."

"They found Annette's phone number in Livingston's cell. Texts back and forth. He knew her."

Trouble had told me dancers contacted customers from time to time. Annette and Livingston. Small world. "What else?"

"He had a great chest. On that chest he wore a tat. The prettiest tat that you ever did see."

"That tat being?"

Venus said, "A burning skull with the letters ECS under it. The picture you gave me."

"So he and Annette?"

"Apparently so."

"Apparently intimately." Lou had said Annette was seeing one of Mikey's boys. Chrome Livingston. Recently deceased.

Venus snapped her fingers. "You fall asleep on me there?"

"Trying to think like you. Which is impossible, given that I'm a man. Does the burning skull mean anything?"

"It means the wearer can look death in the eye. One thing for sure, Chrome Livingston knows what death looks like now."

"You could ask him about the experience, however given the circumstances…"

"He's pretty close-lipped on the subject. Anyway, search gang tattoos and you'll look all day. With his priors I added Texas, and came up with one hit. Enrique Cruz Siempre."

"Is 'siempre' this guy's last name?"

Venus had a mouthful of Coke. She nearly choked, had some drip out her nose, and spent the next few minutes coughing, laughing and wiping up the mess. After she wound down, she said, "Didn't you take high school Spanish with me?"

"Over twenty years ago. I can still count to ten, order a beer, and cuss you out big time, *bruja*. Siempre doesn't ring a bell."

"It means always. Enrique Cruz Always." She leaned back and smiled. She looked pretty smug for a person who had just performed the involuntary soda-out-the-nose trick.

"So genius girl, what else did you discover?"

"Cruz runs his operation out of San Antonio. Drugs and human trafficking from Mexico, guns back in. All the stuff that makes America's free enterprise system so great. For muscle, he employs high-quality recruits from the Texas prison system. In this case, it appears once upon a time Chrome Livingston worked for him."

"And Annette had a picture of this loser with his shirt off? I mean, him scoring a twenty-year-old, that's hot. For her, not so much."

Venus tossed her head and said, "Girl grows up without her father. Maybe she's looking for a daddy figure."

"Bet she never knew who she fell for. Convict. From Texas with love."

"Now headed back to the Lone Star State in a box."

I tapped the desk. "Any idea who paid the shipping cost?"

"Oh my gosh," Venus said, leaning forward and slapping my arm. "When you ask questions like that, you almost sound like a real detective."

"I've been watching you."

She crossed her arms across her chest. "I know, and it's pretty creepy sometimes. Anyway, the ME hasn't released the remains yet. So no dice, smart guy. But good try."

Cash walked in with two cups of coffee and a greasy paper bag. He patted Venus on the head, snooped around the refrigerator and came up empty. He gave me a coffee, sat down on the couch next to her and said, "So, you tell her about Annette?"

"Tell me what about Annette?" Venus asked, the temperature in the room dropping to downright chilly.

I was right. I would know the time when I saw it.

I took a couple of deep breaths and wished I was drunk. "We should have had this talk earlier." I told her about my visit to the church dormitory and how Shari and Annette had run off. I mentioned my suspicion that someone had taken them.

Venus raised her eyebrows. "Why would Shari go too?"

"Maybe to protect Annette. If there's one thing I don't understand, it's the mind of a woman."

"Don't underestimate yourself, amigo," Cash said. "There are lots of things you don't understand. Women are just one of them."

Venus said, "You knew about the girls being kidnapped for days now, and you kept it to yourself? I'd like to hear why."

A crime is a lot like a jigsaw puzzle. When you dump the box out all you have are a jumble of pieces and no idea how they interconnect. It takes a lot of trial-and-error to figure out what goes with what. If I started identifying pieces to Venus I was afraid the cops would begin to understand the pattern in front of them. And those pieces might lead to someone else dying. Like Annette Begley.

Unfortunately that logic, if I tried to explain to Venus, would go over like a fart in church. I said, "I was working for Lou. He paid me to keep his problems on the down low. So I kept things on the down low. But now that he's dead…over to you, I guess."

Her eyes sparked. "Like that? Over to you."

I meekly nodded.

She fumed. "Tell me the truth. Do the girls have anything to do with why Lou was shot?"

Cash piped up. "Honest officer, we don't know anything."

Venus whipped her head around to him. "Knock it off, you clown. Or I swear…"

I said, "Venus, do you trust me?"

She turned toward me and ground her teeth. Deep lines slashed her forehead. She closed her eyes for maybe ten seconds. When she opened them, she didn't look convinced. "Sometimes, okay? Sometimes I trust you. And sometimes it turns out I'm sorry when I do."

"I'm begging you to trust me on this. Don't flip out. Don't shoot me. Don't threaten to have my license pulled. You may not play the hand this way, but right now I don't think I have a choice. It's this way or no way at all."

She walked straight to my desk and put her face maybe a foot from mine. "This way what? By lying to the cops? By withholding evidence?"

"No. This way because I'm trying to keep two girls alive. That's what this is about and nothing else."

Venus straightened. "You screw this up and it's out of my hands. Being friends won't help you one bit."

"Got it." I stood and started for the door. Cash stood as well.

"No!" Venus barked. "You do not dismiss me! You do not walk away until we talk this through. The police are in charge here. Not you."

I took my scolding like a man. "You're right. This is what I'm thinking. The girls disappeared in town, so that is pretty much your ballgame now. You work around the clock. You talk to family. You and your fine team of detectives support State Police Detective Dellacroce on the homicide. You try to figure out how the girls tie in with Lou. You talk to the press and you tell them you're all over this. And while people are watching you dance in the limelight, Cash and I will stay in the shadows and do our shadowy thing."

Venus knew I was right. I knew admitting it was the most difficult thing facing her.

I'd also begun to learn patience is my friend.

After a few seconds, she spoke very precisely. "Don't screw it up or it'll be the last mistake you ever make."

Cash patted Venus on the head. "I guess it's all for one, and…"

She smacked his hand away. "Don't even start with me."

She walked to the door but didn't open it. After a lengthy pause she turned to me. "It appears I have another problem. When Dellacroce and I went to interview Yvette this morning, all we heard were crickets. Not a peep from her, other than to say she'll only speak to you. It's bullshit, but I'll give her some sway after what happened. So will you go with me and talk to her?"

"She a suspect, detective?" Cash asked.

Venus's lips puckered like she'd bitten into a lemon. "No, she isn't a suspect, Mister Cashman. No weapon, no blood, no motive that I can tell. But I need to know what she saw."

I said, "What about Dellacroce? He going to let me talk to her?"

She bobbed her head from side to side. "I'd prefer he doesn't know. The State detectives are stretched thin as hell right now, so he wasn't planning to come back today. Won't matter if she refuses to talk. But if you can play icebreaker with Yvette, maybe she'll be a lot more receptive when he returns."

"Time and place, detective."

"Tomorrow morning. My office. Eight sharp." Venus slammed the door on the way out.

Cash said, "Seemed like you were getting along pretty good until I showed up."

"Yeah. It seemed like that to me, too."

"Well, it sure changed in a hurry. So, what were you kids talking about?"

"You ever hear of a guy named Chrome Elvis Livingston? Forty-one years old, from Lufkin, Texas?"

He laughed until he saw I hadn't joined him. "You're not kidding?"

I shook my head. "And you thought being named Winfield Romero Cashman sucks."

Cash sniffed. "I come from a long and distinguished line of Winfield Romero Cashmans."

"And probably they all thought their name sucked."

He cocked an eyebrow. "But not as bad as Chrome Elvis Livingston."

"You see my point."

"To be honest, I'm surprised you had one."

I would have shot him the finger, but he'd brought us carnitas burritos from Luisa's. I quickly forgave him.

Cash said, "What about this guy named Chrome?"

"He's the guy who was killed at Lou's. He has a record, but not local."

"Where?"

"San Antonio. Assault, times two."

"How far back?"

"Sixteen years ago, when our boy Chrome was just hitting his prime. Two years for that one. He didn't learn so good, so three years later he took a trip down memory lane. He served forty-six months for that. Lot of little stuff on the perimeter, but no other jail time."

"You think he wore out his welcome in the Lone Star State and decided to saddle up and ride into our quaint little town?"

I said, "Why not? You did."

Whenever Cash had nothing to say he ate or drank. He did both.

I waited for an inevitable dose of Winfield Cashman wisdom. When he finished his burrito and coffee he looked at me. "What?"

"I'm waiting for you to decipher our serpentine enigma."

"I got your serpentine enigma right here. I was waiting for you, gumshoe." He walked over to my coffee pot, measured the grounds, and made a pot. "You think Texas is important?"

"I guess a guy might move from Texas to the great state of Maine and settle down. Enjoy the pine trees and the black flies and learn to say 'ayuh' a lot. But our guy was packing. You know guys who pack are hard cases."

"Like you and me," Cash said.

"Damn right." I wiped carnitas from my shirt and pointed to Cash's cheek. "You got a little bit of something right there."

He dabbed at it. "Is the Chrome Livingston angle worth chasing?"

"He dated Annette. He worked for someone who had Lou killed. I'm guessing that someone is Mikey Cross. Short of challenging Mikey again, I'd say a little background check on Chrome Livingston can only help us crack this nut."

Cash said, "I know a friend of a friend. I'll see what I can find."

"Good. And in the meantime we still need eyeballs on Mikey and his guys. If Annette and Shari are with them, maybe they'll show up. When they do, I want them, even if Mikey votes no. Let's go find them." I stood.

"Do you mind if we talk things out in greater detail, just in case we get to put your plan in motion?"

"Men don't talk. We act."

Cash sighed. "But before we act, maybe we should understand the lay of the land a little more."

He's usually right. But I'm careful what I say about it, or it goes straight to his head. I said, "You know, we probably should talk things through a bit before we jump straight down Mikey's throat."

"Good idea."

"Thanks. Glad I thought of it. So Lou was in to Mikey for serious money. Livingston told Annette she was in danger. Mikey threatened to kill her unless Lou gave him the club. So Annette grabbed Shari and ran off to a church dormitory. Where we believe Mikey's boys intercepted them for safe keeping."

"This is like a rerun. I knew everything you were going to say."

I winked. "Mikey kept pushing Lou for the money, but Lou said he suddenly changed his tune. He wanted the club instead. Forget the fifty grand, give him the club and they're good. What's it worth?"

"Four hundred?"

"More," I said. "But let's say four hundred thousand. Who knows what Lou still owed on it? But he wouldn't give it up."

"Maybe Mikey planned on buying it instead. Not to square the debt, but because he wanted to own it. Lou said he'd started to turn the corner and it was making a little money. After all, as Mikey says 'I'm a legitimate bidness man.'"

"Is that the way he said it? Bidness man?"

"That's the way I hear it," Cash said.

"So, if Mikey wanted the bidness—I'm sorry, business—why shoot Lou? Beat him up instead. Wave a knife and threaten to cut off his manhood unless he sells. Except someone pulled a gun and started shooting. But Yvette is still alive and kicking, which makes even less sense than shooting Lou. And here we are. In the middle of a bowl of goulash."

Cash wrinkled his nose. "Goulash?"

"Fine. Kitchen sink soup. Throw everything in and it's a mess."

"Good description of what we have right now. One goulash of a mess."

CHAPTER 23

9:30.

I shifted on the couch and tried to ignore the clock on the mantel. Ecstasy would be on stage tonight. And here I sat, watching Humphrey Bogart on the tube in black and white glory, going crazy trying to figure out how to get his gold from the Sierra Madres.

Ma snored in the armchair to my left. She dragged each wheezing breath out for seconds. How she slept through it, I had no idea. How the pictures stayed on the wall with her room-shaking gasps remained a mystery unto itself.

9:32.

I imagined Ecstasy snuggled up with the handsome young man who had cost me hours of sleep in recent nights.

He had a pocketful of cash and he'd sweet talk her and they'd slip into a crushed velvet booth and he'd sit with a lust-filled look on his face and she'd look at him with a face equally filled with lust and she'd take her clothes off and she'd kiss him and tell him welcome home and come talk to me for three nights in a row and he would and...she'd be gone from my life.

Forever.

9:35.

I focused on Bogie. Why would a man become so consumed with something, so all-fired consumed, that it became the only thing he thought about? Gold, gold, gold. It could drive a man totally insane. Like it drove Bogie insane, right in front of me.

Her smile.

Her touch.

Her eyes.

Ecstasy.

Absolute foolishness, Ma would say. Good men don't fall for bad women. And a stripper, a woman who peels off her clothes for a dollar bill, what other kind of woman could she be?

Bad.

By Ma's narrow definition.

I glared at her. At her loud, snoring self.

Her glasses had slid down her nose. They balanced on the very end, daring her to give one more snort so they could plunge off her face, down her robe, bounce off her knees, and break when they hit the floor.

I dared them to do it as well.

Ma would say Ecstasy was a sinful woman. Ma would say she wasn't good enough for me. Ma would say I could do better.

Ma said an awful lot for someone snoring so loudly.

Ma hadn't approved of Eileen either. Not one tiny bit. Eileen wasn't good enough. She wasn't smart enough. Her clothes were too trashy. Her boobs were too big. She bleached her hair.

While we were together, I don't ever remember wishing Eileen was this or Eileen was that.

And I'm sure Ma had an opinion about that, as well.

However the one thing I'd thought about most since Eileen and I had split, the one thing I'd dwelled on during all the sad, lonely nights, the one thing that had become diamond-cut, crystal-clear in my mind, was that I didn't care one bit what Ma thought anymore.

And that's why I dragged myself out of the chair.

10:02.

The Limit welcomed me like an old friend who'd decided to let bygones be bygones. I stood at the bar and received a beer, a smile, and a half-hug over the counter from Tori.

The story of Lou's death had made the rounds, and I saw many new faces eager to learn about the pleasures The Limit offered. At least thirty men filled the room, along with two beefy, middle-aged women who eyed a sleek black woman on stage two.

I chose the only available table and watched the show.

Soon a kind, gentle hand rested on my shoulder. I turned and looked into Ecstasy's eyes. A gold clip at the base of her neck held her hair back, and she wore heavy, triangular gold earrings that shimmered as she moved in the flashing light. Her black and gold body suit, with strategically-placed cutouts across the front, highlighted her taut, rippling midsection.

I thought about my midsection. Few would consider it taut. Although it always moved. Rippling in a different way, I guess. I appreciated hers far more.

"May I?" she asked.

Over my jackhammering heart I answered, "Yes."

She chose the chair to my left, leaving my right side free for gun work, swordplay or the occasional arm wrestling challenge. Smart girl.

Out of the corner of my eye I could see her studying me. I felt like a bug under a microscope. Or at least as I thought a bug under a microscope might feel.

Just when I started to feel uncomfortable about the scrutiny, she nudged me with her shoulder and asked, "What makes you you?"

"Discarded odds and ends, the sum of which is far less than the value of the individual parts."

Ecstasy's tongue danced across her lips. "Very funny, but not really. Remember Norm from *Cheers*? How everyone yelled his name when he walked in the bar? That's what it's like with you. The people here are happy to see you."

"Fat guy who drinks a lot of beer. I've achieved...notoriety." I drained my bottle.

Ecstasy's eyes sparked and her words were tinged with annoyance. "You can stop with the big, fat comments any old time."

"But..."

"But nothing." Ecstasy touched my hand. "You don't know this yet but it's okay to be you, just the way you are. People genuinely like you. I find that...appealing."

"It's not that they like me, they just consider themselves a whole lot smarter after they compare themselves to me."

"No," she said, and playfully punched me. "I don't meet a lot of nice guys in my line of work. You're one. Debate over. I win."

Ecstasy held up her finger and shook her head when I tried to speak. She turned her soft eyes on mine, and the playfulness disappeared. "Last time you were here you left without saying goodbye."

"Yeah, I had some really important stuff to do."

"Really important? Like what?"

"Like...you know...laundry, or something."

"Laundry," she said, pursing her lips. "You left this awesome female right here...to do laundry. Or something." Her eyes pried deeper. Intense. Full bore.

I'm the intense one. I bring the heat. I make them turn away first.

Me.

Ecstasy continued to lock eyes with mine.

My stomach churned, and my left eye developed a tic.

I looked away, defeated. Weakly I said, "It doesn't do itself."

Ecstasy smiled knowingly. "I guess it doesn't."

Just when I thought I'd wriggled off the hook, she reverted to serious girl. "But you left me."

I shrugged. "I left here."

She touched my hand. "No Paul, you left *me*." Her voice tightened. "You don't understand. You come in and listen to me ramble like it's the most important thing you'll do all day. Some people say 'how you doing?', but they're more interested in watching my shirt come off. But you actually care about how I'm doing."

"I...well, yeah," I verbally stumbled around, trying to say something that'd make me sound like I had a basic grasp of my native language. "It's important to me. That's...that's...that's why."

Her eyes opened wider and she leaned forward. "I know! I know. That's the way it feels sometimes and it feels…so…good. You make me laugh my butt off with the dumbest jokes in the world, and when you touch my face it feels like…you really do care about me. I begin to forget *everything* I think about men. Then you pull a disappearing stunt like this, and I don't know what to believe anymore." She closed her eyes. "You hurt me."

The other guy was young and handsome and I failed both those tests with flying colors. She preferred him over me so I left with my wounded pride intact and that…hurt her? How could I explain? How could I put into words how I woke up to the beauty of her face and how I fell asleep every night thinking about her?

Should I fess up that my first girlfriend became my wife and, to date, she was the sum total of my intimate female experience?

I said, "So you're prepared, I may do a load of whites later if things get totally nutty."

Ecstasy shook her head and chuckled. "Let me know if it all comes out in the wash."

She inched her chair closer to mine.

We sat sardine close, watching an unfamiliar dancer on stage. The girl, a skinny bleached-blonde without discernible curves, eagerly pulled herself hand-over-hand to the top of the pole, hooked her leg tightly around it, and flipped so her head pointed toward the floor.

A little at a time she slipped down the pole, till her head hung about four feet from the stage. With one final shake of her leg, she plunged.

Her head whacked against the stage. She did an involuntary somersault, ending up face down, her skinny butt sticking up in the air.

I stood to help her, but Ecstasy clutched my arm. "She'll survive."

She did. A few seconds later the girl shook her head, rose to her hands and knees, and crawled to the edge of the stage where two graying, heavily-bearded, flannel-wearing men helped her down. She wobbled her way to their table and joined them.

Ecstasy shook her head. "The newest incarnation of the oldest trick in the book."

I wondered how many brain cells the girl had lost. "Huh?"

"Her name's Savannah. Every time money's a little slow, she takes the Nestea plunge head-first into the stage. She figures it's worth an extra two hundred a night."

"What a girl won't do for a buck." I watched Savannah, now in full flirt mode with the lumberjack boys. Oh, the restorative powers of the lure of cold, hard cash.

"That isn't all she'll do. Last week she got caught going down on a guy in her car at the grocery store. But at least she had the decency to move her baby out of the way first."

"Well, you don't want to expose the young ones to the evils of oral sex too early."

Ecstasy snickered. "Boy, you said a mouthful."

I glanced around the club. Checking for faces. Like the face of the handsome young man who had sent me running home. To do laundry.

She touched my arm. "Are you looking for another girl?"

I tried to turn the seductiveness in my eyes up a notch. "Never."

Dimples danced on her cheeks and she wiggled a bit in the seat. "You looking for a guy, maybe?"

In a manner of speaking, yes. So I could rip his arm off and beat him with it. I kept my eyes locked on hers. "Only you."

She bit her lip and drew in a huge breath. When she blew it out she patted my hand. "You better mean it, Paul. I don't specialize in disappearing acts."

I placed my hand on hers and she curled her fingers in mine.

We sat like that for two songs. Absolutely silent.

Then...Ecstasy leaned her head against my shoulder.

She didn't say a word.

She didn't need to.

Girls danced and men watched and music played and lights flashed.

The DJ called Ecstasy up on stage. She looked at him and solemnly shook her head.

He gave her the thumbs-up and called for Angel instead.

Silence always works best for me. In spite of that I said, "You're not going to dance?"

She shook her head against my shoulder. "I need this more."

"I'll pay you for your company."

Ecstasy shook her head again. Harder this time. "Paul, shhh. Please."

So we sat together while my brain tried to wrap itself around what was going on. The girl who I couldn't get out of my dreams had her head on my shoulder.

On one hand, victory dance.

But on the other hand, with the club crowded and the number of men who drooled over her, she'd wasted a lot of lap dances.

Five. I'd cost her five lap dances. A cool hundred.

Ecstasy squeezed my arm. "Excuse me for a moment? Ladies room."

"Sure."

I pulled out some twenties and placed them on the table. Yes.

She walked toward me a couple of minutes later, her eyes joyful and her hips swaying in time to the music. She gave me a huge smile and a wink.

Until she saw the money. Her face froze.

She sat but slid her chair away. No head on my shoulder. No hand in my hand.

"You okay?" I asked.

"Just ducky." Ecstasy glared at the money.

I stammered, "I figured I cost you a bundle, so…"

She held her hand out, stopping me. "Would I sit here with *my* head on *your* shoulder if I was worried about money?"

I didn't know what to do next.

Ecstasy did. "No, I most certainly wouldn't." Her words crackled.

"I thought…"

"Oh, you call *this* thinking? You give the stripper some money, and she'll say 'That Paul Doyle is one hell of a guy.' Was that your objective for tonight? To pull me out of the gutter? Feel better about yourself when you did? Because if you need to feel better about yourself, figure out how to do that without me in the picture."

Ecstasy snatched her purse off the table, stood, and started to stomp off. When she turned toward me, her eyes seemed wet.

With slow, measured words she said, "Don't be that guy, Paul. Don't ever be that guy."

CHAPTER 24

Early the next morning, Venus and I drove toward Yvette's doublewide on a half-acre lot ten miles from Westfield. Venus was pissy the entire way, offering little more than disinterested grunts to my earnest attempts to get myself out of hot water.

It was a fun jaunt.

When we pulled in beside Yvette's brown Toyota Tercel, I looked at the gold '62 Chevy Bel Air sitting in the driveway, engine hanging from a cedar log tripod spanning the car's front end. Lou's project car. Over a beer one night he told me he'd owned a car like it thirty years ago. He'd found this one in an old lady's barn buried under some hay bales. He planned to have a guy do the bodywork and get the engine running right. Then he'd give the Caddy to Yvette. The Bel Air was going to be his.

We walked up the steps. I rang the doorbell, unsure how it would all play out.

When Yvette opened the door her black and white cat slipped by her leg. The road was close. And cats don't do well with roads. At least the cars on roads. I reached down to grab him.

"Oh, don't worry about Bowser," Yvette said. "He's older'n hell and don't never leave the porch anymore."

Bowser looked at me with 'told you so' disdain. He bounced onto a plastic chair on the porch, curled up, then looked at me. Still disdainfully.

Yvette turned to Venus. Her face tightened. "Yeah?" she said around the cigarette that hung in the corner of her mouth.

"Can we talk for a few?" I asked.

She glared at Venus, shook her head and motioned me closer.

I leaned in.

Yvette whispered, "I ain't got nothin' to say to her. She thinks her shit don't stink."

"You know how women can be."

"Yup, that I do."

Venus looked exasperated beyond words. And not just with me this time.

I put my arm around Yvette's shoulders and pulled her closer. "This can't sit any longer. Even if you don't talk to her, the State cops are going to come back. They might not be so understanding."

Yvette leaned back and looked at the Bel Air. "That car is like me and Lou. Nothin' got finished. We didn't get the club runnin' right. Didn't get out of debt. Didn't get married. Didn't raise no kids."

She looked me in the eye. "He wanted to marry me, did you know?"

I didn't.

Yvette took a long drag on her cigarette, dropped it and crushed it out on the damp porch. "Uh-huh. Oh, you didn't know Lou like I knew Lou. He was all tough with other folks around, yellin' and bossin' them like he was the King's right hand. But here, when it was just him and me, he was the nicest, sweetest..."

She looked surprised when a tiny sob escaped.

She quickly steeled herself, glared at Venus and said, "I don't wanna talk to you, so get the hell off my porch, Missy."

Yvette looked at me and softened. "Coffee, Doyle? I got instant." She didn't wait for an answer. She went inside, expecting me to follow. And expecting Venus to get the hell off her porch.

Venus held out her hand, demanded my keys, and stomped off. She started the car and jabbed the accelerator.

The tires on my Nova chirped as she sped away.

Yvette gave me a cup of coffee and placed Nilla wafers on a plate. I took a handful and, while I ate, I studied her.

She appeared tiny, wizened, like a grape well on its way to raisin status. She had a hard face and hard, bony arms. She had a hard way of talking and a hard way of living. And now life would be harder still. Because for as long as I'd known her, Yvette had had Lou to lean on.

They'd always been one of those funny-like-a-duck-walks couples. He was short and dumpy, she was stick-skinny. He yelled at everyone in sight, and Yvette seemed far more interested in the complexity of soap opera plots than what was going on in real life. Lou drank too much, and cigarette smoke habitually ringed her.

He bitched at her. She bitched at him. I wondered how they made it through the day, not to mention the years they'd spent together.

But Lou always helped Yvette on with her coat. She patted his butt when he walked by. He called her Dear. She brought cups of coffee into the office and sat with him while he battled a mound of paperwork and tried to keep their little enterprise solvent.

They found a way. The oddest of odd couples found a way to coexist.

So what the hell was wrong with the rest of us?

Yvette sat motionless. Hers was a face on Mount Rushmore. Then I noticed the first tiny fissures appear. They started around her wrinkled mouth, the lines deepening as her lips moved. Her ever-present cigarette fell, bouncing off her sweatshirt. It landed on the table, still burning, beside an ashtray filled with butts.

Yvette didn't bother to crush it out.

I scooped the butt off the table and dropped it in the ashtray.

She composed herself enough to say, "We gotta do this now? We gotta talk about him dyin'?"

"We do." I patted her hand.

She glanced toward the door. "Them guys told me if I say one word to the cops, they'd start shootin' strippers."

"But I'm not a cop."

She rolled her eyes. "You gotta promise you won't say nothin' to Miss Priss cop and that detective guy who come by yesterday."

I crossed my heart. And my fingers, just in case.

Yvette grimaced. "It's so Christly hard to trust anybody."

"I have that problem too. But we all get to choose who to talk to. You get to choose."

"I already chose," she said. "That's why you're here."

"Whenever you're ready, dear."

She nodded like she was gathering herself to leap off a bridge. "It was a regular mornin' before the girls came in. Just me and Lou sittin' in the parkin' lot and talkin' about how to pull our place out of trouble, when in drove them guys who beat Lou up before. The black one and the ponytail one and some other guy with a knife. The knife guy stood at Lou's door and the ponytail one was by mine."

"The same guys? Mikey said they didn't work for him anymore."

She grimaced. "Well, strippers tell customers they want them real bad, so I'm not sure if what they say really matters. I dunno who they work for, but they're the same guys."

"Okay." Another damn curveball.

"Anyway, the black guy told Lou to roll down the window. He said, 'No more bullshit. My boss wants the club.' Lou told him to get bent, like always. Then the knife guy yanked Lou's door open. He grabbed Lou's arm and pinned it to the steering wheel. And the black guy said to take his thumb."

"Shaft," I said. "The black guy is Shaft. Ponytail is Guido. The knife guy is…"

"Like I give a shit." Yvette lit another smoke. "Lou told them…no foolin', his name is Shaft? Like the movie?"

"Like no other."

It seemed to work for her. "Okay, so Lou told that Shaft guy to bring him Cherry, and they'd talk. That Shaft guy got a funny look on his face. He grabbed his phone and made a call. Said something like 'He said bring the redhead.' Then he listened. Then he said 'How the fuck do I know?' Looked like an argument goin' on, you know?"

"Sure," I said. "Lou changed the game and Shaft didn't know how to play it."

"No, he didn't. He looked some surprised when Lou told him to get Cherry."

"Did she ever show up?"

Yvette scowled. "Nope. She weren't never comin', I could tell by the look on Shaft's face. After a few he came back to the car. Lou looked at him a bit and goes, 'You ain't got no leverage on me. You ain't got nothin', do ya.' Then he started laughin'."

I didn't think I needed to ask, but I did anyway. "Then what?"

Yvette seemed to pale a little more. "Shaft and the knife guy started talkin' about what to do next. Like they forgot Lou and me was there. So Lou grabbed his gun from under the seat and shot the knife guy in the neck. When he fell Shaft shot Lou right in the gut. Lou kinda just…went over."

"I'm sorry."

Yvette rubbed her temples. "Yeah, me too. Lou weren't ever gettin' up again. But that Shaft guy, he kinda hovered. He looked at Lou and said, 'Before you go, all that money you got, why does this place still look like a dump?' Lou groaned somethin' awful, tryin' to speak. Then he said he used the money to win the election instead. That Shaft guy, he said, 'Consider this payback from the Reverend.'" She shook her head. "Fuckin' bastard."

"Are you sure he said it was from the Reverend?"

She set her jaw. "Hard to confuse that with 'Hey, did that bullet hurt?'"

Virdon had lost the vote due to Lou's debate. He'd lost his chance to shut down the club. Mikey Cross was doing the full-court press to take it over. Maybe Virdon had decided, before Mikey became too involved, he wanted one more shot at Lou. So he'd hired Mikey's former boys to take the club.

Maybe.

Of course, equally likely, maybe not.

Yvette scrunched her lips. "Lou didn't know no other way but to fight everyone who came along. His family. The bank. Stupid Reverend. Those guys. And…" Her eyes searched mine.

"And Mikey?"

"Him most of all. Every inch, Lou fought him. Lou didn't take pushin' around very lightly. 'Course, you see where it got him." She pulled a final drag on her cigarette and ground it out. She watched a faint curl of smoke drift from the ashtray and said, "They killed my man, Doyle. Them bastards killed my man. Why would they kill him?" She slammed her eyes shut, trying to stop a few rogue tears from escaping.

I touched her arm. "Mikey took my father's business the same way. Killed him too."

Her eyes widened. "Mikey killed your father? Jesus."

"In a manner of speaking. He wanted our construction business and Pops said no."

"Like he wants to take ours. And I don't wanna let him, but I don't know if I can fight him like Lou did. Did your father fight him? Is that how...hell Doyle, is that how he died?"

"Pops was a stubborn old guy, but in the end the only thing he brought to the battle was words. Kind of like bringing a knife to a gunfight. You do that, you just aren't ever going to win."

Yvette dropped her head to her arms and moaned, soft and low like a siren in the distance.

I let her get it out.

Her shoulders gave one last hitch. When she looked up, she quickly dried her eyes. And looked angry, probably at herself for having a weak moment, especially in front of me.

Yvette grabbed a cigarette from her pack, jammed it in her mouth and lit it up. She caught me looking. "I know, I know. Five more minutes of my life down the drain. But it ain't like I got much to use it on now."

Something still bothered me. "Any idea why Shaft and Guido let you go? You're a witness. Shaft should have shot you, too."

Yvette cocked her head and said, "'Cause I got somethin' somebody wants. Namely the club. Shaft looked at Lou dyin' and told me I'd be the sole owner soon. He said I got thirteen days to get the deal done. Final offer."

"Wonder why he set the deadline at thirteen days?"

She grumbled, "Sometimes I think you focus on the wrong thing. They want the club and you see what they'll do to get it. What else matters?"

She was right. People around me usually are. "What did you tell them?"

Yvette seemed to swell a bit. "I said 'You harm a hair on Cherry's head, and I'll burn the club right to the ground. Then nobody will get shit. That I can promise.'"

"How did Shaft take it?"

"He told me to stop fuckin' around, stop talkin' about Cherry. Then he stuck the gun in my face and said I got thirteen days. And I believed him."

I believed him, too. I'd seen enough of his handiwork to know he meant business, and I didn't want to see any more. It seemed like a good time to pull the plug on Yvette's macho show. "Why don't you get rid of it, get Cherry back, and get this over with? Is keeping the club that important?"

Yvette clamped her jaws shut and brooded for a while. "Crap, you known Lou forever, you know how he was. Before we bought the place, he acted like he didn't deserve to walk on the same street as the rest of the world. Then one day, he's a respectable businessman. Okay, it's just a titty bar, and it ain't never gonna be more than a titty bar. But it was Lou Principi's titty bar, and all of a sudden he weren't a sorry schmuck no more. The Limit made him who he wanted to be, so I gotta hold onto it. It's all I got left of him."

Bowser began to yowl at the door. Yvette stood up. As she walked by me she briefly touched my shoulder.

I sighed. Shaft and Guido were in a funeral-causing mood. I wasn't ready for another.

When she returned I tried to reason with her. "Thirteen days is all you have left…"

She grabbed my hand and squeezed. Hard. "No. That was two days ago, so now *you* got eleven days to get Cherry and find a way to help me keep the club. You like bein' everybody's hero, Doyle. Well, now it's time to be a hero for me, how about? I got nobody else to turn to."

I called Venus. About ten minutes later she came by to pick me up. She refused to move from the driver's seat.

I climbed in the passenger's side.

She chirped the tires again as she drove away, driving far too fast for the potholes we encountered.

After she'd whipped through two rolling stops and flew through Fairfield at least twenty miles over the speed limit, Venus said, "So, you going to spit it out? What Yvette said?"

The moment of truth. Or in my case, half-truth. Because one thing I'd understood very clearly. Yvette talks to the cops, dancers end up dead. I thought about Trouble. Veronica. Shari and Annette.

But really, I thought about Ecstasy.

I said, "Lou shot Livingston."

"We know that! So who's the other guy, the one who shot Lou? Jesus, time's a wasting."

I tried to get the pacing right. To sound like I spoke the truth, while I lied through my teeth. "She said she'd never seen him before."

Venus slammed on the brakes and skidded over to the curb, tires squealing. When she whipped around to look at me, her eyes blazed with fury. "You're telling me she has no idea who shot Lou? He was some out-of-the-blue person who walked up to the car and popped him?"

"Yvette said she didn't know the guy."

I could almost see the smoke rising from Venus's ears. "Well, perhaps you can give me a description of the shooter. If it wouldn't be too much trouble. After all, you were there for an hour, Yvette had to say something." She continued to glare.

As cool as I could be, I said, "The guy was kind of tall and muscular. Maybe brown eyes."

"Well, that's a useful nugget. A guy who is kind of tall and muscular. Maybe had brown eyes to boot. I'll call in the APB right now."

"Hey, that's what she gave me."

Venus snorted. "And she couldn't say that in front of me? Like there's anything I can do with this." Her eyebrows knitted together. "Did she give you any particular reason why she couldn't talk to me?"

At least I could tell the truth this time. Even if it hurt. "She said you think you're better than her."

Venus's mouth clicked closed. She sagged in the seat. Without a word she turned away from me, dropped the car in drive, and drove the speed limit the rest of the way to the police station.

CHAPTER 25

After I dropped Venus off the day had turned unseasonably warm and the sun shone through my office window. I had opened it and a light breeze puffed the drapes and freshened the tired room.

The worn leather couch had beckoned, and I acquiesced.

I don't know how long I'd slept when my jangling phone woke me. "Hullo?" I tried to get the fuzz out of my brain and the cotton from my mouth.

"Paul, get out here." It was Venus.

"Get out where?"

"The field behind the high school track. You pull in there and you'll know where to find me."

"Be there in twenty." I rubbed the sleep from my eyes. Naptime over.

I drove past the football field and down a small hill to the school's back parking lot. In the far corner I could see an ambulance, lights flashing, along with a handful of police cars, marked and unmarked. A crowd of fifty or sixty people stood nearby.

As I neared the ambulance a short policeman stepped from the crowd and held his hand up. "That's far enough, buddy," he ordered.

Overambitious officer Cameron Hedgepeth. Reduced to crowd control.

I exited my car and decided to tower over him. "Detective Robinson?"

"Detective Robinson is here." He eyeballed me. "Not that it's your business."

"Probably is, though. She called me."

"Paul!" I heard Venus yell. I glanced toward the track, where she rapidly walked toward me. "You coming or not?"

I looked at Hedgepeth. "Am I coming or not?"

He set his jaw, stepped aside and let me pass.

When I neared Venus, she turned toward the edge of the field and strode off. "Let's go."

We followed a faint set of tire tracks that made a beeline for the brush-choked stream that marked the edge of the woods.

We stepped over crime scene tape suspended from a couple of small wooden stakes and walked to the creek.

I saw something in the brush. Appeared to be a blue rag. I looked at Venus.

"This is where the kids come to smoke during lunch break," she said.

An uneasy feeling settled over me. I walked closer to get a better look at the rag.

But it wasn't just a blue rag.

No, it wasn't just a blue rag at all.

I saw a mass of purple hair.

Venus and I stood nearby while they removed the body. "You sure it's Gerald Tappey's girl?" she asked.

"Her name's Shari."

"The one who was with Annette Begley?"

I nodded. "How long do you figure she's been here?"

"Couple of days. Be a while before we know, but I'd guess she was dumped here maybe Friday or Saturday. Kids come to school Monday, and there she is."

Maybe Friday. Maybe. I closed my eyes. Thursday was when Cash and I had talked to Mikey.

Possibly Shari's last day alive. Possibly on account of me.

Friends take care of friends, so Gerald and Katherine should hear about it from me first. I dug my phone out of my pocket. "I'm going to call them," I said. Venus left me alone and went to talk to a State Police detective who lingered on the other side of the tape.

There are a million reasons why people don't answer the phone. When Gerald's went to voice mail, when Katherine's went to voice mail, and when the home phone went unanswered, I could only think of one: they already knew.

I flipped my phone closed, turned and studied the storm clouds piling up to the west. Overhead, a flock of geese in a ragged V-pattern winged their way south.

I tried to think of everything good I knew in the world. Beer and pizza. The Red Sox. Ecstasy's gentle eyes and tender touch.

None of it helped. Not a whisker. The green grass that stretched before me blurred and danced.

Until it went away.

Then Venus stood at my elbow. "You all right, Paul?"

It took all the strength I had to shake my head. She patted my shoulder and walked away.

Ten years ago, my father died. I'd been trying to connect the dots of a challenging marriage, so I was focused more on me than him. He had problems. I had problems. We all had problems. Except his problems killed him.

A couple of years ago my sister Vivian died of cancer. Growing up, she was my hero. She was my confidant, my protector, and my best friend. When Pops was too busy at work and Ma was too busy being Ma, Vivian was always there. Until she was gone.

Now Shari.

I needed to talk to someone. A wild thought dashed through my mind: I could call Eileen. I'd drop by my old house, she'd make a pot of coffee and we'd discuss how Shari had died. Maybe, if I was lucky, she'd tell me I wasn't the biggest screw-up in the entire state of Maine.

But it wasn't Eileen's place to hear my problems. Eileen had a new life and a new sweetheart. They talked about stuff now, we didn't.

If I hadn't fouled things up so badly, I could go to Ecstasy. She seemed like a listener, a woman who'd encourage me to talk. A woman who'd listen to me and help me formulate my thoughts. She'd pat my hand and tell me it was okay. And more importantly, I was okay.

Because right this second I didn't feel remotely okay.

And in truth, I doubted anyone could say anything that would make me feel differently.

I went home instead, straight to my room, and closed the door.

CHAPTER 26

When I rejoined the world my head hurt, my back ached, and my eyes felt so sore and gritty I could hardly keep them open. I sat on the couch while Ma remained at the table, drinking coffee. She looked at me and waited.

And waited some more.

When waiting lost its luster she said, "I'm sorry."

I grunted. "Me, too."

My coffee cup had a World's Greatest Dad logo on it. I studied it. 'World's' was black lettering. 'Greatest' was blue.

'Dad' alternated green and purple. The color of Shari's eyes. And her hair. Of course.

"You okay, Paul?"

I hardly recognized the frailty of my voice. "I screwed this up. I can't believe it turned out like this."

"Why do you say that, son?"

Son. I couldn't remember the last time she'd called me that. I wasn't sure why she chose now to hit me with the 'son' tag. I struggled to regain my bearings. "Shari needed me to save her. Instead, I ran her right to them."

She forced herself to stand, and slowly walked over to me. I was too ashamed to look her in the eye.

She placed her hand on my head. "You sound a lot like your father. When those things happened to the business, he couldn't shake it. He blamed himself, and he couldn't let it go. He'd sit for hours night and try to figure out what he could have done differently. And when thinking didn't work, he tried to drink his way to answers."

Ma nudged me to slide over and wedged herself between me and the arm of the couch. She said, "But he never found what he was looking for. He didn't. He just found another way to beat himself up for something he couldn't have changed. You know what it did to him. Don't let it do the same thing to you."

"But…"

Ma shook her head. "Not everything that happens is your fault, Paul. You tend to dwell on the bad and think you cause it. We all do sometimes, but you do it more than most. For once, try to dwell on the good you do."

She stood, patted the top of my head and walked to her bedroom.

I tried to remember something good I'd done. Something I could hang my hat on.

I came up goose eggs.

An hour later, I called Cash. "I acted like an ass with Mikey. Maybe that's why he killed Shari."

"Don't you think Mikey has been cussed out by badder dudes than you? A guy tells Mikey to back off, Mikey tells him to fuck off. They both walk away mad. But they both walk away. And no one dies."

"This time somebody did," I said. "Because I stood up to him."

"Dude, what an ego! Mikey paid you back when he personally split your cranium in the hallway. That threat he made about talking to the cops and a bullet in the brain? Maybe Mikey included you in the off-limits category. And Lou came to you, remember? You didn't go to him."

I slapped my leg. The next time I saw Shari she'd be in a casket. "You think he killed her for that? Because Lou hired me?"

"First, we're still not sure he killed her. We just know someone killed her."

"Fair enough. But Mikey had her."

Cash cleared his throat. "Once upon a time Virdon did too."

"This shit hurts my head. It's easy to say Mikey, but you're right. Reverend Virdon's name keeps popping up like a mushroom."

"Whoever did it, they dumped the body where someone was sure to find it. Message sent and received."

Anger pulsed behind my aching eyes. Through gritted teeth I said, "When I find out who did it, I'm gonna ask him why. Right up in his face. And by God, he's gonna answer me."

Cash remained quiet for a while. "Paul, it's all well and good that you want to square this up, but payback for Shari doesn't equal justice. And don't forget why we started this shindig. Think about Annette. She's still missing."

I thought about Shari Tappey instead. The last time I saw her she was working at her uncle's store. She'd gotten a good belly laugh out of me leaving my wallet in my car when I stopped in for coffee and a donut, and had sixty-three cents and a sheet metal screw in my pocket. She'd told me to keep my windfall. This one was on her.

When I walked out she'd given me a big, friendly wave and said, "See ya around."

She was wrong.

I rubbed my temples and wished Annette hadn't gone to the church dormitory. Or that Shari hadn't gone with her. Or that Reverend Virdon hadn't tried to outlaw adult entertainment. Or that Lou hadn't gone to a prick like Mikey when he needed money.

I had a lot of wishes stacking up.

Mostly I just wished they'd all just go away.

"You going to her funeral?" Cash asked.

"Yeah. Of course. You?"

He hemmed and hawed. "Next one I plan on attending is my own. Maybe I'll climb Katahdin when you're at the funeral and try to remember what it felt like to be young and without a care in the world."

Hiking Mount Katahdin sounded nice, but finding Annette sounded nicer. "Funeral's in a couple of days. We could sneak a bit of work in before then."

Cash said, "This didn't work out so well before, but any chance you want to follow Shaft and Guido around to see if they'll get us closer to Annette?"

I took a couple of deep breaths to get my head together. "I guess we could pick them up and see what we see."

He sounded more enthusiastic. "So…boredom kicked in this morning, and I may have followed Guido when he left Mikey's place and met Shaft. To stay in practice and all."

"Color me surprised. Were they aware you tailed them?"

Cash laughed.

"Sorry Mister Cashman, I withdraw the question. If I may ask, why did you keep me in the dark on this critical piece of information?"

"Knowledge is power, Big Guy. I know things you don't, so you need me."

"And are you still providing clandestine surveillance as we speak?"

He chuckled softly. "In a most surreptitious fashion."

"Where can I find you?"

"Why don't you swing by Marmaduke's for a look see?"

Marmaduke's Bar, a dingy yellow single-story building that does double duty as a convenience store with one gas pump, and triples up as a deer tagging station during hunting season, hovers on the bank of the Carleton River, just south of Westfield. Ever since I'd learned that beer tasted good and Marmaduke's had an endless supply I'd made it one of my favorite watering holes.

When I pulled into the parking lot I didn't see Cash's Caprice. I did, however, see a hand shoot out the window of a dirty gray Ford Escort. I parked behind a ragged bush and walked to the Escort. Cash looked huge in it. I'd look even larger when I got in. If I could get in at all.

I pulled the door open and wedged myself inside.

Cash watched with obvious enjoyment. "Now you know what college kids used to feel like, trying to cram into a phone booth."

I grimaced. "Yeah, but there's only one of me."

"Good thing."

"How long have you been on them?"

"They met up about two hours ago outside of Mikey's, followed the river and pulled in here."

"We have them cornered but it's not going to do us a helluva lot of good. If we go in and give them a beat down, there's no saying they'd take us to Annette."

"Drats," Cash said. "I was ready to exert my will with dire consequences."

"Patience, my friend. You may still get the opportunity. So what do they drive?"

Cash pointed to an Audi parked in front of Marmaduke's. "These boys ride in style."

I patted the Escort's dashboard. "If they decide to run, the only way we can catch them is if we're going downhill. Or off a cliff."

"Never underestimate the power of my lead foot. Where they go, I will follow."

While skeptical, I appreciated his enthusiasm. "We'll tag team them. You in this, me in my hotrod Nova."

Cash coughed. "Talk about something that needs to go off a cliff. For good."

I touched his shoulder. "That's my baby you're talking about. Did you bring food?"

"No. I was hoping you'd feed the help." He eyed the paper bag in my hand.

I pulled out a ham sandwich. "One for you, one for me."

Cash looked like he wanted to cry.

He destroyed the sandwich instead.

I went back to my car and ate the other sandwich. I had nothing to wash it down with. On the other hand, washing the sandwich down meant other impending biological problems. I'd stick with the dry sandwich over an aching bladder any day.

Marmaduke's marquee offered meatball grinders, chips and a drink for six bucks, and two-dollar lunchtime beers. They all sounded better than my dry sandwich. Especially the beer.

Shaft and Guido were probably washing their grinders down with cool, refreshing beer right now. Pitchers of beer.

I picked up the crossword puzzle, found a pen, and hoped they'd drown in it.

About the time I had more cross-outs than correct letters, they came out the door.

Guido slipped behind the wheel. Shaft slid in beside him. I hunched a little lower in my sweet ride as they pulled past me and headed the last direction I thought they'd go. East on Route 155 and a quick right on Lake Shore Road toward the edge of nowhere.

Cash waited for an old Ford station wagon to pass by. He fell in a few hundred yards behind the Audi. I took the rear, about a half-mile back.

Guido drove the speed limit along Lake Shore Road's residential area and into the countryside. He drove past rolling hills, chicken barns and dairy farms. Straight through a no stoplight town, North Vassalboro, then through East Vassalboro on the shore of China Lake.

We'd gone about eight miles and the Audi continued straight and true. As it approached the intersection of Route 3, Cash dropped back. The Audi slowed, rolled through the stop sign, and picked up speed again.

The last time I'd viewed the wooded hills on the far side of Route 3, I'd seen nothing but cows and trees. But it had been a couple of years since I'd been out this way. Today, I saw a spectacular, sprawling, brand-spanking new golf course abutted by a still under-construction housing development.

The course was breathtaking, with duck ponds and burbling creeks throughout. Large pines, maples and oaks dotted the fairways. Dozens of sand traps gleamed as white as snow, offsetting the freshly mowed, emerald grass. The course beckoned me to come and play.

As a golfer, I'm sure I'd have found it irresistible.

But I'm not. So it was eminently resistible.

While I tried to wrap my brain around why some idiot would build not only a fantastic, world-class golf course in the middle of Nowhere Maine, not to mention the semi-palatial estates that stretched past the ridge to the south, Cash turned right on Route 3. So I turned left.

I drove past the crest of a knoll a quarter-mile up the road, pulled off, and walked back to the top. I could see the Audi. It had skirted the security guards manning the massive iron gates separating the course from the housing development, turned off the road and now bounced up a dirt lane, past the golf course toward a wooded hill.

I watched until it entered the pines and disappeared from sight. I surveyed the trees. Nothing...except...except there seemed to be an unnatural clearing on the side of the hill.

I looked south and could see Cash's car tucked in behind an old farmhouse. He was standing on the lawn, staring toward the trees.

I called him. "What do you think?"

"I want to get a quick eighteen in. You?"

"Only if the eighteen in question has hops and fresh-brewed flavor. You see anything else?"

"Besides a golf course Tiger Woods would kill to play on? Nope."

"Past the golf course. From here, it looks like a clearing up there."

"That's funny. From here, it looks like the Taj Mahal up there."

I envied his view. "How big?"

"I dunno. Bigger than a breadbox. Smaller than Fenway Park. Does that help?"

I got in the car, whipped it around, and drove to Cash. He motioned me in to the weed-filled yard of the abandoned house.

"You bring your hiking shoes?" he asked.

"I brought my running shoes. You ready?" I climbed into imaginary starting blocks.

Cash looked at me with skepticism. "I'm a nationally-ranked handicap triathlete. You sure you want to do this?"

I stood up. "Maybe a leisurely hike instead."

CHAPTER 27

With no cars in sight we set out across the road, skirting the golf course by a wide margin. We ran across a couple hundred yards of open field before we reached tree cover. Cash set the pace, way faster than I liked. Despite the cool weather I was sweating like a hooker in church by the time we stopped.

I dropped onto the first rock I saw and tried not to die.

"You gonna make it?" Cash asked.

I took a minute to catch my breath. "I was just hitting my stride," I wheezed. I don't think he was convinced.

When my heart rate dropped to double digits, I stood up. "You ready?"

"Me? Are *you* ready?"

"Ayuh. Let's mosey on up to the Taj Mahal of central Maine."

We climbed a hill that had just enough rise that it burned the hell out of my quads as we progressed. From halfway up, we had a good view of the golf course. A rock-lined stream splashed along the two nearest fairways and pooled against railroad ties that edged the elevated greens.

We worked our way through some juniper and continued to climb. Huge pine trees dominated the hill as we neared the top.

I gave Cash the timeout sign, and he took a few minutes to admire the view while I struggled to regain normal respiratory function.

Cash studied me with the care of a cardiologist until I gave him a weary nod.

We made our way down a small ravine guarded by scattered oaks and pines. When we picked our way over some stones and crossed a tiny creek, through the trees we could see a structure.

We eased closer.

A solid, eight-foot high concrete wall separated us from the building we'd seen from the road. A strand of electric fence was strung across the top.

It looked like the owner didn't particularly want visitors.

Inside the wall we saw the huge building. Certainly bigger than a breadbox. Not much smaller than Fenway Park.

From this close, the sprawling gray and red structure looked like a deranged architect's nightmare. Three massive spires thrust themselves skyward and looked almost as charming as fangs on a cobra. Offsetting those were three short, fat onion-shaped ones, as if the designer couldn't fully commit to one concept or the other and decided 'More has to be better, I'll do both.' Numerous odd-shaped dormers dotted the side of the house nearest us, fracturing the otherwise elegant line of the impressive red, Spanish-tiled roof.

On the lawn, centered between the fence and the house, was a fountain.

Not just any fountain, but one that rivaled the Trevi in Rome. Despite the frigid temperature, water coursed through the two-tiered limestone behemoth that featured writhing horses, soldiers engaged in fierce battle, and angels swooping in to observe the fray. The fountain's centerpiece was an extremely tall, extremely shapely, extremely nude woman.

"What do you think?" I asked after we'd studied it for a while.

"Dude, she's got rock-hard abs."

Despite the encouragement it would provide, I chuckled.

To improve our vantage point we poked around until we came to a partially-exposed granite ledge. Most of the compound was visible. On the far side a dirt road ended at a sliding gate.

Inside the fence a driveway circled in front of the massive building. Parked on the drive were a white van, a flatbed truck with some gardening tools on the bed, a gray Mercedes and the Audi.

"We found your boys, I guess," Cash said.

"What do you figure this place is?"

"Big house. Or a small hotel."

"Big house. It must be fifteen thousand square feet."

"Not so shabby for this vicinity. Wonder who owns it?"

I surveyed the vehicles in the yard. "Looks like there's a sign on the van."

"There is in fact a sign. How's your eyesight?"

"Incredible. How's yours?"

Cash grinned. "Better than your measly incredible. And I can prove it. How about you read the sign? Out loud, so we can share the moment."

I squinted, turned my head and shaded my eyes. After trying everything I knew, I realized my vision was a long way from incredible. "Okay, smart guy, what does it say?"

He pointed at his face. "Fighter pilot eyes. They never cease to amaze me."

"When you finish celebrating your eyes, would you share what it says on the van?"

"If my eyes do not deceive me, and we know they don't, the lettering on the side of the van says Castle View Free Church. Truck says the same thing. In smaller print, of course."

I stared at him.

He said, "I couldn't make up better stuff than this."

I squinted at the yard. "So Shaft and Guido kidnap Annette and Shari from the church dormitory. Someone kills Shari. Annette's still missing. And the boys who we believe took them are at a woodland palace along with a van from the church?"

"Dude, the world's a funny place. One time I went to Tijuana and I saw a woman do things with a…"

I put up my hand. "I don't need to know what you saw. But this doesn't make sense."

"The lady in Tijuana didn't make sense either. That's what made it so fun."

I ground my teeth. "Can we forget about the lady from Tijuana?"

"Her actions are indelibly etched in my brain."

"Can you at least push her to the back burner?"

He gave a tree beside him a sentimental smile. "*Adios, señorita.*" He winked at me. "So, what do you think?"

"We don't know if Annette is here, but the guys who we think took her are. I'm not leaving."

Cash scouted around in the brush and came back with a cracked plastic pail and a metal one with numerous bullet holes. He flipped them over. "Which one would you like?"

I doubted the cracked pail would hold me so I took the metal one. It sat crookedly on the ground, which I knew would bother my back before long. But it was a seat. Cash sat beside me.

Sitting in a car during a stakeout isn't half bad. There's a roof over your head, a heater at your fingertips, a place for food and coffee—in short, most of the comforts of home.

Sitting on a crooked metal pail in the middle of the Maine woods in late October however, sucked.

A cold, angry wind blew out of the north, biting through my jacket. In less than an hour my nose ran like a grade schooler's during cold and flu season, my teeth chattered non-stop, and my butt was so numb I'd forgotten how bad it had been aching.

As I stood to head back to the car, Cash touched my arm and pointed toward the mansion. Shaft and Guido walked out the front door and entered the Audi.

Another man left the house, started the van and drove toward the gate. It slid open and he drove through, followed by the Audi.

"Interesting," I said after the gate closed again. "Did you recognize the guy who drove the van?"

"I did." Extra emphasis on *I*. He turned to me.

"You're a falcon. I get it. I'm freezing my nuts off here, so get to it. Who was it?"

"You've seen him on TV. You've heard him on the radio. He hopes one day to be bigger than Jimmy Swaggart. A Pisces, he likes bubble baths and cuddling on a bearskin rug with that special someone. Ladies and gentlemen put your hands together for Johnny Virdon!" He gave a solemn golf clap.

"Johnny Virdon? Are you sure?" Of course he was. He had eyes like a falcon.

Reverend Johnny Virdon, pastor of the Castle View Free Church, at a mansion with two thugs who used to work for Mikey Cross.

Cash looked perplexed. "How do you want to play this one, Paul?"

"Like an air guitar," I said.

Because I had nothing.

CHAPTER 28

There are many things in life you want to do. There are also things you must do. It's nice when the 'want to do' and the 'must do' piles overlap. Tonight they weren't remotely close.

Calling hours at the Schwartz-Patton Funeral Home. From 6 to 9 PM.

There is little worse than seeing a coffin that holds the body of a twenty-year-old woman. A twenty-year-old woman who hadn't even scratched the surface of life yet. A woman who should be doing anything in the world tonight. Anything other than lying in a coffin.

I hovered outside the viewing room, chatting with old classmates and neighbors. While our conversation bordered on banal, vague memories of football games, children, marriages and divorces, it beat what was coming next.

Because I didn't come to catch up with old acquaintances.

I came to say goodbye to Shari Tappey.

Soft organ music played. Massive floral arrangements dotted the room, including one of red and white, Shari's high school colors. But a simple mahogany casket with the cover open held my attention.

As I walked by Venus, I patted her on the shoulder. A detective's work never ends. She touched the seat beside her but I moved forward instead. I'd come for Shari.

I walked to the front row and looked around the room. Gerald and Katherine Tappey sat near me, stiff-backed, huddled together.

Yvette sat on the right, alone, dressed in black slacks and a frayed black blouse. She'd worn the same outfit to Lou's funeral earlier this afternoon. Black is versatile like that. You can wear the same thing over and over every time you mourn a loved one.

I gave her a quick hug and a peck on her leathery cheek.

She looked up at me, her eyes watery. "They killed Bowser."

I dropped into the chair beside her. "Bowser is dead? How?"

Yvette reached for her cigarette pack, then at her surroundings. She dropped the pack into her purse. "Got his head crushed is how. Oh, they made it look like he got hit by a car. I found him out by the street this morning so that's what you'd guess. Just…you look at it one way, he got hit by a car. You look at it my way, someone dragged him off the porch and stepped on his little head."

"You hear anything? See anything?"

"No," her voice dragged out. "Maybe I heard somethin' on the porch, maybe I didn't. But Bowser ain't left it in two years. Why would he do it now?"

Deep lines creased her brow. "Well, he wouldn't. So they did it."

I sat with her a bit longer, my hand on top of hers.

She slid her hand from under mine, then nudged me. "Go ahead, your girl's waitin'." She nodded across the aisle. "She been waitin' a while."

My girl? I didn't have a…I looked in the direction Yvette indicated.

Ecstasy wore an understated yet elegant knee-length, lacy black dress, black pearls and matching earrings. She'd pulled her hair back in a low ponytail and held it in place with a wide gold clip.

I walked to her and sat in the empty chair to her right. She smiled and hooked her arm with mine. Her makeup showed signs of tears. Her eyes promised more to come.

"Hello Paul," she whispered.

"Ecstasy, I'm sorry about the last time we…"

She hugged me with her eyes. "*No te preocupes.*" Which, although I had no idea what it meant, was all I needed to hear.

I said, "Did you pay your respects yet?"

Ecstasy shook her head. "I saw you arrive. I want to do this with you."

I patted her hand. "I'm going to see her now. Then I have some things to say to her folks. We grew up together. Are you ready?"

Ecstasy squeezed my arm. "Are you?"

I nodded. "I think so."

She took my arm as we walked to the casket and looked inside.

Shari looked like I remembered her in only the vaguest possible sense. Her hair was still purple. The shape of her face hadn't changed. Her crooked nose and the line of her mouth looked familiar. The scar on her cheek remained. Those made her identifiable as Shari Tappey.

However, what made her so memorable to me was the joyous spark that crackled from her eyes. The playful smile that tugged at the corners of her mouth. It was the funny faces she made whenever she saw me.

Those were gone forever.

People say the deceased look like they're sleeping.

Spare me.

Shari Tappey looked dead.

Ecstasy let go of my arm and fished in her purse for a tissue. She wiped her eyes, gave her nose a gentle blow, and took my arm again.

After a while, we had nothing else to do.

We turned and walked a dozen steps.

Gerald and Katherine slowly stood as we approached them. Gerald's face resembled a flat tire that had been driven on. It was shredded beyond repair.

Katherine's face, on the other hand, was an iron mask. I looked for anger. I looked for agony.

Her flinty eyes bored through me, yet I don't think they saw me.

I think they saw her daughter.

When she was still alive, and I was still a friend.

I waited for Gerald to accuse me of killing Shari.

I waited for Katherine to scream at me. Something about how, until I started hunting for Annette Begley, their daughter was alive.

And now she wasn't.

I stared at one of the flower arrangements. I couldn't bring myself to look at Katherine again.

We stood in pained silence for far too long before I whispered, "I'm sorry."

Katherine's breath hitched. She didn't speak.

She didn't need to. I felt every ounce of her loss.

Ecstasy took a quick step toward Katherine and took her hand. "Your daughter was a wonderful person."

Katherine crumbled as if her legs had been swept out from her. She ended up in Ecstasy's arms, their heads on each other's shoulders.

Katherine's breath hitched again, but this breath sounded different.

This one was sodden with tears.

Though I tried not to, my mind drifted to the rocker in the Tappey's living room.

It would remain empty.

The walk away from Gerald and Katherine was the most painful I could remember.

"I know this is hard," Ecstasy murmured, and continued to hold my arm. "So we will do it together."

Venus stood near the door watching the attendees leave. As we approached, her eyes slowly moved from me to Ecstasy and back.

We stopped. "Venus," I said.

Her nod seemed a tad curt for the funereal setting. "Paul."

"I'd like you to meet Ecstasy."

Awkward silence embraced us. Ecstasy shifted her weight from foot to foot.

"What?" I asked, feeling like I had just missed a private joke.

Venus stiffly said, "This…woman…and I have already met."

After that, they were as quiet as church mice with laryngitis. "So…okay," I said when it became apparent it was my job to get everyone off the stage in an orderly fashion. "We gotta go."

Ecstasy nodded toward Venus. "Good to see you again, detective."

Venus didn't waste a smile. "The pleasure is mine."

I could feel her eyes on our backs as we made our way to the parking lot.

As we neared Ecstasy's car I said, "I got it. She interviewed you."

Ecstasy patted my chest. "Nice work, Dick Tracy."

"By the way, thanks," I said. "I'm not talking about the Dick Tracy line."

She looked straight ahead but I could feel her smile. "I know."

When we arrived at her car it was decision time. Go home alone. Or go somewhere together. I hoped for together.

But it wasn't going to happen if I stayed mute. "You want some coffee?" I forced myself to say, expecting fourteen different versions of 'dude, no.'

Ecstasy remained silent.

Words fire-hosed from me. "You have to go. I understand. You're not working tonight are you? Because that'd mean you really have to go, so I don't know why I even thought…"

Ecstasy clutched my arm. "Slow down, sailor. I was trying to think of a coffee shop that's still open."

Through the first snowflakes of approaching winter I followed her down River Road to a place called Uncommon Ground. We bought two lattes and a blueberry muffin to share. We sat on an overstuffed couch near the fireplace and picked at the muffin and sipped our coffee in silence. I felt like we were seated in our own uncommon ground. One that didn't come fully equipped with a roadmap. So we felt our way along.

When we finished eating, Ecstasy wiped the crumbs from her dress. Her eyes seemed to challenge me. "I've been thinking about this since our last blow-up and I just don't…freaking…know. So I'm gonna ask. What do you want from me, Paul?"

No beating around the bush with this woman.

What did I want? Really? Well…the first time I'd met her I wanted the curvaceous young beauty who seemed damned glad to please me, even if I had to pay for it. I wanted the fantasy.

The next time we were together I realized I wanted to see her smile. I wanted to hear her laugh. I wanted to see her eyes gleam like sunrise on the ocean. And I wanted to know I caused those reactions.

A little bit here and a little bit there she'd begun to pull back the curtain from her life, and now I wanted to know who she was. And why.

I touched her hand and blurted, "I just want a chance to know the real you."

She closed her eyes and sat perfectly still while I forgot how to breathe.

Our waitress flipped the sign on the door to 'Closed'. She glanced at us, checked her watch, and began to sweep the floor.

The snow continued to fall.

Ecstasy opened dewy eyes. She exhaled slowly. "Oh…kay."

And our personal teeter-totter, which had occasionally slammed to one side or the other, for the first time seemed relatively balanced.

"Only one thing I ask, Paul."

"Easy."

"You say that," she said, her words turning autumn-crisp in the quiet shop. "But everything is easy to do until you actually have to do it."

I touched the scar on her chin. "I mean it. Anything."

She pulled away. "Do you really?"

I nodded.

Ecstasy watched the waitress put the broom away, then she spoke. "Okay, in the club you touch my hand and you touch my face and one night you kissed me on the forehead and that's nothing next to what I've done…but…that's in the club. Whatever we had in the club, I don't want that here yet. We have to crawl before we walk."

"I fully understand," I said. I had no clue what the hell she was talking about.

She gave me a thin, tight-lipped smile. "The Limit has fewer rules than a cage wrestling match, and it would be easy to say no rules here. We've already established what I am. But…I was a stupid girl a lifetime ago, and I've vowed never to be a stupid woman. But what the hell does that mean? It means I don't know how to act with you right now, okay? So let's put some rules in place. First rule: no touch. Only talk. Let's let it grow from there."

I nodded. "I'm a helluva talker. You're going to be impressed."

She bit her bottom lip to keep from laughing. "I'll be more surprised than anything. It's a talent you've kept hidden very well."

"Pacing myself, girl. A full dose of Paul Doyle might kill you, and then where would you be? In the graveyard, where people are just dying to get in."

Ecstasy laughed lightly, and blushed the tiniest bit. "This is fun and all with your stupid jokes, but knowing me is like walking through a minefield. You'll never know what's going to trigger an explosion. Sometimes I don't know."

She frowned. "Most of the time I don't know."

I smiled. "I guess we'll learn together."   ·

She smiled back. A very tentative smile. But a smile nonetheless. "Not many people have stuck around me for long. First time they hit a mine, they tend to disappear. Usually in pieces."

"You don't need to show me your warning label."

She cleared her throat. "Don't be too certain, mister. But it's getting late, so before we have to leave let's talk about something other than crazy old me. Shari's parents, maybe. I don't know that I've ever seen people that looked more tortured. How well did you know them?"

"Gerald and Katherine and I went to school together. In a small town like this, you watch folks fall in love and get married. And if you stick around long enough, you get to watch their kids die."

Ecstasy's head snapped back.

"I'm sorry," I muttered, shaking my head. "I've known Shari since she was a little girl, and this...this is hard."

Ecstasy touched my hand for a moment before she jerked hers away. I guess no touching applied to her touching me too. "I'm here if you want to talk."

In the silence that followed, something told me to let her in. My ex-wife knew very little about what I did, and as long as the money was there she'd seemed content to keep it that way.

But I sensed Ecstasy's genuine interest. I told her, a little at a time, about how Annette and Shari were at the dorm, and how they'd fled when I arrived.

Ecstasy asked, "Any idea why Shari went to the dorm, too?"

"Maybe she wanted to protect a friend. Maybe she didn't want to be alone. I don't know. All I do know is she didn't deserve to die."

Ecstasy leaned forward. "Do you know who killed her? Or Lou?" Her eyes implored me to confide in her.

In their sincerity, I caved. "This can never be repeated. Not to a friend, not to a sister, not to a mother." I didn't bother mentioning to a customer. I think she tracked with me.

"You can trust me."

In my business you don't trust many people, but I made a snap decision. I would trust Ecstasy. "I don't have proof, but all along I've suspected a man named Mikey Cross. He likes people to believe that he's the greatest guy you'd ever meet, but truth is he's as shady as an elm tree in summer. Lou owed him big money and couldn't pay, so Mikey sent two of his men to gently encourage Lou to give up the club instead. Old school style, so that's why his face looked like raw hamburger a while back."

"People actually do that? Like in the movies?"

"People actually do that. Just like in the movies. When Lou couldn't pay the loan, Mikey said he'd take the club instead. Lou didn't want to let it go. So Mikey threatened to kill Annette. Then she disappeared. And that's where I came in."

"You think Lou was killed because he wouldn't give up his club?"

"You don't say no to guys like Mikey. When he's pushed, he pushes back harder. Like killing flies with a sledgehammer harder. And then bad things happen to good people."

Her eyebrows crashed together. "This is like a straight-to-video movie."

"Most folks don't see this side of life, but trucks get hijacked, cars are stolen, drugs are trafficked. People are smuggled into the country and guns are smuggled out. You forget you owe a tough guy money, he breaks your leg. You forget again, maybe you get a bullet."

"And you're involved with people like this?" Her eyes were those of a little girl who'd just learned the rest of the world isn't as safe as her own back yard.

I tried to play it off. "A lot of the work I do is mundane. A woman thinks her husband is cheating, she hires me to peek through the keyhole. An insurance company believes a person filed a fraudulent claim, they pay me to prove it. It's pretty safe, actually."

"It's not always safe though, is it?"

"Well, no. Sometimes people disagree with what I do."

"Meaning?" Ecstasy bit her lip.

I pulled my jacket back so she could see my .38 in a shoulder harness.

Her mouth dropped open. "You took a gun to a funeral home?"

"My life isn't full of friends. Especially now that Mikey and I are pissing in each other's Cheerios."

She rocked back and forth. "You sure this Mikey guy killed Lou?"

"At first look it was all Mikey, but now I'm not so sure. I thought it was Mikey's guys who took Shari from the church dormitory. The next time anyone saw her, she was dead."

"That's not enough evidence to give to the police?"

Ahh, the sticky wicket otherwise known as the police. "Last time I saw Mikey he told me if the cops became involved in his business with Lou someone would eat a bullet. Shari may have been the first. So I'm trying to string this out as long as I can before anyone else dies. Now you know why."

Ecstasy held her index finger up. "Hold on. Let's think. You said at first look Mikey was the guy, but now you're not so sure. Why do you say that?"

I told her about Shaft's 'Consider this payback from the Reverend' line, and about seeing Virdon with Shaft and Guido.

"Got it," she said. "But even with the whole snafu about the adult entertainment referendum—a Reverend killing people? I don't know."

"I don't know either. Last I knew the knuckle-busters worked for Mikey. Seeing them with Virdon kind of threw me for a loop."

"Think of them like strippers. Maybe it'll help you get your brain around it."

I made it about two seconds down that line of reasoning before I came to a screeching halt. "How on earth are they like strippers?"

Ecstasy snickered. "I know where your mind went, straight to the gutter. Not like that. Strippers are independent contractors. They can dance wherever and for whomever they want. Hire themselves out to the highest bidder. Maybe your guys did the same thing."

"But we have to figure out who they're working for now, and quickly. I believe whoever it is still has Annette. I just don't know why."

"Or she could already be dead too." Ecstasy plucked at her left earring.

I thought about Yvette's hard line with Shaft. "She's a bargaining chip. She needs to stay alive." I hoped I was right.

Because Ma had a saying: bad things come in threes. I pictured Lou as he lay dying. Shari in the coffin. I had to get Annette safe before she completed the trifecta.

Ecstasy said, "So what's your plan?"

I winced. "My plan is set in pretty warm jello—I'm still waiting for it to firm up."

Ecstasy rubbed her hands together. "You're so in luck, planning's my forte. Well, planning and lap dances. But let's focus on planning for now and see what we find."

I told her about the mansion in the woods, and the wall protecting it. "But first things first. We have to know if Annette's there, and we haven't learned that yet. If she is, the next step is to figure out a way to get in and rescue her. I don't think scaling the wall will work very well."

Ecstasy said, "Sounds like you need a little divine intervention."

"I'm not above trying anything that would help. It doesn't matter how I find the clues, I just want them. It's like pulling strings. I'll give each one a little tug and see what unravels."

"Yet there's a pretty important string you haven't tugged on yet," Ecstasy said. She placed her hands on her knees, cocked her head and smiled demurely. "Come on. Think."

"Spit it, sister," I said when I realized I didn't know what she was talking about.

Ecstasy looked at me like I was feeble. "A lot of people rely on faith to get them through the hard times. Maybe you can manipulate that holy string a little."

CHAPTER 29

The next morning I drove to the Castle View Free Church. After talking with Ecstasy I had a whole new way of looking at things, and I wanted Reverend Virdon to try my idea on for size.

A petite blond sat at the front desk, fully ready to meet my every need. "Good morning," she bubbled when I approached. "Praise the Lord."

"If you think it'll help. And after that, I'd like to speak to Reverend Virdon."

She seemed less eager to please. "I'm sorry. Reverend Virdon doesn't see drop-ins. Maybe I can help you instead."

"That's why you're here. So you can help. And the best way to help is to let me speak to Reverend Virdon."

"I don't…I can't…."

I'd asked for a bridge too far. Before today, her biggest challenge revolved around what color nail polish to wear. Thong or panty. Tough stuff like that.

I hoped she hadn't boned up on the art of subterfuge. "Let's try again, dear. What's your name?"

Back to stuff she could do. "Samantha Sutter." She beamed with happiness.

I extended a hand. "Paul Doyle. Where are you from, Samantha?"

"I live over towards Albion."

Aha. "Not Willy Sutter's daughter?"

She giggled. "He's like, my dad."

I needed to be like, twenty-two in a hurry. "No way! I went to school with him."

"No way! That's so weird!"

"Your dad tell you stories about growing up?"

She rolled her eyes. "Always bragging about his hotrods and stuff. Bor-ring." She stuck her finger against the side of her head and pulled the trigger. She lolled her head to the side and stuck her tongue from her mouth, just in case I couldn't keep up with her speed of play.

"He ever tell you about when he streaked through the school auditorium?"

"What?"

I leaned in. "Your dad was a wild man back in the day." I waved her off. "You don't want to know."

Oh, but she did. She clutched the edge of her desk like it might try to escape. "My dad went streaking?"

"We were playing Mount Blue for the conference championship. You remember how they do the pep rallies at the end of the school day?"

Her eyes snapped with excitement. I pictured her front row center. Shoot, she probably brought the pompoms.

"Imagine it, Samantha. The band's playing, the cheerleaders are screaming their lungs out. The players are getting fired up."

She bounced in her chair. Her eyes danced. She was with them. Doing her favorite cheer, right here in her seat.

"So, it's about over. The band plays the fight song. The students are all singing. You know the last line, 'What we can for dear old Lawrence...'"

She loudly finished, "And the good old gray and blue!" Roses bloomed on her cheeks.

"Then the auditorium door slammed open and a guy came charging in, painted blue from head to toe, with a big old bulldog mascot head. Naked as a jaybird."

"My dad?"

"As you never want to see him."

Her eyes widened.

"Don't worry, young lady. It was no big thing."

Samantha blushed furiously. "Mister Doyle!"

"Next time you see the old man, ask him how it's hanging."

She blushed brighter, splotches of red showing on her fair skin. "No!"

"Well, it'll be our little secret. About his little secret."

Samantha shook her head. "My dad a crazy man."

Time to change gears. "I heard Willy had a daughter. I had no idea she was so beautiful."

"Oh my!" She blushed harder, because now she had a challenge to live up to. My assessment of her. She stroked her hair back from her face and tucked it behind her ears. She checked her reflection in a tiny mirror clipped to her computer screen. When she believed she looked presentable she turned back to me, her cheeks still glowing.

I said, "Hard to believe I went to school with your dad, and now I meet his daughter, who runs the Castle View Free Church." I fanned myself. "I must be getting old."

"You're not old at all, Mister Doyle! I think you're...cute." She tittered.

Probably the last thing she'd called cute was a kitten. When she was thirteen.

However, I'd take cute if it kept the ball rolling. "You just made my day, girl."

Samantha dipped her head and studied her nails. I heard the slightest, "Awww." The sound a woman makes when you nail her. Right in the heart.

"Miss Sutter, the problem I come to you with is bigger than both of us. I need your church's help and I bet you're the woman who can make it happen. That's why they put you out front. Because you make things happen."

Samantha spoke slowly. "Reverend Virdon says I'm very diligent."

She glanced over her shoulder at a closed door, and looked back at me. Like she still thought I was cute.

Her smile held a secret. "Reverend Virdon is inside. Writing his memoirs, he says. Sometimes I look in and he's napping."

"Ministering to a flock like his is hard work."

"God Bless the Shepherd."

"Amen to that, sister."

Samantha stood up, walked to the door and quietly opened it. She peeked inside, closed the door, and turned to me. "He's looking out the window. He's not doing anything at all." She seemed disappointed, as if great men should be doing great things. And looking out the window hardly qualified.

I prodded. "So now would be a good time for me to see him, don't you think?"

She nodded. As she opened the door to let me in I said to her, "Tell your dad to keep Little Willy in the barn."

"Okay Mister Doyle," she said, her smile lighting the room.

The Reverend Johnny Virdon stood behind a huge oak desk and stared out a picture window that faced east. The sun remained hidden behind heavy clouds.

He turned to look at me. "May I help you?"

Virdon stood a shade over six feet. He was elegantly dressed in blue slacks, a white shirt, a blue and red-striped tie and a pinstriped vest. A light mist of gray had settled on his close-cropped black hair. He had soft hazel eyes, and his brown skin appeared unlined, as if time had forgotten to burden his face. He looked little like the animated preacher I'd seen bounding around the stage like a peacock with his tail on fire.

He looked serene.

Maybe knowing the Lord did that for you.

I extended my hand and he took it. "Paul Doyle."

Virdon motioned to a chair on the side of his desk. We both sat.

He said, "It takes a determined effort to get by Samantha. You must be very capable."

"Her immovable force met an irresistible object. Me."

He fought a smile. "Yes, quite. Irresistible."

"Reverend, while I could try to sweet talk you about why I'm here, I doubt my charm will get me as far as it did with Samantha."

Virdon motioned me to continue.

"I'm here for your help."

He shrugged. Rather modestly, it appeared.

"I'd like to take Annette Begley home now."

Virdon leaned toward me. "And you mention this to me because?"

I spread my hands toward him. "I was hired to find her."

"So...you are *here*...with *me*...because..."

"I am *here*...with *you*....because she used to live in your dormitory. Now she doesn't. I know where she was. Now I don't know where she is. I feel like I'm in the middle of a Johnny Virdon three-card Monte game."

He stood and paced the room. Like he was trying to get his head on straight. When he turned to face me, I sensed a sermon coming on.

"Mister Doyle," he said. "You live in a world of unfounded mistrust. Mistrust you veil in accusation. Because...you fear what you do not understand. And, ah, the fear that you feel is...well it is manifested in your attitude right now. About Annette. Toward me."

He looked at me like he expected a stirring chorus of hallelujahs.

Or at the very least, a handclap of praise.

"I hope you do better when you preach from a script," I said. "That sucked."

He stammered, "I speak the word of the Lord. What he inspires me to say, I do not edit. I believe."

"I believe, too. I believe he needs a new scriptwriter."

Virdon's words crackled as he spoke. "The world is full of doubters. It is because of people like you that the world needs people like me."

"Wow, and all the time I thought you did this for the glory of God."

He scowled. "*I* provide protection to the helpless. *I* provide nurture to the empty-hearted. *I* provide food where there is hunger. *I* provide a roof where there is no shelter."

"There you go again. I'd always heard there is no I in God. You can see my confusion."

Virdon gritted his teeth and fought to compose himself.

A sudden ease came over him. He placed his hands palm down on his desk and leaned toward me. "Maybe we started off on the wrong foot. My church has enough adversaries. I do not need another."

"Why do you have adversaries, Reverend? People have bought The Word for two thousand years. Maybe it's the way you peddle it that's the problem."

His face tightened. "I do not peddle anything. I am a servant of the Lord. He directs my actions. I do not do this for me. I do this for them." He glanced at an ornate cross on the wall. "In his Holy name," he quickly added.

"You say you're a good servant, but Annette and Shari disappeared from your care nonetheless. I attended Shari's calling hours last night. I'd love to tell you she looked beautiful, but she just looked dead."

Virdon twisted his hands. "I heard this, and I truly grieve her passing. We lose some of our flock along the way and each one saddens me. But it is freedom we ultimately provide, and freedom and safety are often at odds. Still, it is upon those very principles that our forefathers founded our country hundreds of years ago. And these principles are as alive today, and as necessary today, as when our ancestors first came here seeking freedom from the tyranny of their oppressors."

"Huh," I said. "That was a better speech than your last one. But the time for speeches is over. That freedom thing you mentioned didn't work out so well for Shari, did it? Or Annette. You have a thing against strippers, Rev?"

"I have a 'thing', as you call it, against indulging in the lust of defiling passion. I will do everything I can to shut that abomination down."

"I can see that. You picked a fight with The Limit and you got your holy ass kicked in the voting booth. All of a sudden, the guy who beat your referendum...dead. Wonder how that'll play out in the court of public opinion."

Virdon's nostrils flared. "What exactly are you saying?"

"I'm saying you have your nice, shiny side of the coin that you show everyone. But everyone has another side that they pray no one sees. Everyone. Even you. You can't hide that side from the Lord, and you sure as hell can't hide it from me."

Virdon slammed his hand on the desk. "I have nothing to hide! I am what you see!"

I leaned back in my chair. "What an interesting thing to say. Because I watch folks when they don't know they're being watched. Lately, I've been watching you. I see you skittering around, thinking nobody cares what you do. And one day where do you pop up? At a mansion in the middle of nowhere with Mikey Cross's former boys. You borrowing them for something? Any other strippers you need knocked off?"

Virdon angrily shook his head. "That's ridiculous!"

I reached out and tapped two fingers in his chest. "You think that's ridiculous? Well here's more. I say you're the one who owns that mansion in the woods, and there's some funny shit going on."

"What? What?"

"You own that mansion, don't you? Is that where your congregation's money goes? 'I'm Johnny Virdon and I'm on TV and I'm holier-than-thou and I want you to give me every penny you have to help me celebrate the glory of God.' Then little old ladies drop their cat food money in the offering plate so you can slap another god-awful *spire* on your palace? You know what those things look like? They look like you're flipping off the big guy."

Virdon struggled for composure. "You fool. One word and I could have you..."

I grabbed him by his vest and yanked him close. "Let me guess the one word. Kill. Judging by the hole in Shari Tappey's head you've used it before."

Virdon twisted away from my grasp. "I may not be who..." He shook his head. After a moment he gained control of his emotions and quietly said, "Everyone falls short in the eyes of the Lord, including me. But my shortcomings do not justify your wild accusations."

"Yeah, well I have a shortcoming too. When I beat the shit out of the idiot who killed Shari, I won't feel a bit of remorse. And here's something else. When I figure out what the hell is going on with your church you'll sink faster than a fat man in quicksand. So maybe it's time you pull your head out of your ass and start praying for your own damn salvation."

I gave him a healthy shove. He stumbled against his desk before catching himself.

When I walked out I slammed the door. Extra hard.

Samantha squealed and knocked over her tea. It spread rapidly, soaking the papers on her desk.

She looked like she might cry.

I leaned next to her and said, "I just told the Emperor he has no clothes. He comes walking out, you may want to avert your eyes."

CHAPTER 30

I had a little time before I went to Shari's early afternoon funeral so I stopped by the police station to see Venus. "We good?"

She seemed less than cuddly around the edges. "We're like a rubber band. We snap back pretty fast. Any updates on the case? Something you'll share with me for once?"

I ignored the barb. "What do you know about the Castle View Free Church?"

Venus poured herself a cup of coffee and one for me. When she sat at her desk she said, "Reverend Virdon moved here about ten years ago. Bought some land up on the ridge by the Interstate. Pretty soon construction vehicles showed up and before I knew it the largest church in the state was in our back yard."

She sipped her coffee. "Why do you ask?"

"Yesterday I saw Virdon with…" Warning bells went off in my head. "Yesterday I saw Virdon with some persons of interest."

"Persons of interest? Is that the best you can do? Paul, why are you still holding back? Tell me who these 'persons of interest' are. Ongoing police investigation here."

I pictured the bullet wound to Shari's right temple. Halfway between the ear and the eye socket. No exit wound. Small caliber. A perfectly neat and tidy killing. Likely done by one of these 'persons of interest.'

"I can't right…"

"Enough of this 'I can't' bullshit! Who do you think you are?"

"Venus. Venus. Trust me. Please. A couple more days."

She exhaled loudly. "Trust. You. You make it sound so easy."

Very slowly I said, "Another 'person of interest' told Lou no outsiders, or strippers would die. Shari's body tells me he means it."

Venus placed both palms on her desk. "You sonovabitch, you know who the killer is, don't you?"

I chose silence.

"You have no privileges when it comes to the law. Friend or not, you have no privileges with me."

"I'm not sure I'm asking for any."

"But you are, Paul! You are!" She slumped in her chair. "You got to understand, I'm getting heat too. Lou killed. A dancer at his club killed. Before them we had one homicide the entire year. Now we have two this week. Give me something to chase. Give us something to chase."

"I'll give you Chrome Livingston."

Venus rolled her eyes. "Oh thanks. I already have him."

"So peel back the onion a little more. Why do you think Livingston was at The Limit in the first place?"

"From what happened, it appears he was there to kill Lou."

"I respectfully disagree.'

She rolled her eyes. "Of course you do. Because you think you're smarter than the rest of us."

"Yeah, I am, but I'm not trying to be difficult. But think it through. What weapon did he carry?"

She thought about it. "The knife."

"There's easier ways to kill people. But threaten to use it on extraneous body parts and folks become compliant pretty quickly."

"So you're saying Livingston was there to threaten Lou?"

I shrugged. "Seems plausible."

"You think Livingston had Annette?"

"No. I think Livingston was a foot soldier who died the way foot soldiers do. I think Livingston's boss still has Annette. The big question is why."

"I'll bite. Why?"

We were getting awfully close to the truth. Maybe too close. But if I could give Venus a little nudge, and if Venus could be subtle about her investigation…and if the detective the State Police assigned could be subtle in his investigation…

I said, "I think Livingston's boss wants something. If I had to guess, I'd say it's The Limit. That's why Yvette is still alive, and why Livingston's boss still has Annette. He wants Yvette to sell him The Limit, and he's using Annette for inspiration."

Venus groused, "You're giving me half the story, which is half more than you've given me in the past. I suppose I should be grateful." She stood and walked to the window.

When she turned, the beginnings of an idea played on her face. "You said you saw Virdon and your 'persons of interest' together. I went straight past Virdon. Time to double back and see what he's up to."

She sat and snatched up her phone.

I placed my hand on hers and pushed the phone down. "He might not say much. I just came from the church."

Venus's eyes bored into mine. "Why, pray tell, were you at the church?"

"To get Virdon's help. Ecstasy and I worked out a plan to…"

"What!" She threw up a hand. "You and who?"

I'd never felt more naked. "Ecstasy?"

Her face was tighter than my jeans after they've been washed. "Let me get this straight. You've done everything you can to keep the police a mile away from this case, but you've chosen to confide in…a stripper? I like the sound of this." She threw herself against the back of her chair.

"Hey, she's a very smart…she's very smart." The surge of anger I felt toward Venus surprised me. It was a feeling I'd never felt toward her before.

"I've interviewed her, Paul. For heaven's sake, she's a…"

I put my hand up. "Don't say it."

We swapped contemptuous glares and unspoken curses.

Venus said, "Fine. Okay. You and Ecstasy devised a plan. Care to share its brilliance with me?"

"I thought Virdon might know something about Annette, so I decided to leverage that 'man-of-the-cloth' thing he trumpets. Get him to do the Christian thing. If he helps, I don't care if it's due to guilt. I don't care if he's looking for absolution. I don't care if he's so scared shitless about saving his own soul that he begs me to let him help. But he's the key, I'm positive."

"That's the plan you and the…" Venus swallowed hard. "That's the plan you and Ecstasy devised? Muscle up on a Reverend and scare him into helping you? Yet you don't even know for sure he's involved."

"Oh, Virdon's involved. I don't know why and I don't know how, but that mother is involved."

Venus slapped her desk. "You know that, huh? So if you and your little friend had such an airtight plan, why are we having this conversation?"

I ground my teeth and growled, "Because I screwed up with Virdon! Does that make you feel better? Is that what you want to hear? And to top it off, I may have spilled the beans about something else."

"And what, pray tell, could that have been?"

I hissed, "You're so frigging smart, you tell me."

"Don't tell me you mentioned seeing him with your 'persons of interest.'"

"Okay, I won't."

She stood and paced the room. When she turned, he face was twisted with frustration. "You think Virdon is involved, and now he knows you know, and who knows what will happen next?"

"Fine, sure. You ever see a plan that seems perfect, but you get a little excited, a little hot under the collar, and your plan goes poof?"

"The fact you had a plan at all surprises me to no end. The poof part, that doesn't surprise me in the least."

"Jesus, Venus, shit like this probably doesn't happen to superstars of the detective world. But to the rest of us not named you, it occasionally does."

She leaned closer to me. Her angry breath beat against my face. "But keep your mouth shut with Virdon for more than two seconds and we're not having this discussion."

"Yeah, I could have kept my mouth shut. I could have waited till the cows came home, trying to find the connection between Virdon and my 'mysterious persons of interest,' which still may not help me find Annette. But the whole time I'm screwing around, it's tick-tick-tick-tick-tick. And I already saw one girl in a creek, so I'm not ready to sit around with my thumb up my ass, only to find Annette in the next creek I see."

Venus jabbed me in the chest. "So you and your girlfriend come up with this plan. Now you've gotten Virdon stirred up and he'll get your famous 'persons of interest' stirred up, and look where it's gotten you. But that's Paul Doyle in a nutshell, isn't it? Smashing the hornet's nest and acting surprised when they sting you."

We both took a second to catch our breath. Venus sat down and stared at me. No forgiveness in her eyes. She lowered her gaze and rubbed her temples. "Paul, Paul, Paul," she said, shaking her head. "What were you doing? Be a detective instead of a wrecking ball. Now they're on to you and you have nothing to work with."

"Maybe I was a little impulsive."

Venus rocked forward in her chair. "A little? You're being a bit too lenient on yourself. There's no way I'd pull a stunt like this."

That simple 'Once again I'm smarter than you' sentence that she trotted out from time to time cranked my flame from simmer to boil. I bolted from my chair and glowered at her. "I'm sure you wouldn't. You'd wait. You'd hope. You'd file your nails and do your hair and pray a clue would come floating your way. And if nothing did, you could always call on your old buddy Paul Doyle to beat the daylights out of someone until he talked. After all, it's worked before, hasn't it?"

I shoved my chair. It skittered across the floor and slammed into the wall.

Her eyes grew wide. As I stormed out her door, she started to speak.

But I was too mad to listen.

Besides, it would have ruined a perfectly dramatic exit.

And to top it off, she may have been right.

After I left Venus's office I called Ecstasy. I could tell I woke her, for weariness dripped from her voice like honey. "So tell me how it went with the Reverend." I could hear her sigh as she stretched.

"Not good. I never got to ask him where Annette is."

"What do you mean, you never got to ask him? That's why you went. All you had to do was blurt it out."

"The blurting out part I did real well." I told her how our conversation had been in freefall almost from the first words I'd uttered.

She sighed. "Unfortunate turn of events. Tell me about his face when you mentioned killing Shari. What did he do? How did he react?"

"Pure shock, like he couldn't believe I was accusing him."

"Maybe his shock was because you put the pieces together. A man like him, he has a lot to protect. A lot to lose."

"Either way, our plan to motivate him has gone by the wayside."

She said, "My dad was in the Army and he liked to say 'No plan survives first contact with the enemy.' I guess ours didn't either."

"Got any other tricks up your sleeve?"

"Let me sleep on it." She laughed through a soft fog, like she was already halfway there. "Paul, one last thing. There is some good in how your day has gone so far."

I groaned. "How do you figure?"

"I'm pretty sure it will only get better from here."

After the funeral I drove to the abandoned farmhouse on Route 3. I pulled in behind it and got in Cash's car.

I handed him a cup of coffee and sipped my own. After I explained what had happened he said, "So you're not any closer to solving this case."

"It's Virdon. Or Mikey." I had a little more coffee. "No…Virdon. Or Mikey."

"Pick one, Paul. It can't be both."

"Okay. I picked."

Cash chuckled. "You have to say it for the record, or I won't be able to laugh at you when you're wrong."

"Thanks for having my back. I'm leaning toward Virdon. He makes me sick the way he stands up there and preaches about holiness and righteousness and whatever the hell else a preacher preaches. But we know he had Shari, and she's dead. We've seen him with Shaft and Guido. How do you feel about guilt by proximity?"

Cash sucked in a long breath before he spoke. "When I was sixteen, my folks found some weed in my sock drawer. They didn't ask any questions, they just assumed I was guilty. Weed in my sock drawer. It had to be mine, right?"

I could feel a curveball coming on. "It wasn't yours?"

He sipped the coffee. "My older brother. But two things. If I told them, would they believe me anyway? And even if they did believe me, I'd just be ratting out family. In my mind that would have been worse."

"So?"

"So they grounded me for the entire summer. And they checked my sock drawer every day. But not before I did."

I got it. "So I shouldn't believe what I see in the Reverend's sock drawer?"

"Believe the facts. After you verify them."

I considered myself sufficiently chastened. Even if I didn't like it. I asked him about Virdon's latest trip to the mansion.

"You spun him up, that's for sure. After you left, he busted his ass getting out here. I had trouble keeping up, and you know how I drive."

"Did Virdon go straight there?"

Cash shook his head. "No, he went antique shopping and got a pedicure."

"You're right. Stupid question. Did you find out who's building the development?"

"Someone named Cantu Constantine. Never heard of him before. You?"

"Must be a guy with more dough than brains. Who would build a golf course like that out here? He can't make a go of this."

"Can too."

"What?"

Cash looked like the cat that ate the canary. "You said he can't make a go of it. I said he Cantu. As in Cantu Constantine."

When I didn't even approach a laugh, he looked concerned. "Talk to me."

"Yvette and I spoke after the funeral."

Cash tensed. "Problems?"

"I think so. You know she lives out in the sticks by herself, no neighbors around. Sometimes that's best, no neighbors in your business. But when your guy has been killed and your niece has been kidnapped and your cat just died and you've been threatened, maybe living alone isn't the best thing after all."

Cash rubbed his chin. "What happened now?"

"Remember that old Chevy Lou had out front? Someone smashed the windows last night. Shredded the interior. She said she's scared, and she may give in whether she gets Cherry back or not."

Cash lurched forward. "Dude, I knew I should have been there. I could have…"

"I know. I think the same thing. Yvette talked a good game about being strong, but it's different when they bring the fight to you."

"So she's not going to stand up to them?"

I tossed my empty coffee cup onto the backseat floor. "Honestly, I don't know. I'm sure they feel they rattled her. No reason to let up now. Continue to turn the heat up a little at a time, eventually she's going to crack. On top of this, the State Police detective went back to see her. He wasn't quite as understanding as Venus when she said she had nothing to say to him. She may have bought herself a day, but she's getting shoved pretty hard from both sides."

Cash's brow wrinkled. "I'd say this is a good time to hide Yvette away for the duration. If they can't find her, they can't hurt her. One less person in the line of fire."

Made sense to me. "Where are you going to take her?"

"Plausible deniability, man. Don't you worry your little head, I got this."

CHAPTER 31

I waited all day and didn't come up with any more bright ideas about who was involved in Annette's disappearance. Cash had left with Yvette until we could figure the whole thing out, so I didn't expect to hear from him for a while. I'd pretty much exhausted all the leads I could think of. So I grabbed a beer from my fridge on the off-chance it would exponentially increase my brain power. I felt so much smarter after I finished it I immediately grabbed another. I sat at the dinner table and kicked the problem around, swig by swig.

Everyone has a weak spot. One thing that makes them vulnerable. Superman has kryptonite. Spiderman has Mary Jane. Pumpkin pie with whipped cream slays me. So if guys like us can be had, Mikey and Virdon had to have weaknesses, too. A thing they'd bend to that would allow me to catch them unawares.

Something I could use to rescue Annette. I just had to hit on it.

I glanced at the calendar. I had seven days left. Seven days before Shaft said all hell would break loose.

What did I really know about the case? Anything that I'd overlooked?

A guy from Texas was involved. Chrome Elvis Livingston. So what?

I dunno. It was a question I'd never asked before. Why would a man from Texas find his way to Maine? Christ, even Knob Noster, Missouri is more appealing than Westfield. And it's only half as far away.

Texas floated in the foggy background of my mind. I finished the beer, closed my eyes and tried to bring the idea to the front.

Something about Texas. It hung tantalizing close, yet refused to leave the shadows.

I'd recently seen something about someone from Texas.

What? And who?

It wasn't Livingston. I already knew he came from there.

Annette and Shari had been born and raised in Maine.

I hadn't thought too much about anyone else.

Not true. I'd thought endlessly about Ecstasy. But she came from Santa Fe. That was Arizona. Or New Mexico. One of those western states. I took another chug of beer. New Mexico. Highly likely.

The only other people I'd thought about were Johnny Virdon and Mikey Cross.

Something flickered in my brain. A story I'd read on the Internet.

About Johnny Virdon.

And Texas.

Johnny Virdon and Texas.

Bingo.

Desperate times call for desperate measures.

The phone rang four times before Venus picked it up. "Hullo?" she mumbled.

"Hey Veenie, you remember anything about Johnny Virdon and Texas from awhile back? 'Cause this guy right here on the telephone talking to you does."

I heard a mumble in the background. Then to me, "Hold on a second."

I had half a beer of patience left.

I heard a door close. Venus came back on the phone. "You talk any louder and I won't need a phone to hear you. And do you know what time it is?"

"It's case-cracking time, girl."

"Well, it's also after midnight."

I looked at the clock.

At the table. Five empties indicted me.

"Ah...yeah. It wasn't earlier."

"Well, it is now."

Her voice sounded cold. Not sweet and friendly like when we usually talked.

Of course. She had family troubles. She'd told me about family troubles.

Nice try, but that wasn't it and I knew it. I had a fully-prepared concession speech ready to go when she said, "Is it important?"

"Sorry, Veenie. I got carried away."

"You only call me Veenie when you drink, so I won't ask. I'm up, so talk to me."

I took a deep breath. Broaching the subject hadn't gone so well the last time. But she said go ahead, so I did. "Remember when I told you about seeing Reverend Virdon and my 'persons of interest?' I've been trying to find the thing that ties them together. Then I thought about Lou shooting Chrome Livingston. We know Livingston's from Texas. Now why would he come from Texas all the way to Maine? Shoot, I wouldn't, except I was born here."

Venus yawned. "I can see why this kept you up all night. You're riveting as usual."

"Hey, it took Picasso a while to paint the Sistine Chapel. I don't think the Pope stood there with a stopwatch."

She snickered. "Picasso? You're an idiot."

"Maybe, but you won't think so after you hear this. Livingston worked for Virdon. And Virdon had Lou killed. I believe this to be true. Case cracked."

She muttered a curse. "The most famous Reverend in the state had a strip joint owner killed? Please tell me you woke me up in the middle of the night with facts to support this. Real evidence. Not your famous beer theories."

"It's gotta be him. I just know it."

"Paul, it's pretty hard for us to arrest Virdon in the middle of a sermon based on 'It's gotta be.' Why on God's green earth does it have to be him?"

"Livingston's from Texas. Then I remembered reading about the Castle View Free Church, and one article said Virdon was originally from Texas, too. Livingston worked for someone, right? Common sense says a guy from Texas. Remember Science class? Molecules cluster for a reason."

Venus grumbled, "Facts, Paul. Not bullshit about molecules. What else?"

"Okay, here's a fact you can try on for size. Shaft and Guido used to work for Mikey. Those boys will kill you in a heartbeat. But lately I've seen them with Virdon. If it was only one time I'd call it a coincidence, tip my hat and be on my way. But today I drove by Virdon's church and Shaft's car was parked outside."

"Good night, Paul."

"Wait, wait, wait! There's more."

"This reeks of desperation, and I'm out of patience. I want the truth about this case or we're done."

The truth. As if I even knew what the truth was anymore. The slope I was sliding down seemed painfully steep. "I know it was Virdon or Mikey. I just don't know which one. And that's the truth."

Venus cleared her throat. "A minute ago you told me it was Virdon. But it could be Mikey. Hell, it could be neither. For all you know it could be both. Whoever it is, you don't have the first clue. You have to stop accusing people based on a knee-jerk reaction."

"It's not a knee-jerk. It's just…the clock is ticking and I'm afraid it's going to strike midnight before I find her."

"Okay, okay," Venus said. "I understand. I do, Paul. But even if one of them is involved in a kidnapping or murder, you just can't go throwing accusations around. You've been impulsive before, and it hasn't worked out great."

I could have told her to get bent, but she was right. About five years earlier, a woman hired me to find her ex-husband. She'd come to me with a black eye, a broken collarbone and a sob story about how he'd roughed her up when she wouldn't allow him to see their kids for Easter. She asked me very sweetly if there was any way I could please find him so the police could take him into custody because she couldn't go through life afraid of him any longer.

So I found him. And before I turned him over to the cops I might have roughed him up a bit. Because you don't beat women just because you can't get your way when it comes to your kids. Someone had to teach him the way of the world.

Then the truth, as it usually does, came out. He had joint custody. And it was his weekend to have the kids. And she was a bitch. And it was her new boyfriend who'd roughed her up. And she'd conveniently decided the bruises would be just the ticket to go back to court and be awarded sole custody of her children.

Although I was never arrested, that little stunt had cost me a few brownie points with the Westfield police department. Because I was impulsive. Which, given Venus's analysis, still seemed to be my M. O.

"Paul, I don't mind kicking this around to see what comes up. But no guesses. I need facts. There probably are some facts rattling around in that brain of yours. Let's talk about Annette first. Who do you think has Annette, and why?"

"I was positive Mikey had her. He was trying to take over The Limit and his guys took her when she left the dormitory."

"Think or know?"

"Think. I saw tire tracks in the mud by the dorm. A lot of footprints. I was positive it was Shaft and Guido."

Venus sounded more energetic. "Why did you think it was them? And why are you unsure now?"

"I thought it was them because Mikey had threatened to harm Annette unless Lou sold him the club. But I changed my mind when Mikey said Shaft and Guido didn't work for him anymore. I saw them with Virdon and that clinched it."

"Anything else you can think of that has to do with Annette?"

"When I saw Mikey, he told me if the cops were involved in his little situation with Lou someone would know what a bullet in the brain feels like. I always thought he was talking about Annette. But maybe he meant Shari."

She exhaled loudly. "Losing that girl is a damn shame. I can't imagine what it's going to do to Gerald and his wife."

"I think Shari was the glue that held them together."

Venus sighed again. "I think you're right. They wake up one morning as parents and go to bed with no idea who they are anymore. Think they'll make it?"

I thought about it. "I think I'll pass."

"Let's talk about Shari a bit more. Do you think Virdon killed her?"

"When I saw the body, I assumed Mikey killed her. He still needed Annette as collateral until he got the club, but he didn't need Shari. And he'd threatened to kill strippers. Someone put Shari where she would be found. That's a pretty big 'See, I told you so' in my book."

"How does Virdon fit in with Shari?"

"Could be two ways. She was at his dormitory. Plus the guys who took her work for him now."

"Fact or opinion about them working for Virdon?"

I sighed. "Opinion. I saw them with Virdon, plus Mikey said…"

"Plus Mikey said they didn't work for him anymore."

"Fact."

Venus chuckled. "It's a fact that Mikey said it. But it may or may not be true."

"Now we're getting somewhere. You wanna try the 'fact or opinion' game with Lou?"

Venus said, "Did Virdon have a motive for killing Lou?"

"Well…Lou was responsible for Virdon losing the adult entertainment referendum." I thought about it. "Opinion."

"But let's follow that. Why did Virdon want to shut the club down in the first place?"

"The bastard hates boobies. Opinion."

Venus groaned. "Playtime is over, Paul. Why did Virdon want to shut the club down?"

"He said it was a den of iniquity. Bad for you, bad for me. Something like that. It was so catchy I began to beatbox. Then the congregation started chanting for the key to lock the place up."

"So, in your mind that was his objective. Shut the club down. How would killing Lou help him shut it down? Only the voters, or the lack of customers, would do that."

"You should see the place now," I said. "Packed to the gills, the last time I went."

"Like a car accident, right? Everyone driving by stops to look. Now let's talk about Mikey. You said he wanted the club. Why?"

I exhaled like a deflating balloon. "Question I've been trying to get my brain around. Because it makes money? Because he wants to own a strip club?"

Venus asked, "Anything else?"

"Huh."

"Huh, you didn't hear me, or huh, you have a thought?"

"Maybe Mikey wants the site. Knock the club down and build something else on it."

"Good," Venus said. "Any of those are viable options. So how would killing Lou help Mikey get what he wants?"

"Yvette said Lou would only sell over his dead body. Maybe Mikey called him on it."

Venus said, "Huh."

"Was that a 'did you hear me' huh, or a 'thought' huh?"

"While we did this I made a chart. Mikey and Virdon across the top, Annette, Shari, and Lou on the side. I put a checkmark by who would benefit the most by each of them dying."

I didn't need a chart to know the answer. "For every one of them, Mikey Cross."

"Time we go see Mikey and let him know we're serious."

I said, "If Mikey's involved, strong arm doesn't work. Speaking from experience."

"Strong arm didn't work for you. That doesn't mean we can't..."

"Can't what? Have the State Police or Augusta cops go barging into Mikey's office and demand he stop killing people and give Annette back? He's already made it clear. If he sees the cops around you'll get Annette back, all right. In a box."

Venus cursed a blue streak. "You're buying his threat?"

"Not sure we have a choice. If he ordered Lou shot, and he had Shari killed, that's a pattern even I can follow. Still, we don't have to rush this. If it's Mikey that's truly doing this, he appears to have a very specific date in mind, and it's seven days from now. Until then we don't use brute force. We tiptoe."

"I don't like Mikey calling the shots one little bit. Are you telling me, in your professional opinion, he has us over a barrel?"

"Venus, in my professional opinion, Mikey *thinks* he has us over a barrel. It's in our best interest to keep him thinking that for as long as we can. We use the seven days we have left. And while he's celebrating how he's screwing us, we figure out a way to screw him right back."

"Okay, Mister Smart Guy. How do you propose we do that?"

I twisted the top off another beer. "If I was you, I'd start with Elvis."

CHAPTER 32

I woke up the next morning with the same questions I'd gone to sleep mulling over.

Was it Mikey? Or Virdon?

Virdon? Or Mikey?

It had to be one of them. Unquestionably. Unless…

Venus had said one thing that planted the tiniest seed of a thought in my mind, and it had floated around in the beer all night. By the time the sun came up an idea had begun to blossom. But I'd need a little help nurturing this to full bloom.

When I was a boy Pops told me, 'Paul, you don't have to be the smartest person in the room, you just have to know who they are. Then get them to work for you.' So while I might not be able to slay this dragon on my own, I had no compunction against asking an old friend to kick in a little effort on my behalf.

Hard to believe the guy whose chin I split open on a football field many years ago would be the person I turned to first.

Lieutenant Simeon Mathers, who ran the State Police Major Crimes Unit North office, was one of Maine's best high school football players of my generation. Back then the state had an annual all-star game, with northern Maine farm boys coming down to Portland to get our asses kicked by the city boys from the south. That's where Mathers and I met.

I played offensive tackle. As I settled down in my stance on the first play, I found myself facing an equally large and twice-as-fierce looking defensive end from Deering.

"I'm gonna make you eat dirt all day!" he snarled before the first snap.

"I prefer pizza."

He rocked back in his stance and looked at me. We snapped the ball, I leveled him, the running back blew by and went sixty-five yards for a touchdown.

We celebrated like we'd just gotten laid.

And never scored again. We lost, 42-7.

When we went through the handshake line after the game most of the southern boys tried not to laugh as they said 'good game.' Except for the defensive end. When he came to me he said, "You suck, 73!"

I lowered my shoulder, lunged forward, and my pads caught him dead on the chin. He fell backwards and blood gushed all over his commemorative all-star game jersey. He tried to claw his way back to me.

I rapidly jogged to the bus. Lucky for him, I made it.

And now I needed a favor.

"What's up, 73?" he said when I leaned into his office.

"How's the chin?"

"Chicks dig scars, man. I tell 'em I earned it snuffing ragheads in the war."

"Your National Guard unit never left the state."

"You know that, and I know that. Chicks don't know that." He grinned, prominently displaying the jagged line on the left side of his chin. Who said Paul Doyle would never leave his mark on society?

Mathers wore his light brown hair in a flattop, which accentuated his nearly square head. He still looked like a fire-breathing defensive end. Or G.I. Joe as a cop.

He picked up a coffee cup with a picture of his wife on it, leaned back and rested his mirror-polished black shoes on the desktop. "I haven't seen you since last summer. Must be important."

"I'm organizing a touch football game for Thanksgiving. You in?"

Mathers laughed. "My football days are long gone. You?"

I shook my head. "This old lineman can hardly touch his knees anymore. But you won't believe it. I'm a jogger now."

He dropped his feet to the floor, leaned around the desk and looked a little too long at my bulk. "It shows."

"Hey, don't judge. Up to five miles a day."

Mathers snickered. "Just yanking your chain. Maybe ten-twelve years ago I was as heavy as a boat anchor and didn't give a rat's ass if I sunk, until one day I met my sweetie." He pointed at her picture on his cup. "So I bought myself a treadmill. And worse, I started using it for more than a clothes rack. Now I'm this fine piece of man-flesh you observe in front of you."

He looked at me kind of funny. "I'm banking that you have a new woman in your life." Mathers knew Eileen, and I didn't think he'd disapprove one bit at an upgrade. Or even a one-for-one replacement.

I hemmed and hawed a bit. "I met her a little while ago, and…"

"And you became a jogger?"

"Yeah."

"You spend a lot more time checking the mirror before you see her? Don't drink like you used to? Stopped cussing so much? Try not to fart in public? You think about her from the time you wake up until you fall asleep, and then the thoughts get better?"

I'm pretty sure my cheeks glowed.

Mathers smiled like a big brother. "Who'd a thunk it? Paul Doyle's in love."

"I'm not sure what it is," I said, feeling like a tenth-grader. "It *is* something, though. She's something else entirely."

Mathers grinned broadly. "I look forward to meeting her. But you didn't drive down here to talk about women, even from the Casanova of cops. So what can I do for you?"

"You hear about that new housing development and golf course up on Route 3 by China Lake?"

Mathers leaned forward. "I heard some houses were going up. Last time I drove by the course it was still being built. Is it done?"

I told him what we'd seen.

Mathers leaned toward me. "No shit? Maybe I can get a round or two in before winter."

"You better take out a loan. Membership starts at two hundred thousand, and that's before you pull your clubs out of the trunk. Another ten grand a year for annual fees. Their website says they let twenty-four non-members play there on Mondays. Two hundred bucks a round. Still interested?"

Mathers looked deflated. "Maybe I'll take my kids to putt-putt."

"Now that we've gotten golf out of your system, what do you know about Mikey Cross?"

"You on to something with him?"

I shook my head. Innocently.

Mathers studied my handsome visage for an extra beat before he said, "Mikey's clean as a whistle. Except not really. Okay, most of his stuff is clean. Apartments and office buildings. Nice park downtown that I drive by every day. But other stuff…shit. He's bad and we all know it. Proving it's been a bitch, though. Few years back rumor was the Feds had a guy with a wire and thought he was in with Mikey. They didn't hear shit until the guy hit the ground. Then all they heard was 'thump.'"

"Lucky Valentine."

"Not so lucky after all. Now, I don't know if it was fact or fiction that the Feds were involved, but the story tells well around the cop campfire." Mathers tapped his foot on the floor and studied me. "Why? You know something about Mikey that maybe I should know?"

"Not a thing. Making small talk."

"I believe that…not at all."

"Okay, correction. Nothing to tell you right now, Sim. Just kicking a thought around."

"Seriously, he's no good. If you help us get closer to him, we'll probably let you speed on the Interstate for a year free of charge."

"With my car, speeding's not an option. But I'd like to hold my ideas to myself for now. Something comes up, we'll talk. Okay?"

"Paul, of all people, you know how Mikey is. Reminds me of a used car salesman. You see him on the street and he gives you his cheesiest grin. But when he slaps you on the back, it could be a dagger going in."

"I know." Boy, did I ever.

Mathers said, "I didn't see it up close, but I remember the story about your dad. You have your beef with Mikey, and I hope you square up with him before he gets rejected at the Pearly Gates. I have other problems with Mikey and they're not getting better with age. So if you have information that can maybe close the loop around his neck, I'd appreciate it. We know he's as crooked as a rattler, but it's been hell to prove."

"Fair enough. How about Johnny Virdon?"

Mathers sputtered, "How'd we get from a jerk like Mikey Cross to old holier-than-thou Johnny Virdon?"

"I'm in the favor-asking business. Got any spares?"

Mathers pulled on his nose. "I'm listening. I'm not promising, but I'm listening."

"I'm still involved in the Lou Principi case."

His eyebrows shot up.

"Unofficially," I quickly added.

"Of course."

"Remember the girl they found behind the high school in Westfield?"

"Gerald Tappey's daughter. I see him here and there. Helluva thing when your kid dies."

I forced out a breath. "Before she was killed, Shari and her friend Annette were living in Reverend Virdon's dormitory."

"I hadn't heard that yet. Sounds like you're a little ahead of us on this unofficial thing."

"I've been chasing it for a while now. Started with a stripper who went missing. Simple little case, right? Find her and be home before dinner. Now Lou's dead and Shari Tappey is dead, and I still haven't found the stripper. But everywhere I turn, I keep tripping over Mikey Cross and Reverend Virdon. That's an awful big coincidence in my book. It's possible one of them is involved, Sim."

Mathers bounced a pen on his desk. "So what's your favor?"

"Crazy idea I got all of a sudden, courtesy of a late-night talk with Venus Robinson. It may not be one of them playing this game after all. It may be both."

CHAPTER 33

Venus called me at noon, just after I'd returned from seeing Mathers. "You awake? I hate to disturb your beauty rest. You need that more than anything."

"Hey, be pleasant. Lots of women are. I ran five miles. A hundred pushups, a hundred situps. What did you do to improve yourself today?"

She scoffed. "Venus is the goddess of love and beauty. Hard to improve on that."

She had me there. "Any luck with the boys down in Texas?"

"First time I called down there I didn't make much headway. No one seemed to know anything, or maybe they just weren't talking to a chick city detective from East Podunk. So I called Simeon Mathers an hour or so ago. We compared notes, mostly about you by the way."

"Must have been a fascinating discussion."

"Endlessly. Seems Mathers is doing some digging, too. Apparently at your request."

"Do you blame him? I'm so freaking irresistible."

Venus chuckled. "I say delusional, but to each his own. Anyway, Mathers gave me the name of a detective from Austin who he knows, and the detective helped connect a few dots regarding the checkered history of Chrome Elvis Livingston."

A heartbeat of hope blipped in my chest. "Whoa. I feel all shook up."

"I hope that'll be your last Elvis reference. Not sure I can stomach another."

"Come on, it's fun. Give it a try. Just avoid a blue suede shoes reference. That's my specialty."

She sighed, then said, "Don't be so cruel to me. Okay?"

I leaned back. "Ahh, that's the spirit. What else you got?"

"If we're done playing Name That Tune, as you deduced, Texas appears to be the fertile breeding ground for a whole lot of things currently going on here."

"Not just Livingston?"

"Not remotely. The Austin detective referred me to a Sergeant Raymundo Vasquez in San Antonio, who waxed rhapsodic when talking about Livingston's relationship with a 'person of interest' named Enrique Cruz."

"Our Enrique Cruz? The one made famous by Livingston's burning skull tattoo?"

Venus said, "I can only assume that's the Enrique Cruz he was talking about. Vasquez and I spoke for quite a few minutes, and one particular story caught my attention."

"Is it a story you'd care to share?"

"I like to collaborate on police work whenever possible. Do you like to collaborate, Mister Doyle?"

The trap had been sprung. I rubbed my forehead and grumbled, "More and more, I've come to learn collaboration can be an effective Catch-the-Bad-Guy technique. Wonder why we never tried it before?"

Venus sighed. "God only knows."

"What else did Sergeant Vasquez tell you?"

"He told me enough to pique my interest. And left out enough to make me giddy about the information a good detective could learn."

"Jeez, you don't know one, do you?"

I could sense a smile on her end. "I know one feller seems to fill the bill. This one's right up your alley, Paul. Vasquez alluded to a link forged in San Antonio many years ago that we might be able to use to put Mikey over a barrel. For good."

"He didn't tell you the secret?"

"Vasquez said he knew few actual details and he wasn't interested in discussing what he knew on the phone. But he did say if someone came down there he would try to set up a meeting with a 'person of interest,' and we all know how much you like those. All off-the-record, though. He said there might be some lives at stake so it had to stay hush-hush, at least down in Texas. He said the guy you might meet wouldn't talk to the cops. He said that a couple of times."

"If I learn something, is it a secret I can keep all to myself?"

Venus gave me one of her best laughs. "I think you've done more than enough of that already. So on the off-chance you're inclined to sniff around in the Texas sun, I'm sure your friendly local and State law enforcement officials would love to hear what you learn."

CHAPTER 34

Cash and I left Portland that day in a late afternoon snowstorm and landed in sunny San Antonio, where it certainly wasn't snowing. It felt like a hundred degrees, although the rental car shuttle driver told us it was only eighty-four. I removed my jacket and wished I'd worn a short-sleeved shirt instead of my Intrepid Maine Woodsman sweater.

Over long johns.

Cash, adorned in khaki slacks and a loud Hawaiian shirt, sighed pleasantly. "This is the life." He looked me up and down. "Hey, you're pretty fair skinned. You bring sunscreen?"

"That was on your list of things to buy."

"No, I bought the plane tickets."

"That's right. You buy the plane tickets, I get the sunscreen. Even Steven."

Cash rolled his eyes. "Relatively speaking."

A window behind Sergeant Raymundo Vasquez's desk near the southwest corner of the San Antonio Police Department's central substation provided him an obstructed view of South Frio Road. A less obstructed view, had it been available, would have revealed heavily-traveled railroad tracks to the west, a vacant lot, a hospital and the ragged edge of low-income housing. An unobstructed view east wouldn't have been much more preferable. An elevated section of Interstate 35 hovered nearly overhead, providing a persistent rattle and hum from thousands of passing vehicles each day.

The town I grew up in had no traffic lights. For me the vast city of San Antonio was next to intolerable.

Sergeant Vasquez didn't appear to mind. He told us he'd worked on the San Antonio police force since 1987. I doubt much about the traffic caught his attention anymore. It was just another daily slice of life passing him by on the way to his retirement.

Vasquez, heavy-jowled and pot-bellied with thinning black hair combed straight back, pointed to a chair beside his metal desk. I took it. Cash hovered expectantly. Vasquez pointed to an unused chair at the desk beside his. "You can stand, or you can sit. Makes no difference to me."

Cash took the chair and pulled it near mine. "I choose sit."

Vasquez said, "Your persuasive friend, Detective Venus Robinson, is she as beautiful as her voice?"

I beamed. "She's as beautiful as her name implies."

Vasquez sighed. "As I age, once more I dream of my youth. Of the women I knew and loved and wish I might love once more. The beauty of these women I cannot forget. And when a voice such as hers I hear, I wonder, is she another angel of my dreams?" Vasquez looked out the window toward the railroad tracks.

"We could maybe get her to send you an autographed picture. I own the collector's set," Cash offered, before I applied an elbow to his ribs.

Vasquez turned back to us. "The perfection of Venus Robinson I hold in my mind is preferable to me."

Cash started to speak. I held up my hand. "Detective Robinson told you we'd like information on a man you arrested years ago. Chrome Elvis Livingston. You remember him?"

Vasquez looked pained. "Would you remember such a name? Of course you would."

"What can you tell us about him?"

"Unfortunate circumstances brought Mister Livingston and me together. Unfortunate for him, at least. While on patrol I received notification of a domestic dispute. What I found was not domestic, although it was certainly a dispute. I observed Mister Livingston assaulting a working woman outside a club on Flores Avenue."

I asked, "Can you tell me who he worked for?"

Vasquez tapped his fingertips together. "So many years later, perhaps you would first tell me your interest in a man such as Livingston."

"We're interested in why he's dead," Cash said.

I patted his leg. "As Mister Cashman said, Livingston is dead. It appears he was performing the same type of work in Maine as he did here many years ago."

"And you will explain your involvement with Mister Livingston?"

"My former client killed him."

Vasquez rubbed his forehead. "Perhaps we should not speak of this further."

"There is a young woman involved," Cash said, his first intelligent input since I could remember. "She is a tall redhead with deep blue eyes and skin like the richest cream. She moves with the grace of a dancer. She is…"

"*Es bella?*" Vasquez asked.

Cash smiled. "Beyond your imagination."

Vasquez walked toward the front of the office. For a long time he watched the trucks rumbling by on the interstate. He spoke to the window. "There are some stones you may pry up and glance underneath without disturbing the surrounding earth. It will appear as if the stone was never moved at all." He sighed. "I do not believe this is such a stone."

Cash jumped up. "There a can around here?"

Vasquez pointed toward the hallway. "Last door on the right."

He watched Cash leave. "He is impulsive."

"A good man, but quick with his words."

"And, I fear, quicker to deed."

I sensed his reluctance. "Do you believe his impulsiveness may cause problems?"

Vasquez tapped his finger against his lips. "Can he be trusted with a secret?"

"He can." I hoped.

Vasquez spread his hands. "Visions of a redhead with skin of cream clouds my judgment. As does the beautiful Detective Venus Robinson of Westfield, Maine. I am forever a fool, so that I will share this with you is inevitable. You ask me about Chrome Livingston, but it is not his story at all. In actuality it is the story of Enrique Cruz, of his greed and his pride. It is also the story of his family, which means it's a story of heartbreak and sadness. It is a story I cannot properly tell."

Vasquez seemed troubled. "You may find answers with this man." He scribbled a name on a notepad, tore it off and handed it to me.

He tapped the name on the paper. "You will quickly form an opinion of him. Yet I ask you to understand, he has suffered much. If you choose to judge him, please judge him kindly."

CHAPTER 35

Steady hands poured their first drink of the day just past 8 AM. Whiskey and water with minimal ice, for the man who knows where he wants to go and the fastest way to get there. Ken Bartholomew motioned us to the deck of his small house, perched among rock, cactus and scrub oak on the edge of the Texas Hill Country.

Ken sat in a faded white lounge chair that faced east. It overlooked a small canyon that wound its way from the edge of his property and intersected a shale ledge below us.

I took the remaining chair, a cedar plank one. Cash sat on the railing and faced us.

I sipped coffee and watched a coyote slither through the brush.

When I looked at Ken, his drink was nearly gone.

He gave me a crooked, careless grin. "Whiskey each day keeps the demons away." He tipped his glass toward me.

I clinked it with my cup.

He took another sip. "So, you came to hear my little secret."

"From what I hear, there's nothing little about it."

Ken pursed his lips. "I've never shared the complete story before. But Detective Vasquez told me you might be the one to help me make some sense of it."

"I'll try." Which, given that I had no idea what he was about to tell me, seemed like the best I could do.

The shadows on his face were as deep as those beneath the thick oaks nearby. "From the time Vasquez called me until you showed up in my driveway, I debated telling you. I have been fearful for years." He shrugged. "But coddling this fear hasn't changed my lot in life. So we will talk, my friends."

My 'Thank you' sounded wholly inappropriate. But at least it was sincere.

Ken grimaced. "Writers, we learn to string words together in a way that stirs emotion. Some consider it art. Of course, artistry can be Rembrandt. Artistry can be Salvador Dali." He took another sip. "Or it can be spray-painted graffiti."

"Eye of the beholder, huh?" Cash offered.

Ken leaned forward. "Yet it's still art, regardless of its form. And of its acceptance by the wider community."

I said, "Sergeant Vasquez told us you're a brilliant writer."

Ken shook his head. "Sergeant Vasquez is a foolish romantic."

"Maybe so, but he led us to believe your story is significant."

Ken's laugh dripped with bitterness. "A significant story stands the test of time. It is irrefutable. The story Sergeant Vasquez refers to isn't one of those. It exists in my heart, and it exists in the memory of those it touched. But like art, it relies on the viewer to assess its true value."

Ken freshened his drink and topped off our coffee. He sat down and gazed out over the scrub brush. "I will tell you a story of ambition, deceit, and greed. More than a little of it mine." He pointed to me. "You're a detective, so you know how it is. You poke around, figuring it's better than napping on the couch. And one day you trip over a morsel. It doesn't seem like much at the time, but with nothing better to do you follow it. You ask a question, you hear things. In the end, most things you hear are a lark. One day I heard a crazy story. Too incredible to be true. I almost dismissed it as pure folly. But when I saw the earnestness on the woman's face...I listened."

Cash wandered away and inspected the barbecue grill.

Ken said, "Her name is Gabriela. A breath at a time, a laugh at a time, she became the joy in my life. She became my reason to wake every morning. Before I knew it, I fell in love."

He shrugged. "Merely calling it love sorely undersells what I felt, for I found myself intoxicated to the point of irrationality." His face seemed flushed. Maybe from the whiskey, although for a professional drinker I had a hunch it would take more than the two he had so far.

Ken said, "When you're in love you want to learn everything about the person you're in love with. You want to know their favorite color, the name of their first puppy. Are they captivated by the moon and the stars? Is it beach walks or mountain views? These are the things you want to understand about your love. Inevitably, as you seek to find who they are, you also want to discover who they *were*. And here I made a foolish error. For more than anything, I wanted to know who Gabriela was before she came into my life."

Cash stepped off the porch and walked around the back of the house. Ken seemed not to notice. My ears were his canvas.

"Tell me about her," I said.

"Close your eyes."

I did.

"Now, picture the most beautiful woman you've ever loved. Think of what you loved most about her. Her smile perhaps. Her eyes. The way she touched you. Possibly you remember the urgency with which she made love. Or the way she whispered your name. The way she made you dream. Now," Ken said, "can you remember every single thing about a woman such as this?"

A month ago, I would have thought about Venus. Today, all I could see was Ecstasy. "I can," I mumbled. I kept my eyes closed. Now that I had her I was unwilling to let her vision slip away.

"Good," Ken said, resting his hand on my shoulder until I opened my eyes. "So now you know what I felt for Gabriela. In my love, I coveted her. In her love, she chose to please me."

"How?"

Ken sagged in his chair. "One night she told me a story about a poor girl of fifteen from a small Texas border town. A girl who lost her parents and came to the city, where she hoped she'd find enough work so she could support her sisters back home. A girl who found little, except for hunger and poverty. Until one day when a man offered her a new life."

His eyes questioned me. "What else could a child of the streets hope for? Where she knew despair, he offered hope. Where she knew loneliness, he offered fellowship. It seemed too good to be true."

We sat in silence and watched the sun crawl higher and the birds flit from bush to bush as the rough landscape came alive.

Ken said, "Gabriela went to a house east of the city where she was bathed and clothed and fed. And for the first time since her parents died she felt the onset of happiness. But happiness is a temptress that calls to us and we chase it. It is often close, but seldom attained."

I was familiar with the concept. Having been married.

Ken ran his finger over the rim of his glass. "Gabriela believed she stood on the cusp of happiness. And after a few days the man who found her on the streets took her away to a place on the plains and showed her where her new life would begin. A spectacular palace, a building of chandeliers and circular staircases, of deep carpets and expensive artwork. And he told Gabriela, 'This is your home now. This is El Palacio Rojo.'"

"The Red Palace."

"Yes, my friend, a palace but nowhere near a home. What seemed so rich was in truth a façade. Gabriela joined dozens of young women there. White, black, Hispanic, Asian. Inside the high walls shielding them from the outside world these women were coerced into prostitution. For all of them there was some type of threat. Leave, and a family member would be killed. Leave, and you yourself may die. Gabriela…most of all she feared for her sisters, so for five years she remained there. Through the years she received various offers of marriage. One man in particular was very insistent in declaring his love for her. The more she denied him, the angrier he became. One night the man said she must marry him, or he would kill her himself."

Ken made no effort to wipe his tears away. "Gabriela dying in the Red Palace? To her this seemed very real, because she did not love him and refused to marry him. But that night another man came to her. He promised he'd help her leave, and that her sisters would remain safe. He remained with her all night. When morning came, they left."

"Getting away from El Palacio Rojo was that easy?"

"In retrospect, no. Gabriela told me her heart raced as they first stepped out the gate. A helicopter seemed so close, yet she feared she'd never make it. Each step she took, she imagined a hand would fall on her shoulder and pull her back. But he stepped into the helicopter. He held his hand out, helped her aboard, and strapped her in. She said her eyes were squeezed so tightly shut that her head throbbed. As the engine rumbled, as the rotors spun, and as it lifted off the ground, she prayed she'd be free."

"They made it, right?" Cash said as he poked his head around the porch. "He freed Gabriela?"

"One would think," Ken said. "But this is where the tendrils of deceit first exposed themselves. The man who rescued Gabriela explained it was his brother who threatened to kill her, and he could not allow that to happen. He urged Gabriela to flee and never look back. So she ran."

"But the story didn't end there," Cash said.

"Of course not. Here is where the story truly began. For a year Gabriela lived on the streets in constant fear, afraid she might be caught. Afraid the man who threatened to kill her would find her and take her back. Afraid something would happen to her sisters. But, inexorably, time moved on. Eventually she found work and contentment. When she met me she believed her life would once again be happy."

Ken rubbed his forehead. "God, if only I could have ignored every word she spoke. We could have been…I really thought…" Ken exhaled heavily. "I think to this day we could have been happy."

I rested my hand on his shoulder and waited.

He gave me a tight smile. "But I chose to follow her story because I selfishly wanted this story to become mine. And I discovered two men named Constantine owned El Palacio Rojo."

My mouth felt too dry to speak. "Constantine?" I croaked.

Ken nodded. "Yet when I searched for the history of the Constantines, I learned they were myths and nothing more."

"You never found out who they were?"

Ken shook his head. "You're getting ahead of my story. What I discovered instead was mindboggling. I learned that the man who showed up on paper as Elihu Constantine preached under his given name at Our Church of Eternal

Hope two hundred miles away. I flitted around the church like a moth to a lightbulb. Why would a preacher use an assumed name, and why would he own a brothel? One day I got too close, for I received a not-so-friendly visit from a man who told me if I valued anything in my life, I would stop looking. Of course I redoubled my efforts, as any good journalist would."

"As would a detective."

"We have a kinship, detectives and reporters. We seek the truth, and seldom stop until we find it. So I continued grasping at straws. Try as I might, it seemed I would come up empty. I thought I was doomed to write a story about a Reverend whose assumed name appeared on the title of a brothel. It would touch the evening news and quickly be replaced by the changing price of beef cattle.

"Then one day, I stumbled across a piece of good fortune in the person of Enrique Cruz. If he was involved my story had legs. I found new energy. I dug deeper and discovered the Constantines were in fact front men for him. Cruz dumped his money into companies owned by them, his money came out clean on the other side, and three men became rich. Well my friends, now I had my story. Thanks to Gabriela."

"Okay, but how did the brothel fit in?" I asked.

"The brothel. The brothel was…" Ken shook his head. "I have a friend who works in the Middle East, and he would call the brothel *baksheesh*. Like offering a tip or a bribe to get what you want. See, the Constantines had decided the big money was in building a championship golf course and selling memberships. But in order to build the course they were mortgaged to the hilt and the memberships weren't selling worth a damn. You know how the economy goes."

Cash said, "So they built the brothel to help sell golf memberships?"

Ken tapped his nose. "What can I tell you? The right woman can sell ice cubes to Eskimos."

"Talk about your high-priced ball washers."

Ken ignored Cash.

I tried to, as well. "That plan worked?"

Ken shrugged. "Apparently. The course was going great guns when I saw it."

"You wrote this story?"

"In the end, yes. I wrote the story of a poor girl from Del Rio Texas who came to the big city. A girl who was, for all intent, kidnapped and held for five years in a brothel prison. I wrote the story of mysterious brothers Elihu and Cantu Constantine. I outlined their involvement with Enrique Cruz. I wrote about the money laundering side of his organization. I'd found my golden ticket. My fifteen years of fame. My Pulitzer. And yet…"

He pointed his empty glass toward Cash. "It became my untold secret. For one day Cruz decided to end my folly himself."

I walked to the rail. As I looked out over the canyon, Ken joined me. "Few stories end happily," he said. "This is one of those. I came home one night to find a car parked by our apartment. A man told me to get in. He blindfolded me and drove me around until I was hopelessly lost. When he stopped he took me inside a building. And there I saw Gabriela with a man I didn't know. Next to them stood a man I knew all too well. Enrique Cruz."

Ken's voice knotted, as if the words did not want to be spoken. He forced them out. "Cruz said, *You wrote a story of lies about me?* I said I captured the truth. He laughed. *I captured something of yours as well.* He rested a hand on Gabriela's shoulder. *If you tell your story, I will return her head to you as a reminder of what you deem most precious. However I offer another choice.* Cruz sat very close to me, like he needed an ally. A way to alleviate his pain. He pointed to the man next to Gabriela. *Years ago my youngest son fell in love with this* puta, *only to have her escape. But this pitiful wretch of a son could not forget her. Now he pledges his love for her against my wishes. I cannot abide a man who disobeys his father, so for this he will leave me and my name behind. As for you, I believe you will find me a fair man. So my deal is this. If a word of your story is never spoken to the press or the police, she will live. As will you. However, one wrong word and she dies.*"

"You didn't try to publish the story?"

Ken flinched. "My story died the night Enrique Cruz took my wife from me."

Cash whipped his head around. "Your wife?"

"On that day she was carrying my child. Now I sit here alone, dreaming of them, until I'm fortunate enough to die."

"Do you think she's still alive?" I asked.

"Every so often Enrique Cruz reminds me how alive Gabriela truly is."

Ken walked into the house and out of sight.

Cash cocked an eyebrow. "You believe this old drunk's story?"

I wasn't sure.

Until Ken brought us a shoebox full of pictures. Each photo had a date scribbled on the back. And each showed a petite, beautiful woman with dark brown eyes, raven hair and delicate features. As we sifted through the pictures the years played across her face. Yet while youth slowly ebbed from her, her beauty did not.

Some of them showed her in a house. A few showed her walking the streets of a large city. Some were taken in a heavily wooded area. In two, she stood in the snow. And numerous pictures showed a curly-headed boy grow from toddler until maybe eight years old.

Ken stuffed the pictures into the shoe box. "She lives with a man who raises my son, and I am convinced Enrique Cruz sends me these. From time to time money accompanies the photos."

That part didn't add up to me. "Why does Cruz send you money?"

Ken sighed. "I believe it's because he wants me to live forever, so I'm constantly reminded of the price of my foolishness."

"But you could still say something."

"Say what? He would kill them. He knows that would be my ultimate tragedy."

"Did you ever try to find her?" I asked.

"I did enough harm to her by forgetting what I truly loved. Now, every day I remember. So out of love for her, and fear for what might happen, I have let her go."

"Is that the story Raymundo Vasquez wanted us to hear? We asked him about a man named Chrome Elvis Livingston. And he sent us to you."

Ken spoke like a patient teacher to youthful pupils. "Each part of a spider web is critical, no matter how insignificant it seems. Livingston was merely a small part of a much larger web. A web that stretches in many different directions yet was inevitably spun by Enrique Cruz. I told you about Livingston, I merely omitted his name. He worked for the Constantine brothers, which ultimately means he worked for Enrique Cruz. It was he who found Gabriela on the streets of San Antonio and brought her to the brothel."

Cash stood. "One thing I'm confused about," he said. "The Constantine brothers. I thought you said they weren't real."

"Their true name isn't Constantine, however they are very real. Are you familiar with the story of the Emperor Constantine, who saw a vision of a cross in the sky? He put it on his men's shields going into battle, a battle which they won against a formidable foe. These two men, half-brothers, saw their own cross in the sky and under it they built a fortune."

"You learned their real names during your investigation?"

"I saw the man also known as Elihu Constantine preach. He was… spellbinding."

"Is he still at the church?" Cash asked.

"No," Ken said. "When Enrique Cruz drove his youngest son away, I am sure he thought the oldest son would continue to run the Constantine businesses. However the oldest son chose to accompany his brother out of Texas, as did Livingston and a few others. I've heard no more of them, and believed they'd disappeared for good. Now, it appears you've found one of them."

"Lot of good it did. Livingston being a stiff and all," Cash said.

"Tell us the Constantine's real names," I said.

"I have never uttered them. When Enrique Cruz spoke, I listened. I believed my silence extended to the affairs of Chrome Livingston. To the fraudulent Constantine brothers. To my Gabriela. And most especially, to anything having to do with Enrique Cruz himself. I wanted it all to go away."

I said, "Things may dip under the surface for a while. But they are still there."

"Hence, you."

"Hence us."

Ken tapped the railing as if counting down to the moment. "I lost the love of my life. I lost the son I never knew. I lost my career and I lost my dignity. Finally, I feel I'm losing my will to live. There is nothing else I can lose by telling you. The Constantines are in fact half-brothers, and Enrique's sons. Miguel Cruz is the brother who fell in love with Gabriela and took her from me. The half-brother who freed her? Johnny Virdon."

I remembered enough Spanish to know Cruz meant Cross. As in Mikey Cross.

Touchdown. And the crowd goes wild.

CHAPTER 36

While I stood at the luggage carousel in Portland later that evening, Yvette called me. "I done what you said," she rasped. "I talked to your lawyer friend."

"He drew up the papers?"

She wheezed a laugh. "He drew up somethin', that's for sure. But when I read 'em I wasn't sure if I was preparin' to sell The Limit or donatin' my body to medical science."

"Did he send them to Mikey's lawyer?"

Yvette waited a minute before replying. "You ain't plannin' to screw me, are ya? You ain't helpin' nobody take my business?"

I'd used the words 'trust me' an awful lot in the past week or so. I'd used them so much I wasn't sure how much value they carried anymore. Still, I found myself saying, "Trust me."

She softly said, "You ain't got much to lose. I got everythin' to lose. Everythin' else I got."

"I know." I picked at my fingernail and thought about all-time great bluffs.

It was time to play mine out.

"Busy?" I asked Ecstasy after she'd stuffed her purse full of bills, wrestled a red stretch top over her head and came off the stage. The leather miniskirt she wore left very little to the imagination. Which played to my strengths.

She looked at the nearly full club. Four guys hovered close by, waiting for her to make eye contact so they could get down to business. "No, Paul. No I'm not. This is like a vacation."

"Well good. Can you spare a few minutes for me?"

A small smile slipped out. "I used to make time *with* you. Now I make time *for* you. Let's celebrate the ongoing metamorphosis of me."

Ecstasy gave her paramours the wave-off and joined me at a table far from the stages. I motioned to Kassie, the waitress working the floor. She gave me the thumbs-up and brought a beer and a drink for Ecstasy.

I looked at Kassie. "You don't ask? You just bring us what you think we want?"

Kassie wrinkled her nose. "I'll play your silly game. How did I do?"

I slid her a twenty. "You nailed it, sister."

She walked away with a big smile plastered on her face.

A twenty does wonders, if administered to the right person at the right time. As long as it wasn't Ecstasy. Especially when she was in full woman mode.

Ecstasy traced her finger along the outside of the glass.

I knew the move. I just didn't know what it meant.

She looked up and caught my eyes. "What?"

I threw out my shy, little boy smile. "We still seem undefined."

She laughed. "Don't try to get fancy with the English language, Mister. We are…you and I are…I guess I'd call us…" She thought for a moment, then frantically waved her hands like she had exhausted her vocabulary. She shrugged. "Undefined?"

"Well said." I studied the petite lady in front of me. Physics dictated my sheer size would dominate her. Newton identified that in one law or another. But his scientific law had been trumped by Cupid's Law, stating any woman can move any man of any size at any time.

Oh, that crazy Cupid.

I asked, "You remember the last time we sat here? This table, no less?"

"Of course. Out of the goodness of your heart you slipped me some money. I overreacted and left."

"Nice of you to remember it that way, but I should have known better than to be my stupid self. It's just so natural for me."

Ecstasy touched my hand. "I guess I should have known better, too. This is different, you and I. I don't quite understand it, and it has me off-kilter."

My head hummed. And my heart. And my stomach. I pretty much hummed all over. "Different?"

She said, "Sometimes I think I'm ready for us to feel more like a man and a woman."

"A man and a woman?"

Ecstasy said, "Let me make it easy. You have a penis, right?"

I nodded my head. Dumbfounded.

She said, "And I have a vagina. That makes us a man and a woman." Ecstasy looked around the club at the customers, and focused on one who motioned her to join him. She shook her head firmly and didn't waste a smile. When she looked back to me she said, "I decided it's time I dip my toe in the truth pool. I need to tell you something. It may come straight out, and it may get kind of messy, but if we move…"

She bit her lip. "If we move…forward…or sideways or backwards or wherever we move, I have to share my little burden. It's taken a long time but…I trust you, Paul."

I nodded because I didn't know how else to react. "I've heard that's what friends do."

She enthusiastically nodded. "Friends. I know. I feel like we're friends. When you look at me I can tell I'm special to you. Not because of how I look with my clothes off, or what you might get from the deal, but because you like plain old me, bumps and bruises and bitchiness be damned. You see the good in me. Not many others do." Ecstasy's eyes dropped to the table.

She was right about me seeing the good in her, and because of that what I felt went far past what I first saw, the great body and her willingness to share it with me. With other women I felt relatively useless. Paul Doyle, the worn out couch, easily replaced by any other couch in the furniture showroom. But Ecstasy treated me like I was worth something.

And she…she was smart, funny, gorgeous…and strong-willed. I'd seen that up close the night I tried to pay her. She had a hard edge. She wouldn't melt when the going got tough. And one thing I'd learned in life, even when the going got tough, you still had to get up and face the day. More and more, Ecstasy seemed like a woman to face the day with.

Yet I'd been doing the famous Paul Doyle 'avoid your feelings at all cost' soft-shoe for too long. Because if you don't avoid them, they are conveniently available for any old Sally or Jane or Ecstasy to smash to bits on the sidewalk. Showing your feelings meant you'd be vulnerable. Like a crack in a dam. The water building up behind it would find that one little crack, one area of weakness, and it would come blasting right through. And then what would you have? Not a dam thing.

I sipped my beer and snuck a glance at the lady across the table. Would she blast through my dam? Or would she help me keep it in one piece?

I could almost hear Venus offer an alternative. *Or you can tell a girl how you really feel and you might find you don't need a dam at all.*

Whoa.

I couldn't wait for the right time to talk to Ecstasy, for as I'd learned with Venus many years ago, if you wait for the right time it may never come at all.

I wished I could write a note and leave it in her locker, or have Cash slip it to her in study hall. Instead I went with the weak high school standby, "I really like you, Ecstasy."

She did a tricky thing with her eyes and they seemed to brighten. "I like you, too."

That immediately made things easier, and infinitely more complicated. Because my repertoire was shot after five words.

I drank my beer and hoped she didn't change her mind in the silence that followed.

The music switched and the dancers rotated.

Ecstasy stayed beside me. After a few quiet minutes she said, "The last person I said that to asked me to marry him. And that's what I need to talk to you about."

"How'd it go?"

"Some people likened our marriage to a train wreck." Her eyes drifted away from me. "They were far too kind."

My spidey-sense began to tingle. "A husband. You haven't mentioned him before."

She twisted a strand of hair around her finger. "Ex-husband, but still. A girl has to have a few secrets."

"Yes, I've heard that's true. So he's gone now? Out of your life?"

Ecstasy nodded. "He's out of my life. Not fully out of my head, but he's out of my life."

"Why is he still in your head?"

She scowled. "Because I let him stay there, even though I know I shouldn't. When we were together he fed me a steady barrage of 'girl, you suck' and after a while it sunk in pretty deep. I was stupid, I was ugly. My feet were too big, my boobs were too small, I sucked at sex, I laughed too loud, I slurped my coffee, I got too drunk when we went out with friends. No matter what I did, I did it wrong. So instead I tried to make sure I was perfect. That became ridiculously impossible."

I cupped her hand. Ecstasy gave my fingers a tiny squeeze.

She said, "I'd be up before him in the morning and I'd wait for it to begin. Then I'd hear the floorboards creak upstairs…and my stomach would knot up so tight I wanted to puke. Because I knew…I *knew* he'd say something. About how I should be different. Or better. Or just something…else. Anything but me."

"How long did you put up with that?"

She grabbed a coaster and began tearing it. "Longer than I should have, but I was dogged. Couldn't fail at this marriage thing. But then when the truly crazy shit happened we decided it was best to go our separate ways."

"Truly crazy shit?" I asked, not fully sure I wanted to know the depths of the truly crazy shit she had to endure.

She shook her head. "Nothing for you to worry about. Not like they're going to show up and take me away in handcuffs or a straightjacket or anything. Just…stuff happened, and then we weren't married anymore. And here I am today, the wonderful phoenix that rose from the ashes of me." She tried a bubbly, don't-you-worry-about-me laugh, but it didn't work very well.

For either one of us.

I said, "Maybe…maybe you haven't put this experience all the way in your rearview mirror yet. You want to talk about it?"

"I don't know if talking will help. I can't seem to get past hearing his voice telling me how bad I am."

"Just as likely he was talking about himself. A woman as beautiful as you, he probably felt he couldn't compete. So if he dragged you down to his level…"

Her body tensed. "You think I'm beautiful?"

'What are you, an idiot,' I almost said. But I thought that might backfire in light of her previous revelation. Instead I said, "Eminently," and brushed her cheek with my fingertips.

Her face clouded over. "You're aware I'm a stripper, right? That's a pretty big minus in the beautiful column. Always has been. Always will be."

"I'm aware you make me laugh. You look at me like I'm a fool when I try to make you laugh. You pick on me and challenge me and you never give me a free pass and I adore that about you. So, yeah. You ain't half bad."

"Though I'm a stripper."

"Girl, I spot a recurring theme. Dancing bothers you?"

She whipped her head furiously from side to side, causing her hair to explode around her face. "Paul, wake up. Dancing is what teenage girls in their underwear do when they listen to music in their bedrooms. What do I do now that I'm grown? I've raised dancing in my underwear to a whole new level. So don't patronize me. Let's call it what it is."

I watched Ecstasy make the coaster pieces even smaller. I considered getting her a phone book in case she wanted a real challenge.

When she looked satisfied that all the bits were sufficiently torn she said, "When I was growing up I always thought I was going to be someone special. I plateaued at stripper." She pumped her fist. "Yes."

I tried to sound intelligent. "Are you sure you've plateaued? I think of a person as a wall that's being constructed, and each experience is a brick that we add to our wall. But not all of them are going to be set straight. So step back and see if you like the wall you're building. You can always pull the crooked bricks out and put new ones in."

Ecstasy mulled over what I said, then nudged me with her shoulder. "Ain't you a smartie?"

"Takes one to know one."

She tossed her head again, but less violently this time. Her eyes bored into me. "But now that you're seeing my dirt, what do you think of me?"

"You trusted me enough to tell me your most intimate secret. I'm impressed as hell that you did."

"Well…" Ecstasy cupped the shreds of paper into a tiny mound on the table and continued to shape them as she talked. "Okay, sure. That's my most intimate secret. Now you know. But did I let my slip show too much?"

Her skirt stopped where her thigh met her butt. "There's room for a slip under there?"

She giggled like a teenager. "Sweetie, I barely have room for anything under here."

"Underwear?"

She patted her butt and laughed, happier than I'd heard her all night. "Under here, you nut. Even a marginally good detective would have already discovered this."

"So consider me a great one. But as great as I am, sometimes even I need help, and I think you're just the girl to solve my problem. You know I'm trying to find Annette Begley. But I'm running out of time and I've hit a roadblock, one I think only a woman can help me with."

"Yes."

"As simple as that? Yes?"

"Come on, Paul. I strip. I sleep late. I eat Froot Loops and watch TV and wait until the next time I strip. This isn't the epitome of my dreams."

"So compared to that, private eye stuff is pretty hot?"

"Keep telling yourself that." She laughed and clutched my arm. "No, it sounds like fun. And it's sweet that you asked. One important question, though. Do I get to shoot anyone?"

"Probably not this time. You want the details now?"

Ecstasy shook her head. "It's back to job one. Flashing boobs for the working man. When do you want me?"

'Always and forever' was dying to come out. What I heard from my mouth instead was, "We can talk over breakfast."

"Okay. I get off at four. Would that be a good time for you?"

I shook my head. "I'll be snoring like a grizzly at four."

Ecstasy smiled. "I sleep till noon. How about then?"

"Funny time for breakfast."

"Not if you work until 4 AM."

She had me there. "Will you want Froot Loops?"

"Oh no. If I work for you, I want the moon. You're buying me waffles."

CHAPTER 37

Thank heaven for 24-hour pancake houses. Ecstasy showed up at 1 PM, slightly after the rest of the eating world had already finished breakfast. She wore a snug-fitting red turtleneck and black, skinny-leg jeans. A wide black elastic belt outside the sweater, just above her waist, accentuated the all-too-alluring curves of her breasts and hips.

She wore minimal makeup, just a touch around her eyes and a whisper on her cheeks, dark red lipstick and nice perfume. Once I'd heard a stripper say she couldn't send men home with perfume on them. So Ecstasy could be a real girl today. While she'd looked elegant and understated at Shari's calling hours, this Ecstasy, by the light of day, was spectacular.

"Been waiting long?" she asked as she slid into the booth across from me.

"Earth has been around for about four billion years, so against that back-drop…" I glanced at my watch. "Not long at all."

"I had to…my makeup…it took longer than I thought…and…"

I remembered Ecstasy's explanation about her ex-husband's assessment of her. "As always, you're worth waiting for."

She twirled her hair with her index finger. Hesitantly she said, "Okay."

The waffles didn't happen. Instead she ordered stuffed French toast covered with powdered sugar and strawberries. Afraid of following her into a sugar coma, I opted for a spinach and cheese omelet.

Ecstasy ate her first piece of toast in silence, took a sip of coffee and dabbed her lips, careful not to smudge her lipstick. After she finished her routine she looked expectantly at me. "You going to lay out the caper, boss man? Do we hit a bank? Boost an armored car?"

She slapped her forehead. "No wait, we're the good guys. I know. You want me for surveillance at a makeup counter. They have mascara disappearing right in front of their eyes, right?" She laughed like it was the funniest thing she'd heard all day. It wasn't bad for a rookie.

"No, I'd like you to talk to a friend of mine. Samantha Sutter. Hopefully she'll help us find Reverend Virdon."

When I finished explaining, Ecstasy said, "Fear not. I will be your Mata Hari."

"My mother who?"

Ecstasy choked down a laugh. "Surely you know of Mata Hari."

"I know 'Hello Mudda, Hello Fadda, Here I Am At Camp Granada.' Am I close?"

"Not remotely. Mata Hari is a spy who was shot. If we can avoid the shooting part, that would work best for me. But what if Samantha doesn't tell me where the Reverend is?"

"Bond with her. Girl talk. Do that fancy stuff guys always fall for. Anything, just get her talking until she coughs up his whereabouts. Then Cash and I will jump into action."

"Is there a backup plan? I'd hate to think all your eggs are in my basket."

I stalled a moment by drinking my coffee. But she wouldn't let me off the hook, I could tell. "I think the best way to find Annette is to use Reverend Virdon against his brother. We have a few days until Mikey's deadline. That gives us a few days to deftly massage the problem. If that doesn't work…we go to the cops with what we know. They do what they do. And we hope Annette survives."

Ecstasy bit her lip, then looked at me. "So it's pretty much on me then? If I fail…Mikey may kill her?"

"Always been that chance," I said. "Let's go do the best we can and we'll figure out how to play the cards as they're dealt to us. Fair enough?"

She nodded. "Fair enough. When would you like me to do this?"

"Tomorrow?"

Ecstasy grinned. "Tomorrow's perfect. Early?"

"Depends on whether you're working tonight. I think early hinges on that, doesn't it?"

"I'm not working tonight, Paul." And the way she said it, the way it almost sounded like an offer, an unasked 'Do you want to do something together,' made my heart skip.

Or maybe I was imagining it. I…I…I didn't have the guts to find out. I stammered, "I'm going to watch the Celtics game on TV."

"Oh-kay. Well, enjoy watching your game."

I mentally booted myself in the ass. Because a smart guy would have asked her to dinner. A walk along the river. A drive to see the stars.

A semi-smart guy would have asked for her phone number. Her astrology sign. If she wanted to fool around. Anything.

I said, "Good luck tomorrow."

Her eyes dimmed a bit. "You want me to do my spy thing solo?"

"Oh. No. I'm going to help. Of course."

Ecstasy tapped the side of her nose. "And you do this for a living?"

"Cash does most of the thinking. It frees me up for the real hard stuff."

"Is he available? It's starting to look like things might get a little complicated from here on out."

I looked at the beauty in front of me, my heart spinning and my brain dog-paddling to stay afloat. "I think they already are."

She gave her mouth a delicate touch with her napkin, then placed the napkin on the table. "So, how about I play Cash? You pick me up at my apartment tomorrow morning, say nine o'clock. You drive me to the church. I do my thing. And when I come out, you will treat me to a nice lunch. We'll build the rest of the plan from there."

I nodded.

She pinched my cheek. "Now isn't this thinking stuff easy?"

True to her word, Ecstasy strolled down the stairs and climbed into my car the next morning. She wore a pair of gray paint-stained Husson College sweatpants, a torn white Reebok hoodie and blue flip flops. Her hair was a mess and she wore no makeup.

"You're living proof of what a good night's rest will do," I said.

Ecstasy leveled haunted eyes on me. "I didn't sleep a wink. I decided total exhaustion look would be most effective. Method actor here."

"I like the hair the best. It's so...you."

"I spent about an hour with gel and a blow dryer to get it perfect."

"When I try a disguise, I usually stop shaving for a couple of days. Wear a different hat. I slouch. Sunglasses work."

Ecstasy shook her head. "You didn't play dress up much as a kid, did you?"

I parked a quarter-mile past the Castle View Free Church and looked at Ecstasy. "Once more. This time with feeling."

She popped a salute. "Yes, sir. I walk in. First door on the left. The one that says Main Office. Duh. I shuffle my downtrodden booty to the receptionist desk, operated by the formidable Samantha Sutter. I tell her I need a place to get away from my abusive boyfriend."

She cut an accusing eye at me and ran her tongue over her teeth. "My abusive boyfriend who won't stop until he finds me. I'll say please baby please. I'm at the end of my rope and I must talk to Reverend Virdon. Only he can help me in my time of need." Ecstasy flicked a fake tear from her cheek.

"Understated approach. I like that. Go get 'em, kid."

She lunged across the seat and gave me a quick kiss on the cheek. She left the car and began the slow walk toward the church while I struggled to remember my name.

A private investigator is ever vigilant, so I couldn't have drifted off while Ecstasy was gone. I was therefore involved in intense surveillance on one thing or other because her approach eluded me until she threw the passenger door open and slid in. She slammed it shut, grabbed my arm and said, "I love this shit!"

My brain lagged a half-lap behind her. "How'd it go?"

She leaned away from me. "Let's see. I jump in the car and say 'I love this shit!' and you want to know how'd it go? Freaking awesome is how it went!"

"I'm sorry you didn't have more luck. Maybe it will be better next time."

"Paul, that was better than an orgasm." She clutched the dashboard with both hands and closed her eyes. "Oh. Oh! Oh God! Oh God!" She stopped. "It was that good."

"No faking?"

"Not this time." Ecstasy bounced around on the seat like a kid who had to pee. I headed toward a restaurant with a working bathroom, just in case.

We decided on a small place just down the street from my office and beat the lunch crowd by a mile. After we ordered I said, "I thought you might burst on the way over here."

Ecstasy dismissed me with a wave. "I wanted to make sure you bought me lunch, so I oversold it big time."

When she saw the look on my face, she slapped the table. "Just playing! I can't believe it! I shake my boobs for farm boys and you do this for a living!"

"I similarly revel in the euphoria. Almost daily." I patted her arm. "Whenever you're ready, just crank up your story and let it go."

She couldn't contain herself. "So I walked up to the church and the whole way I was working on my this-is-the-most-miserable-day-of-my-life face. But when I came to the door all of a sudden I thought there was no way I could do it. Paul, I couldn't breathe! I thought about running away. Then the door opened."

"It's hard to get in otherwise."

She gave me her one thousandth 'Oh my God you're an idiot' look. "Guess who opened the door? Samantha Sutter you'd say. And you'd be...wait for it...wrong!" She giggled.

It was a nice giggle. I let her ride it out.

"No," she said, "Reverend Virdon himself let me in. He told me Samantha was taking a three-day weekend and he was keeping an eye on the front office. He looked like a helpless grandpa. I wanted to ask him to type a letter. No. No! I should have told him to sit on my lap and take a memo, sweetie. Get him totally flustered. But he seemed pretty flustered anyway. He kept glancing out the window like he expected the Big Bad Wolf to come barging in at any time."

"I think he was afraid of the big bad me."

Our waitress placed bowls of chicken vegetable soup in front of us, along with roasted turkey breast sandwiches with asiago cheese, bean sprouts and tomatoes. After we'd put an impressive dent in the food Ecstasy said, "So anyway, Reverend Virdon brought me into his office, and I told him my story. And the whole time he looked at me like some of the creepy guys at the club. Like I can't ever get a second to fix my lipstick or pull my thong out of my...adjust my thong without them watching. So I know when a guy's scoping me out, trust me."

"I'm sure you do. Especially when you look like this."

Ecstasy waggled her finger at me. "A woman's beauty comes from within, Paul. Don't fixate on the fancy wrapper. It's what's inside that's important."

"Consider me rebuked."

"Okay Rebuked, I told Reverend Virdon if my boyfriend finds me he'll beat me and make me go back home. The Reverend seemed very upset and said he would protect me. He wanted me to stay right then so I'd be safe. Hoo, I thought I was up the creek! So I said I own a cat that I need to give away. My bastard boyfriend isn't going to keep my cat."

"You made all that stuff up? I'm impressed."

She blushed. Her eyes plummeted toward her plate.

I took it as a compliment. "Did Virdon tell you where he was planning to take you?"

Ecstasy looked up and froze me with her stare. "Mister Doyle. You hired me to do a job. You counted on me to deliver the goods. Now what kind of employee would I be unless I brought...this...shit...all the way home?"

"I assume that means you got the information?"

"Did I?" She smiled like a queen looking at her subjects. "I said 'I'm so frightened. He always finds me. And he beats me.' Reverend Virdon said he runs a dormitory for people in need. Many of his congregation lives there, and it's a wonderful place to hide. He said I'd be safe. Then we prayed."

"When did you tell Reverend Virdon you'd be back?"

Ecstasy pushed the crust of her sandwich around the plate. "I told him I'd be back before he went home tonight. He's expecting me."

I gulped. Our timeline had just changed. I'd promised Venus and Simeon Mathers that I'd meet them tomorrow. I was going to lay out everything I knew to them then, and then we'd figure out the next move together.

Sounded like I'd be giving them a backbrief instead.

Ecstasy grabbed her napkin and twisted it beyond recognition. "Wrong thing to say?"

"Naah," I said, fighting to keep my face neutral. "You picked the song. Cash and I will dance to it." And we'd be doing the quick-step.

Ecstasy squirmed in her chair. "I didn't know what to say, and I had to say something. So I said I'd be back today." She continued to work the napkin. "I screwed your case up, didn't I?"

I gave her my best smile. "In thirty minutes you did what we haven't been able to do for days. You brought Virdon to the table."

I could tell she wasn't buying what I was selling.

I brushed the hair from her pained eyes. "Come on, I'll take you home to get some sleep."

It didn't sit well with Cash. He didn't say much one way or the other. That's how I knew.

"You don't like it," I said.

"No. I don't. You're going to keep her in the game?"

"I don't see any other way. She goes to see Virdon. He drives her out to the dormitory. And we meet him there for a little us on one."

"What if he doesn't take her to the dorm? What if he takes her to the compound? Once she gets in there, she might be a little hard to get back out. It'll be like Hotel California, man."

"I've been thinking about what Ken Bartholomew told us regarding how Virdon helped Gabriela escape El Palacio Rojo. I'm not sure the good Reverend's a full partner in the game."

"Yeah, I think something, too," Cash said. "I think the Reverend and Mikey are lower than whale shit and I wouldn't trust them with anyone. Not to mention a complete stranger."

Cash sipped his coffee and leaned back on the couch. "And speaking of a complete stranger, what's with you recruiting outside the agency?"

"I needed a little feminine guile. With you being so macho…"

"I hardly qualify. You're right. So who is she, Paul?"

"Just a woman."

"A woman who you've never mentioned before. Don't forget, secrets kill friendships. What's her name?"

"Her name…" I froze. People form opinions about strippers. They aren't good women. They use their bodies for money. I heard one guy call Ecstasy a heartless bitch because she wouldn't give him her phone number. I felt she was anything but heartless, so she'd won me over. But Cash?

They felt like the hardest four words I ever said. "Her name is Ecstasy."

Cash nodded. "I like her optimism."

"She has a co-worker named Forna Kate."

"Now that's my kind of girl."

I shook my head. "False advertising."

Cash carefully placed the coffee cup on the table in front of him. "Ecstasy, huh?"

"Ecstasy."

We were silent.

I bounced a pen on the desk.

Cash drummed his fingers on the couch. Then he slapped his hands on the cushion and pushed himself up. "She like Chinese?"

"Of course. She likes everyone."

"Not people. Food. Chinese food. And you're not funny."

"Now you tell me. But I have no earthly idea about the food."

Well, you could call and ask her."

I shook my head. "She's napping right now. She has to work tonight."

"Factory, I imagine."

I winced. "The Limit."

Cash gave a quick nod. "Yeah, you won't find many girls named Ecstasy on the assembly line."

"Or Forna Kate, either."

Cash walked over and put a hand on my shoulder. "Well, when we nail Johnny Virdon to the cross and rescue Annette Begley and roll Mikey over in the clover for fun, you tell Miss Ecstasy we're going to celebrate by going all out. As in take out."

CHAPTER 38

When I picked Ecstasy up an hour later I could sense her reluctance. The first go with Reverend Virdon had been fun, just a girl play-acting.

This visit to Reverend Virdon would be for keeps.

"In a few minutes, you're going to meet Cash," I told her. "You'll love him."

She leaned against the door. "I'm scared."

"Of Cash? He's a teddy bear. A teddy bear who shoots people, mind you."

She blew a breath upwards, causing her bangs to dance away from her forehead. "I'm not afraid of Cash. I'm afraid of seeing the Reverend again. All I can think about are bad things happening."

"Cash and I will be close. There's nothing Reverend Virdon can do to hurt you."

Ecstasy tensed. "You think that, but you don't really know that."

"No, I don't. But I do this for a living. I put myself in dangerous situations, and I always find a way to get out of them."

"Okay, but now I'm the one in the dangerous situation."

Touché.

We pulled in behind my office. Ecstasy stayed glued to the door.

"Come on," I said. "It'll be okay."

Ecstasy hesitated, as if any movement from the car could only be bad. Because after the office, no more safety valves remained.

I put a hand on her shoulder. "Trust me."

We climbed the stairs and went through the open door that said Paul Doyle, Investigations.

Cash stood when we walked through the door, and stuck his hand out to Ecstasy. "Winfield Romero Cashman the Third."

"Ecstasy." She paused and seemed slightly embarrassed. "I didn't vote for your dad last time he ran."

He chuckled. "Neither did I, and he's still unemployed. But enough about him. You ready to join our little crime-busting club?"

Ecstasy displayed more enthusiasm than I believed she truly felt. "I am."

She sat on the couch and I filled her in. "Our goal is to get Reverend Virdon alone. He's the key to the plan, but we need to talk to him first, in a place where he can't escape. Let's say he saw us come up to the church with you. He'd go deeper into seclusion and we'd never find him. Let's say we try to stop him on the road to the dormitory. Lots of ways for him to get away. And lots of ways others might get hurt in the process."

I put my hand on her shoulder. "I'll be at the dormitory, and Cash will follow you. When the Reverend brings you inside he'll meet me there. Cash will come in as well to keep the odds the way I like them, decidedly in our favor. And we will learn the true story about Mikey Cross. And Shari Tappey. And hopefully, the whereabouts of Annette Begley."

Ecstasy wrung her hands. "What do I do when you're talking to him?"

Cash jumped in. "You get nervous, little lady, you stand by me. If that's not enough you get behind the Big Guy. That way Reverend Virdon will never even know you're there."

The sun was creeping toward the horizon when I took Ecstasy to the church. While I drove she shredded a tissue into tiny bits and built an impressive pile in her lap. Her own form of stress relief. I used to eat, but since I'd taken my belt in a notch and had no intention of backsliding, I chewed gum.

Not that I felt stressed or anything.

I crammed another stick of Spearmint in my mouth.

As I drove by the church she slid across the seat, took my arm and pulled it around her.

We parked in the same turnoff as before and sat like that for about five minutes. Ecstasy pressed against me.

Me with my arm around her.

Her wrestling with herself.

She patted my chest, pushed away, and looked up at me. "This is better than a nude lap dance. I keep reminding myself that."

She opened the door, stepped out, and shuffled toward the church with her head down and hands jammed into her pockets.

Cash called me about thirty minutes later. "They left the church. I have good news and bad news. Which do you want first?"

My stomach tightened. "I'm an optimist. Give me the good news."

"They turned on North Scofield. My guess is they're headed your way."

I exhaled, relieved. "What's the bad news?"

"Flat tire. I pulled off to change it. So you've lost your eyes."

Shit. Double shit.

But if it went like we thought, Virdon would stay on North Scofield. Turn left on Tremaine Avenue. Turn left on Memorial Drive. Follow it past the college. Turn left on Armstrong Road. Pull into the dormitory's circular drive. And walk Ecstasy inside.

However, if Virdon turned right on Tremaine Avenue or Memorial Drive or any other street in the urban Westfield maze, we might never find Reverend Virdon again.

Or Ecstasy.

A minute ticked by. I closed my eyes. I saw them pull up to the stop sign at the intersection of Memorial Drive. They sat, the third car in line, waiting for the traffic to clear. The radio played. The Reverend looked like a classical music kind of guy. I had no idea if Maine had a classical station. Christian. I knew about the Christian station. Reverend Virdon had his own show. Of course that's what they were listening to. The Christian radio station.

They turned. They climbed the hill toward Aberle College. Past the cross-country trail on the left. Past a soccer field on low, swampy ground on the right. Past the college's signature white-steepled administration building.

The football stadium loomed on their left. Past it, Armstrong Road. I pictured two cars approaching them. A red GMC pickup. A Subaru with

Massachusetts plates. They passed. Reverend Virdon and Ecstasy turned. Toward the dormitory.

Toward me.

30 MPH. Reverend Virdon was a speed limit driver. The dorm was about a mile up Armstrong Road. I waited for two minutes.

At three minutes, I called Cash. "You coming?"

"You know what I hate when you buy a car? They give you one of those little donut-looking tires as a spare. Nobody in their right mind wants one of those. Nobody, I tell you."

I sighed. "How does your car look with the donut?"

"Please. I have a full-size spare. Matching rim and everything. Cool, huh?"

Some days I wanted to strangle him. Most days. Today. "They're not here yet."

"They're coming, Paul. Have a little faith. Where else would they go?"

From the corner of my eye I saw a flicker. I turned to see a slim blonde girl soundlessly slip from a room two doors down the hall. She jumped when she saw me.

"You want to get downstairs with the rest of them," I said. "It may get a little wacky around here real soon."

I had warned Cory to leave us alone and he'd spread the word to the rest of the tenants. Since it'd worked so well with him before, I'd once again flashed my gun for reinforcement. Didn't Irmalee love that one, me brandishing my gun in front of her kids. Still, after seeing my tough guy encore they were only too happy to follow orders. They were all in the basement.

Except for this stray.

She stood in the middle of the hallway, openmouthed, and stared.

"Go ahead," I said, motioning her away with my gun. "You'll be safe. Stay with the rest of them."

She looked at me a few seconds longer, then she walked to the staircase and disappeared toward the basement.

I heard tires crunching on the gravel driveway. I stepped into a nearby room and peered out the window.

Reverend Virdon climbed out of a white church van. He walked around the passenger's side and opened the door.

Ecstasy took his hand and stepped down.

Virdon and Ecstasy walked to the front door. When they stepped inside he told her, "Many people come here. The door is always open to those in need."

Her fragile voice said, "If the door is always open and many people come, won't my boyfriend be able to find me? How can I possibly be safe here?"

"I have learned that it is often best to hide in plain sight. People see what they expect to see. No one expects to see you here. Trust me."

"How can I trust you? I don't even know you."

"Then trust in the Lord, my child."

They came out of the small foyer and turned into the hall. They nearly walked into me.

"Howdy, Reverend," I said, my gun pointed at his chest.

CHAPTER 39

Reverend Virdon turned to Ecstasy, his eyes darting from her to me. "I'm sorry, I promised to protect you."

I took her elbow and pulled her close. "Ask Shari Tappey how that promise feels."

Virdon's brow furrowed. "I had no idea you were the one who beats her."

I looked at Cash. Virdon thought I was Ecstasy's abusive boyfriend. This could play to our advantage. I nodded.

Virdon scowled. "The last time I saw you, you accused me of kidnapping and murder. Is it any better, what you do?"

I pointed to the closest room. "This isn't about me. It's you who's got some 'splainin' to do, mister."

Virdon glanced at Ecstasy, who I still held, then he entered the room.

I gave Ecstasy's elbow a quick double squeeze and said, "Up against the wall, sugar britches. Stand by Mister Handsome over there and don't make any trouble." I nodded toward Cash.

She jerked her elbow away. "You better not hurt me again, you bastard," she said, in a tone that would play well on the big screen.

Cash latched onto her and held her close.

Virdon stood where he could see all of us.

"You value human life?" I asked him. "From all appearances, I say no."

Virdon muttered, "I value hers. Let her go, and I will help you with the source of your struggle." His eyes pleaded with me.

I didn't give in that easily. "What I'm struggling with is your failure to tell the truth. That's what I want, the truth, Elihu Constantine."

He flinched. "That's not my name!"

I put my left hand up. "See now, we're starting off on the wrong foot already. You lie again and I'm going to hit her with something more than a fist. You got it?"

Virdon nodded.

"That's better," I said. "Mister Cashman and I recently returned from a Texas fact-finding trip. You were born Johnny Virdon. Son of Miriam Virdon. The illegitimate offspring of Enrique Cruz from his oat-sowing days."

Virdon didn't sit on the bed. He dropped on it, as if I'd swept his feet out from under him.

I gave him time to develop his defense.

It quickly became apparent he had none. "You win. If it will save her, I will talk."

"Good," I said. "I like the sound of your voice."

He eyed Ecstasy before returning his gaze to me. "It all started with my father. He could have ignored me. Instead he honored me by raising me. I felt I owed him everything for that."

I said, "Fast forward, he recruited you to work for him. As one of the brothers Constantine. Starring nasty little brother Miguel Cruz. Better known as..." I pointed to Cash.

"The one and only Mikey Cross."

Virdon shook his head. "How do you know all this?"

I smiled. "Doyle and Cashman. When you pay enough to get the very best."

Cash said, "I always tell my mom it's Cashman and Doyle. I think you may have it backwards."

"I probably do," I said.

Virdon smirked. "Whatever you're called, do you think it's right to accost me and this innocent woman?"

Cash said, "Naah, but this is an extra added benefit where we can explore our dark side." He held a pistol, and started to lift it. Toward Ecstasy.

"Don't!" Virdon yelped. "There's been enough of that already."

"So keep talking," I said. "Your words are the only thing keeping her alive."

"And that," Cash said, "is what's called playing from a position of power."

Virdon sagged. "Please put the gun away. Stop threatening this woman."

Cash looked at me. When I nodded he complied.

I said, "The Constantine brothers were quite busy in Texas. Construction company. Real estate development. A golf course. With a sweet little brothel as the nineteenth hole."

"Our father directed us to build El Palacio Rojo," Virdon blurted. "It was his dream."

Cash said, "Father or not, you can't run from your involvement."

Virdon slowly shook his head, his eyes cast on the floor. "Nor can I run from family."

I said, "You housed two girls in your dormitory. One earned a bullet. I imagine the other girl is at the mansion in the woods. Beautiful redhead?"

"The girl who was killed lived there. About the redhead, I cannot say."

"You're saying she isn't there?" I said.

Virdon's lips twitched. "I'm saying I don't know her whereabouts, therefore I cannot say."

"And why, pray tell, don't you know her whereabouts? You've been to the mansion. We saw your van there."

Virdon appeared to be formulating an answer. When he spoke, his words were very precise. "I haven't seen the redhead in quite some time."

I looked at Cash. "I don't have time for this. Do her."

Cash grabbed Ecstasy and pulled the pistol from his waistband. "Can you say where she is now?"

Virdon shook his head. "I honestly do not know where Annette is. Threatening this woman will not change that."

Cash lowered his pistol and released Ecstasy. "Sometimes we have to go on a hunch, Paul. I have a hunch she's at the mansion. Shari was there, and they were together. I say we get her now. Then we shut Mikey down. Permanently."

I thought about it. "Makes sense to me."

"Is Mikey running the same setup as you boys had in Texas?" Cash asked. "Using hookers so guys can get their shafts straightened?"

Virdon scowled. "We built the Texas golf course with dreams of riches, but it was dying on the vine. Our father made a business decision to try and save our investment. It was only business."

Cash weighed in. "Monkey business if you ask me. And now you baboons are at it again."

Virdon glanced at Ecstasy. "Miguel learned a valuable lesson in Texas. A man may or may not pay for the pleasure of golf. But he will always pay for the pleasure of a woman. Miguel combined the two yet again, only earlier this time, before we were swimming in debt." He held his arms wide, as if he were a poor-man's Jesus on the cross. "But it is Miguel, not me."

I said, "Well Reverend, there are people up here in the sticks who might think otherwise. We tell them about your gig back home, and we show them how things appear to be shaping up the same way. So the more talking you do, the better the chance you won't find your ass in a sling. Anyway, guys like you say that confession is good for the soul."

Virdon said, "Maybe it is. Forgive me if I am long-winded."

"Sermonize your black heart away," Cash said.

Virdon took a deep breath. "As a child I had no idea who I truly was, for I did not know my father. My mother never spoke a word of him, no matter how often I pleaded with her. Then when I was thirteen, my mother passed. At her funeral I met my father for the first time. He called me his son and told me I was to live with him. I was grateful. For the first time in my life I had a father."

Reverend Virdon paced the room, shaking his head as he walked around. "As we grew older Miguel and I often talked about our father and his business. Miguel begged him to be a part of it. I, on the other hand, chose a different calling. One day I told our father I dreamed of serving the Lord. He said a small prayer and hugged me. I've reflected many times over the years. Was I was the good that balanced his evil? His support for my endeavor, it may have been his conscience speaking."

"What did Mikey think about it?"

"Miguel watched men step out of the way as our father came near. He wanted them to do the same for him, and would do whatever it took to make it so. I was never sure about his conscience, one way or the other."

"I can imagine interesting conversations around the dinner table."

Reverend Virdon grimaced. "You have no idea. One day our father told us his vision. His sons would expand his business dealings. I was apprehensive, yet Miguel was euphoric. After much pressure, I was convinced to listen to their version of logic."

"Which was?"

"We would buy real estate. Over time we would sell the properties to other companies we also owned. When our father wanted something built, he would hire us to do so. His illicit money went in. Clean money came out. Even the golf course helped us do this. It is what families do, he assured me. They take care of each other. They asked me to select the name of our company."

"Constantine. United under the cross."

"Exactly," Virdon said. "Your research is thorough."

Cash grinned, rather immodestly for my taste. "I'm not gonna lie. Cashman and Doyle rock."

I couldn't get past one hurdle. "You're a Reverend. You preach against sin and all that. Why was it so hard? No, forget hard. Why was it impossible to stand up to your father and tell him you didn't want any part of the family business?"

Virdon's shoulders sagged. "I have spent many hours debating this in my mind, and I believe two things affected me. First, my father treated me as an equal son. I held such strong gratitude toward him for taking me as his own, this clouded my judgment. The second thing was Miguel. There is ruthlessness in him that I've seen in no other man. As a brother I chose to stay near him, to try to tame him. I felt only I could save him."

Cash piped up. "How did that brilliant decision work for you, Rev?"

"Miguel's journey is not complete. There is still time."

"Great," Cash said. "So while you try to save him, Shari Tappey died. Lou Principi. Your old fishin' buddy Chrome Livingston. And God only knows who else."

Virdon seemed to shrink slightly in front of my eyes. "Miguel desperately wants to be loved by those around him. You've seen his park, and his charities. But donations and parks alone do not buy love. When Miguel does not feel appreciated, he finds another way to gain what he wants. He does not seem to accept the word 'no.'"

I said, "Yes, we've seen the body bags. And I have a suspicion Mikey's still filling them."

Virdon looked down. "Miguel continues on the path of our father, while I follow the path of my Holy Father. I hope one day to convince him to follow the Father I serve."

I sat on the bed next to Virdon and glanced toward Ecstasy. "I'd go easy on the 'serve the Lord' references, what with you screwing around with a brothel. Again."

Virdon quietly said, "What I do and who I am…they are not the same."

"Awfully convenient of you to absolve yourself, yet you continue to preach about the evil at The Limit, as if the women who work there are the scourge of the earth."

"It is God's will that man avoid sexual immorality. A house such as that should not…"

"Zip it, Rev. You owned a whorehouse, so we'll compare sins later. Even worse, you're tangled up in a mess with a couple…" I stopped short. "When I saw you with Mikey's boys, I thought they worked for you. Shaft and Guido. Mikey said he fired them."

Virdon looked lost. "Shaft?"

"Tall black guy. Leather jacket. Bald. You know, Shaft."

"His name is Rumeal Bentley."

Cash whistled. "Man, we were close."

"I am not sure why Miguel said they worked for me," Virdon mused. "They have always worked for him."

"Sounds like misdirection on his part," I said. "We watch them and Mikey makes us think we're watching you. You betray him, he betrays you. Some family you got there. Should have called yourselves Cain and Abel, Incorporated."

Virdon sighed. "I can see why you'd say that."

"Not that I'm judging," I said. "Anyway, Bentley shot Lou."

"I suspected as much," Virdon said.

"But when Lou said he'd spent the money Mikey loaned him to win the election, Bentley said 'Consider this payback from the Reverend.' Now I know why. Brotherly love. Mikey's money paid for you to lose."

Virdon ran his hands over his coarse hair. "It is somewhat ironic. Dirty money defended a dirty thing. After we lost, Miguel said he had another plan to gain control of the club. I did not understand any of it at the time."

"Easy enough to follow now. Killing Lou and this girl was part of it." I handed him Shari's crime scene photos. He thumbed through them.

"Did you show him the one with the hole in her head?" Cash asked. "You can see it…" He stuck his index finger against Ecstasy's temple. "Right here."

She ripped a vicious elbow to his gut, then spun away and glared at him from the corner.

Cash rubbed his belly. And grinned.

Virdon said, "You've heard my story. You got what you wanted. Now I want this woman released."

"Not quite yet," I said. "You still have a significant role to play. I want those girls out of Mikey's little pleasure palace. And then Mikey and I have some other topics on the agenda. Knowing him, this won't end with the girls being released."

Virdon said, "I've told you everything I know. I held up my part of the bargain. Now it's your turn. I want this woman safe, and I want her safe now."

I crooked my finger and motioned Ecstasy to stand with me. "She's perfectly safe. She's with us."

Virdon's brow crinkled. He looked at Ecstasy. "Is that true? You weren't in any danger?"

She shook her head. "Not from them."

Virdon looked helpless. "No boyfriend you were trying to escape?"

She shook her head again.

Virdon looked defeated. "I believed what you told me."

Hers was a winsome smile. "I hear that from men a lot."

CHAPTER 40

Ecstasy walked with me toward Cash's car.

"I'm going with you," she said. Her hopeful, soulful eyes searched mine.

I brushed her bangs back. "Fun stuff we do, huh? Big talk and big threats make for big fun. But the next step won't be fun. The next step will be guns and bullets and people may die, and you..."

She threw her hands up. "I know. Girl can't cut it. I'd be a liability. You'd spend so much time watching me you'd forget about Mikey."

I pressed my finger against her lips. "No. You told me you were working tonight."

She bit her teeth down hard, deep creases shredding her brow. "Son of a..."

I grabbed her hand and decided to say something that'd been on my mind for a few days. "Why don't you walk away from there, Ex? I've been thinking about it, and you don't have to do this to yourself anymore."

Her eyebrows shot up. "Do what?"

"You know." My stomach felt like I'd just boarded a rollercoaster. "Strip."

She yanked her hand away from me. "Oh, you have a problem with me stripping?"

"No." The rollercoaster steadily climbed the first big rise. She pursed her lips. "Sounds like it. Let's chase that thought, how about we do?"

"How about...no?"

"Oh yeah," she said, her words crackling. "You kicked the door open. Be a man and walk on through."

Her goading worked. I took the plunge. "So...I've been thinking that maybe you strip...to punish yourself."

She placed her palms together in front of her face. "How judgmental of you to analyze me when you don't know what the hell you're talking about."

"I mean…I was thinking…" I tried to come up with something to extricate myself from the increasingly hot water I found myself in. "Okay, I don't know for sure, but with your brain you could be anything. Yet you choose to strip. I guess I sometimes wonder why."

She tapped her forehead with her index finger. "Hmmm, why do I strip? There must be a reason. Let's see if I can hit on it. Wait, it's coming to me now. Could it be because I usually clear over a thousand a week? Could that be it? Maybe? You're a smart guy, is that a good enough reason for me to take my clothes off for the viewing public? I don't really see the punishment in making a good living, but then I'm not as morally centered as you."

"Forget it," I said. "It isn't important."

"Oh, apparently it's real damn important," she snapped. "While you're imparting so much unsolicited wisdom my way, you have anything else to get off your chest?"

I felt helpless.

"Come on Paul. You were doing so well. Don't disappoint me now."

That's the thing about getting on a rollercoaster. Once you're on it you have to ride it till the end. "Maybe…there are other things you could do to make a living."

"Of course you're right. There are myriad options for a girl with skills like mine. Here's one. I'm not half bad on my back. I got that going for me." She gnawed on her lower lip, her eyes welling with tears.

"No," I said, unable to stop the avalanche of idiocy pouring from my mouth. "That's not what I mean. But stripping, it's like you're determined to prove your ex-husband's opinion of you every time you dance. You could change. It doesn't matter what you did in your old life. You can still be anything you want to be."

"Pffft," she blew a hard breath upwards. "So that's your opinion about what I do? Shit," she said, her lips quivering. "I guess the shine is off the apple. We're telling the truth now."

"That's not it at all," I said, looking to clutch onto anything that resembled a life preserver. "What I'm trying to say is stripping is what you do. It's not who you are. You're Ecstasy."

She stepped closer and clapped me on the chest with a very firm right hand. "Well said, detective! Ecstasy is a stripper name. I'm only a lowly stripper. Let's say it together so we both understand. Come on, you can do it. Stripper."

Her eyes teetered between angry and tear-filled. "Any suggestions for my outfit tonight? French maid stripper? School girl stripper? Birthday suit? I have a really awesome birthday suit. You've seen it before. Not that you'll ever see it again, I can tell you that."

"Ex, please," I started.

She waved her hand and cut me off. "Don't sweat it, Doyle. Oh, I almost forgot. Thanks for nothing." She motioned to Cash.

When he came near, her voice dropped to a low growl. "Take me home. I have some very important stripping to do."

Without a look back, Ecstasy climbed into Cash's car and he took her away.

The rollercoaster slammed to a halt. I meekly disembarked.

I left my car at the dormitory and rode with Virdon back to the church. Soon after we arrived, Cash joined us. He entered the side door of the van. "So boys, we ready to get us some women and have a good time tonight?" He leaned toward Virdon, wrapped an arm around his neck, pulled out his nine millimeter and stuck it against Virdon's forehead.

Hard.

Virdon tried to roll his head away, but Cash held him firm. "You pull a fast one on us, you miserable prick, and I will send you straight to Hell."

"That," Virdon said, "is my biggest fear."

Cash gave Virdon a firm shove and let him go.

We exited the van, opened Cash's trunk and surveyed the weapons inside. He'd brought two shotguns, a Beretta 9mm, a .380, and my personal favorite to stop a charging rhino, a .44 Magnum. With Cash's pistol and my .357, we were better armed than many third-world countries.

"Those clean?" I asked.

"As a baby's butt," Cash said.

"That doesn't instill the greatest confidence." But I took the .380 and placed my .357 in the trunk.

Virdon uneasily eyed the weapons. "You are prepared for a fight."

"Mikey won't go easy," I said.

"Do you plan on killing him?"

I could picture a couple of outcomes for tonight. I could rescue Annette and Mikey would still demand the club. And he'd do what it took to get it. Problem unsolved. I could fail to rescue Annette and die in the process and Mikey would still demand the club. And he'd do what it took to get it. And a lot of innocent people could be hurt. Problem unsolved.

Only one other option came to mind. Stop Mikey.

Problem solved.

I sighed. "I plan on saving the girls at his place, and then we'll see what happens next. How this plays out is entirely up to him."

Virdon's jaw muscles danced as he worked on what I said. "If I help you get Annette to safety is there any way you can stop this without anyone else getting hurt?"

"I think we're way past that now. Mikey had Lou killed. He had Shari killed. He's threatened to kill other strippers from The Limit. My opinion is, as long as Mikey is alive he'll continue to kill to get what he wants. And we can no longer allow that to happen."

"So even if I help you get Annette it won't be over."

"Mikey's objective is The Limit. To him, Annette is merely a means to an end. Like Shari was. And we all know how that turned out."

Virdon sighed, long and loud. "I understand."

While Cash and I loaded the van Virdon made a quick sketch of the house. When he was done he joined us. "The house opens up into a large marble foyer. Two sets of curved staircases here and here, lead you upstairs to the girls' rooms. Downstairs is an office, common rooms, the kitchen and such."

"Did Mikey build it to match El Palacio Rojo?"

Virdon rubbed his chin. "He built it to exceed El Palacio Rojo. Miguel has everything, but everything he has is not enough until it is more than our father achieved. What a ridiculous thing to chase, the shadow of your father."

Cash cleared his throat.

Virdon spread his hands, pleading with us. "I don't understand the demons that hound Miguel. Above all he has a beautiful wife and son. Why isn't that enough for him?"

Cash clutched his hands to his chest and in his best voice-over tone said, "Theirs is a heartwarming story of boy meets girl in a bordello, boy one day takes her from her husband and calls it true love." He dabbed at his eyes.

I pondered what Virdon said. "His wife and son won't be there, will they?"

"Gabriela would never set foot in a house like this. Maybe it is because she once…" Virdon shook his head. "She is a silent wife. She knows what Miguel does, but she doesn't speak of it."

No family at the mansion. Good. "Are many other people there?"

"The house isn't fully staffed yet. There is a cook, a woman who cares for the girls, and of course the men. Two of them you know. The ones you call Shaft and Guido. The other is an older man, Rene, who manages the daily operation. He looks very mild, however he also worked for my father and I can assure you Rene will kill without a second thought."

"We met some fine gentlemen at Mikey's office. Quade, Acie Doucette, and a couple of others. Any chance they'll be at the mansion?"

Virdon said, "They are another rung down the ladder. They don't get to come inside the house."

So the numbers didn't suck. "Reverend," I said, "two of us against four of them, in a regular fight I call it fair. But when it comes to guns, especially in their territory, we need to separate them. When you see Mikey, how does it go down?"

"Rene meets me at the door. He walks me into Miguel's den. There, Miguel and I share a drink and talk by the fireplace."

"Do the men accompany you?"

Virdon scoffed. "We are brothers. He's perfectly safe." He looked down. "Until now."

"What do Shaft and Guido do when you're with Mikey?"

"You've seen the size of them. They sit in the kitchen and eat."

Cash stroked his chin. "What do you think? Get them out in the yard where we can do our thing? Now it's two on two. We go inside and stop Rene before he relives his glorious past. Then it's on to Mikey." He rubbed his hands together. "How hard is that?"

Virdon said, "When the diversion begins, Miguel will suspect I am involved. When the shooting starts, he will know I betrayed him." He slowly walked around the parking lot, scuffing his feet as he went.

"He isn't used to failing people," Cash said. "At least not up close and personal. And betraying a brother, that's pretty personal."

"He's done it once before and survived," I said. "He sounds like he wants to do the right thing. But if he chooses to betray us too…"

Cash jumped in. "That tin can we're riding in will seem awfully small if the lead starts flying."

As darkness slipped around us we prepared to depart the churchyard. Cash, who would park his car by the old farmhouse and join us before we entered Mikey's place, left first.

I climbed into the front seat. We were nearly out of the city before Virdon broke the silence. "Your friend, Mister Cashman, is intriguing. I would call him a blithe spirit."

"I've considered calling him far worse. But there's something…a type of innocence…" I'd never tried to capture Cash in a nifty sentence or two. Now I knew why. "It's almost like he's oblivious to things the rest of us obsess about. Maybe he has a clear conscience. Or no conscience at all. It's debatable."

"I wish I had the same."

I was surprised at his openness. "I have that conscience thing too. A few years ago I killed a man who shot me. I beat myself up about it every day. But eventually I realized I can't change who I was in the past. I can only shape who I'm going to be."

He smiled. "Is that a Paul Doyle original?"

"Fortune cookie. So it has to be true."

"I overheard you saying almost the same thing to the woman." He turned serious. "Am I to assume she is a stripper?"

"She's the most wonderful person I know."

"But does she…"

I cut him off. "Does it really matter? She's sweet and warm and funny and beautiful and compassionate and…" I paused to get my words right. "She makes me want to be better than I am. I can't find the bad in that."

Virdon inhaled deeply. "Her profession contradicts every value I hold dear."

"Bit of a pill for me to swallow too, what she does for a living. But in the end, who am I to judge?"

"Judging," Virdon mused. "We fall into patterns in our lives where it seems so easy to judge a person by what they do. But you've found a way to see past that. Few people can. Is this woman that important to you?"

I closed my eyes for a moment and pictured her anger as she walked away. That might be my last glimpse of her. I turned to Virdon. "She's…she's that important to me."

Virdon pursed his lips. "She needed to know that. If you'd brought her along, she'd have known."

"But how could I have done that?" I said, my mind chasing an elusive concept. "I was trying to protect her. Doesn't that tell her I care about her?"

Virdon placed his hand on my forearm. "You tried to tell her in your way. In the future, learn to say it her way. You wanted her to be safe, but to her it felt like rejection."

"Yeah, I received that message loud and clear. And all that foolishness I said about how she didn't need to strip anymore…now she's gone."

Virdon patted my arm, and then returned his hand to the steering wheel. "I saw the way she looks at you. She isn't going anywhere. You offer her something she needs, even if you don't know what it is yet."

"Is it always going to be like this, me and her? I think I'm doing one thing, and she reads it another way? I try to say something that I think is kind and it ends up with the worst possible result?"

"With relationships, communication is usually the biggest challenge. Just remember while you're trying to figure out who she is, she's trying just as hard to understand you."

Forty seconds slipped by as we waited at a traffic light. A minute.

Virdon said, "Men will die tonight."

"Yes. Which ones, I'm not sure."

As we eased away from the light he said, "Regardless of what he's done, I don't wish to see my brother harmed." He drummed his fingers on the steering wheel. "You've talked about Miguel killing people. Are you sure? Do you have unquestionable proof?"

"Look in that heart of yours, Reverend. You don't need me to provide proof. You know who he is."

As we wound our way deeper into the countryside, Virdon studied the road. When he spoke, it was to the windshield. "It all started out so innocently. We were young men who bought things and built things. Tinker Toys, erector sets and Monopoly money, that's what I convinced myself it was. Then we built El Palacio Rojo. That is where I could no longer draw the line and say we remained clean. I, a man who preached against sin, owned a brothel. I confronted my values and lost. Maybe this is why I am so fervent about closing The Limit. I am taking a stand now to make up for my failures in the past."

"Trick is, we can't ever make up for the past. And bigger picture, you came to Maine to stop your brother from becoming your father. Today is the day you can be successful."

Virdon exhaled. "The Bible says if my brother trespasses against me, I should tell him his fault. If he hears me, I gain my brother. I have counseled Miguel endlessly. He nods, he smiles, and he continues along this path he's chosen."

"He's had many chances to listen."

"He does not hear me. I truly know I have lost my brother." As we stopped at the red light at the intersection with Route 3, Virdon bowed his head, closed his eyes and said a brief prayer.

When he opened his eyes I asked, "What are you praying about?"

"I asked God to forgive my treacherous soul."

CHAPTER 41

Virdon left the main road, drove past the golf course and turned onto the dirt road that led to the mansion.

He slammed on the brakes as Cash stepped from behind a tree. Cash opened the side door and I slipped into the back of the van with him. He looked at me. "You ready for this?"

"Kind of late to ask now, isn't it?"

"Sure. But in every war movie, just before the attack one joker asks his buddy, 'You ready for this?' I wanted to stick to the script."

"Well good for you. There's the gate."

As Virdon said it would, the gate slid open when we approached. He drove through.

"There's no turning back now," Cash said.

"You get that from war movies, too?"

"Execute the plan. Do unto others before they do unto you. Kick ass, take names. Bomb them back to the Stone Age. Kill all the bastards, let God sort 'em out. I have a million snappy quotes. One to fit every occasion."

A floodlight shone in front of the house. The yard behind the house was dark. Virdon rolled to a stop, exited the van and walked to the door.

A short man in a white shirt and black pants, with a slight potbelly and thinning hair, opened the door and greeted Virdon. After they embraced, the man let him inside.

I looked at Cash. "Doesn't look like a setup, or they'd have started shooting by now."

"Still, I'd feel a whole lot safer outside this coffin on wheels."

We smeared on face black and donned black gloves. Cash opened the van's back door and we slipped out.

I sprinted to the house and flattened against it while Cash, with his arms full of gear, melted along the compound's outer wall. Within a few seconds, all I saw was a black expanse in front of me. But I knew he was there. Cash always did what he said he'd do.

Except when he improvised.

I hoped like hell he wasn't going to improvise tonight.

I followed the wall as I crept along. When I came to the corner I stepped around to the back of the house. A faint light from two kitchen windows dimly illuminated a wide porch with many wooden rockers.

About twenty feet from me I saw the back door. Shaft and Guido would come out there. I wanted to be as close as possible when they did. I worked my way toward it.

The woods were silent. We were too far from the road for traffic sounds. I heard only my breathing, slow and easy. It was me, my feet and the grass. Me, my feet and the...

The wire over the back wall rattled. Cash had thrown a fully-clothed dummy onto it.

Game on.

A bright flash and a boom shattered the evening serenity. Two seconds later, another. Another. My ears rang from the concussions. M-80 firecrackers will do that to you. Every time.

I heard a shout from inside and a chair thump to the floor. The porch light came on, momentarily blinding me. I dove to the ground and looked toward the nearly-invisible wall. Apparently no one had thought about installing lights that shined that far from the house. Even I couldn't tell what was happening, and I was in on the plan.

Footsteps pounded on the porch as two men charged out. Shaft and Guido.

"Fucker's comin' over the fence!" Shaft yelled. He assumed a spread-legged firing position and threw lead at the barely-visible figure.

Guido took a knee about twenty feet from me. He watched the figure twitch as Shaft's shots peppered it. Guido didn't shoot.

Something wasn't right.

"Over here," I said.

Guido spun. I fired three rounds into him while his only shot barked over my head and thudded into the house. As he fell, I sprinted past him toward the porch door.

Shaft turned and fired where I'd been.

I crouched fifteen feet away and squeezed off three more. Shaft jerked, then jerked again.

He looked at me, stunned, but he remained standing. His gun hung at his side. He struggled to raise it.

Cash stuck his pistol behind Shaft's ear and pulled the trigger.

We ran for the door. I dove inside and hit the floor. Cash cut left.

I hid behind an island in the kitchen. I couldn't see Cash, but he knew where I was. I trusted that would be good enough.

While I reloaded, I peered around the island. I saw the dining room and a hallway. The hallway that led to the foyer and Mikey's study.

My ears still rang. I would see my attacker before I heard him. If I could see him at all. Right now, I only saw half of the dining room. And a hallway that led to the foyer.

Nothing moved.

I thought about the time when I'd moved too quickly in Mikey's darkened office building hallway. That had gone poorly for me.

So this time I waited.

Because he who moves first dies.

And he who waits best wins.

Think.

I could do that.

What would I do if I was under attack?

I'd assume I had two men down.

I'd assume my attackers would work their way through the house to find me.

Therefore I'd put myself where my attackers wouldn't think to look for me. Where they had just been.

I spun around in time to see the briefest shadow slip by the window. If he made it to the door, he'd shoot me in the back.

Which made it imperative I didn't let that happen.

I scooted around the side of the island. I could see the door, but a person looking in couldn't see enough of me to get off a good shot.

On the other hand, the first living thing I saw would get a chest full of dead.

I licked my lips.

He who waits best…

The barrel of a shotgun slowly eased into the door opening. A left hand. A shoulder. The side of a bald head. Craning around the corner toward me.

When I saw his shirt pocket, I raised my gun. But before I could shoot, Cash fired. The pocket disappeared and the shotgun clattered to the floor.

I waited forever, and saw no additional movement. I heard no sound.

I crept around the island and saw Rene on his back, his eyes, mouth and chest open. Threat neutralized.

A moment later, Cash appeared. He glanced at Rene. "He was watching the right hand, and the left hand knocked him out."

I looked toward the hallway. "I don't like going through there."

"If Mikey's watching it, going down that hall might suck a little. How you want to do this?"

"One at a time. You get behind the china buffet and cover me. I'll go down the hall lickety-split, followed by you."

He studied me. "You have a lickety-split speed?"

"When folks are shooting I sure as hell do."

Cash seemed satisfied. "Let's roll." He stood up, took a dozen quick steps and hunkered down behind the buffet. He looked back at me. "C'mon, boy. Get your lickety on."

I scooted through the kitchen, the dining room, and down the short hallway to the foyer. I slid to a stop beside the marble staircase. A moment later Cash joined me.

I looked at the large door on the other side of the staircase. "That's where Mikey is."

"Be a brave man who opens that door."

"You feeling brave?"

"I was thinking you. But since you asked so nicely, I'll go first."

"Keep your head down, Bud."

"Why do I suddenly feel like The Sundance Kid?" Cash said, before he went around the staircase, to the door, and turned the knob.

He yanked the door open. "Mikey, you got company!"

No answer.

"Mikey, you goddamn coward!" Cash hollered. His words echoed through the foyer. Cash looked at me. "I think he's ignoring me."

Before I could stop him, Cash stepped around the door and into the room.

CHAPTER 42

A moment later Cash said, "Paul, come here."

His tone said it was bad. I walked through the open door and into the room.

Johnny Virdon stood near a cherry desk, cautiously eyeing his brother.

Mikey Cross was in front of an ornate, marble and teak-framed fireplace that was enthusiastically burning.

His arm was wrapped tightly around Ecstasy's neck.

His right hand held a pistol. He stroked the business end of the barrel along the side of her face. "Given the timing of her arrival I can only assume she's with you."

Ecstasy's terrified face searched mine.

My stomach felt like I'd swallowed concrete, but I fought off weak-in-the-knees and went with false bravado. "Who she's with doesn't matter. This is over, Mikey."

Mikey sneered. "It isn't over till I say it's over!"

"So say it, douche bag," Cash urged. He slowly slid to Mikey's left, hoping to improve his line of fire.

"Uh-uh!" Mikey said, blocking Cash's movement by pivoting Ecstasy. "You take one more step and I'll shoot her." Mikey tapped his pistol against her skull.

"You could," I said. "But when you shoot her you'll have lost your coward shield. And you're not man enough to stand there without one."

Virdon spoke. "Miguel, no more threats. No more death."

Mikey glared at him. "Shut the fuck up, you spineless imbecile!"

"Mikey," I said, "you had Lou killed. Fair enough. Price of doing business with a dirtball like you."

Mikey seemed a trifle remorseful. Not nearly enough to suspend an impending death sentence, but a trifle. "I never planned on killing him."

"What you planned is irrelevant, since your boys shot him anyway."

"They responded in self-defense. We are all innocent."

"Says the guy with a gun to a woman's head." I wished mine was against Mikey's head. Perhaps his definition of innocent may change a little. "I'm not sure your version of events matches the truth. The way I hear it, your boys blew things a bit out of proportion when they found out Lou Principi used your money to beat your brother's referendum."

Mikey's eyes flashed fiery hate. "He tried to double-cross me."

"He tried to save his business."

Anger slowly ebbed from Mikey's face. "Yet he ultimately failed. He was not my equal."

I snarled, "You don't do equal, asshole. You play a fixed game. Like with my father. You burned up his trucks. You jerry-rigged scaffolding. You put two guys on disability. You…"

My head was on fire. I couldn't see straight. I couldn't think straight. I only knew Mikey deserved to die. Tonight. Now. "You…you…" I tried again. "You murdered Shari and you're not walking away from that. Why'd you kill her?"

"Ah, the odd purple-haired girl. Her death was an unfortunate by-product of a larger undertaking. But do you understand a threat?"

"You mean like me saying, 'I'm going to kick your ass?'"

Mikey smirked. "Sure. But a threat, especially a threat like yours, is hollow. Unless the threat is backed by proof of intent. I said I would kill strippers if anyone talked. Principi talked to you, so I used the girl to reinforce my point. Tonight…" He again tapped the pistol against Ecstasy's skull. "I'm sure you see how this will play out."

Ecstasy twisted against him, trying to pull away.

Mikey tightened his grip on her and laughed. "What you don't know are a few things I must share with you. First, I've already called the State Police to report a breaking and entering. They should be here soon."

"Well, we didn't actually break in," Cash said. "We kinda snuck in through an open door. Technically it may not count."

"Shut up!" Mikey said. He rested his chin on top of Ecstasy's head. "This woman, this associate of yours, tells me you're here to rescue Principi's red-headed niece. You are such a fool, Doyle. She has never set foot in this place. I would let you inspect my property, but..." He glanced between me and Cash. "I just don't see the value in it for me. You will have to take my word for it."

"For real?" I said. "You never had her?"

Mikey said, "After she disappeared from the church dormitory I never found her. I thought you had hid her away and, as it turned out, I didn't need her to achieve my aims. But still..." His face slackened as if he were puzzled by this turn of events.

"Sorry to disappoint you," I said. But I felt as confused as Mikey looked. If Annette wasn't here, where was she?

Mikey shook his head slightly. "It is of no matter now. The next thing I say will make you look even more foolish."

I waved my pistol back and forth like a baton. "I'm guessing it's about the club or something."

"Ah yes, my beautiful club," Mikey said. "That's where this all started." He glanced toward Virdon. "You wanted to shut the club down and politics couldn't fix it. But I could."

Virdon's face tightened. "You did this for me?"

Mikey's smile grew. "Of course. It is two days before your birthday, but this is worthy of an early surprise. As the new owner, my gift to you is The Limit."

When Virdon spoke his voice sounded flat. Emotionless. "You killed Principi and the girl to give me the club?" He looked utterly exhausted. With him being Mikey's big brother, I could understand.

A smile burned across Mikey's face. "I would do it again."

"Let me get it straight," Cash said. "This all happened because Principi out-smarted you? What a dumbass."

Mikey jammed the pistol hard under Ecstasy's jaw. "Do not insult me! Or I will kill her!"

I held my left palm out as a peace offering. "Again I'll remind you, bullet in her head means your coward shield is gone. But no kidding, you think the club is yours?"

Mikey nodded toward his desk. "The papers are in the middle drawer. I am the owner."

Cash sidestepped to the desk and withdrew a sheaf of papers.

"Read them," Mikey commanded.

Cash unfolded the papers and handed them to Virdon. "I'm kind of busy trying to shoot your brother. You want to read for us?"

Virdon took the papers. He rapidly scanned them. When he finished, he looked at Cash, who hadn't taken his eyes, or his gun, off Mikey. "I don't know what you want me to say."

I coaxed him along. "Tell us what day Yvette supposedly sold the club to your brother."

"Yesterday."

I pondered this. "No shit?"

Mikey's jaw twitched. "As of yesterday, the club is mine to do with as I wish. And I wish to give it to my brother." Mikey looked Virdon's way. "Take the key that is also inside the envelope. The Limit is finally yours. I have already contacted the local media. They will be there tomorrow at noon when you…"

"Whoa!" Cash bellowed. "You said yesterday."

Mikey snapped, "You are an incessant jerk."

"You say it like you're surprised." Cash exhaled loudly. "Boy, you had us going there for a second. Till I understood the 'yesterday' part. I feel a whole lot better now."

Mikey glared at Cash. "You keep talking about yesterday. Yesterday, yesterday. It's in the papers. Yvette Monfort sold me The Limit yesterday."

Cash said, "And after that, I'll bet your troubles seemed so far away. But now…" He pointed his pistol at the sheaf of papers Virdon held. "Now I think they're here to stay."

I nodded thoughtfully. "Gonna have to agree with Cash on this one. But I gotta know. What did she soak *you* for, Mikey?"

"I paid off her note. Would it please you to see the receipt?"

"Naah, I'm good. One hundred eighty-three thousand, two hundred forty-seven dollars. And some change."

Mikey's glare appeared darker than the night. "How would you know that?"

I tapped my jacket pocket and looked at Mikey. "May I?"

Mikey scowled. Nodded.

I pulled some papers from my pocket and pushed them toward Virdon. "Since you did so well last time."

When Virdon seemed confused, Cash reassured him. "Go ahead. I think we all know where this is headed."

Virdon ran his eyes over the document. When he read the last page, he cocked his head. "This says Yvette Monfort sold The Limit to Paul Doyle on October 28th. Four days ago."

I smiled. "I paid her a buck for it. I was the legal owner three days before Yvette took you to the cleaners. I changed the locks already, so that key doesn't mean much. Jeez, you got screwed good."

I looked at Mikey, whose skin seemed to have paled considerably. "Remember that day in your office when you told me you were forever a giver? Yvette says thanks."

Virdon gently said to his brother, "I ask you to look for the deeper meaning in all this, for life inevitably finds its balance. Maybe the Lord decided this is atonement for your past sins."

Mikey spat, "Do not judge me. You were part of this! You stood beside me through this entire thing!" Fury sparked from his eyes.

"Until now." Virdon looked over at Cash, and back at me. "I can stand beside you no longer. What these men said is true. They did not break in. I let them in."

Mikey's jaw tightened. "No. You would not do this to me."

"It is time you know the truth. I hid the redhead you've been looking for. You were never going to find her, my brother. Knowing you, I could not risk her life."

Mikey stared at Virdon. "I don't believe you."

"Believe him," I said. "But this isn't new behavior for the good Reverend. Remember when Gabriela vanished from El Palacio Rojo years ago? Inside job." I hooked a thumb at Virdon. He nodded.

Mikey moaned. "You are my family. You would not betray me."

Virdon solemnly said, "I have given you all that I can give. Our destiny is in the Lord's hands now." He closed his eyes, clasped his hands and prayed.

In the near-quiet room nothing moved.

Then Mikey shook his head. "No. I control our destiny. *Perdóname, hermano. Perdóname.*"

Very deliberately, he shot Virdon in the chest.

Virdon melted to the floor.

Ecstasy drove her left heel onto the top of Mikey's foot and whipped an elbow that cracked him in the chin. As he jerked his head away, she spun from his grasp.

Cash dove and yanked her down as Mikey fired high.

I fired as well.

Twice.

Into Mikey.

Center mass.

Mikey looked for a moment at the holes in his shirt.

Then dropped, face down on the floor.

Virdon strained to look at the floor in front of him.

He studied the distance.

He rose up on his knees began to crawl.

Six inches.

Virdon hung his head and drew in a ragged breath.

He moved six inches more.

Then he dropped like a bag of flour, slamming onto the boards.

Moaning deeply, Virdon struggled to lift his head.

His face was painted with resolve.

His shoes slid against the hard wood, begging for a toehold.

His fingers dragged in vain along the polished boards.

So he wriggled like a snake.

And moved.

A bit more.

Again.

He was at Mikey's side.

Virdon slid his right arm out. As far as he could reach.

He found Mikey's lifeless hand and squeezed.

"*Te perdono, Miguel,*" he whispered.

It was done.

CHAPTER 43

I heard a muted gasp from the corner. Ecstasy leaned against the wall, her eyes closed. Her head slowly weaved back and forth.

When I touched her arm she opened her eyes and said, "You shot Mikey."

"Yes."

Her breathing hitched. "I think they're both dead."

"They are."

She looked at the bodies and shivered before she spoke. "I can do a lot of things, but I can't do 'dead,' Paul. I can't do dead."

I took her hand. "Ex, what are you doing here? How…"

Cash stepped out of the room.

Ecstasy looked at the door. "I made Cash bring me. He didn't have a choice, so don't get mad and blame him. I snuck in behind you when they opened the gate for the van. I had to come. I had to do this. After our blowup…I didn't mean what I said. I had to fix it."

"Nothing to fix, Ex," I said. "And you being here…well, at least no one was hurt." I looked at the bodies in the room. "Scratch that. None of *us* were hurt."

"Still," she said, "people did die. When you told me about your job, you said that people die and I believed you. I really did. But believing and seeing are two different things. And no matter what I want, I can't…do…this." She seemed frozen in place.

She could have leaned closer to me, but she'd already spoken her piece.

I didn't move toward her either, so that probably clinched the deal.

Ecstasy pulled her hand away. "Just go. Find Annette. I have to go now too."

She was right. Of course. We took the stairs two at a time.

I knocked on the first door we saw. A woman of fifty or so, dressed in a heavy white nightgown, met us. She carried a fluffy white thing that may have been a dog in the crook of her arm. Despite the ruckus and our black-smeared faces she didn't seem overly concerned. "What's going on? I heard shooting."

"Change of management," I said.

The dog yipped. The woman closed the door.

True to Mikey's word Annette Begley was nowhere to be found, but we discovered nine other girls in the house. After we explained in brief detail what had happened, every single one voted for the 'go home' option we proposed. They huddled around the dining room table, torn between laughing, crying and peering furtively around every time they heard an unusual noise. We woke the cook and persuaded her to feed the girls while we slipped out and worked our way as far from the memory of Mikey Cross as possible.

After we'd gone out the front gate and climbed past the rocky outcropping where we'd first observed the mansion compound, Cash turned to me. "Watching Mikey die, I have to know…how does revenge taste?"

I leaned against a tall pine and sampled my emotions. I wasn't glowing like an ember. I wasn't hoping to give out high fives. No. I felt like I'd just finished reading a book and didn't particularly like the ending. Because no matter how dead Mikey was, it didn't change what he'd done. "It isn't the tasty morsel I once hoped it would be. And…let's not call it revenge, okay? It sounds like we did this for the wrong reason. We did it to stop Mikey from killing more people. Let's say the right thing happened, even if we swerved a little out of our lane to do it. I'm okay with that."

"Just one thing. Lot of shooting tonight, and no Annette to show for it. Have any guesses as to where Virdon might have stashed her?"

I'd thought about it a bit since Virdon sprung the surprise a few minutes earlier. I nodded. "I know exactly where she is."

"Are we heading there next?"

"If we get off this ridge without the cops catching us." I picked up the pace.

"By the way, Gabriela is a widow now," Cash said.

"I know. I made her one."

"Ever think about filling Ken Bartholomew in on this fascinating turn of events?"

"Well no," I said. "She's only been a widow for about twenty minutes. I wanted to give her time to grieve. But maybe…"

"Tomorrow?"

"Yeah. Maybe tomorrow."

We listened as the police sirens turned off Route 3 and headed toward Mikey's.

"I noticed the gate was open," Cash said.

"Yup."

"It was closed when the fun started."

"Yup." I pictured a slim young woman pressing the button, opening the gate, and walking away without a backwards glance. I'm not sure I blamed her.

"Ecstasy didn't take it well?"

"She…the guns, you know? She learned that what we do isn't like a movie or a book. This shit tonight was real." The darkness deepened. It matched my mood to a T.

Cash cleared his throat. "'Tis better to have loved and lost…"

"Shut up or I'll shoot you too."

If walking through the woods during the daytime is hard, doing it in the dark while lugging an armful of weapons and a fully-clothed dummy added an exponential degree of difficulty I could have done without.

By now the cops would have found the bodies. They'd have rescued the girls. They'd have discovered a few stray shell casings, none of which matched any ballistics they had on record.

They'd also have noticed a confounding lack of assailants.

While the face black would have helped some, we'd also asked the girls to be less-than-specific when they described our size, shape, and general demeanor. Given how their quality of life had improved in the last hour, we were pretty sure they'd comply.

Cash and I were nearly back to the old farmhouse when my cell phone went off.

Maine State Police Lieutenant Simeon Mathers. "Want to hear some good news?"

"That's my favorite kind."

"I'm looking at the body of Mikey Cross, and some extensive collateral damage. This place looks like some B-grade slasher movie."

I hummed. "Slasher movie, huh? You think Mikey cut himself shaving?"

Mathers said in a rather testy tone, "I don't know, Paul. You tell me."

"I don't know, Simeon. I'm not looking at him. You are."

Mathers cursed. "This frigging place looks like a shooting gallery. A goddamn war zone. The girls we found here said some husky guys wearing black face paint were involved. You wouldn't know anything about that, would you?"

Cash and I stood beside the road and waited for a car to pass. "From what you've told me, I have no further interest in the affairs of Mikey Cross."

We scurried across the road before an oncoming semi caught us in its headlights.

Mathers cursed again. "So that's it? That's all you've got to say about this goat rope I'm observing as we speak?"

"Just one more thing."

"What is it?"

"Good night, Lieutenant."

⚔

We drove straight to the church dormitory. The front door was unlocked. I led the way.

To the same door I'd seen the slim blonde girl exit earlier in the evening.

I tapped on the door.

After a few moments, a blue-eyed girl with freckles looked out. Though her hair was bleached there was no mistaking the face.

Annette Begley.

Cherry Delight.

Take your pick.

⚔

When Cash dropped me off at my car, I felt exhausted. But I wasn't too tired to drive to the cemetery and climb over the locked gate. Or to walk to Shari

Tappey's grave. And sit for a while and watch clouds dance past the moon and think of a beautiful young woman who was far too young to die.

I wasn't too tired to call Venus, either. Though it was after midnight. Again.

I kept it to the point. Annette was safe. Mikey wasn't.

Venus didn't ask a single question.

We were quiet then, not quite sure what to say and not quite ready to say goodnight.

I watched the stars wink on and off as the clouds slipped by. I hoped she could see them too. I finally said, "I always thought our midnight chats would be pillow talk."

She sighed. "Once upon a time, so did I."

CHAPTER 44

Days went by, as days tend to do.

I re-sold Yvette the club for a buck. She was some thrilled to break even on the deal.

I jogged religiously.

I slept when I could.

I stuck with the healthy diet and dropped a few more pounds.

I picked up two new cases and wrapped them up in a week.

I, Paul Doyle, had the world by the balls.

So why did it feel like it had me the same way?

I was somewhere along the path to fitful sleep when the doorbell jarred me awake. I glanced at the clock. 3:07.

Ma's feet thudded to the floor as I grabbed a pair of sweat pants. I hopped on one foot, trying to get my stubborn right one in, when I heard her open the door.

"Yes?"

"Is this Paul Doyle's house?" A voice I thought I'd never hear again.

Ecstasy's.

"Who are you?" Ma said.

I pulled the sweats on and charged out of the bedroom. "She's a friend, Ma."

Ma ran her eyes over Ecstasy.

Her unbuttoned coat flapped in the windy night, and she clutched her platform heels in her hand. She'd been working while I'd been sleeping, and she was still dressed for the occasion. She wore a miniscule black miniskirt that hugged her hips tighter than bark on a tree, accompanied by a fashionable white see-through blouse with no bra. Even an arm modestly thrown across her chest was no match for Ma's prying eyes.

"Lookin' good, Ex," I said, because it seemed far too late to say anything remotely appropriate. We were playing strictly for laughs now.

Ma snorted. "We will not make a habit of your lady friends coming over here like this, will we?"

I never knew what the final push out of the nest would feel like. Now I did. "Been meaning to tell you, Ma. There's a nice little place I've been looking at on Hudson Street. About time for me to mosey."

"I didn't mean…you don't have to go…"

I looked at Ecstasy, then back at Ma. "Yeah. I do."

Ecstasy smiled and stuck out a hand to Ma. "So pleased to meet you."

Ma surveyed Ecstasy's outstretched hand, then spun on her worn out slippers and stomped off to bed. She gave the bedroom door a house-shaking slam.

Ecstasy looked at her shirt, and then at the bedroom door. "I wish I were dead."

"I believe Ma wishes you were, too."

Ecstasy scanned the living room and the kitchen. What she thought when she saw a thirty-year-old couch that I too often frequented, or Ma's chair with the broken arm, I couldn't tell.

What I saw when I looked was the place that had been my home. Twice.

Ecstasy nudged me. "You're going to leave because I showed up?"

I ran my index finger from her scalp line, down her nose, over her lips and briefly circled the scar on her chin. "No. I'm going to leave because I ran back home to Mommy when my life went south. Well, it's been a year. It's time to stop relying on Mommy." I tapped Ecstasy on the nose.

She patted my chest. "What a big boy you are."

I looked at her closed bedroom door. "Ma may not agree. But in the morning…"

"In the morning you'll get your own apartment."

"Yes. In the morning I'll get my own apartment. Because this place is ridiculous. People dropping in at all hours of the night."

Ecstasy watched her foot draw circles on the floor. "I'm sorry. I needed to see you standing in front of me. I needed something…real."

I thought about the last 'real' thing we'd shared.

She forced a smile that wasn't a real smile at all. "So here I am."

"You want to talk about it, girl?"

Ecstasy turned her gentle, tender eyes on me. "I want you to hold me."

We walked into the bedroom and closed the door.

She dropped her six-inch heels in the corner, climbed onto the bed, and waited.

When I lay down, she scooted next to me. She put her head on my shoulder, her hand on my heart and crossed her legs over mine.

I flipped the quilt over us.

I watched her head move. I felt her breathing slow. It became shallow.

She slept.

And I wondered what the hell this was all about.

A weak gray light shone through the window. Ecstasy's luxurious brown hair cascaded over her face, covering her left eye. I could only see part of her cheek and her chin.

If this was the last time I'd see her, I needed to see more. I brushed some stray locks away.

She slept like a child. Peaceful. Soundless.

Seemingly without a care.

I had a few.

Ecstasy mumbled, burrowed deeper into my chest and wrapped her legs around mine.

I kissed the top of her head and dreaded the moment when she would wake. Because waking dramatically increased the chance that she would leave the bed, put her shoes on, walk out the door and disappear forever.

While she was asleep, she was still mine.

When Ecstasy stirred next, it wasn't gentle. She threw the quilt back and stared at the bedroom door.

I heard it, too. The sound of a frying pan being placed on the stove. Good old Ma. I inhaled. "You like coffee?"

"Your mother hates me," Ecstasy said, her eyes wide, her face contorted.

"Don't feel so special. Ma hates everyone."

Ecstasy scowled. "It isn't funny, Paul. I can't leave with her out there."

"Why do you want to leave now? She makes a mean French toast. And I know how much you like French toast."

"I can't eat breakfast here." She looked down at her blouse. "Not like this."

I studied her. "I have a sweater that will hang fashionably to your knees and cover your…bountiful harvest."

She gritted her teeth. "Everything is a joke to you, isn't it? Well, it's not a joke to me."

I went to my closet and took out a striped robe, a brown sweatshirt and a red shirt.

I held the shirt up. "Red is definitely your color. Here, slip this on."

She took it.

"Ma gave it to me."

Ecstasy slammed it down on the bed. "You're such an ass." She waved off the clothes I'd laid out, stood up and walked to the armchair in the corner. She pulled it near the bed, spun the chair around, hiked her skirt up and straddled it. She crossed her arms on the chair's back and faced me. That left me the bed.

"Before we think about breakfast maybe we should talk first," she said. "I bet you're wondering why I'm here."

"The thought has crossed my mind."

Ecstasy grimaced. "That night at Mikey's…I found blood in my hair, Paul. Girls don't like blood in their hair. Maybe that's why I flipped out and ran. One of the many reasons, as it turns out."

Clouds blew across her face. She started to say more but seemed to think better of it. Say it, I wanted to scream. Whatever it is, say it.

Then I thought about Reverend Virdon. 'Let her do it her way,' he would have said. Be patient with her. "It doesn't need to be perfect, Ex. Throw it out there when you're ready. We can always make it pretty later."

She blew out a huge breath. "So, after you and Cash went to find Annette, I ran out to the main road. I bummed a ride back to town. And then I took a shower, put on a trashy little outfit, and went to The Limit. I gave seven nude lap dances. Given all that had happened, it seemed like a fitting way to end the evening."

I wasn't sure if I should say 'good for you,' or 'I'm sorry.' To be on the safe side I didn't say anything.

Ecstasy slowly shook her head. "That doesn't shock you? Me giving all those nude lap dances? Guys seeing me that way?"

I decided to go bold and try to explain what I felt. "I should have said this a while back when I made a mess of things. There is no sin in stripping. You do what you do and I accept it. Plus, you saw me kill a man. I'd like to think that puts your work in perspective."

She looked relieved. "Every time I tell you worse and worse things I expect you to run for the hills. But you never do. Of course that all may change, because I saved the punch line for today."

"Ex," I said, thinking about Ken Bartholomew uncovering Gabriela's back-story. "I don't have to know about your past. I accept you as I see you today. Unequivocally."

She slapped the back of the chair with her hand. "We shall see, Paul Doyle. We shall see. Ever hear the one about how I killed my unborn child? It's a real page-turner."

I finally understood what 'utterly speechless' felt like.

She touched my arm. "What, no witty one-liners? No snappy comebacks?"

I shook my head, more than a little bewildered. "I got nothing."

She said, "With an opening line like mine I hardly blame you. Still, here we go. Remember that night when I told you about being married and you assumed that was my deepest secret? Please. That was amateur stuff. Pull up your seats, boys and girls, and lemme tell you a humdinger."

I hitched closer to her.

A grim smile briefly graced her face. "My husband's name was Dan. Whatever we married for, it didn't take long for Danny Boy to decide love wasn't it. First rule for a college girl to follow: never fall in bed with a rich white boy who only wants something different than the white girls he's had. But I forgot that rule as soon as I saw his bedroom eyes. We eloped to Vegas right after graduation. Made it almost a year before he decided it was more fun to be an eternal frat boy than a husband."

A tear slipped down Ecstasy's cheek, and she took a gulping breath to steady herself. Softly she said, "When I found out he had a girlfriend…that was the cherry on top of our breakup sundae, don't ya know. God, I was so desperate to be loved by him."

She cocked her head and frowned. "Silly me, did I say loved? What I meant to say was I couldn't accept being rejected by my absolute shit of a husband. So one day I played my trump card and told him I was pregnant." She traced the scar on her chin. "He was not a happy prospective father."

I stroked her hair until her breathing once again steadied.

She lifted her eyes to mine. "Some days I was so sad I couldn't get out of bed. Couldn't shower, couldn't eat, couldn't even brush my teeth. Couldn't. Hardly. Breathe. So I finally went to a pill-pusher and he diagnosed me with depression and gave me a medicine cabinet full of help. Of course, he didn't know I was two months pregnant at the time." She cleared her throat. "Looking back, I guess I should have brought that up."

I half-nodded, half-shrugged.

"How we doing so far, Paul? Still with me?"

I leaned forward and patted her shoulder. "Still here, Ex."

"Good, I don't want you nodding off, we're just getting to the juicy part. So one day, in a fit of sheer boredom and morbid curiosity, I counted all the pills in the house. Twenty-one Vicodin we'd collected over time, twenty-three Prozac and nineteen Wellbutrin of my very own. Then I sat on the floor and placed them in a neat, tidy circle around me. But then I decided the odd numbers weren't at all symmetrical, so I took five Vicodin, seven Prozac and three Wellbutrin and washed them down with a light, crisp Chablis I'd been saving for just such an occasion. That left me sixteen of each pill. Square root of sixteen—four. Square root of four—two. Like the two of us, my little fetus and me. Now we were symmetrical as hell. I rearranged the remaining pills in a circle around us. Then I lay down and waited for us to die."

My deep exhale surprised me. "Luckily you didn't."

Ecstasy squinted her eyes and locked her jaw so tightly shut her facial muscles twitched. "I wouldn't call it luck," she finally said, "because I was supposed to die, too. When it was over I told them I didn't know I was pregnant and they bought it. Still, I received a lot of counseling over my little indiscretion. Quality fucking counseling, boy let me tell ya. There were times when I felt I was just barely hanging onto my sanity by my fingertips and they looked at me and said 'You're researching suicide tips online? How nice. So, see you same time next week, dear?' It was always 'Same time next week, dear?' until one day I screamed 'What will it take to make you realize what I'm feeling is real? When I put a gun to my head? Or maybe it will take my sixteen Vicodin, sixteen Prozac, and sixteen Wellbutrin. I'd like them back now, please.' That's when I had their full attention."

I took her hand. She let me hold it while she stared at the wall.

After a few moments she pulled her hand away. She fished around her purse for a tissue and dabbed at her eyes. After she stuck her tissue back in her purse she said, "We have this game where we say I'm almost cured now, me and my therapist who can't take his eyes off my tits when we talk. But I'm just telling him what he wants to hear so he won't push any pills toward me. To tell the truth I'm scared to death about having more to place in a circle around me. Because if I'm having a really shitty day maybe this time I won't leave any behind and we all know what the square root of that is. Nada." She shuddered.

Though I had no idea what to say I decided to try something. "You've endured more pain than I can imagine. The fact that you can get through the day at all is incredible. And to do it as wonderfully as you do…"

"Pfft," she said. "I think we've both determined there's nothing wonderful about me."

I cupped her cheek in my hand. "Gonna have to disagree with you there, Ex. Your smile is like the sunrise after a very long night. It gives a person hope. Your eyes flash like lightning storms rolling across the desert. Your heart is the deepest well of compassion I've ever seen. You…you're my…I…"

Her face scrunched up. "Lightning storms rolling across the desert? That's a little over-the-top, don't you think? I'm just a skinny girl who takes her clothes off for a buck."

"Fair enough," I said. "And I'm just a dumb fat guy who was on his way to being one of those people you see wandering around town. You know, the ones where you say 'Didn't expect he'd amount to much, and I was right.' Sad thing was I was at the point where I just didn't care anymore. I was ready be a loser and be done with it. Then I met you. And all of a sudden, it was like I had something to strive for. Something that maybe I could achieve. Something like…you."

She twisted her cheek from my hand. "You should aim a little higher, Paul. I'm not much in the grand scheme of things."

"Says you. Try to see yourself through my eyes."

Ecstasy closed her eyes for a time. When she opened them, she mini-shrugged. "I only know how to look at me through my eyes. And that view makes me cringe. You want to know why I came by your house this morning? You want to know what put me over the top and sent me crawling over here? This may add a little context to the me that you think you know."

I wasn't overly sure I did. But given she was going to tell me regardless, my opinion on the issue didn't seem to matter much.

"A couple came into the club last night," she said. "Man and woman. I usually only do singles, but he was insistent. His wife singled me out, he said. From all the girls in the club, she chose me. And she was…exotic. Long brown hair. Expensive perfume. Beautiful dress. Perfect makeup. Cute shoes. Long legs. Great body."

A flush rose on her cheeks. "I've never been touched by a woman before. Never even wondered what it would be like. But she caressed my face and she told me I was beautiful. And when she kissed me…"

"You let her touch you? Kiss you?" First rule at a strip joint—no touching the talent. Keep your hands and lips to yourself or you end up on your ass in a snowbank.

She chuckled. "Right on the lips, mister. I've never, ever let a customer kiss me before, never mind a woman. I started thinking, 'This is too good to be true.

They bought me my own bottle of champagne. They're paying me five hundred dollars to do this, and I'm having a good time too. Ain't life grand?'"

Her eyes drifted away from me and looked toward the wall. "Her fingers were like feathers on my skin. Up and down my arms. Dancing along my ribcage. Circles on my stomach. Her lips along my jawline, to my ear…down my neck…" She dropped her eyes, shivered and bit her lip.

When she looked up, a sad smile brushed across her face and settled in her eyes. "I was in heaven. And then I looked over at her husband."

Her voice became rock-hard. "And the look of contempt I saw on his face…I disgusted him. I was crap. I was…worthless. Then I looked in my heart…and I believed him."

Teardrops slipped down her cheeks and landed on her thighs.

I tilted her chin up and used my thumbs to wipe the remaining tears from her cheeks.

"But you'd be awful proud of me," she said, "because I kept my game face on. I finished with her and kissed her like I cared and thanked her and said 'Gosh that'd be swell' when she said she'd like to do it again sometime and I took the five hundred dollars the husband shoved my way and I watched him kiss her like I had and I watched them leave hand-in-hand…and then I went to the can and I puked, the classy girl that I am."

Her eyes brimmed again. "My life story just keeps getting better and better, huh?"

I brushed her new tears away, then swept the bangs from her eyes. "To use a line a very smart woman once told me, you don't know it yet but it's okay to be you, just the way you are."

She hung her head, and a huge sigh shook her. "God you're an idiot." She slowly stood and walked to the edge of the bed where I sat. She motioned me to stand. When I did she nestled her head against my chest and wrapped her arms around me. She held me like she might hold on forever.

And I was okay with that.

Then the pressure slowly subsided. "Thank you," she whispered. "Nobody else believes that about me. But you really do, don't you?"

I looked down at her. "Yeah. I do."

She dabbed quickly at another tear on her cheek, then brushed the back of her fingers along my jaw. "I'm sure I'll pull that sentiment from my memory scrapbook from time to time. But it's time for me to be going now. Because after meeting the real Ecstasy I know that, no matter what you say, deep in your heart your opinion of me has changed. For the very worst."

Which was a mile off-base. Thoughts pinballed in my mind. What would Johnny Virdon tell me to say? Something to let her know that, despite how she felt about herself, I felt something entirely different. Something that would let her know there was room for her in my world. I settled on, "I've never met a woman like you before. And now that I have, I never need to meet another."

Seemingly dazed, she backed away. She felt for the chair. Once she found it she again sat, leaned forward on the chair back, and faced me. As I sat on the bed her eyes searched mine.

I rested my hand on her shoulder. She rolled her head and rested her cheek on my hand.

We sat like that for a long time.

Ecstasy lifted her head. "I don't ever talk about my life."

I waited.

She said, "Because I don't trust people."

I waited.

"Apparently I trust you."

"Apparently," I said.

She intently studied my face. "I just told you that I killed my unborn child, and that I made out with a woman last night."

"I heard."

"You didn't scream."

"Neighbors might be sleeping. It's a Sunday, after all."

"Still with the jokes," she said. "I hope one day they'll get funnier."

"Me, too."

She blew out a huge gust of air. "So, Paul Doyle, I think I figured something out, but I'm not sure if I can get the words right."

"Take your time, dear."

Ecstasy half-smiled. "You calling me Dear is nice. So…once upon a time you asked me why I strip. I guess I'd never really thought about it before you asked. One day I didn't dance, and one day I did. But what turned me from a wife with a job to a single girl whose clothes kept falling off? I called my sister and after we chased it around a little and cried a lot, we came to the same conclusion you did. I'm punishing myself for something I can't change, but I keep making myself a punching bag just the same. Then I deliver the knockout blows myself."

"Maybe today is the day you stop beating yourself up."

She searched my face. "Maybe you're right. But it won't be easy alone."

"Any chance you're looking for a teammate?"

She bit her lip. "Yeah, I think I am."

I sang in my perfectly pitched, ultra-manly baritone, "Wherever we go, whatever we…"

She squeezed my arm. "Please don't ruin the moment by singing. I'll take your word for it." A small smile found her face. And stayed a while. "I've already decided that the first step of the 'Ecstasy Reclamation Project' is I'm out of the dancing business, Paul. Of course, I'm not real sure what I'll do now that my nights and weekends are free. Got any suggestions for the newly unemployed?"

Pops always said when opportunity comes knocking, be ready to open the door. I grabbed the handle and pulled. "I've watched you work, kid. I'm not going to lie, I see potential. Shoot, now that you're unemployed I can snap you up as a student at the Paul Doyle School of Private Investigating."

Ecstasy cocked her head and cracked a lopsided grin. "You run a school?"

"I will now. And you'd be perfect. You wear ratty clothes anyway. You don't like to brush your hair. You only shower on the weekends. You'd be like one of the guys. Pay's not great, but you can't have everything in life."

"Money's not super-important to me, Paul. When you agree to become un-married to a rich white boy, especially after you try to kill yourself, the former in-laws are very appreciative financially. Even more so if you agree to leave their family name behind."

"Nice sucker punch to the kidneys, huh?"

She seemed a trifle sad. "My lips are officially sealed by court order. Still, you won't have to raid the petty cash to pay me, at least not for a while. But for real? You want me to join you and Cash?"

"Yeah. Trust me. It's for real."

She did her world-famous Ecstasy-staring-into-my-soul contest. "Not pity?"

It seemed to be an important distinction for her. "Not hardly. For now, be here. With me. We'll figure the rest out as we go."

She bit her lower lip. "I don't have the slightest idea how to be a private investigator."

"Don't sweat it, neither do we. For now you can follow us around and we'll do our best to make you the next great Magnum P.I. One request, though. Lose the mustache."

Her cheeks grew rosy pink as she rubbed below her nose. "Consider it gone." She grew instantly somber. "But you'd do all this for me even though I've never told you my real name?"

"Been mulling that over," I said. "Before I rush out and put your name on the door, calling you something other than Ecstasy might be best. Customers may develop unrealistic expectations otherwise."

Her laugh was musical. "You say my name every time you talk to me. My initials, at least. XTC. That's me."

"You used your initials?"

"Sure, why not? Who the heck would ever figure that out?"

Not me, for one. "You want to enlighten me about the mystery of you?"

"Xiomara Talia Cordoba."

"I must be half-deaf. I didn't hear much that sounded like an X in there."

"I pronounce X-I-O like 'See-oh'. See-oh-MARR-uh." She shrugged. "I'm Xiomara."

Xiomara. It was so worth waiting for.

She said, "When I started dancing I picked my stripper name as a joke. Ecstasy, right? No ego there. But...the way you say it, you make Ecstasy sound beautiful. Way more beautiful than it was supposed to be."

"Then you'll still hear it."

Her dimples approved.

"Let's say you join us, Ex. Does that mean you're going to retire your awesome wardrobe?"

She looked down. "I guess I will need new shoes. A looser-fitting skirt."

"And a shirt where I can't see your…bountiful harvest quite so much."

Ecstasy leaned away from the back of the chair, looked down, then looked at me and smiled. "Yes. That too."

"It's not that I object to seeing your…but the customers might get distracted."

"Well we can't have that, can we?" Her smile deepened. "I believe it's the things we don't do in life that we end up regretting the most. If you looked back at this moment in ten years, would you regret not kissing me right now?"

My throat felt too tight to speak. I gave nodding a try. It seemed to work.

She smiled as we stood. Her eyes closed as I neared her.

And she quivered as we kissed.

When we finished, she opened her eyes. "That wasn't so bad, was it?"

"No," I gasped. "It wasn't."

"Maybe we could try it again, just for fun?"

I touched her cheek. "I think I'd like that."

Ecstasy beamed. "I think I'd like that, too."

Acknowledgements

I'm very fortunate to have wonderful critique partners who provided no-holds-barred comments and advice as Easy Street took shape. A deep debt of gratitude to **Ron Cree**, **Bob Spiller**, **Kirk Farber**, and **Barb Nickless** for their warmth, friendship and wonderful mentorship, and to my online writing partners **Lynde Iozzo**, **Pamela Prockish** and **Betty May**, who were very supportive throughout the journey. To all my wonderful author friends at **Pikes Peak Writers**, thanks for inviting me into the family.

Thanks to **Felicia Chavez** for her invaluable assistance as I wrestled with early drafts, **Annie MacFarlane**, whose ongoing support and enthusiasm never failed to fire me up, wonderful graphic artist **Dave Fymbo,** and **DeAnna Knippling** for her expert work on the layout.

Special thanks to a generous team of technical advisors: **Sergeant Michael Benecke** and retired **Sergeant John Gould** from the Waterville Maine police department, **Lieutenant Christopher Coleman** from the Maine State Police, and **Dr. Margaret Greenwald**, Maine's Chief Medical Examiner. While I'm sure they quickly tired of my 'Is this within the realm of possibility?' questions, they answered every one I threw their way with patience, kindness, and wonderful insight.

Thanks to my mother **Shirley**, who is an accomplished writer herself, and to my father **Bill**, who prefers Westerns to tough-guy detective stories. Dad, I owe you a Western. Soon. I promise.

To my children: **Stefanie**, **Laura**, **David Ryan**, **David Edward**, **Mary** and **Renee**—thanks for being the frosting on my cake of life.

And always, to my loving wife **Peggy**, thank you, dear.

About the Author

Born in Massachusetts, raised in New Hampshire and finally Maine, Michael Shepherd stopped moving north when he ran out of country. An unabashed Red Sox fan who follows *Spring Training* games online, he recently retired from the Air Force after a 29-year career. He continues to work for the government and is still trying to come to grips with how he married a Yankees fan.

www.ingramcontent.com/pod-product-compliance
Lightning Source LLC
Chambersburg PA
CBHW062117170626
46813CB00002B/481